M cA
M

H

SMOKE IN THE WIND

By Peter Tremayne and featuring Sister Fidelma

SMOKE IN THE WIND

Peter Tremayne

 St. Martin's Minotaur 🐾 New York

www.minotaurbooks.com

ISBN 0-312-28780-1

First published in Great Britain by HEADLINE BOOK PUBLISHING
A division of Hodder Headline

First St. Martin's Minotaur Edition: July 2003

10 9 8 7 6 5 4 3 2 1

God arises and his enemies are scattered;
those who hate him flee before him,
driven away like smoke in the wind . . .

Psalm 68

HISTORICAL NOTE

The Sister Fidelma mysteries are set mainly in Ireland during the mid-seventh century AD.

This story, however, takes place while Fidelma and her companion in adventure, the Saxon Brother Eadulf, are en route to Canterbury, the primacy of the Anglo-Saxon kingdoms. They have been forced ashore by a storm in the kingdom of Dyfed, in the south-west of what is now modern Wales.

Sister Fidelma is not simply a religieuse, a former member of the community of St Brigid of Kildare. She is also a qualified *dálaigh*, or advocate of the ancient law courts of Ireland. As this background will not be familiar to many readers, my Historical Note is designed to provide a few essential points of reference to enable the stories to be better appreciated.

The Ireland of Fidelma's day consisted of five main provincial kingdoms; indeed, the modern Irish word for a province is still *cúige*, literally 'a fifth'. Four provincial kings – of Ulaidh (Ulster), of Connacht, of Muman (Munster) and of Laigin (Leinster) – gave their qualified allegiance to the Ard Rí or High King, who ruled from Tara, in the 'royal' fifth province of Midhe (Meath), which means the 'middle province'. Even among the provincial kingdoms, there was a decentralisation of power to petty-kingdoms and clan territories.

But in this story we also encounter the emergent Welsh kingdoms, still in a state of flux, as the original Britons, whom the Saxons called *Welisc* (foreigners), were pushed westward from the territories they had occupied for nearly fifteen hundred years by the invading Jutes, Angles and Saxons. In Fidelma's day, Devon (Dumnonia) and Cornwall (Curnow) were still Celtic, as was Cumberland (Rheged). North Wales was divided between two main kingdoms, Gwynedd and Powys; but south Wales was divided between eight smaller kingdoms of which Dyfed and Ceredigion were in conflict over who should be dominant.

Dyfed, the home of the famous abbey of the patron saint of Wales, St David (Dewi Sant), had actually been settled by the Irish of the Dési. Its early kings bore Irish names. The Welsh

ix

King Lists show that the famous Hywel Dda (AD 905–950) descended from King Eochaid of Dyfed who ruled c. AD 400. Hywel Dda was arguably the greatest of Welsh kings whose authority extended over all Wales. It was Hywel Dda who called a great conference in Dyfed which lasted for six weeks during which representatives of all the territories of Wales, under the chairmanship of a lawyer called Blegywryd, set forth the laws of the country in their first known codified form. These law books were popularly known as 'The Laws of Hywel Dda'. However, they represented an ancient legal tradition among the Celtic peoples so that comparisons between the Brehon Laws of Ireland and the Laws of Hywel Dda can clearly be made.

It was this common legal tradition that catches the interest of Fidelma in the current story.

However, we should remind ourselves of Fidelma's own culture, from which she views this kingdom of Dyfed, and discover how she could be an advocate of her country's legal system.

The law of primogeniture, the inheritance by the eldest son or daughter, was an alien concept in Ireland. Kingship, from the lowliest clan chieftain to the High King, was only partially hereditary and mainly electoral. Each ruler had to prove himself or herself worthy of office and was elected by the *derbhfine* of their family – a minimum of three generations from a common ancestor gathered in conclave. If a ruler did not pursue the commonwealth of the people, they were impeached and removed from office. Therefore the monarchical system of ancient Ireland had more in common with a modern day republic than with the feudal monarchies which had developed in medieval Europe.

Ireland, in the seventh century AD, was governed by a system of sophisticated laws called the Laws of the Fénechus, or land-tillers, which became more popularly known as the Brehon Laws, deriving from the word *breitheamh* – a judge. Tradition has it that these laws were first gathered in 714 BC by order of the High King, Ollamh Fódhla. Over a thousand years later, in AD 438, the High King, Laoghaire, appointed a commission of nine learned people to study, revise and commit the laws to the new writing in Latin characters. One of those serving on the commission was Patrick, eventually to become patron saint of Ireland. After three years, the commission produced a written text of the laws which is the first known codification.

It will be seen that the Welsh law system was not codified, so far as is known, for another five hundred years but, nevertheless, like the Irish system, it was the result of a sophisticated oral tradition or of a manuscript codification long since lost. Certainly, influences by the Roman occupation and then by contact with the Roman Church coloured the Welsh law. Yet still the vibrant Celtic origin shows through.

The first complete surviving texts of the ancient laws of Ireland are preserved in an eleventh-century manuscript book in the Royal Irish Academy, Dublin. It was not until the seventeenth century that the English colonial administration in Ireland finally suppressed the use of the Brehon law system. To even possess a copy of the Irish law books was punishable often by death or transportation.

Welsh law survived until the Acts annexing Wales into England which also enforced English language, law and custom there in 1536 and 1542. Some eighty law manuscripts in Welsh and Latin survive, mainly from the twelfth to sixteenth centuries.

In Ireland, the law system was not static, and every three years at the Féis Temhrach (Festival of Tara) the lawyers and administrators gathered to consider and revise the laws in the light of a changing society and its needs.

Under these laws, women occupied a unique place. The Irish laws gave more rights and protection to women than any other Western law code at that time or until recent times. Women could, and did, aspire to all offices and professions as co-equals with men. They could command their people in battle as warriors, be political leaders, local magistrates, poets, artisans, physicians, lawyers and judges. We know the names of many female judges of Fidelma's period – Bríg Briugaid, Áine Ingine Iugaire and Darí among others. Darí, for example, was not only a judge but the author of a noted law text written in the sixth century AD.

Women were protected by law against sexual harassment, against discrimination, against rape. They had the right of divorce on equal terms from their husbands, with equitable separation laws, and could demand part of their husband's property as a divorce settlement; they had the right of inheritance of personal property and the right of sickness benefits when ill or hospitalised. Ancient Ireland had Europe's oldest recorded system of hospitals. Seen from today's perspective, the Brehon Laws seemed to enshrine an almost ideal society.

This background, and its strong contrast to Ireland's neighbours, should be understood in order to appreciate Fidelma's role in these stories.

Fidelma went to study law at the bardic school of the Brehon Morann of Tara and, after eight years of study, she obtained the degree of *anruth*, only one degree below the highest offered in either bardic or ecclesiastical universities in ancient Ireland. The highest degree was *ollamh*, which is still the modern Irish word for a professor. Fidelma's studies were in both the criminal code of the *Senechus Mór* and the civil code of *Leabhar Acaill*. Thereby, she became a *dálaigh* or advocate of the law courts.

Her main role could be compared to a modern Scottish sheriff-substitute whose job is to gather and assess the evidence, independent of the police, to see if there is a case to be answered. The modern French *juge d'instruction* fulfils a similar role. However, sometimes Fidelma is faced with the task of prosecuting in the courts or defending or even rendering judgments in minor cases when a Brehon was not available.

In those days, most of the professional or intellectual classes were members of the new Christian religious houses, just as, in previous centuries, all members of the professions and intellectuals had been Druids. Fidelma became a member of the religious community of Kildare, founded in the late fifth century by St Brigid. But by the time the action in this story takes place, Fidelma has left Kildare in disillusionment. The reason why may be found in the title story of the Fidelma short story collection *Hemlock At Vespers*.

While the seventh century AD was considered part of the European Dark Ages, for Ireland it was a period of Golden Enlightenment. Students from every corner of Europe flocked to the Irish universities to receive their education, including the sons of many of the Anglo-Saxon kings. At the great ecclesiastical university of Durrow at this time, it is recorded that no fewer than eighteen different nations were represented among the students. At the same time, Irish male and female missionaries were setting out to return a pagan Europe to Christianity, establishing churches, monasteries, and centres of learning throughout Europe as far east as Kiev, in the Ukraine, as far north as the Faroes, and as far south as Taranto in southern Italy. Ireland was a byword for literacy and learning.

However, the Celtic Church of Ireland was in constant dispute with Rome on matters of liturgy and ritual. Rome had begun to reform itself in the fourth century, changing its dating of Easter and aspects of its liturgy. The Celtic Church and the Eastern Orthodox Church refused to follow Rome, but the Celtic Church was gradually absorbed by Rome between the ninth and eleventh centuries while the Eastern Orthodox Church has continued to remain independent. The Celtic Church of Ireland, in Fidelma's day, was much concerned with this conflict so that it is impossible to write of Church matters without referring to the philosophical warfare existing at the time.

One thing that was shared by both the Celtic Church and Rome in the seventh century was that the concept of celibacy was not universal. There had always been ascetics in the Church who sublimated physical love in a dedication to the deity, and at the Council of Nice in AD 325 clerical marriages had been condemned (but not banned) in the Western Church. The concept of celibacy arose in Rome mainly from the customs practised by the pagan priestesses of Vesta and the priests of Diana.

By the fifth century, Rome had forbidden its clerics from the rank of abbot and bishop to sleep with their wives and, shortly after, even to marry at all. The general clergy were discouraged from marrying by Rome but not forbidden to do so. Indeed, it was not until the reforming papacy of Leo IX (AD 1049–1054) that a serious attempt was made to force the Western clergy to accept universal celibacy. The Celtic Church took centuries to give up its anti-celibacy attitude and fall into line with Rome, while in the Eastern Orthodox Church priests below the rank of abbot and bishop have retained their right to marry until this day.

An awareness of these facts concerning the liberal attitudes towards sexual relationships in the Celtic Church is essential towards understanding the background to the Fidelma stories.

The condemnation of the 'sin of the flesh' remained alien to the Celtic Church for a long time after Rome's attitude became a dogma. In Fidelma's world, both sexes inhabited abbeys and monastic foundations, which were known as *conhospitae*, or double houses, where men and women lived and raised their children in Christ's service.

Fidelma's own house of St Brigid of Kildare was one such community of both sexes during her time. When Brigid established her community of Kildare (Cill Dara – church of the oaks) she invited a bishop named Conláed to join her. Her first surviving biography, completed fifty years after her death in AD 650, during Fidelma's lifetime, was written by a monk of Kildare named Cogitosus, who makes it clear that it continued to be a mixed community in his day.

It should also be pointed out that, demonstrating their co-equal role with men, women were priests of the Celtic Church in this period. Brigid herself was ordained a bishop by Patrick's nephew, Mel, and her case was not unique. In the sixth century, Rome actually wrote a protest at the Celtic practice of allowing women to celebrate the divine sacrifice of Mass.

Unlike the Roman Church, the Irish Church did not have a system of 'confessors' where 'sins' had to be confessed to clerics who then had the authority to absolve those sins in Christ's name. Instead, people chose a 'soul friend' (*anam chara*) out of clerics or laity, with whom they discussed matters of emotional and spiritual well-being.

To help readers more readily identify personal names, a list of principal characters is given.

To some English readers, the Welsh names may look confusing. I will attempt to explain the most difficult Welsh phonetics which English readers apparently encounter. C is always hard as in '*c*at' but CH is as in the composer '*Bach*'. DD is pronounced 'th' as in '*th*em'. LL as in '*Ll*anwda', '*Ll*anpadern' etc is a sound that does not occur in English. To make it correctly, one places the tongue on the roof of the mouth near the teeth as if to pronounce 'l' then blow voicelessly. In desperation one might resort to the sound 'ch'lan'. TH is pronounced as in 'clo*th*'. U is usually as in '*t*ea' or '*t*in'. W is as in '*b*oon or '*c*ook'. Y as in '*t*ea' or '*r*un'. For example, Cymru (Wales) is Kum-ree. Thus the name of the chieftain Gwnda is pronounced 'G'oon-da'.

Finally, some readers have written to me arguing that I am being anachronistic by giving distances in the modern metric system. In this respect the historian must give way to the storyteller to translate for his readers a modern equivalent of the Irish measurements of Fidelma's day. It would otherwise be too cumbersome to explain what was meant by an *ordlach*, *bas*, *troighid*, *céim*, *deis-céim*, *fertach* and *forrach*.

How to Pronounce Irish Names and Words

As the Fidelma series has become increasingly popular, many English-speaking fans have written wanting assurance about the way to pronounce the Irish names and words.

Irish belongs to the Celtic branch of the Indo-European family of languages. It is closely related to Manx and Scottish Gaelic and is a cousin of Welsh, Cornish and Breton. It is a very old European literary language. Professor Calvert Watkins of Harvard maintained it contains Europe's oldest *vernacular* literature, Greek and Latin being a *lingua franca*. Surviving texts date from the 7th Century AD.

The Irish of Fidelma's period is classed as Old Irish which, after 950 AD, entered a period known as Middle Irish. Therefore, in the Fidelma books, Old Irish forms are generally adhered to, whenever possible, in both names and words. This is like using Chaucer's English compared to modern English. For example, a word such as *aidche* ('night') in Old Irish is now rendered *oiche* in Modern Irish.

There are only eighteen letters in the Irish alphabet. From earliest times there has been a literary standard but today four distinct spoken dialects are recognised. For our purposes, we will keep to Fidelma's dialect of Munster.

It is a general rule that stress is placed on the first syllable but, as in all languages, there are exceptions. In Munster the exceptions to the rule of initial stress are a) if the second syllable is long then it bears the stress; b) if the first two syllables are short and the third is long then the third syllable is stressed – such as in the word for fool, amadán = amad-**awn**; or c) where the second syllable contains **ach** and there is no long syllable, the second syllable bears the stress.

There are five short vowels – **a, e, i, o, u** and five long vowels – **á, é, í, ó, ú**. On the long vowels note the accent, like the French acute, which is called a **fada** (lit. long), and this is the only accent in Irish. It occurs on capitals as well as lower case.

The accent is important for, depending on where it is placed, it changes the entire word. **Seán** (Shawn) = John. But **sean** (shan) = old and **séan** (she-an) = an omen. By leaving out the accent on the name of the famous film actor, Sean Connery, he has become 'Old' Connery!

These short and long vowels are either 'broad' or 'slender'. The six broad vowels are:

a pronounced 'o' as in cot
á pronounced 'aw' as in law
o pronounced 'u' as in cut
ó pronounced 'o' as in low
u pronounced 'u' as in run
ú pronounced 'u' as in rule

The four slender vowels are:

i pronounced 'i' as in hit
í pronounced 'ee' as in see
e pronounced 'e' as in let
é pronounced 'ay' as in say

There are double vowels, some of which are fairly easy because they compare to English pronunciation – such as '*ae*' as in s*ay* or **ui** as in q*ui*t. However, some double and even triple vowels in Irish need to be learnt.

ái pronounced like 'aw' as in law (dálaigh = daw'lee)
ia pronounced like 'ea' as in near
io pronounced like 'o' as in come
éa pronounced like 'ea' as in bear
ei pronounced like 'e' as in let
aoi pronounced like the 'ea' as in mean
uai pronounced like the 'ue' as in blue
eoi pronounced like the 'eo' as in yeoman
iai pronounced like the 'ee' as in see

Hidden vowels

Most people will have noticed that many Irish people pronounce the word film as fil'*um*. This is actually a transference of Irish pronunciation rules. When **l, n** or **r** are followed by **b, bh, ch, g** (not after **n**), **m**, or **mh**, and is preceded by a short stressed vowel, an additional vowel is heard between them. ie **bolg** (stomach) is pronounced bol'ag; **garbh** (rough) is gar'ev; **dorcha** (dark) is dor'ach'a; **gorm** (blue) is gor'um and **ainm** (name) is an'im.

The consonants

b, d, f, h, l, m, n, p, r, and **t** are said more or less as in English.

    g is always hard like 'g' as in gate

    c is always hard like the 'c' as in cat

    s is pronounced like the 's' as in said except before a slender vowel when it is pronounced 'sh' as in shin

In Irish the letters **j**, **k**, **q**, **w**, **x**, **y** or **z** do not exist and **v** is formed by the combination of '**bh**'.

Consonants can change their sound by aspiration or eclipse. Aspiration is caused by using the letter 'h' after them.

    bh is the 'v' as in voice

    ch is a soft breath as in lo*ch* (not pronounced as lock!) or as in Ba*ch*.

    dh before a broad vowel is like the 'g' as in gap

    dh before a slender vowel is like the 'y' as in year

    fh is totally silent

    gh before a slender vowel can sound like 'y' as in yet

    mh is pronounced like the 'w' as in wall

    ph is like the 'f' as in fall

    th is like the 'h' as in ham

    sh is also like the 'h' as in ham

Consonants can also change their sound by being eclipsed, or silenced, by another consonant placed before it. For example *na mBan* (of women) = nah *m*'on; or *i bpaipéar* (in the paper) i *b*'ap'er or *i gcathair* (in the city) i *g*'a'har.

    p can be eclipsed by **b, t**

    t can be eclipsed by **d,**

    c can be eclipsed by **g**

    f can be eclipsed by **bh**

    b by **m**

    d and **g** by **n**

For those interested in learning more about the language, it is worth remembering that, after centuries of suppression during the colonial period, Irish became the first official language of the Irish State on independence in 1922. The last published Census of 1991 showed one third of the population returning themselves as Irish-speaking. In Northern Ireland, where the language continued to be openly discouraged after Partition in

1922, only ten-and-a-half per cent of the population were able to speak the language in 1991, the first time an enumeration of speakers was allowed since Partition.

Language courses are now available on video and audio-cassette from a range of producers from Linguaphone to RTÉ and BBC. There are some sixty summer schools and special intensive courses available. Teilifís na Gaeilge is the television station broadcasting entirely in Irish and there are several Irish language radio stations and newspapers. Information can be obtained from Comhdháil Náisiúnta na Gaeilge, 46 Sráid Chill Dara, Baile Atha Cliath 2, Éire.

Readers might also like to know that *Valley of the Shadow*, in the Fidelma series, was produced on audio-cassette, read by Mary McCarthy, from Magna Story Sound (SS391 – ISBN 1–85903–313–X).

Principal Characters

Sister Fidelma, of Cashel, a *dálaigh* or advocate of the law courts of seventh-century Ireland
Brother Eadulf, of Seaxmund's Ham, a Saxon monk from the land of the South Folk

At Porth Clais

Brother Rhodri, of Porth Clais

At the Abbey of Dewi Sant, Menevia

Abbot Tryffin
Gwlyddien, king of Dyfed
Cathen, son of Gwlyddien
Brother Meurig, a *barnwr* or judge of Dyfed
Brother Cyngar, of Menevia
Cadell, a warrior

At Pen Caer and environs

Mair, a victim
Iorwerth the smith, father of Mair
Iestyn, his friend, a farmer
Idwal, a youthful itinerant shepherd
Gwnda, lord of Pen Caer
Elen, Gwnda's daughter
Buddog, a servant in Gwnda's hall
Clydog Cacynen, an outlaw
Corryn, one of his band
Sualda, another of his band
Goff, a smith
Rhonwen, his wife
Dewi, his son
Elisse, the apothecary

Osric, thane of the Hwicce

Chapter One

The girl looked as if she were merely resting among the bracken lying with one arm thrown carelessly behind her head the other extended at her side. Her pale, attractive features seemed relaxed; the eyes, with their dark lashes, were closed; the lips were partially opened showing fine, white teeth. Her dark hair formed a sharp contrast to the pallid texture of the skin.

It was only by the thin line of blood, which had trickled from the corner of her mouth before congealing, and the fact that her facial skin seemed discoloured, mottled with red fading into blue, that one could see she was not resting naturally. From that, together with her torn, bloodstained, dirty clothing, a discerning observer might realise that something was clearly wrong.

The youth stood before the body, gazing down at it without expression. He was thin, wiry, with ginger hair and a freckled face, but carrying a tan which seemed to indicate that he was used to being outside in most weathers. His lips were too red and full, making his features slightly ugly by the imbalance. His pale eyes were fixed on the body of the girl. He was dressed in a sleeveless sheepskin jacket, fastened by a leather belt. Thick homespun trousers and leather leggings gave him the appearance of a shepherd.

A deep, long sigh came from his parted lips; a soft whistling sound.

'Ah, Mair, why? Why, Mair?'

The words came like a curious sob yet his expression did not alter.

He stayed there with fixed gaze for a few more moments until the sound of shouting came to his ears. He raised his head sharply, tilting it slightly to one side in a listening attitude, and his features changed. A wild, hunted expression came on his face. People were moving in his direction. Their cries came clearly to his ears, moving closer and closer through the surrounding trees. He could hear them beating through the gorse and bracken.

The youth glanced once more at the body of the girl and then turned quickly away from the approaching sounds.

1

He had gone barely ten or twenty metres when a blow across the shoulders felled him to the ground. The momentum of the blow caused him to pitch forward. He dropped on his hands and knees, gasping for breath.

A burly man had emerged from concealment behind a tree, still holding the thick wood cudgel in his hand. He was dark, thickset and full-bearded. He stood, feet apart, above the youth, the cudgel in his hands, ready and threatening.

'On your feet, Idwal,' the man growled. 'Or I shall strike you while you are still on your knees.'

The boy looked up, still smarting from the pain of the blow. 'What do you want with me, lord Gwnda?' he wailed. 'I have done you no harm.'

The dark-haired man frowned angrily. 'Don't play games with me, boy!'

He gestured back along the path, towards the body of the girl. As he did so a group of men came bursting through the trees onto the forest path behind them. Some of them saw the body of the girl and howls of rage erupted from them.

'Here!' yelled the dark-haired man, his eyes not leaving the youth, his cudgel still ready. 'Here, boys! I have him. I have the murderer.'

The newcomers, voices raised with fresh anger and violence, came running towards the kneeling youth who now started to sob as he saw his death in their expressions.

'I swear, by the Holy Virgin I swear I did not—'

A sharp kick from one of the leading men landed on the side of the boy's head. It sent him sprawling and, mercifully, into unconsciousness because several others among the new arrivals started to kick viciously at his body.

'Enough!' shouted the dark-haired man called Gwnda. 'I know you are full of grief and anger, but this must be done according to the law. We will take him back to the township and send for the *barnwr*.'

'What need have we of a judge, Gwnda?' cried one of the men. 'Don't we have the evidence of our own eyes? Didn't I see Idwal and poor Mair with voices raised in fierce argument only a short time ago? There was violence in Idwal, if ever I saw it.'

The black-bearded man shook his head. 'It shall be done according to law, Iestyn. We will send for the *barnwr*, a learned judge from the abbey of Dewi Sant.'

*   *   *

2

The monk was young and walked with that confident, rapid stride of youth along the pathway through the encompassing forest. He wore his winter cloak wrapped tight against the early morning chill and his thick blackthorn staff was carried not so much as an aid to walking but to be turned, at a moment's notice, into a weapon of defence. The woods of Ffynnon Druidion, the Druid's well, were notorious for the highway thieves who lurked within its gloomy recesses.

Brother Cyngar was not really worried, merely cautious in spite of his confident gait. Early dawn on this bright autumnal day was, he felt, a time when all self-respecting thieves would still be sleeping off the excessive alcohol of the previous evening. Surely no thief would be abroad and looking for victims at such an hour? Not even the infamous Clydog Cacynen who haunted the woods; Clydog the Wasp, he was called, for he stung when least expected. A notorious outlaw. It was fear of meeting Clydog Cacynen that caused Brother Cyngar to choose this hour to make his way through the wood, having spent the previous night at a woodsman's cottage by the old standing stone.

There was frost lying like a white carpet across the woodland. Behind the soft white clouds, a weak winter's sun was obviously trying to extend its rays. The woodland seemed colourless. The leaves had fallen early for there had been several cold spells in spite of its not being late in the season. Only here and there were clumps of evergreens such as the dark holly trees with the females carrying their bright red berries. There were also some common alders with their brown, woody cones which had, only a short time before, been ripened catkins, and a few silver birch. But everything was dominated by the tall, bare and gaunt sessile oaks.

Now and again, along the track that he was following, Brother Cyngar espied crampball clinging to fallen trunks of ash; curious black and inedible fungi which he had once heard prevented night cramp if placed in one's bed before sleeping. Cyngar had the cynicism of youth and smiled at the thought of such a thing.

The woods were stirring with life now. He saw a common shrew, a tiny brown creature, race out of a bush in front of him, skid to a halt and sniff. Its poor eyesight was made up for by its keen sense of smell. It caught his scent at once, gave a squeak, and then disappeared within a split second.

As it did so, high above came the regretful call of a circling red kite who must have spotted the tiny, elusive creature even through

3

the canopy of bare branches and, had it not been for Brother Cyngar's appearance, might have taken it as its breakfast.

Only once did Brother Cyngar start and raise his stick defensively at a nearby ominous rustling. He relaxed almost immediately as he caught sight of the orange-brown fur coat with white spots and broad blade antlers that denoted a solitary fallow deer which turned and bounded away through the undergrowth to safety.

Finally, Brother Cyngar could see, along the path ahead of him, the trees gradually giving way to an open stretch of bracken-strewn hillside. He began to sense a feeling of relief that the major dark portions of the wood were now behind him. He even paused, laid down his stick and took out his knife as he spotted an array of orange at the edge of the footpath. He bent down and carefully inspected the fungus with its white, downy underside. It was not difficult to recognise this edible species which many ate raw or soaked in honey-mead. The little harvest was too good to miss and Brother Cyngar gathered it into the small *marsupium* he wore on his belt.

He rose, picked up his stick again and began to walk on with the renewed energy which comes with knowing one's objective is almost in sight.

On the far side of the next hill lay the community of Llanpadern, the sacred enclosure of the Blessed Padern, where nearly thirty brothers of the faith lived and worked in devotion to the service of God. It was to this community that Brother Cyngar was travelling. He planned to seek hospitality there, an opportunity to break his fast, before continuing his journey on to the famous abbey of Dewi Sant on Moniu, which some Latinised as Menevia. The abbey was the authority over all the religious communities of the kingdom of Dyfed. Brother Cyngar had been entrusted with messages for Abbot Tryffin by his own Father Superior. He had left on his journey shortly after noon on the previous day and hence his overnight stop at the woodsman's cottage, after completing nearly twenty kilometres of his journey, before venturing through the notorious woods of Ffynnon Druidion. He had left the woodsman's cottage too early for breakfast but, knowing that the hospitality of Llanpadern was a byword among pilgrims journeying south to Moniu, he did not mind delaying his morning meal.

Brother Cyngar walked entirely at ease now. The sun, while not exactly breaking through the clouds, was warm enough to

4

dispel the early morning frost. Birds wheeled and darted about the skies on their many food-gathering tasks and the air was filled with their cacophony; plaintive, angry, argumentative, depending on their natures.

He came over the shoulder of the bare rocky hill called Carn Gelli. On its height stood a heap of stones, one raised upon another, to denote an ancient grave, which gave the place its name. Brother Cyngar halted and, from the vantage point, peered down into the valley beyond. A short distance below him was the grey stone complex of buildings. Smoke drifted reassuringly from a central chimney. He walked down the pathway, his speed increasing, his body propelled more by the steepness of the path than a desire to reach the gates in a hurry.

As he followed the path to the main gates of the community he noticed, surprisingly, that they stood open and deserted. This fact made him frown. It was unusual, even at this early hour, for it was the custom of the brethren of Llanpadern to be out in the surrounding fields, beginning their work at first light even on such a cold autumnal day as this one. There was usually some activity about the gates and the fields.

He came to a halt at the gates, compelled by a sudden feeling of unease. No one stood in attendance. After a moment's delay, he went to the wooden pole to ring the bronze bell which hung there. The chime echoed eerily but there was no movement in answer; no responding sound followed the dying peal; there was no sign of anyone beyond.

Brother Cyngar waited a few moments and then caused the bell to send out its clanging demand again, this time ensuring that its peal was long and insistent. Still there was no response.

He moved slowly inside the deserted courtyard and looked round.

Everywhere was as quiet as a tomb.

In the centre of the courtyard stood a great pyramid of branches and logs piled high as if waiting to be ignited into an immense bonfire. The dry wood was structured so that it stood fully four metres or more in height. The young man rubbed his chin thoughtfully as he examined it.

He suppressed the shiver that threatened to send its icy finger down his spine. He marched across the quadrangle to the chapel door and swung it open. The chapel was shrouded in gloom, in spite of the brightness of the morning. Not even the altar candles were alight. He could discern nothing among the shadows.

5

Having been a visitor to the community on several occasions, Brother Cyngar knew the layout of the community's buildings, and turned through a small door which he knew led to the main living quarters. The brethren shared one large dormitory that now stretched before him. The beds were all neat, tidy and undisturbed. Their occupants had either risen very early and made them or not slept in them at all during the previous night.

Brother Cyngar's lips had become slightly dry and his feeling of disquiet began to grow as he walked between the rows of empty beds. Some unconscious prompting caused him to move lightly on the stone-flagged floors, trying not to let his leather sandals make a sound.

Beyond the dormitory was the refectory, the communal dining room.

It was deserted, as he now expected it would be. But he was not expecting the manner of its desertion. It was lit by several flickering, smoking candles and, to his amazement, Brother Cyngar observed that each place was laid, each platter contained a half-eaten meal. By these platters, knives and spoons were laid down as if the eater had been disturbed. Jugs and beakers containing water and wine stood at each place setting.

A sound made him start nervously and drop his blackthorn stick with a loud clatter on the floor. A few feet away on the table, a black rat dragged a piece of food from a platter and went bounding away with it. With mouth firmly compressed to keep his lips from trembling, Brother Cyngar bent down to retrieve his stick.

There seemed no disarray anywhere to explain why the meal appeared to have been deserted halfway through the eating of it. Stools and benches were pushed back as if everyone had risen, but he saw nothing that indicated any confusion or panic. He walked up and down the tables searching for something to account for the scene that met his incredulous eyes.

He realised that the candles were burning low and deduced that they must have been alight for a long time before he arrived because, in one or two places, the candle grease had spilled onto the wooden table top. This must have been the evening meal and, so it seemed to Brother Cyngar, at a given moment, before the meal had ended, the brethren had simply stood up, leaving everything in an orderly manner, and . . . and vanished! Brother Cyngar exhaled sharply. This time he could not suppress the shiver.

Steeling himself, he turned and began to explore the rest of the buildings of the community, one by one. The quarters of the Father Superior were neat and tidy, the bed not slept in, and, again, there was no sign of any commotion to account for the disappearance of the occupant. The tiny *scriptorum* was also undisturbed, the books arranged neatly on the shelves. Outside, across the quadrangle, in the storerooms, nothing was out of place, and when Brother Cyngar went to the animal sheds he found all in order.

It was only when he had returned halfway across the flagged courtyard on his way back to the chapel that he realised the significance of this. There were no animals in the barns; no chickens, no pigs, no cows nor sheep, not even one of the two mules which he knew the community kept. They, like the brethren, had vanished.

Brother Cyngar prided himself on being a logical young man and, having been raised as a farmer's son, he was not frightened of being alone. He was not one given to easy panic. All the possible facts and explanations should be examined and considered before one gave way to fear. He walked carefully to the main gate and gazed intently at the ground in search of any signs indicating a mass exodus of the community with their animals. Cows and mules in particular would leave tracks in the earth outside.

There was no sign of the earth being unnecessarily disturbed by the passage of men or animals. He did note some deep cart ruts, but that was not unusual. Plenty of local farmers traded regularly with the community. The roadways to the north and west were stony, so the tracks soon vanished. He could see a few traces of the flat-soled sandals used by the monks but there were few other signs. Without an alternative to consider, he return to the conclusion that the community had vanished like a wisp of smoke dispersed in the wind.

At this point, Brother Cyngar felt the compulsion to genuflect and he muttered a prayer to keep all evil at bay, for what could not be explained by Nature must be the work of the supernatural. There was no temporal explanation for this desolate scene. At least, none he could think of.

Could Father Clidro, the Father Superior of Llanpadern, and his fellow monks have stood up in the middle of their meal, left their candles burning, gathered all the animals and then . . . then what? Simply disappeared?

As a conscientious young man, Brother Cyngar forced himself

to return to the refectory and extinguish the candles before going back to the main gates. He gave a final glance around and then swung them shut behind him. Outside, he paused, uncertain of what he should do next.

He knew that a few kilometres to the north lay the township of Llanwnda. Gwnda, the lord of Pen Caer, was supposed to be a man of action. Brother Cyngar hesitated and wonder if he should proceed in that direction. But, as he recalled, there was no priest at Llanwnda, and what could Gwnda and his people do against the supernatural forces of evil which had caused the brethren of Llanpadern to vanish?

He concluded that there was only one thing to do.

He should continue as quickly as possible to the abbey of Dewi Sant. Abbot Tryffin would know what to do. He must inform the abbot of this catastrophic event. Only the brethren of the great abbey founded by Dewi Sant had the power to combat this enchantment. He found himself wondering what evil sorcery had been unleashed on the poor community of Llanpadern. He shivered almost violently and began to hurry away from the deserted buildings, moving swiftly along the stony road towards the southern hills. The bright, autumnal day now seemed gloomy and heavy with menace. But menace of . . . of what?

Chapter Two

In the few seconds between unconsciousness and awakening, there is a moment of vivid dreams. Eadulf was struggling in dark water, unable to breathe. He was attempting to swim upwards, threshing with his arms and legs, feeling that death by asphyxiation was but a moment away. No matter how desperate his efforts, he had that feeling of complete powerlessness. Just as he had given up all hope, he became conscious; the transition came so abruptly that for a moment he lay shivering, sweat pouring from his forehead, not sure what was reality. Then, slowly – so it seemed – he realised that he had been dreaming. He tried to make a sound, some articulate noise, but succeeded only in making a rasping breath in the back of his throat.

He became aware of someone bending towards him.

He tried to focus but the image was blurred.

A voice said something. He did not understand. He made a further effort to peer upwards. He felt a firm hand behind his head, lifting it slightly. Felt a hard rim against his lips and then a cold liquid was splashing against his lips and dribbling over his teeth. He gulped eagerly. All too soon, the hard rim was withdrawn, the hand eased his head back to a pillow.

He lay for a second or two before opening his eyes again and blinking rapidly. The figure seemed to shimmer for a moment and then harden into sharp focus.

It was a man; short, stocky and clad in the robes of a religieux.

Eadulf tried hard to think what had happened and where he was. No coherent thoughts came to his mind.

The voice said something again. Again, he did not understand, but this time he recognised the tone and realised that the voice was speaking in the language of the Britons. He licked his lips and tried to form a sentence in the language which he knew but inadequately.

'Where am I?' he finally managed to say, realising, as he said it, that the words had actually come out in his own tongue.

The lips in the round face of the religieux pursed in an expression of disapproval.

'*Sacsoneg?*' The man went off into a long, fast torrent of words which was just sound to Eadulf's ear.

With an effort of concentration, for his head was still throbbing, he tried to form a sentence in the language of the Britons. It would not come and, finally, he resorted to Latin, realising that he had a better knowledge of it. It was many years since he had spoken any word of the British tongue.

The religieux looked relieved at the Latin. His round face became wreathed in a smile.

'You are in Porth Clais, Brother Saxon.'

The man reached forward and again held out the beaker which contained water. Eadulf raised his head by his own efforts and eagerly lapped at it. He fell back on the pillow again and some memories began to return.

'Porth Clais? I was on board a ship out of Loch Garman. Where is Porth Clais, and what happened . . . ? Fidelma? Where is my companion, Sister Fidelma? Were we shipwrecked? My God! What has happened . . . ?'

He was struggling to sit up as memories flooded his mind. The stocky religieux laid a restraining hand, palm downward, on his chest. Eadulf was pressed gently but firmly back onto the bed. He realised that he must be very weak not to be able to counter the strength of the single firm hand that held him.

'All in good time and in good order, Brother Saxon,' replied the man gently. 'You have not been shipwrecked. All is well. You are, as I say, in Porth Clais in the kingdom of Dyfed. And you, my friend, have not been so well.'

Eadulf's head continued to throb and he raised a hand to it, registering some surprise as he felt a tender swelling at his temple.

'I don't understand. What happened?'

'What was the last thing that you recall, Brother Saxon?'

Eadulf tried to dredge the memory from the confused thoughts that swam in his mind.

'I was on board ship. We were hardly a day out from Loch Garman and sailing for the coast of Kent . . . Ah, I have it. A squall arose.'

The memory clarified in a flash. They had been scarcely half a day's sailing from Loch Garman. The coast of Laigin, the south-easterly of the five kingdoms of Éireann, had dropped below the horizon when a fierce wind hit them from the south-west, sending great waves cascading over the ship. They had been tossed and buffeted without mercy. The sails were shredded by the powerful wind before the captain and his crew were able to haul them down, so unexpected was the onslaught of the storm. Eadulf recalled that he had left Fidelma below deck while he went to see if he could give some assistance.

The captain had curtly dismissed his offer of help.

'A landlubber is as much use to me as a bucket with a hole to bail out,' he shouted harshly. 'Get below and stay there!'

Eadulf remembered hauling himself back, hurt and disgruntled, across the rocking, sea-swamped decks to the steps which led down to the cabin below. Just as he started down, the mighty seas seemed to lift the vessel up and toss it forward. He lost his hold and his last memory was of being tumbled forward into space and then . . . then nothing until he awoke a few moments ago.

The stocky monk smiled approvingly as Eadulf recited these memories.

'And what is your name?' he asked.

'I am Eadulf of Seaxmund's Ham, emissary of Theodore of Canterbury,' Eadulf replied immediately and then demanded with irritation: 'But where is Sister Fidelma, my companion? What has happened to the ship? How did I get here? Where did you say it was?'

The round-faced monk grinned and held up his hand to halt the rapid succession of questions. 'It seems that the blow to your head has damaged neither your mental faculties nor your lack of patience, Brother Saxon.'

'My patience is wearing thin with each passing second,' snapped Eadulf, attempting to sit up in bed and ignoring his throbbing temples. 'Answer my question, or I shall not answer for my lack of patience.'

The stocky man shook his head in mock sorrow, making a disapproving noise with his tongue. 'Have you never heard the saying, *Vincit qui patitur*, Brother Saxon?'

'It is not one of my maxims, Brother. Often patience does not bring results. Sometimes it is merely an excuse for doing nothing. Now I require some explanations.'

The monk raised his eyes to the ceiling and spread his hands as if in surrender to greater forces. 'Very well. I am Brother Rhodri and this, as I have explained, is Porth Clais in the kingdom of Dyfed.'

'On the west coast of Britain?'

Brother Rhodri made an affirmative gesture. 'You are in the

land of the Cymry, the true Britons. Your ship ran in here yesterday in the late afternoon to shelter from the storm. We are a little port in which many a ship from Éireann make their first landfall. You were, as you now recall, knocked unconscious in the storm and could not be roused. So you were carried off the ship when it harboured here. You were placed in this little hospice which I run. You have been lying unconscious nearly a day.'

Eadulf lay back against the pillows and swallowed. 'Unconscious for a day?' he echoed.

Brother Rhodri was serious. 'We were worried for you. But, *deo juvante*, you have recovered.'

Eadulf sat up again with an abruptness which made him dizzy. He realised that one of his questions had not been answered.

'My companion, Sister Fidelma . . . what of her?'

Brother Rhodri grimaced wryly. 'She was very worried for you, Brother Saxon. She and I shared your nursing. This morning, however, she was summoned to go to our mother house to see Abbot Tryffin.'

'Abbot Tryffin? Mother house?'

'This is the peninsula known in Latin as Menevia where the abbey of Dewi Sant is situated.'

Eadulf had heard of the great abbey of Dewi Sant. He knew that those Britons who dwelt in the west of the island which they now shared with the Angles and Saxons regarded the abbey as almost as important as Iona, the Holy Island, in the northern kingdom of Dál Riada. It was accepted that two pilgrimages to the abbey was the equivalent of one pilgrimage to Rome and a pilgrim could acquire enough indulgences – pardons of temporal punishment due for sins committed – to last them for many years. Eadulf realised that he was thinking in terms of the teachings of Rome, where the Holy Father granted indulgences out of the Treasury of Merit won for the Church by Christ and the Saints. Eadulf knew well enough that the churches of the Irish and the Britons did not believe in such things as indulgences nor in absolving oneself from one's responsibility by their acquisition.

He suddenly pulled his wandering thoughts sharply back to the present.

'She was *summoned* there? Sister Fidelma? Is the abbey near here, then?' he asked.

'Near? It is within walking distance, less than two kilometres. The good sister will return by this evening.'

'And you say that we are on that peninsula of Dyfed known as Menevia?'

'In our language, it is called Moniu,' Brother Rhodri confirmed.

'Why was Fidelma . . . Sister Fidelma summoned there?'

Brother Rhodri raised his shoulders and let them fall expressively. 'That is something that I cannot help you with, Brother Saxon. Now, perhaps, as you are in a better state, you might like to sip some herbal tea or some broth?'

Eadulf realised that he was feeling famished. 'I could eat something more substantial, Brother,' he ventured.

Brother Rhodri grinned approvingly. 'Ah, a sure sign that you are recovering, my friend. However, it may be unwise to have more than a broth for the time being. Nor should you move. Lie there and relax for a while.'

Some hours later, Eadulf felt more himself. He had sipped a meaty broth and his headache was diminishing thanks to a poultice which Brother Rhodri had placed on his forehead. It appeared that Brother Rhodri was a trained apothecary and Eadulf, who had himself studied at the great medical centre of Tuam Brecain, had identified the poultice as being comprised of foxglove leaves which, he knew, were excellent for calming headaches. He had gradually dropped into a soporific state and then fallen into a natural sleep.

He awoke to the sound of Fidelma's voice and came to his senses as she entered the room. The concern on her face lessened as Eadulf rose up on his bed. She came swiftly to him, both hands held out, and sat on the edge of the bed.

'How do you feel? Are you all right?' she asked anxiously, examining him quickly. 'The swelling on your temple seems to be going down.'

Eadulf returned a wry smile. 'I suppose I feel as right as anyone who has been knocked unconscious for a day.'

She gave a sigh of relief but she did not let go of his hands, making a careful visual examination of his wound. When she was satisfied, she visibly relaxed and a smile crossed her features.

'I was worried, but the swelling is definitely diminishing,' she said simply. Then, becoming aware that Brother Rhodri had appeared in the doorway, she let go her grip on his hands and sat back. 'Has Brother Rhodri explained to you where you are and what happened?'

'I gather the ship put into Porth Clais to escape the storm.'

'A harbour on the coast of Dyfed,' agreed Fidelma. 'It really was a bad storm. I insisted that you be brought ashore to this hospice as soon as we came into harbour, for there was no telling what injuries you might have sustained in your fall.'

'I seem to have had a good nurse.' Eadulf smiled. 'We can return aboard the ship and continue our journey as soon as you like.'

To his surprise, Fidelma shook her head. 'Our ship sailed on this morning's tide. The captain was impatient to be away as soon as the storm passed and he had replaced his shredded sails.'

'What?' Eadulf pushed himself up stiffly into a sitting position. 'He has marooned us in this place? We paid him to take us to the kingdom of Kent. You mean he went away and left us stranded here?'

Fidelma pouted her lips in reproof. Her eyes flicked quickly to Brother Rhodri. They had been speaking in Fidelma's native tongue, which Eadulf spoke as fluently as his own, perhaps more fluently than Latin. Was there a warning in her eyes?

'We are not stranded, Eadulf. The kingdom of Dyfed has good links with other lands and kingdoms. Anyway, the captain refunded some of our passage fee.'

Eadulf followed her glance towards Brother Rhodri. It seemed that Brother Rhodri knew something of the language, for he seemed to be following their exchange.

'I only meant that we are a long way from Canterbury,' Eadulf pointed out. 'It is vexing that the captain did not have time to wait.'

'The wood will renew the foliage it sheds,' Fidelma reassured him, quoting an old proverb.

Eadulf shrugged reluctantly. 'We are not so well endowed with money that we can afford to lose any,' he admonished. 'We have to find a new ship and will have to pay more for the journey to Canterbury.'

Fidelma made a dismissive gesture. 'What we have to do now,' she corrected him with emphasis, 'is for you to rest and regain your strength, Eadulf. Remember the saying that there is always another tide in the sea.' She made to rise.

'Stay awhile,' Eadulf urged. 'I am not sleepy.'

Fidelma glanced at Brother Rhodri, who was lighting a lamp, for the dusk had crept up while they had been talking.

'It is time for the evening meal,' he said. 'Shall I bring some food to you here on a tray, Sister?'

14

'Thank you, Brother. It would be most kind of you.'

The monk smiled briefly and turned to Eadulf. 'You seem well enough to take a little more broth, Brother. I shall see to it.'

When he had gone, Eadulf grinned sheepishly at Fidelma. 'I am sorry that I have precipitated you into this predicament.'

'Predicament?' She paused and shook her head. 'It is always fascinating to see a new land, even when it is done without intention.'

Eadulf's features dissolved into a glum expression. 'The land of the Britons may be fascinating for you but not for me.'

'What do you mean?'

'Saxons are not exactly welcome among Britons in spite of Brother Rhodri's Christian charity.'

'Do Britons have a reason to dislike Saxons?'

Eadulf glanced at her sharply. Was she mocking him? She was well acquainted with the recent history of these islands.

'You know that nothing happens without reason, Fidelma. And you know your history as well as anyone I know. You will be aware that the Britons once lived all over this land but two centuries ago the ancestors of my people came from beyond the eastern sea to conquer and colonise – the Jutes, Angles and Saxons. They began to push the Britons westward and northwards and take over their lands. I can understand the feelings of the dispossessed. My people are a warrior people who have only just accepted Christian values. I think, behind their professed acceptance of the new faith, they continue to fear Woden, the old god of war. They still believe that the true way to immortality is to die with a sword in their hand and Woden's name on their lips. Only along that path do they think they have a chance to pass into the Hall of Heroes, where all the immortals live.'

Fidelma was puzzled at the intensity in his voice. 'You sound as if you also believe this, Eadulf?'

Eadulf regarded her with a sour expression. 'I was a young man when I was converted to the new faith by missionaries from Éireann, Fidelma. I went to study it in your lands before I went on to Rome. You know that before my conversion I was the hereditary *gerefa* of Seaxmund's Ham. It is hard to forget the culture in which one has been brought up. Within living memory did King Eadbald of Kent revert to the worship of Woden. People are alive today who can remember when the East Saxons killed or chased into exile all Christian missionaries there.'

15

'That's true,' agreed Fidelma. 'But most of the Saxon kingdoms are now firmly converted to the Faith.'

Eadulf sighed and shook his head.

'There are still many kingdoms where the Christian faith is only tolerated. Mercia, for example, is still not entirely Christian. Even with the acceptance of the Faith there has been a constant war between my people and the Britons. Since we carved out our kingdoms with the sword there has always been such warfare. Christian Briton against Christian Saxon. It is also within living memory how Athelfrith of the Saxons defeated the Briton, King Selyf son of Cynan. After that battle, Athelfrith went to the great abbey of the Britons at Bangor and slaughtered one thousand Christian monks to celebrate his victory. Do the Britons forgive us such slaughter, Fidelma? I think not. I cannot rest easy all the while that I am in the kingdom of the Britons.'

Fidelma considered his fears with some sympathy. 'You are not to blame for the misdeeds of your people, Eadulf. I think that you should reflect on the fact that the Britons are not so narrow-minded that they would blame all Saxons for the events caused by previous generations. The Britons have adhered to the Faith for many centuries, even during the time when the Romans occupied their lands. They do not inflict harm without just cause. The massacre of the monks at Bangor took place in the kingdom of Gwynedd in the north and we are in the kingdom of Dyfed, which is in the south. Dyfed has close links to Éireann. And tomorrow Abbot Tryffin of Dewi Sant has invited us to break bread with him.'

Eadulf looked at her in surprise. 'We have both been invited?'

Fidelma grimaced. 'Well, the invitation was primarily to me but it was made clear that if you were sufficiently recovered then you would accompany me. I believe that something is worrying the abbot. He seems a kindly soul. I think that he wants to ask for help but did not feel comfortable about doing so at our meeting this afternoon.'

Eadulf was bewildered. 'Why would the Britons ask for your aid?'

'As I said, there are close links between Dyfed and Éireann.'

'Such as?' Eadulf, always keen to learn some new knowledge, asked her to explain.

Brother Rhodri entered at that moment bearing a tray with bowls of steaming broth and bread. He set it down on a table beside the bed.

Eadulf regarded the broth wryly. 'I could eat a side of venison,' he sighed, glancing at Fidelma, still speaking in their common tongue.

Brother Rhodri regarded him in disapproval. 'You may try some cuts of cold meat and cheese on the morrow, Brother Saxon, but I would advise you not to fully indulge your appetite for a day or so.'

Eadulf grinned a little in embarrassment at the man, now realising just how fluent the Briton's knowledge of the language of Éireann was. Perhaps he should have been more circumspect in his utterances.

'I am grateful both for your nursing and for your advice, Brother Rhodri.'

The round-faced man smiled suddenly. It seemed his natural expression. 'God never ordained a mouth to be without food,' he quoted as he left the room. 'So remember that advice is never the law.'

'What are these links, Fidelma?' Eadulf demanded as they began their meal after Brother Rhodri had departed.

Fidelma was nothing loath to explain the history and folklore of her people.

'According to the old scribes, it was over two centuries ago that a chieftain of the Déisi, Aonghus of the Terrible Spear, made a cast in temper and knocked out the eye of the High King, Cormac Mac Art. Because the cast was an accident, the punishment was not as severe as it might have been. The punishment was that Aonghus and his entire clan were to be banished from their rich lands in the kingdom of Midhe. Part of the clan was settled in my brother's own kingdom.'

Eadulf nodded, remembering that a tribe called the Déisi did, indeed, dwell in the southern area of Muman. 'And the others?'

'Another section of the clan went across the sea. One was led by Eochaid. He settled his people here in this area, which was the lands of the Demetae. He became the ruler here, though it is said that he achieved it by peaceful means and not by war. Since then there have been ten kings of his line and many of the nobles of this place are the actual descendants of the Déisi. That is why you will find many of this kingdom still able to converse in the language of Éireann and why many of our religious come to study here.'

Eadulf had not heard the story before. He considered the history before returning to the main point.

'If this Abbot Tryffin seeks your help, why do you think he did not say so when you went to see him this afternoon?'

Fidelma paused, a spoon halfway to her mouth. 'I don't know. He was cordial and concerned that you were well treated. He asked about our journey and then asked me, and you if you were well enough, to attend him tomorrow at noon.'

'Why would he seek your help? Indeed, how would he know who you were? I presume he knew that you were a *dálaigh*?'

'A good point to spot, Eadulf,' she observed appreciatively. 'He knew precisely who I was and of my qualifications as a *dálaigh* of the courts. The Britons share a fairly similar legal system with us. Apparently news of who I was reached him soon after our landing. I have told you that many religious from my country come to study at the abbey of Muine.'

'Muine?'

'It is what we call Menevia in our language. It is called Moniu in the local language.'

'Oh yes, Bother Rhodri told me,' Eadulf remembered.

Fidelma smiled mischievously. 'You might not like to be reminded of Fearna, Eadulf, but the Blessed Máedóc, who founded that abbey, was also a disciple of Dewi Sant and studied here.'

Eadulf shivered slightly, remembering how he had recently come close to meeting his death at the abbey of Fearna.

'Anyway,' Fidelma was continuing, 'Abbot Tryffin had been told of the reputation that we have achieved in solving mysteries . . .'

Eadulf felt an inward pleasure at the way she had naturally included him. 'So you believe he wants to consult us about some problem which confronts him?' he asked quickly.

'I believe that is his intention.'

'It seems very strange.'

'We will know soon enough. It is no use speculating without knowledge.' She reached forward impulsively and took his hand in both her own. 'It is good to see you recovered, Eadulf. I was worried.'

Chapter Three

The following day was bright and clear. Eadulf took a few tentative steps out of the hospice building and found, as Brother Rhodri had warned him, that he felt slightly weak and a little dizzy. In spite of that, he felt the better for the sharpness of the fresh air and soon the giddiness vanished.

The harbour of Porth Clais was situated where a river made its way to meet a long narrow inlet of the sea, with hills rising on either side. A few small fishing craft rode at anchor there, rocking gently on the waters, and there were isolated buildings dotted amidst gorse and heather covered hills.

Almost at once, Eadulf became aware of the seabirds for whom the inlet seemed a natural haven. Their noise and constant swooping, darting and soaring was all-pervasive. He was also aware of seals splashing in the sheltered waters just below the spot where he was standing. The place seemed almost idyllic. He could see a seal pup scrabbling about on a muddy flat on the opposite side of the inlet. Then, even as he watched, the dark shadow of a bird came, dropping down by curious stages like a falling stone. There came a combination of cries, and the seal pup's grey head became bloodied where the bird's talons had raked it. Yet the bird had not succeeded in carrying it off. There was a splashing as the mother seal came anxiously from the waves, crying to the pup to join her. Eadulf saw the russet and brown bird, which he recognised as a kestrel, climbing and turning for a second dive. The pup, encouraged by the mother, had made it into the water. Eadulf was sharply reminded that life was never idyllic.

He turned, walking along the pathway until he found a tree stump and sat down. The sun, though weak compared to summer sunshine, was warm and pleasant. One or two people passed by and greeted him in their own language and he replied, regaining his meagre knowledge of it. During his time studying at Tuam Brecain, two of the brethren there had come from the kingdom of Powys and he had spent time trying to learn their language. He was keenly aware of the antagonism that existed between the Britons and his own people. In moments of calm reflection, Eadulf could clearly understand the roots of the enmity between them.

In his father's day, the British kingdom of Elmet had been destroyed when Ceretic, its king, had been slain and the population driven westward by a Saxon war chieftain named Snot who had built his township or *ham* on the west bank of the river that had marked the tiny kingdom's border. Now Snotingaham was a thriving Saxon town where once Britons had flourished. Of course, he could understand why Britons hated Saxons. And did not most Saxons return that hatred? The conversion of the Saxons to Christianity had, if anything, pushed Briton and Saxon even further apart instead of joining them together.

Eadulf had heard the stories from the old ones of how, just over sixty years before, the Roman cleric Augustine, with forty monks from that city, had settled in the kingdom of Kent to help in the Christianising of it. He found only Irish missionaries, mainly in the north, trying to bring the Faith to the pagan Saxons, teaching them how to read and write. At Canterbury he found a church dedicated to St Martin of Tours, originally built by the Britons before the Jutes drove them out. The Frankish Christian wife of the king of Kent and her chaplain were worshipping there. Knowing that the Britons had been Christian from the time of the Roman occupation, Augustine demanded a meeting with their bishops on the borders between their remaining territories and the Saxons.

By all the accounts which Eadulf had heard, Augustine was a Roman who was still full of the old Roman arrogance. He viewed the Britons in the same manner as had the generals of the Roman legions in the old days of the empire. To him they were worthless barbarians. He had demanded of Deniol, the bishop of Bangor, why the clergy of the Britons had failed in their duty to the Faith by not bothering to convert the Saxons. Deniol had sarcastically pointed out that it was hard to preach love and forgiveness to a man when he was in the process of slaughtering one's wife and children. Augustine had gone further in his arrogance and blustered that if the Britons did not accept his authority and that of Rome, then he would bless the Saxon arms and they would suffer vengeance. It was a fact that some years later, Bishop Deniol was one of the thousand clerics who died during the wholesale slaughter of monks at Bangor.

Eadulf stirred uncomfortably from his reflections as a tall

Briton, clad in the robes of a religious, walked by and greeted him with a smile and some unintelligible word. Eadulf automatically returned the smile and gave such greeting as he could remember in the language. Eadulf had no wish to be an enemy to anyone, but what was the proverb of his people which came to mind? There is no safety in trying to make a friend of one's enemy. Surely that could not be right? There were the teachings of the Faith to take account of. What was it that the Blessed James had written? 'What causes conflicts and quarrels among you? Do they not spring from the aggressiveness of your bodily desires? You want something which you cannot have, and so you are bent on murder; you are envious, and cannot attain your ambition, and so you quarrel and fight.' Was that the main reason behind the last two centuries of war and bloodshed since the Saxons had landed in Britain? He shuddered. What was it that Christ had said? 'I give you a new commandment; love one another.' Well, so far as the decision rested with him, that is what he was prepared to do. However, it did not calm his mind; calm his fears of being in a strange land surrounded by a people whom he mistrusted.

Some hours later, when Fidelma came to find him and ask him if he thought himself fit to accompany her on the walk to the abbey of Dewi Sant, he found that the few hours in the fresh air had renewed his vigour. He answered in the affirmative. The giddiness had vanished and apart from a tenderness around the bruising on his forehead, which was still painful to touch, he felt revived.

The great abbey dedicated to Dewi Sant lay not more than a kilometre and a half to the north-east of the small port. They left Porth Clais walking at an easy pace, maintaining a steady gait, along the bracken-covered banks of the river. According to Fidelma, who had traversed the path the day before, it was called the Alun. Along this track came cargoes of gold, mined in Ireland, landed by ship at the port. The gold was taken to the abbey to be constructed by the goldsmiths there into sacred objects for veneration. Further upriver, the track ran into moorland, but Fidelma was able to pick her way through the boggy ground with confident ease. The day was still generally bright and, although the wind was rising, not too chill for the time of year. The journey was an easy one.

In no time at all the great abbey complex came in sight. Eadulf had to admit that it was an impressive collection of buildings, equal to any he had seen anywhere except in Rome.

The buildings were a combination of grey granite and local woods.

They were greeted at the gates by one of the brethren, who seemed to have been expecting their arrival for he led them, without delay, directly to the chambers of Abbot Tryffin himself.

The abbot rose from his chair and came forward to greet them warmly in Fidelma's native tongue. He obviously spoke the language as fluently as Brother Rhodri did. His tonsure was in the fashion of St John, the manner adopted by the churches of the Britons as well as those of Éireann. The head was shaved from the front to a line running from ear to ear, which some said was but a continuation of the tonsure adopted by the Druids, the wise men and sages of old. In his late forties, he was gaunt of face, thin-lipped and with a large nose, crisscrossed by tiny red veins, like a spider's web. He smiled readily and there seemed a genuine warmth in the greeting. Yet his dark eyes held an anxious expression.

They were seated before a fire and served with mulled wine which Eadulf found welcome and comforting.

'Are you in good health now, Brother Eadulf?' the abbot asked as he settled in his chair. 'Are you none the worse for your accident on board ship?'

'None the worse,' affirmed Eadulf solemnly.

'And I suppose, as you informed me yesterday, Sister, that you are still both anxious to continue your journey to Canterbury? Is that so?'

'We are,' replied Fidelma. 'As soon as we can find a ship sailing there, of course.'

The abbot nodded absently, drumming his fingers on the arm of his chair without apparently being aware of his action. It was obvious that some matter of importance was distracting him and he was having difficulty in articulating it.

'However . . .' he began.

'However,' interposed Fidelma, 'there is some problem which you require our help with.'

The abbot glanced at her in surprise. His eyes quickly narrowed. 'How did you know? Has someone told you?'

'Your concern is quite obvious,' replied Fidelma.

Abbot Tryffin gave the answer some thought, relaxed and shrugged. 'I suppose it is. It is true that we are confronted by a mystery which needs the advice of such an expert as yourself to explain it.'

Irritated, Eadulf looked up from contemplating the goblet of mulled wine.

'Before I say more about this matter, may I ask you a question, Sister?' asked the abbot.

Fidelma glanced towards Eadulf and replied with solemn humour: 'Not every question deserves an answer.'

The abbot shifted uncomfortably. 'That is truly said, Sister. I will ask, anyway. If I were to show you a mystery which intrigued you, would you remain a few days in this kingdom seeking an explanation of it?'

Fidelma indicated Eadulf, making it clear that the answer lay with him. 'I am here merely accompanying the emissary of Archbishop Theodore of Canterbury. Your question is best put to him.'

Eadulf set down his wine, considering the matter. It was true that he had delayed in Muman for nearly a year before finally deciding to return to Canterbury. What difference would a delay of a few more days in the kingdom of Dyfed make on this return journey? It would probably take a few days before they could find a ship anyway. But what mystery was there to so distract the abbot that he would invite strangers to solve it, and a Saxon at that? Eadulf was still acutely mindful that he was in the land of the Britons. He became aware of the abbot's close scrutiny as the latter waited with barely concealed impatience for the answer.

'There would be a remuneration for your services,' the abbot said quickly, as if payment were Eadulf's concern.

'Why would you seek our help? Surely there are enough wise heads in the kingdom of Dyfed to resolve the problem without calling in strangers?' Eadulf's tone indicated his vexation.

There was a movement beyond a screen at the far end of the room, and a tall, elderly man emerged from behind it. He had the build of a warrior, despite his age, and his features still retained the handsome mould of his youth. His white hair was tightly curled and beset by a gold circlet. His eyes were a striking, vivid blue, almost violet, with, at first glance, no discernible pupils. He wore clothes of rich satin and woven linen and wool. It was clear that he was a man of rank.

Eadulf noticed that Fidelma was rising from her seat and so he rose reluctantly as well.

The abbot coughed nervously. 'You stand in the presence of—'

'Of Gwlyddien, king of Dyfed,' interrupted Fidelma, bowing her head in acknowledgment.

23

The elderly king came forward, smiling broadly, his hand held out in greeting. 'You have a discerning eye, Fidelma of Cashel, and a quick wit, for I am sure that we have not met before.'

'We have not, but the son of Nowy has been spoken of with respect among the religious of these islands. Was not your father also famed for the support he gave to the Church?'

Gwlyddien inclined his head. 'Yet such as my reputation is, it provides little enough information by which to recognise me.'

'True enough.' Fidelma's eyes held a twinkle. 'It was by the royal symbol of Dyfed which you have embroidered on your cloak and by the gold signet on your finger that I inferred your identity. It was an elementary deduction.'

Gwlyddien slapped his thigh in appreciation and chuckled. 'All I have heard of you seems true, Fidelma of Cashel.' He turned with outstretched hand to Eadulf, who stood slightly alienated by this exchange. 'And, of course, where Fidelma goes, one hears of her companion, Eadulf of Seaxmund's Ham. Our bards tell us that two centuries ago the land of the South Folk, the very place from where you come, was once the kingdom of those Britons called the Trinovantes. From that tribe came one of the greatest of our kings – Cunobelinos, the Hound of Belinos, against whom not even the Roman emperors would dare to wage war.'

Eadulf shifted his weight nervously. '*Tempus edax rerum*,' he muttered, remembering the line from Ovid.

Gwlyddien stared disapprovingly at him for a moment. Then he sighed and bowed his head as though accepting the inevitable.

'Indeed, time does devour all things. Yet does not Virgil say that the Fates will find a way? What was once may yet be again.'

Eadulf restrained a shiver. He had heard that the Britons had not lost hope that one day they would drive the Saxons back again into the sea. He wondered how to respond but the moment had passed. Gwlyddien had seated himself in the chair vacated by the abbot, who took another.

'Sit down,' the king instructed with an impatient gesture. Fidelma and Eadulf resumed their seats. 'The answer to our Saxon friend's previous question is simple. Among the stories that we hear from travellers passing through this kingdom from Éireann, and the many brothers and sisters from your country who come to study here at this abbey, are tales of how Fidelma of Cashel has solved this riddle or unravelled that mystery. Having discussed the matter with Abbot Tryffin, I believe that

God himself put you on a course to this place so that you may help us.'

Eadulf tried to suppress his feeling of annoyance that the king did not include him. It was clear that it was only Fidelma's reputation that had prompted this summons to the abbey of Dewi Sant. The Britons barely tolerated him. He tried to keep his features impassive.

Fidelma was sitting back, regarding Gwlyddien with a studied expression. 'My mentor, the Brehon Morann, used to say that compliments cost nothing, yet many pay dear for them. What cost follows these compliments you now bestow on me and on Brother Eadulf?' The slight emphasis on Eadulf's name implied a rebuke at their exclusion of him.

Gwlyddien was obviously not accustomed to being questioned so directly and the abbot was looking anxious. However, Gwlyddien kept his humour.

'Believe me, Fidelma of Cashel, I am not an idle flatterer.'

'Of that I am sure,' Fidelma replied quickly. 'So let us get down to what it is that you want of us rather than proceed with the inconsequential matters.'

At a gesture from the king, Abbot Tryffin took charge of the narrative.

'Some twenty or more kilometres to the north of here is one of our sub-houses, the abbey of Llanpadern. Abbey is, perhaps, too important a title to give the little community that dwells there.'

When he paused, Gwlyddien exhaled in exasperation. The abbot continued hurriedly.

'One of our brethren, Brother Cyngar, was journeying here from his community. His route took him to Llanpadern where he had planned to ask for hospitality on his way. Brother Cyngar arrived here yesterday in a state of great consternation and anxiety. He is young and impressionable. It appears, from what he tells us, that when he arrived at Llanpadern it was deserted. Completely deserted.'

He sat back as if expecting some reaction to his statement.

After a pause, Fidelma asked casually: 'How many normally live in this abbey of Llanpadern?'

'It is a male house of twenty-seven brothers. They work the land and run a small farm and are thus self-sustaining.'

Fidelma's eyes widened a little. 'Twenty-seven? Was that figure chosen deliberately?'

Abbot Tryffin was puzzled and said so.

'Then it is of no consequence if it needs to be explained,' Fidelma said dismissively. In her culture, the number had a mystic symbolism. 'So Brother Cyngar found the abbey deserted and, presumably, could discover no explanation which accounted for its being abandoned?'

'He could not.'

'Did he examine all the buildings thoroughly?'

'He did. He found that candles were lit, food was on the tables, half eaten, but the place had been deserted for some hours. The rats were quite noticeable. But even the livestock were all gone.'

Fidelma turned to Gwlyddien with a sharp look of interrogation. 'And why is it that this case particularly interests you?'

The elderly king blinked in surprise. 'What makes you say that it does?' he demanded.

'I am interested in why the king of Dyfed is so concerned with this small religious community and its fate. Such inquiries could easily be left to your abbot here. But you seem overly concerned in soliciting our help.'

The king sat back, blinking a little at her directness. 'You have a sharp mind; a keen perception. It is true, Fidelma of Cashel, that I am particularly interested in the fate of this community.' He hesitated, as if trying to organise his thoughts into an articulate form.

'I have a son, my eldest son, Rhun. Rhun decided to enter the community of Llanpadern about six months ago. He was a bright lad. I once thought him ambitious for this kingdom, ambitious to succeed me one day. But then he became frustrated with his life and decided to join the religious.'

Fidelma leant forward a little in her chair. 'And your son, Rhun, is among the brethren who are now missing from Llanpadern?'

'That is so.'

There was a brief silence and then Fidelma asked: 'Do you have any thoughts on this matter, Gwlyddien?'

The elderly man shook his head. 'I do not believe in sorcery, Sister Fidelma. I have to ask the question: other than sorcery, how else can an entire community vanish into thin air?'

Fidelma smiled wryly. 'And do you think you have an answer to that question?'

'There is an answer.'

They all turned at the strange commanding voice that interrupted. A young man stood at the door, which he had opened

26

unobserved. He was tall with fair hair fixed in place by a silver circlet. The handsome features echoed those of Gwlyddien, the eyes reflected the striking colour of those of the king. Gwlyddien indicated him with impatience as the young man entered.

'This is my younger son, Cathen.'

Abbot Tryffin completed the formalities by introducing Fidelma and Eadulf.

'You say that there is an answer to the question which your father posed?' Fidelma queried.

'Do you know anything of the politics of this land?' Cathen replied with a question, as he sprawled into a chair.

'Little enough,' conceded Fidelma.

'During the last decade this kingdom had been under constant attack from the ambitions of our northern neighbours, the kings of Ceredigion. Their current king, Artglys, is an ambitious and ruthless man. His son and heir is hardly any better. The pair of them are evil. Once Ceredigion was ruled by the kings of Gwynedd but there was an internal struggle among its ruling dynasty. A generation or so ago King Artbodgu managed to unite Ceredigion as an independent kingdom. Since the rise of Artglys, the son of Artbodgu, Ceredigion have endeavoured to expand by raiding the territories of their neighbours. To annex the kingdom of Dyfed to Ceredigion is Artglys's dearest ambition.'

'How does that explain the disappearance of the community at Llanpadern?' demanded Fidelma.

'Ceredigion have raided our territory before and taken hostages.'

'So you are saying that Artglys of Ceredigion is somehow responsible for what has happened? That the entire community were seized in a raid?'

'I do not know for certain. I merely say that it is possible that the Ceredigion raided Llanpadern in order to take my brother, Rhun, as a hostage.'

'Possible but not likely,' his father added. 'When Rhun went into the religious, he gave up all claim to the kingship. Why take him hostage? To use as an emotional lever against me? My enemies know that I am not so weak. My oath of kingship and the good of my people come first. As for Ceredigion raids, why, Saxon ships have also been known to raid along our shores.'

'What is it that you expect of us?' Fidelma asked quickly to hide Eadulf's embarrassment at the mention of Saxon raids. 'Solving the politics of warfare is not what we are best at.'

27

Abbot Tryffin appeared uncomfortable. He also did not seem to agree with Prince Cathen's views.

'I believe that this affair has absolutely nothing to do with Ceredigion nor with Artglys's raids across the border . . .' He glanced at Cathen and his voice trailed off.

Fidelma intervened, seeing Cathen tensing himself for an argument. 'You say that this place – Llanpadern – is north of here? How far from the border with Artglys's kingdom of Ceredigion?'

'At least another twenty kilometres or more.'

'A raid coming some forty kilometres into your territory is a long distance for an enemy host to move unnoticed,' Fidelma observed.

'This might be a raid by sea; they could have come ashore on the coast which is only a few kilometres away from Llanpadern,' Cathen insisted.

'There is much power in the word "could",' Fidelma said reflectively.

The abbot had compressed his lips as if wishing to say something but uncertain whether to contradict his prince. Fidelma noticed his expression.

'I am sure that your contribution to this matter would be welcomed, Abbot Tryffin. What point do you wish to make?'

The abbot looked even more uncomfortable but seemed to summon his courage. 'The abbey is situated at the foot of the western slopes of Carn Gelli. If the warriors of Ceredigion made a raid on the abbey by sea, there are only a couple of places they could land. They would still have to march three kilometres from either landing place to the abbey. There are two townships on these routes and such a force would have raised some alarm. Indeed, Father Clidro and his community would have been warned of the arrival of hostile raiders in the territory long before they could reach the abbey. From the way Brother Cyngar describes the orderly way in which the abbey buildings were left, I cannot believe it was the work of warriors carrying off protesting prisoners. There was no sign of an attack, no bodies, nothing to indicate violence.'

Cathen gave a grunt of derision only to be silenced by a gesture from his father.

Fidelma waited for a moment, but as the king said nothing further she asked the abbot: 'Then to what do you ascribe this disappearance?'

The abbot of Dewi Sant was clearly worried. His eyes were slightly haunted as he stared at her. 'As Christ is my witness, Sister, I cannot think of any explanation in keeping with natural law that would account for it.'

Cathen let out a derisive hoot. 'Sorcery! Are you saying that it comes back to magic? I will not have that, Abbot Tryffin. There is no such thing as supernatural forces. You are as bad as that young Brother Cyngar! Evil forces do not exist.'

'I would disagree.'

They all looked at Fidelma in surprise at her softly spoken interjection. Her glance embraced them all.

'The supernatural is the natural which is not yet understood. And what of the mysteries of our faith? Are they not supernatural to us? If we recognise that there is good then we must accept that there is evil.'

'They are mysteries ordained by God!' pointed out Cathen defensively.

'And are you the judge of what is ordained by God and what is not?' Fidelma said quietly.

Cathen opened his mouth as if to disagree but snapped it shut as he found no ready answer would come. He stood flushed-faced for a moment and then said stiffly: 'Your pardon. I have duties to attend to.' He turned and left the room.

Gwlyddien stirred uncomfortably as the door slammed.

'I beg your pardon, I appear to have upset Prince Cathen,' Fidelma said, although her tone was far from apologetic.

'He is my youngest son and is inclined to be hot-headed,' muttered the elderly king. 'He means no disrespect.'

'There is none taken,' replied Fidelma. 'But, considering what has been said, I am intrigued by this mystery. It seems that we have a few days before the likely appearance of a ship by which to continue our journey to Canterbury, so perhaps we may usefully occupy our time.'

King Gwlyddien's face brightened. 'Then you will undertake the task?'

Fidelma glanced at Eadulf. He had already realised that Fidelma would not refuse; almost as soon as he heard the nature of the mystery and the conflict of interpretation between Prince Cathen, his father and the abbot. Mysteries to Fidelma were like the addiction of wine to another person. He grimaced with resignation, hoping that she could not read the resentment and jealous anger in his eye.

'We will,' Fidelma confirmed, apparently not observing anything amiss.

'Then it is a commission of the king,' Gwlyddien said with relief in his voice. 'All your expenses shall be met and whatever fee you demand shall be paid in gold or silver, as you wish.'

'Very well,' agreed Fidelma. 'But we must have some token to show we act on your authority, something bearing your seal; plus a sufficient sum to cover our expenses during our stay in this kingdom. If we succeed in finding a solution, we will accept ten gold pieces. If we do not succeed, we will accept five gold pieces. Agreed?'

'It is agreed.'

'Then we shall want to speak with Brother Cyngar. We would also need a guide to take us to this abbey of Llanpadern.'

Eadulf suppressed a groan at the enthusiasm in her voice.

'That presents no problem,' Abbot Tryffin agreed. 'Would you be able to leave for Llanpadern tomorrow morning?'

'Why so soon?' queried Eadulf, not wishing to be rushed into decisions.

Abbot Tryffin was apologetic. 'I mentioned two townships that might have raised the alarm had warriors of Ceredigion landed on the shores near Llanpadern. It so happens that one of these townships has asked me to send them a *barnwr*, a judge. Tomorrow morning, Brother Meurig, who holds that position, is setting out to the township. You could go with him and he could act as your guide.'

'An excellent idea!' agreed Gwlyddien.

Fidelma was thoughtful. 'Why did this township . . . ?'

'The township of Llanwnda,' supplied the abbot.

'Why did this township of Llanwnda,' she stumbled a little over the pronunciation, 'ask for a judge? I presume that a *barnwr* occupies the same position as a *dálaigh* in my country? Is there any connection between that request and the disappearance of the religious community?'

Abbot Tryffin shook his head firmly. 'The lord of Pen Caer, whose township it is, sent for a judge on an entirely unrelated matter. A young girl was raped and murdered by her boyfriend. She was a virgin. In such rural townships this is a most serious crime. The boy was apparently lucky not to be beaten to death by the outraged locals. No, there is definitely no connection between the two matters.'

'Then I see no reason to delay. We can be ready to depart for Llanpadern with Brother . . . ?'

'Brother Meurig.'

'. . . with Brother Meurig in the morning. However, you have said that it is a journey of over twenty kilometres and Brother Eadulf has not been well . . .'

'I shall be coming too,' interrupted Eadulf coldly. 'I am not so infirm or without talent that I cannot be useful in this matter.'

'Horses can be supplied for the journey,' Gwlyddien offered, ignoring the ill-temper of Eadulf's tone.

'Then we are agreed.' Eadulf looked defiantly at Fidelma, who was wondering why he seemed upset at her attempt to make matters easy for him.

'We are agreed,' she echoed.

'Excellent. It is well beyond midday and our meal awaits.' Abbot Tryffin rose from his place. 'After you have both eaten and rested, we will go in search of Brother Cyngar. Brother Meurig is also in the abbey. Ah . . .' He turned to look at Fidelma and Eadulf as a thought suddenly struck him. 'I forgot. Among the nobles and the religious, we can speak the language of Éireann and, indeed, Greek, Latin, and some Hebrew, but the ordinary people speak only the language of the Cymry. You will need an interpreter.'

'Your language presents no problem to me,' Fidelma replied, lapsing into Cymraeg. 'I served my novitiate with several sisters from the kingdom of Gwynedd and learnt from them. However, there will be much in the way of your legal language that I might not be able to understand, although I shall try my best.'

Eadulf was not asked if he understood, nor did he volunteer that he had any knowledge.

'Then there seems no impediment to your progress,' Abbot Tryffin said in approval. 'Brother Meurig will be able to advise you if you have difficulties.'

'We should be grateful for that,' agreed Fidelma.

'Then let us adjourn to our meal.'

Chapter Four

It was cold but no frost lay on the ground when the three horses moved out of the gates of the abbey of Dewi Sant. The horses moved in line, led by a tall figure on a grey mare. Brother Meurig rode at a steady walking pace, while behind him came Sister Fidelma and Brother Eadulf on two spirited cobs, short-legged, strong beasts. Meurig was wrapped against the early morning chill in a great cloak that was almost the colour of the horse he rode. His companions were also enveloped in heavy woollen mantles.

Abbot Tryffin had sent a man to fetch the travelling bags of Fidelma and Eadulf from Brother Rhodri's hospice at Porth Clais. This gave them the time to question Brother Cyngar about his visit to Llanpadern and be ready to depart with the *barnwr*, Brother Meurig, as soon as the early morning light began to appear over the easterly hills.

Fidelma and Eadulf had both been impressed with the serious and practical attitude of Brother Cyngar. However, the young monk was unable to add much more than they had already been told by Abbot Tryffin. Fidelma had questioned him closely on the detail of what he had observed. He was certainly pragmatic, and showed his eye for detail as he patiently went through a description of the abandoned buildings and their condition.

The young monk, far from being overwhelmed by the idea of sorcery and evil, simply accepted the idea that what could not be explained by natural means must, therefore, be attributable to supernatural ones.

After leaving Brother Cyngar, Fidelma and Eadulf had been conducted to the abbey's *scriptorum* where Brother Meurig was checking some books of law. Brother Meurig was a tall man, towering even over Fidelma who was considered to be of more than average height. He was gaunt, with hollow cheeks and high cheekbones. His hair was greying and his dark eyes were sunken, the right eye carrying a caste which gave him a slightly sinister appearance. His mournful features were not reflected by the bright friendliness of his greeting.

He spoke to Fidelma in her own language, turned to Eadulf and spoke an equally fluent Saxon to him. In fact, it appeared that Brother Meurig spoke several languages and all fairly fluently.

'How do you speak Saxon so well?' queried Eadulf, surprised by the man's ability.

'I was a prisoner among the Mercians for several years.' Brother Meurig pointed to a scar which ran round his throat and had been disguised by the cowled robe he wore. 'See here, the mark of the Saxon slave collar. That was over ten years ago when Penda ruled that kingdom. He was an evil man, that one. Penda was born a pagan and died a pagan, serving none other than his god Woden.'

'But you escaped?' Eadulf asked, trying not to feel embarrassed, although Meurig spoke without rancour.

'After Oswy of Northumbria defeated Penda and slew him at Winwaed Field, when Mercia was thrown into disarray, that was when many of the slaves he had taken, particularly Christian monks such as I, were released and allowed to return to their own lands.'

'And now you are a *barnwr* . . . a judge of the courts of Dyfed,' Fidelma concluded.

Brother Meurig smiled in satisfaction. 'Even as you are a judge, Sister Fidelma,' he said. 'A *dálaigh* is the equivalent of a *barnwr*. We have much in common.'

'I have heard that many of your laws are similar to the laws of the Brehons of Éireann. I am sure that I will have much to learn from you, Brother Meurig.'

'Your reputation precedes you, Sister. I doubt whether I shall be able to teach you much,' pointed out the *barnwr* affably.

'Have you have been told what has happened at Llanpadern?' Eadulf asked.

Brother Meurig nodded swiftly. 'But the matter is not in my hands.'

'Do you have an opinion about it?' Eadulf pressed.

'An opinion?' Brother Meurig sniffed deprecatingly. 'I have heard that Prince Cathen believes that it might be a raid by Ceredigion for hostages. My opinion is that the idea is possible although unlikely.

'Is there another logical explanation?'

Brother Meurig shook his head.

'No other explanation presents itself to you?' Fidelma queried.

'None that I can think of.'

34

'Then you do not believe, as Abbot Tryffin seems to suspect, that the community might have fallen foul of some black art – spirited away by the forces of darkness,' Eadulf asked in all seriousness.

Brother Meurig chuckled dryly.

'The forces of darkness have better things to do than waste time in performing conjuring tricks, Brother Eadulf.'

There was a ghost of a smile on Fidelma's lips. 'When you have eliminated all other explanations, whatever remains, no matter how incredible, must be the answer,' she observed. 'Even the black arts.'

'From what I have heard of your reputation, I believe that the realms of darkness would be the last place where you would seek answers, Sister.'

'Ah, you are so wrong, Brother Meurig. The realms of darkness are the first place to search when you are dealing with evil. The evil condition of the human mind is such a place of darkness that the entities of the Otherworld are but drifting ethereal smoke by comparison.'

Brother Meurig seemed amused. 'I intend to leave for Pen Caer at first light, so that we may be there by dusk. You may spend the night at the township and go on to Llanpadern in the morning. That would be the safest thing to do.'

'Safest?' Fidelma caught the word.

'Pen Caer is an area which has been beset by highway thieves of late. Even religious are not immune from their attentions.'

'On our journey tomorrow, you will have to tell me more about the place,' Fidelma said as they left.

'There it is! That's Llanwnda! That is the seat of the lord of Pen Caer.'

They had been riding most of the day, taking the journey in an easy fashion without tiring their mounts, stopping now and then for water and once for the midday meal. The track along which they rode was parallel to the coastline and the countryside offered such a variety of scenery as to be impressive. Moorland and crag, rolling cultivated lands and deep wooded valleys, river gorges and even tidal marshes bordered their road. Now and then they came close to where Meurig pointed out towering sea cliffs lining the shore between the land and the restless seas beyond.

35

It was late afternoon; the sky was a solid mass of grey-tinged clouds and dusk was not far off. They could feel it in the chill, gloomy air. Brother Meurig brought his mare to a halt on a rise at a crossroads marked by an ancient round-headed stone with a cross inscribed on it, set back in the hedgerow. He gestured towards some buildings which could just be made out through the trees, standing less than a kilometre away.

'That is Llanwnda!' Brother Meurig called again.

Eadulf found the name difficult to pronounce. 'Clan-oo'n-da,' was the closest he could come. 'What's the name mean?' he asked.

'A *llan* is an enclosure,' replied Brother Meurig. 'The chieftain here is called Gwnda and it takes its name from him.'

'G'oon-da?' Eadulf tried to repeat the name phonetically.

'That's right. Gwnda.'

'And the large hill beyond,' interposed Sister Fidelma. 'What is that? Is that the hill where the community of Llanpadern is situated?'

Brother Meurig shook his head. 'No, that hill is Pen Caer, from which this district takes its name. The community of Llanpadern is on the lower slope of Carn Gelli just to the south of us. Can you see the hill far over to your left?'

The area was so wooded that it was difficult, but she could just make out the contours.

'We shall find lodgings in the township. Probably Gwnda himself will provide us with hospitality, and then you may be able to pick up some gossip on what people think has happened at Llanpadern.'

'A sound approach,' conceded Fidelma. 'I hope we will also have time to observe some of your inquiries on the case that you have come to judge. It would be a good opportunity for me to observe the practice of the law of Dyfed.'

'I would like nothing better than to have you sit alongside me in trying this matter,' agreed Brother Meurig. 'But the practice is little different from the one you use.'

'What's that?' demanded Eadulf suddenly. He had been watching a strange glow from among the trees surrounding the township. It seemed like a reddish, flickering light.

'It looks like a fire,' Brother Meurig replied, his eyes widening.

'We must see how we can help!' Fidelma cried, kicking her horse with her heels, moving quickly forward.

'What if the cause is raiders?' Brother Meurig yelled desperately after her. 'Should we not be more circumspect in our approach?'

But Fidelma was already out of earshot with Eadulf chasing after her. Raising his eyes heavenward in resignation, Brother Meurig urged his own mount forward. They cantered along the track through the woods, for it was dangerous to move more quickly, and came to a bridge leading across a swiftly flowing stream into the township.

'I don't think it is a building on fire,' called Eadulf as they halted on the bridge itself.

It was not.

Beyond the bridge they saw a square among the buildings. A crowd was gathered there, facing a central tree with their backs towards the newcomers. Men, women and children were standing in a subdued stillness, each male holding aloft a burning brand torch to create the eerie, red glow which was like a large fire. No sound at all arose from them, the flickering flames of their torches the only movement. Then a restless shudder went through the small crowd. Two men appeared out of the shadows. They seemed to be dragging a third man between them; a figure which struggled and writhed in their grip. The sounds of his sobs came clearly to the watching trio. He cried like a baby, in a high-pitched tone, wailing almost hysterically.

With a muttered oath, unfitting for a religieux, Brother Meurig suddenly sent his horse bounding forward over the bridge and into the square. The people scattered this way and that in surprised terror.

Eadulf cried a warning to Fidelma but she simply shrugged and urged her mount to emulate Brother Meurig's example. Reluctantly, Eadulf followed.

Brother Meurig had halted and Fidelma and Eadulf pulled their mounts up on either side. It suddenly became clear to Eadulf what Meurig had realised was about to happen. The struggling figure was about to be hanged on the tree.

'In the name of God, what do you think you are doing?' Meurig yelled. 'Stop this!'

The people shrank back but a few stood their ground in defiance. The two men who still clung to their unfortunate captive did not move.

A thickset man, his moon face made red by the light of the burning brand torch he held, came forward to glower up at

Brother Meurig. He stood, feet apart, in a belligerent attitude, his free hand resting on the hilt of the knife at his waist.

'This is none of your concern, Brother! Get to your business and leave us alone.'

'This is my business,' replied Brother Meurig calmly, his voice stentorian, showing authority. 'Let Gwnda, the lord of Pen Caer, step forward.'

A second man had come to join the first. He carried a cudgel which he held carelessly in one hand but with such obviousness that he clearly meant it as a threat.

'You'll find the lord Gwnda probably praying in his hall should you wish to join him, Brother.'

The man punctuated his statement with a curious barking aggressive laugh.

Fidelma, following this conversation, caught the word *llys* and realised that it was the equivalent of the word *lios* in her own language. It meant more than a simple dwelling, more of a courtly place where a chieftain dwelt. Perhaps 'hall' was the best translation.

Brother Meurig looked down at the man with an expression of repugnance.

'In his hall, while anarchy rules in this place? He will answer to Gwlyddien, the king, if harm comes to any person without cause.'

The moon-faced man blinked and glanced towards his companion with the cudgel before turning back to Brother Meurig.

'There is cause enough, Brother,' he cried in angry voice. 'But who are you to make threats against our lord in the name of our king?'

'I am sent here by the king at the request of your lord, Gwnda. I am the *barnwr* from the abbey of Dewi Sant.'

This time the moon-faced man seemed less certain of his position. It showed in a slight dropping of the shoulders, a rapid blink and a quick shifting of his weight. His companion, with the cudgel, also looked less sure of himself now. Brother Meurig took the advantage.

'Bring that man here!'

He beckoned sharply to the two men who were holding the prisoner. They glanced at the moon-faced man but, receiving no counter instruction, they moved slowly forward with their captive still held between them. He was sobbing more quietly now, head hung low.

'He is hardly more than a boy,' muttered Fidelma, observing the prisoner closely. She had addressed Brother Meurig in her own language, but the moon-faced man glanced at her distrustfully. It was clear that he also understood her tongue.

'Boy or not, he is a killer and will be punished,' he stated in the local speech.

'This is not our way of punishment,' returned Brother Meurig. 'What do you mean by it?'

'This boy raped and killed my daughter! I will have my vengeance!' the moon-faced man said determinedly.

'You will not have vengeance.' Brother Meurig's tone was biting. 'However, you may see justice done. What is your name?'

'I am Iorwerth the smith.'

'And this boy's name?'

'He is Idwal.'

'Very well, Iorwerth the smith. You will lead us to Gwnda's hall. You two men, bring the boy, and see that he is not harmed otherwise you will answer to me.' His sharp commands allowed for no dissent. Brother Meurig glared at the crowd who had retreated some yards away as if to distance themselves from Iorwerth and his friends. 'The rest of you will disperse to your homes.' He glanced towards the man who held the cudgel, who now appeared crestfallen. 'And what is your name, my friend?'

The man's eyes were still sullen. 'I am Iestyn. I am a farmer here.'

'Well, Iestyn, what justification do you have for your involvement in this affair?'

'I am a friend to Iorwerth.'

'Well, friend to Iorwerth, I shall make it your duty to ensure that these people disperse to their homes in safety. If there is any sign of unrest or further rebellion here . . . why, I would hold you personally responsible. You would not like that, I am sure.'

Without another glance, Brother Meurig turned his back and motioned the man called Iorwerth to lead the way. There was a hesitation and then the moon-faced man shrugged and began to move forward. Brother Meurig started after him, still on his horse, while the two men followed, propelling the boy before them.

Bringing up the rear, Eadulf glanced towards Fidelma and smiled grimly. 'It seems that Brother Meurig has more of a commanding personality than I gave him credit for,' he whispered.

Fidelma grimaced. 'He is what he is; a *barnwr*,' she replied in a tone which implied rebuke.

The procession wound its way along the short distance between the buildings towards a large enclosure of barns and outhouses. Among these stood one tall edifice whose imposing structure marked it as the hall of the lord of the area. Two men stood outside the door. They seemed surprised by the arrival of the procession. One of them came forward as he recognised Iorwerth.

'What has happened?'

'It is the *barnwr*,' the smith explained curtly, jerking his head towards Brother Meurig.

'Where is your lord?' demanded Meurig, still seated on his horse.

The man glanced towards the house and then, surprisingly, his companion turned and ran off. The remaining man called a curse after him. Brother Meurig ordered him in a sharp tone: 'Bring forth your lord. Quickly! And woe betide you if he has been harmed.'

The man went to the door and knocked upon it. It did not seem to have been secured. There was a movement inside and the man turned and scurried off into the darkness.

A moment later a thickset man with a dark full beard appeared in the doorway. He carried a sword in his right hand as if ready to defend himself from attack.

'What does this mean?' he growled, glancing suspiciously around. 'I, Gwnda, demand to know!'

Brother Meurig bent forward in his saddle. 'Are you Gwnda, lord of Pen Caer?'

'I am he,' the man responded, not lowering his sword. Then his eyes narrowed suddenly as he recognised the robes of the religieux.

'I am Brother Meurig of the abbey of Dewi Sant, the *barnwr* for whom you have sent. These are my companions, Sister Fidelma and Brother Eadulf. They travel under special commission of Gwlyddien of Dyfed.'

Gwnda looked startled for a moment. Then he saw Iorwerth and the two men holding the boy. He rested the point of his sword lightly on the step before him, hands on the pommel. His features relaxed but it was hardly a smile of greeting.

'I wish I could bid you welcome to my hall in happier circumstances.'

Brother Meurig swung down from his horse. 'These circumstances will suffice, Gwnda, providing that they are explained to us.'

Gwnda regarded Iorwerth with a sour expression. 'Does this mean that your rebellion is over, Iorwerth?' he asked.

'It was never meant as rebellion,' replied the man, defensively. 'My aim was justice.'

'Revenge was your aim and rebellion it was; rebellion against your lord. Yet I am kindly disposed to you and will forgive your transgression against the law because you let your emotions misguide you. Get to your home and we will discuss reparation for your act later.' Gwnda turned to Brother Meurig as an afterthought: 'That is, if this has your permission?'

'You appear to be a man of liberal judgment, Gwnda,' said Brother Meurig. 'I see no reason to object until I have an explanation. And if everyone has now come to their senses, perhaps these two men will remove this boy to some secure place where he may be confined until I can question him?'

Gwnda turned to the two men and his voice was sharp: 'Return Idwal to my stables. When you have done that, you may take the horses of our guests here and see that they are well cared for.' He smiled briefly to encompass them all. 'Come into my hall, my friends, and I will do my best to explain the sorrow of this evening.'

'Lord Gwnda . . .' One of the two men still stood hesitating.

'Well?' snapped Gwnda.

'Shall I . . . shall we be punished?'

Gwnda nodded towards Brother Meurig. 'You will have the opportunity to present your defence. I shall leave the subject of punishment to the judgment of the *barnwr* here.'

'But it was Iorwerth the smith. He told us . . . told everyone . . . that we should support him. He said it was justice.'

'Everyone?' jeered Gwnda. 'Enough. You will have time to justify yourself later. Now get about the task that I have set you, unless you wish to compound your rebellion?'

The two men, heads hung morosely, moved off with the youth while Meurig, Fidelma and Eadulf dismounted and hooked their reins to a nearby post. Gwnda was ushering them into his hall. Inside, some women, looking apprehensively at the newcomers, were huddled in the corner.

'Have no fear,' called Gwnda cheerfully as he hung up his

41

sword. 'This is the *barnwr* and his companions. They come directly from the court of Gwlyddien.'

A young girl, about seventeen years old, dark-haired and attractive, came forward with an eager look on her face.

'This is my daughter, Elen,' Gwnda announced.

The girl spoke immediately to Brother Meurig. 'Is the boy, Idwal, safe?' she asked. Fidelma registered the concern in her voice.

'He is. Are you a friend of his?' asked the *barnwr.*

Gwnda snorted indignantly. 'My daughter is no friend of the boy!'

Brother Meurig continued to look at the girl. He made no comment but simply raised his eyebrows in interrogation.

'I was a friend of Mair,' the girl said hesitantly, the colour rising in her cheeks. 'Everyone here knew Idwal.'

'You should be more concerned with Mair's fate and in seeking justice for her,' muttered Gwnda sourly. 'Now, you may leave us to discuss matters.' He turned, raising his voice. 'Buddog! Where is Buddog?'

A handsome, blonde-haired woman of middle years, her features still bearing what must have been the stunning beauty of her youth, came forward.

'Bring refreshments for the *barnwr* and his companions. Quickly now!' Gwnda's tone was one of an arrogant master to a servant.

The woman, Buddog, stood for a moment, glaring at Gwnda. Fidelma noticed the intensity of her stare, which seemed to her to be one of malignancy, and realised that her companions had not observed it. Neither had Gwnda, who was occupied in showing Brother Meurig to a comfortable seat. Only then did he notice that Buddog had not obeyed him. He frowned, momentarily puzzled that his order had not been obeyed.

'Our guests need refreshment now, not tomorrow!' he snapped sharply.

Buddog paused for a fraction of a second before she dropped her gaze and moved away without saying anything.

Fidelma then noticed that Elen was also standing at the door, observing the scene. As Buddog brushed by her, the two seemed to exchange a meaningful look, and then Elen turned and closed the door behind them. Fidelma was intrigued by the veiled drama. There was tension in the household of the lord of Pen Caer and its mystery drew her like a moth to a candle.

Gwnda indicated that Fidelma and Eadulf should join Brother Meurig before the roaring log fire. One of the serving girls, not the woman Buddog, entered bearing a jug of local mead, which she served to them.

'We seemed to have arrived at an opportune moment,' Fidelma said, as she sipped the honey-sweet mead. 'It appears that you were a prisoner of your own people.'

Gwnda gave her a swift glance of appraisal and then nodded slowly. 'Rebellion, no less,' he confirmed with irritation. 'I can understand why some have allowed anger to mislead them. Feelings are running high on this matter.'

Brother Meurig regarded him with a serious expression. 'Your understanding is most commendable, Gwnda. But rebellion is still a grave matter. How did this revolt manifest itself?'

Gwnda gestured with one hand, a curious motion as if dismissing matters. 'My own people, stupid and misguided, imprisoned me and my household here. Then they seized the prisoner and intended to execute him.'

Brother Meurig's expression was bleak. 'That is outrageous. They imprisoned you and your family and took the boy from your custody by force? It is unheard of.'

The lord of Pen Caer's features formed into a grim smile.

'If it was unheard of, then I fear that it will now be a chronicler's historical note. Iorwerth, who led this stupid attempt, was the father of the girl whom the boy, Idwal, raped and murdered. It is understandable that vengeance was his motivation. I cannot be harsh on him.'

'Then you are most charitable,' observed Brother Meurig.

Fidelma intervened, however, her voice sharp. 'It sounds as though you have already judged the youth's guilt, Gwnda. What need did you have of a *barnwr*?'

Gwnda turned a patronising smile on her. 'I observe that you are a stranger to our country, Sister. I should be most happy to explain the law later. Law is a complicated business.'

Brother Meurig coughed dryly as if embarrassed for Fidelma. 'Lord Gwnda, Sister Fidelma is not only blood sister to the king of Cashel, but she is also a qualified *dálaigh*, of equivalent rank to me in her own country. It is to her that Gwlyddien, our king, has turned with his personal commission to seek a solution to the mystery of what transpired at Llanpadern.'

Gwnda flushed and made a non-committal sound.

'You have not answered my question,' pressed Fidelma without mercy. 'It seems, from what you have said, that you have already concluded that the boy is guilty.'

The lord of Pen Caer appeared uncomfortable for a moment. 'I sent for the *barnwr* because I believe that one should follow the law. However, my opinion is that the boy is guilty.'

One of the women interrupted by bringing in a tray of refreshments, which she placed on the table. Gwnda took the opportunity to motion them to take seats there. There were cuts of meat, cheeses, savoury cakes and oat bread among the dishes. Jugs of mead and fresh water were added to the meal.

Fidelma took the opportunity of this distraction to ask Eadulf if he were able to follow the conversation well enough. Eadulf was able to understand the general flow, but he confessed that he was too unsure of his knowledge to actually take part in any more tangible form than as a listener.

Gwnda had restarted the conversation. 'So you have been sent to solve the riddle of the disappearing community?' he said, addressing Fidelma.

'You have been told about it?' asked Brother Meurig.

'Llanpadern is only three kilometres from here. We saw and heard nothing until one of our shepherds came by and told us the news.' He was suddenly thoughtful. 'In fact,' he confided, 'it was Idwal who came through the township and told my servant that the community had disappeared. That was on the very morning that he killed Mair.'

'Did you send anyone there to confirm his story?'

Gwnda shook his head. 'By the time Buddog, my servant, told me what Idwal had told her, the murder of Mair had taken place. Idwal was a prisoner. Our concerns were about him and that was when I sent to the abbey for a judge. It was not until this morning that I was reminded about Llanpadern. Of course, it was then too late.'

'Too late? What do you mean?' demanded Fidelma.

'You do not know?' Gwnda seemed surprised. 'Young Dewi, son of Goff the smith at Llanferran, came to the township this morning and told us that the community had been carried off by sea-raiders. Some of their bodies had been left on the shore nearby. They were probably slain while trying to escape.'

The news silenced them.

Brother Meurig asked quietly: 'Was Brother Rhun among those who were slain?'

'I don't know. Young Dewi said that the folk at Llanferran buried the corpses of the dead brothers. If Brother Rhun had been among them, I am sure that he would have said.'

'And did this Dewi of Llanferran identify who these sea-raiders were?' Fidelma quietly asked.

'Oh yes. They were Saxons.'

Chapter Five

The ensuing silence was broken only by Eadulf's stirring uncomfortably. He had been able to follow the conversation clearly. He avoided Fidelma's eyes.

'This lad called Dewi, is he a reliable witness?'

Gwnda inclined his head in affirmation. 'His father, Goff, is well respected. His forge, at Llanferran, is not far from here should you wish to confirm the story.'

'Did you have much contact with the community at Llanpadern?'

'Not really. I knew the Father Superior, Father Clidro, fairly well. He was a charitable man, a holy man and a good scholar. But we did not trade much with the brethren.'

'You say that it was Idwal who first brought you the news?' Fidelma finally asked reflectively. 'That must have been two days ago?'

'He told my servant Buddog that the community had vanished.'

'I shall need to speak with Idwal about what he saw.'

'He is not a reliable witness,' Gwnda said sarcastically.

Fidelma's eyebrows rose a little at the assertion. 'On what do you base that statement? His present predicament?'

'Not at all. Idwal claimed that the community had simply vanished. Puff! Like smoke in the wind. That there were no signs of violence. If the Saxons raided Llanpadern, as Dewi reported, then there would be some sign of their attack.'

Fidelma considered the matter. She did not refer to the fact that Idwal's story was the same as that told by Brother Cyngar.

'Is it unusual that Idwal would be at Llanpadern that morning?' she asked.

'Unusual? No, the boy is an itinerant shepherd and is often wandering the hills.'

'Are you sure, forgive me for asking again, that he brought the news on the same morning that he is supposed to have raped and killed this girl?' Eadulf interposed for the first time in the conversation. It was also the first time that he had spoken in the language of Dyfed. It was harsh and accented, the grammar not

47

quite polished. But it was understandable. Gwnda regarded him in surprise.

'Ah, and I thought you were dumb, Saxon. Yet you do speak. Not well, but you speak nevertheless.'

'Brother Eadulf is an emissary of the Archbishop of Canterbury,' Fidelma pointed out sharply. 'And my trusted companion. He speaks several languages.'

Gwnda smirked in a patronising manner. 'I had heard that there was a new archbishop among the Jutes of Canterbury. A Greek, isn't he?'

'Perhaps we should continue with the investigation first before exchanging gossip,' said Fidelma. 'I believe Brother Eadulf asked a question.'

The lord of Pen Caer shrugged indifferently. 'Indeed, Brother Saxon. It was on the same morning on which Idwal raped and killed Mair.'

'A coincidence?' pressed Eadulf.

'What else, my Saxon friend? What else?'

Brother Meurig cleared his throat noisily. 'There is time enough to attend to the mystery at Llanpadern tomorrow,' he said in a censorial tone. 'I have a more pressing matter to pursue, and would like to hear more of this murder. Perhaps, Gwnda, you would outline the story as you know it?'

'As I know it?'

'The facts, as you know them. In the first place, who was murdered?'

Gwnda sat back in his chair, his hands folded before him. 'A girl called Mair was murdered. As you now know, she was the daughter of Iorwerth, our local smith. She was his only daughter. In fact, his only child. She meant much to Iowerth as his wife is also dead. Mair was young, sixteen years old. And she was a virgin.'

Brother Meurig clicked his tongue several times. When he saw that Fidelma was frowning slightly he offered an explanation.

'I believe that we share the same system of honour prices with you, Sister. A young girl's honour price, the *sarhaed* as we call it, would be high. Indeed, a share of that honour price would also be vested in the king himself for, as a virgin, her safety is his responsibility. It is called his *nawdd*.'

Fidelma inclined her head as she followed his explanation. 'You are right, Meurig. In our law, we call it the *snádud*. The king's protection. All virgins in the territory fall under his protection and a payment must be made if that protection is violated.'

'Shall we proceed to the circumstances of the murder?' asked Brother Meurig.

Gwnda continued: 'It was noticed that Idwal appeared to be seeking Mair's company more than is usual in such circumstances.'

'Such circumstances?' queried Fidelma, quickly picking up on the inflection.

'Idwal, as I have already remarked, was an itinerant shepherd. More than that, he was a bastard child. A nameless child. No one knew his father or his mother. A boy of no worth. That is why Iorwerth warned the boy away from his daughter. He also told Mair that she should avoid the boy's company.'

'And did she?' asked Fidelma.

Gwnda seemed surprised at the question. 'Mair was a dutiful daughter. You see, Iorwerth was a smith and, as his only child, he could expect to make a good match for her. I believe that he meant to marry her to Madog, the goldsmith of Carn Slani.'

Fidelma turned to Brother Meurig. 'I presume that we share the same system of dowries?' she inquired.

'We do,' he confirmed. 'The murderer will become responsible for the payment of the *sarhaed*, to her family, that is to Iorwerth. There is the payment of the *amob* to the lord of Pen Caer, and payment of the *dirwy tais* to King Gwlyddien himself. The payment and compensation of the fines involved would constitute a very large sum of money.'

'More than, say, an itinerant shepherd boy can pay?' Eadulf was able to intervene again with a simple sentence.

Gwnda made a dismissive gesture with his hand. 'The youth, Idwal, could not pay any such fines. That is why there was such anger in Iorwerth.'

'Are you saying that Iorwerth was only angry at the financial loss caused by the murder of his daughter?' demanded Fidelma swiftly.

Gwnda shook his head. 'Of course not, but it would enhance the anger for any man. That anger built up and he forgot his duty to his lord. He persuaded some companions to imprison me in this hall while he and others snatched the boy and were about to mete out summary punishment when you arrived.'

'That is barbaric and against our legal code,' Brother Meurig pointed out.

'Yet satisfying to a man who has been wronged and sees no other way of exacting retribution,' rejoined Gwnda.

Fidelma's brows drew together. 'It sounds as if you approve?' Gwnda lips twisted into a thin smile. It was more a moving of facial muscles than an expression of what he really felt. 'I cannot approve in law. But I can understand his motivation. I have said so before. Therefore, if I judge him on his rebellion, I shall not exact punishment for his action.'

'His action was still unprecedented and without the law,' insisted Brother Meurig.

'The circumstances of the murder have not been explained yet,' Eadulf pointed out quietly, seeing the conversation going down a cul-de-sac away from the main subject.

Brother Meurig regarded him in annoyance for a moment and then realised that he was being logical. 'You are right. Such legal arguments can be more usefully aired at a later time. Let us hear the circumstances of the actual killing, if you please, Gwnda.'

The lord of Pen Caer rubbed the bridge of his nose as if the action aided his thoughts. 'Little to relate. It was two days ago. As I said, young Idwal came to the township and told Buddog that the community had abandoned Llanpadern. That was not long after dawn. It was about then that Iorwerth sent Mair on an errand to her cousin's place at Cilau. About an hour later Iestyn, who is a friend of Mair's father, arrived at Iorwerth's forge and told him that he had seen Mair and Idwal arguing on the forest path. He came straight away to tell Iorweth as he knew that Iorwerth had forbidden them to meet.'

'Why didn't Iestyn intervene in this argument he witnessed? He was a friend of her father,' Brother Meurig pointed out.

'That is something that you would have to ask Iestyn himself,' replied Gwnda.

'Continue,' pressed the *barnwr*. 'What happened then?'

'Iorwerth fell into a rage. He, Iestyn and a few other men from the township went off swearing that they would give Idwal such a beating that he would never molest another girl again.'

'Molest?' queried Fidelma. 'I thought Iestyn only said he had witnessed an argument? How would Iorwerth interpret this as molestation?'

Gwnda turned to her. 'Again, you have to ask him, Sister. I only report what I have heard.'

'When did you hear that Iorwerth and his friends had set off in search of Idwal?' asked Brother Meurig.

'By chance, I was in the forest that morning. That was how I came upon Idwal standing over the body of Mair. He did not see me but it was clear what had happened. For the boy still had his fists clenched in anger and he was shouting out her name in a shrill voice.

'I was making my way towards him when there came the sound of Iorwerth and Iestyn coming through the woods. Idwal heard them also and he turned to run. By coincidence, he came running straight for where I was hidden behind a tree. As he passed me, I hit him across the shoulders with my cudgel and knocked him down. Then Iorwerth and his companions arrived. When they saw what he had done they wanted to kill him there and then. I prevailed on them, at that time, telling them that a judge should be sent for.'

'Let's get this straight,' Brother Meurig said slowly. 'Do you claim that you saw the boy in the act of . . . ?'

Fidelma cleared her throat and was about to speak when Gwnda pre-empted her obvious comment. 'I saw the boy standing over the body. That is all. But it does not take a sharp mind to understand what had happened.'

'In my country, the laws of evidence are strict. You cannot swear to what you did not see,' Fidelma observed dryly.

'The same laws apply here, Sister,' agreed Brother Meurig. 'Opinions or interpretations of witnesses do not constitute evidence. Gwnda knows this well. A judge will draw his own conclusions from the evidence. How was the girl killed?'

'Strangled after she was raped. There was bruising on the neck. The body was seen by Elisse, the local apothecary. He says that heavy pressure was applied and the girl was prevented from breathing long enough to kill her.'

'How did this apothecary deduce that the girl was a virgin but had been raped before death?' queried Fidelma.

Gwnda appeared momentarily embarrassed by the subject. 'There was a great deal of blood . . . you know, on her nether clothing.'

'Was the body warm when you came upon it?' asked Eadulf, once again trying to phrase his question in an intelligible form.

Gwnda stared at him as if he were a half-wit.

'Brother Eadulf means, did you examine the body yourself?' interpreted Brother Meurig.

'I did not touch it. I saw that the girl was dead. That was obvious without an examination.'

'But you cannot say if she had been dead for some time by the time you came on her and Idwal?' Fidelma asked, having seen the point that Eadulf was making.

'The boy was still standing over her. It was obvious that the killing had only just happened.'

'It is not obvious to us,' Fidelma sighed. 'You did not see the killing and there are many ways to interpret what you saw. Has Idwal actually admitted that he killed the girl?'

'Of course not.'

'Of course?'

'I have not known anyone to voluntarily admit to murder.'

'So he had denied that he killed her?' Brother Meurig did not sound happy. 'Did he admit that he raped her?'

'The boy denied that as well.'

'Has he consistently denied being responsible for Mair's death?' pressed Fidelma.

Gwnda nodded slowly.

'Has he volunteered any explanation?' asked Eadulf. 'What does he say happened?'

Gwnda was nonplused.

'Was he ever asked for his explanation of events?' Brother Meurig was worried.

Gwnda saw the disapproving expressions on their faces. 'He was not,' he admitted. 'I am no lawyer.'

There was a short silence which Fidelma broke by observing: 'A pity that you did not touch the body to see how long she had been dead. We might have learnt something from that.'

Gwnda chuckled grimly. 'Only the boy's guilt.'

'At least that would have been something, wouldn't it?' returned Fidelma icily.

Brother Meurig rubbed his chin, his face creased into a frown of irritation. 'Everyone seems to have condemned the boy without asking his story. What motive is he accused of having? Why had he killed the girl?'

'Easy to answer,' replied Gwnda. 'The girl rejected his advances. He raped her in uncontrollable passion and then, realising his crime, he killed her. I would have thought that much was obvious.'

Fidelma had expected his answer. 'Are we sure that Mair, as a dutiful daughter, which you assure us was the case, rejected the advances made by Idwal, if, indeed, he made any?'

Gwnda stared at her in distaste. 'You will not be welcome

in this community if you impute things about those who cannot now defend themselves.'

Fidelma's expression did not change. 'I am sorry if you think I am doing so, Gwnda of Pen Caer. I do not speak frivolously and I thought the purpose of Brother Meurig's inquiry was to ascertain the truth. In pursuit of truth, questions have to be asked and answers given. Sometimes the questions might imply things that are distasteful. It is not the questions that are distasteful but occasionally the answers.'

Brother Meurig rose from his seat, shaking his head sadly. 'In this matter, I agree with Sister Fidelma. It appears that we have arrived just in time to guide this matter into the proper legal strictures. We must question the boy, Idwal. However, the hour grows late and we must find hospitality for the night.'

'You are welcome to the hospitality of my hall, of course,' Gwnda said, trying to exude courtesy once he saw Meurig supported Fidelma.

'Then we shall accept it,' Brother Meurig replied, speaking for all of them.

'Should you need anything, please inform Buddog. I am without a wife and my daughter is still too young to take on the duties of running this household. Buddog will see to your wants. I myself must go to have a word with Iorwerth about the disgrace that he has brought on Pen Caer this night.'

'We would like to question the boy Idwal before we retire for the night,' Fidelma said quickly.

'Then Buddog will show you to the stables where he is held. It is a dark night.'

Chapter Six

Buddog met them at the door with a lantern. She held the light high in strong, capable hands as she conducted them across the yard to the dark stables. Fidelma had a passing thought that the hands did not go with the handsome features of the woman, for they seemed hard and calloused by manual work. Buddog did not seem relaxed or friendly towards them. She spoke only when spoken to and then was monosyllabic, holding her head with jaw jutting upwards slightly aggressively.

'Have you run this household for a long time, Buddog?' Fidelma asked pleasantly as they began to cross the yard.

'Not long.'

'A few weeks?' There was a tone of mockery in Fidelma's voice. She disliked imprecise answers.

She noticed the servant's lips tighten a little.

'I have been in this household for twenty years.'

'That is a long time. So you came here to work when you were a young girl, then?'

'I came here as a hostage,' replied the woman shortly. 'I am of Ceredigion.'

They had reached the stable door. Buddog paused with her hand on the latch and turned to Brother Meurig.

'You will need this lantern, Brother. I know the yard in the darkness so I can find my own way back.'

Brother Meurig took the lantern.

The woman hesitated and then said with a quiet intensity to the *barnwr*: 'If the boy did kill Mair, then she was deserving of death!'

With that, she turned and became a shadow in the darkness.

Fidelma broke the surprised silence. 'I think, Brother, you will have to ask Buddog to explain her views.'

Brother Meurig sighed softly. 'Undoubtedly, Sister. She seemed rather vehement.'

The boy, Idwal, was chained in an empty stall. He strained away from them as they entered, moving into the furthest corner like some frightened animal. He could not move far for he was

55

still bound with his hands behind him and had the chain around one ankle. Fidelma wrinkled her nose in disgust.

'Does he have to be contained in this fashion?' she demanded.

Brother Meurig did not support the idea of loosening his bonds. 'If the boy is a killer, then there is no cause to release him in case he does further harm.'

'*If*? And if he is not a killer?' pressed Fidelma.

'The evidence we have heard hardly supports that contention,' replied Brother Meurig in annoyance at having his opinion challenged.

'We have only heard part of the evidence, so far,' Fidelma reminded him.

Brother Meurig was impatient. They been travelling all that day and he was tired. 'Very well. I will have a word with Gwnda after we have finished.'

He moved forward but Idwal gave another animal-like cry and cowered back, turning his head away as if expecting a blow.

Fidelma laid a hand on Brother Meurig's arm. 'I would like, with your permission, to question him, Brother Meurig. I know I am here only to observe and this is stretching your generosity, but the boy might respond better to questions from me.'

Brother Meurig was about to object. He was beginning to feel that Fidelma might be interfering too much in his office, but he was also an intelligent man and realised that the boy might be more forthcoming to a woman. He indicated by a gesture that she might do so and seated himself on a nearby bale of hay. Eadulf took up a similar position. There was a three-legged stool, used for milking cows, nearby. Fidelma picked this up and went to sit near the boy.

'Your name is Idwal, isn't it?' she began gently.

The boy started back, staring at her with large frightened eyes. It soon became obvious to Fidelma that Idwal was not the brightest of youths. He was a slow-wit. Above all, he was very frightened.

'I am not going to harm you, Idwal. There are just a few questions that I must ask you.'

The youth searched her features as if seeking reassurance. 'They have hurt me,' he whispered. 'They tried to kill me.'

'We are not going to hurt you, Idwal.'

The youth was undecided. 'You are not one of us, the Cymry – the compatriots?'

'I am a Gwyddel.' She used the word which denoted an Irish person in the language of the Cymry.

Idwal glanced beyond her to Brother Meurig and Eadulf. Fidelma saw his swift examination of them.

'Brother Meurig there is the *barnwr* come to hear the charges against you. He has asked me to put a few questions to you. You see, we want to help you. Brother Eadulf is my companion. We all want to help you.'

The youth gave a long sobbing cry. 'They tried to kill me. Iorwerth and Iestyn and the others. They were angry with me. They tried to hang me on a tree.'

'They were angry but they were very wrong to do what they did,' said Fidelma. 'However, we came along and stopped them. Do you remember that?'

Idwal cast a glance at Meurig and Eadulf from the corner of his eye before returning his gaze to her. 'I remember,' he agreed reluctantly. 'Yes. I remember.'

'Good. Now, you do understand that they are saying that you killed a girl called Mair? That you raped her and killed her. Do you understand that?'

Idwal began to shake his head rapidly. 'No, no, no! I did not do it. I loved Mair. I would do anything for her . . .'

'Mair's father, Iorwerth, told you to keep away from her, didn't he?'

The youth hung his head. 'He did. He did not like me. None of them here in Llanwnda liked me.' Idwal's voice was suddenly flat, without emotion. He made a simple statement of fact.

'Why wouldn't they like you?' Fidelma pressed.

'Because I am poor, I suppose. Because I never knew my parents. Because they think that I am stupid.'

'But you were born in this territory?' Fidelma asked the question because in her society the community always looked after its weakest members and it was unusual that resentment was ever demonstrated against those without ability or means.

Idwal responded with a frown. 'I don't know where I was born. I was raised in Iolo's over at Garn Fechan. Iolo was a shepherd. He wasn't my father. He never told me who my father was. When he was killed, his brother, Iestyn, kicked me off the land and I had to fend for myself.'

'Iestyn?' The interjection came from Eadulf. 'Where have we heard that name?'

Fidelma glanced warningly at him. 'Is Iestyn the same person who was one of those trying to punish you this evening?' Idwal nodded quickly. 'Iestyn has always hated me.'

'You said Iolo was killed. How was that?'

'Sea-raiders.'

'Who were they?'

Idwal shrugged and shook his head.

'Tell me what happened between you and Mair,' went on Fidelma. 'Why did you come to be accused of killing her?'

'Mair didn't treat me like the others. She was friendly towards me. She was nice.'

'And you liked her?'

'Of course.'

'In what way did you like her?'

The youth looked puzzled by her question.

'She was my friend,' he asserted.

'Nothing more?'

'What more is there?' The youth was ingenuous.

Fidelma compressed her lips as she gazed into the boy's guileless eyes. 'You were seen having a row with her a short time before her body was found.'

Idwal flushed and he dropped his gaze. 'That's my secret.'

'It is not a secret, Idwal,' she said sharply. 'You were seen arguing with her and a short time later she was found dead. People might say that you could have killed her because of that argument.'

'I promised her that I would not say.'

'But she is dead,' Fidelma pointed out.

'My promise still holds. It was a personal thing between us.'

'So personal that she is now dead?'

'I did not kill her.'

'What happened, then?'

The youth's reply was guarded. 'After I had said that I would not do what she wanted me to . . .'

Fidelma's eyes narrowed quickly. 'That was what the row was about? She asked you to do something and you refused?'

Idwal blinked in confusion. 'Are you trying to trick me? I will not say what the row was about.'

'I am trying to get to the truth of the matter. If you tell me the truth, then you have nothing to fear.'

'I am telling the truth. I did not kill her.'

'What did she ask you to do?' pressed Fidelma relentlessly.

The youth hesitated. Then he gave a little sigh. 'She wanted me to take a message for her, that's all. And that's all I can tell for I swore an oath not to tell anything more. I swore an oath to her; an oath to Mair. I will not break it.'

Fidelma sat back in contemplation. 'It must have been some terrible secret that you would swear such an oath about taking a message. Why would your refusal create an argument?'

'Because I did not want to take her message. I thought it was wrong,' blurted Idwal.

'Why was it wrong?' demanded Fidelma.

'I will not tell any more.' Idwal was certainly a stubborn youth.

'Tell me how you came to be standing over her dead body if you did not kill her?' Fidelma decided to change tack. 'Come on, Idwal, speak sharply now.'

The youth gestured helplessly with his shoulders, a difficult motion with his hands still bound behind him. 'After the argument, I left her. It upset me. She was my friend and treated me nicely. But I could not do what she asked. I went to sit by myself and thought for a while. I felt that I should go to find her and apologise . . .'

'How long did you sit on your own?'

'I do not know. It seemed a long time.'

'So you went back to find her. Did you?'

'It was near to the very place where I had left her. She looked as though she was sleeping. At first, I thought she was.' Idwal gave a sob.

'Then you saw that she had blood on her?' Brother Meurig suddenly intervened, causing Fidelma a moment of irritation.

'She had no blood on her,' replied the boy. 'That's why I thought she was asleep.'

Brother Meurig leant forward from his hay bale. 'Yet the apothecary, according to Gwnda, said the girl had blood on her clothes,' he pointed out, more to Fidelma than the boy.

'Are you sure that there was no blood on her clothes, Idwal?'

The boy closed his eyes, as if trying to remember. 'I saw none,' he said emphatically.

Fidelma glanced at Brother Meurig.

Gwnda had said that the girl was a virgin who had been raped. If so, one would expect blood to make staining on the nether clothing, just as had been reported to them.

59

'What did you do then?' she prompted, deciding not to pursue the matter for the moment.

'I knelt beside her to see what I could do. I realised that she was dead. I stood up. I felt . . .' He paused, unable to express his feelings. 'It was then that I heard angry shouting. People were coming though the bracken. I was scared. I started to run.'

'Then?'

'I remember being hit. I was on the ground and there was Gwnda standing over me with his cudgel. Then the others came and started to kick and beat me. I think I lost consciousness for a long time. I do not recall any more until I awoke here and I was bound.'

'You cannot remember anything else?'

'I do not know how long I was kept here. I know it was more than a day and a night. Buddog came and gave me water. She said she was sorry for me. I have not eaten for a long while. Then early this evening, Iestyn came with two others and dragged me out. They dragged me towards the tree in the square . . . then you came.'

Fidelma sat back in silence for a while, looking at the youth. She turned to Brother Meurig. The *barnwr* was frowning. He indicated with his head towards the door.

Fidelma turned back to the youth. 'All you need do, Idwal, is tell the truth. Do you swear that you have told me the truth?'

Idwal raised his eyes to her. 'I swear it by the living God, Sister. I swear it. I did not kill her . . . Mair was my friend. My good friend.'

'And you still will not say what was the message that she wanted to entrust to you?'

'I have taken an oath to her. I will keep the message a secret. I cannot break my oath.'

Fidelma patted him on the shoulder, rose and followed Brother Meurig and Eadulf to the door.

'The boy has a ring of sincerity in his voice,' Brother Meurig observed reluctantly in a quiet tone. 'But his statement raises as many questions as it answers.'

'I agree that he is speaking the truth so far as it goes,' replied Fidelma.

'Then, like me, you are not sure that he has spoken the whole truth?'

'What message could the girl have wanted to entrust to him which would cause him to argue with her?'

'Maybe he was lying about it?' Eadulf suggested.

'For what purpose? It is obvious that the youth is immature for his age. I doubt that one so simple could make up such a story,' replied Fidelma.

'It seems strange, though. What message could have been important enough for her to make him swear an oath not to mention it?'

They were silent for a moment and then Eadulf spoke thoughtfully. 'The most puzzling thing is that Idwal claims there was no blood on the girl's clothes. Gwnda and the apothecary have said that that was what denoted that she had been raped.'

'That is something we will have to follow up with the apothecary himself. What was his name? Elisse?' agreed Fidelma.

'It is clear that Idwal is claiming that he was not the girl's lover . . . not even a would-be lover,' Brother Meurig observed. 'However, the evidence from the apothecary does indicate rape. The position of the blood on her clothes would confirm it.'

'I would also pursue the matter of this secret message,' Eadulf suggested. 'Often such messages are the means by which lovers communicate. Did Mair have such a lover? Was that the reason why Idwal refused to take her message?'

Fidelma stared at Eadulf in surprise for a moment and then her features broke into a smile of approval. 'Sometimes, Eadulf, you have the ability to see the obvious while we are looking for something else.'

Brother Meurig was intrigued. 'If the message was to a lover, then Idwal, who has admitted that he loved Mair, even though it seems we are not talking about a physical love, might have been stirred to violence through jealousy. Let us tax the boy immediately.'

Fidelma turned back into the stable. 'Idwal, one further question arises. About the message—'

The youth's features were set firmly. 'I have told you that I will not say anything more.'

Fidelma's voice was calming but assured. 'Very well. I suppose, however, you refused to take it because you did not approve of Mair's lover? Is that it?'

Idwal's expression told her what she wanted to know.

'You see, Idwal,' she went on kindly, 'truth has a habit of revealing itself. Who was this man?'

61

The youth shook his head. 'I have given my oath.'

'Your future might depend on your telling me the man's name.'

'I have given my oath.'

Fidelma was a shrewd judge of character and realised that Idwal would not be budged. 'Very well, Idwal. So be it.'

She rejoined Brother Meurig and Eadulf at the door, shaking her head. 'Eadulf was right. The youth insists on saying nothing but his face spoke the truth when I put it to him that the message was for Mair's lover. However, he would not name him.'

'There is one thing that we are overlooking,' Brother Meurig pointed out. 'About this unknown lover – we are talking only of a lover in emotional terms and not physical terms. The evidence confirms she was a virgin. It still gives the boy a motive. Revenge on the girl because she had rejected him for another.'

'I think it is best to wait until morning before pursuing the matter further,' Fidelma replied. 'Tonight, Idwal is determined to keep his oath. He might have reflected on the matter by the morning.'

They left the stable but outside Brother Meurig paused. His face was troubled in the light of the lantern which he held. 'The boy might be more cunning than we give him credit for. He might be misleading us.'

'If he is not,' replied Fidelma, 'it might not only confirm the reason why Iestyn saw the girl and boy arguing, but, again in the boy's favour, it might confirm that someone else had a motive for encompassing her death.'

Brother Meurig looked doubtful.

'At this stage,' Fidelma reassured him, 'it is not so much a matter of getting the right answers as of asking the right questions of the right people. You heard Gwnda's daughter, Elen, say that she was a friend of Mair's? She was also concerned for Idwal. Perhaps she knows something? However, if I may offer advice, I would ensure that you questioned her without the presence of Gwnda. He did not seem at all happy at his daughter's concern.'

Brother Meurig gave her an appreciative look. 'And there is the servant Buddog,' he added. 'She was quite severe about Mair.'

'I had not forgotten. Let us go and have a word with her before we retire.'

Buddog was in the kitchen. She was in the process of wringing the neck of a chicken. She glanced up dourly as they entered, her large hands giving the final quick twist to the bird's long neck. Then she pushed it aside. Three more carcasses lay ready to be plucked for the next day's meal.

'I will show you to your rooms,' she said, rising and wiping her hands on a cloth.

Brother Meurig replied by suggesting that food should be taken to the boy and his restriction eased.

'Food I will take,' replied the woman woodenly. 'Ask Gwnda about his bonds.'

'I shall,' agreed Brother Meurig. 'We were wondering what you meant when you said that Mair was deserving of death?'

Buddog's features distorted with a little grimace. 'I gave you my opinion,' she said, volunteering no further information.

'But on what is that opinion based?' demanded Fidelma.

Buddog hesitated. Her lips thinned, and she pulled a disdainful grimace. 'It is known throughout this township that the girl liked to flirt, to tease any man she thought she could provoke and make gain from.'

'Are you saying that she was promiscuous?' Fidelma asked.

'I thought I had spoken plainly.'

'A promiscuous virgin? It sounds like a contradiction in terms,' muttered Brother Meurig.

'Virgin?' Buddog gave a harsh laugh.

'You do not think she was a virgin?'

'I only have an opinion,' replied the servant. 'I am not a physician.'

'What men did she provoke?' queried Fidelma. 'You said that she would tease and provoke them.'

Buddog pursed her lips, perhaps regretting that she had made the comment. Then she said: 'Why not ask Iestyn? I once saw him coming through the woods with a smile on his face. I heard that he had just seen Mair.'

'When was this?' demanded Brother Meurig.

'A few days ago . . . oh, the very day she met her death.'

'And what were you doing in the woods at that time?' Fidelma asked quickly.

'I was picking mushrooms that morning for a meal I was preparing.'

'Buddog!' It was sharp voice of Gwnda, who had appeared in the doorway. 'What are you doing here chattering? Take our guests to their rooms immediately. Can't you see that they are tired, woman?'

Buddog shot him a resentful glance but said nothing. Gwnda started to apologise to them but Brother Meurig cut him short.

'It is we who were asking questions, Gwnda.'

The lord of Pen Caer frowned. 'Then you should address your questions to me and not to my servants,' he said stiffly.

'That would be futile, for it is the answers of Buddog that we wanted,' Fidelma said. She disliked the overbearing lord of Pen Caer, especially the way he seemed to treat the women of his household. 'I think Brother Meurig does have a request for you.'

Thus prompted, Brother Meurig told him that he expected food to be taken to Idwal and that his bonds should be removed except for the ankle chain. Gwnda grunted and turned away. Brother Meurig took it as an affirmative response and did not pursue him.

'A pity,' the *barnwr* said a short time later as he, Fidelma and Eadulf stood in the corridor outside the rooms to which a now taciturn Buddog had shown them.

'Perhaps you can resume your questions tomorrow?' Fidelma suggested. 'However, it might well be that Buddog was making conjectures about Iestyn. Certainly she seems to dislike Mair. Anyway, we should retire now.'

'Thank you for allowing me to observe your method of interrogation,' smiled Brother Meurig. 'I can see why you have won your reputation.' Then he hesitated and glanced towards Eadulf. 'I mean, why you both share the reputation.'

Eadulf did not bother to respond to Meurig's belated inclusion of him.

'Eadulf and I need to make an early start for Llanpadern in the morning,' said Fidelma.

'Will you not stay and see this matter through before you go? I thought you were interested in this case?' Brother Meurig was surprised.

Fidelma shook her head. 'I am very interested, for I fear the youth is innocent and that something deeper lies behind this. But our commission from King Gwlyddien is to find out what happened at Llanpadern and to his son Brother Rhun. That is our main task. We will ride on to Llanpadern first thing tomorrow. But I will look forward to hearing your news on this matter when we return.'

Brother Meurig's face softened a little. Eadulf realised that Fidelma's announcement probably came as a relief to the *barnwr*.

Fidelma's natural authority seemed to have almost taken over his investigation. Nevertheless, the *barnwr* was gracious.

'I am most grateful for the help given by Brother Eadulf and yourself. It appears that our methods of investigation are similar.' He paused and then added almost reluctantly: 'But won't you need a guide in the morning – an interpreter?'

Fidelma smiled. 'I don't think so. If Llanpadern is just a few kilometres in the direction of the hill which you pointed out to me earlier, then it will not be difficult to find. And as for an interpreter, though it is a few years since I spoke the language of the Cymry, I find that I seem to have retained a fair portion of what I learnt.' She smiled at Eadulf. 'Eadulf, too, appears to understand enough to get by.'

'I understand more than I speak,' confirmed Eadulf.

Brother Meurig certainly appeared relieved that they were no longer calling on his service as guide and interpreter. 'Then I shall remain here and continue the investigation.'

Fidelma smiled. 'We shall look forward to hearing your resolution when we return after our inquiries at Llanpadern.'

Chapter Seven

It was a bright, crisp autumnal day, with a pale blue sky and no clouds to block the tepid warmth of the early morning sun. Fidelma and Eadulf had bidden farewell to Brother Meurig and to Gwnda, the lord of Pen Caer, and begun their journey south-west towards the distant peak of Carn Gelli. The countryside was a mixture of moorland and crags, and isolated farmland surrounded by wooded valleys into which gushing streams, too small to be called rivers, cascaded from the surrounding hills.

It was an ancient landscape with a variety of cairns, cromlechs, standing stones and abandoned hillforts. Fidelma had noticed that there were also a fair number of burial chambers where only chieftains or men and women of high rank would be laid to rest. It was a landscape that showed signs of a wealth of wild flowers amidst the gorse and various species of ferns and heather. At the moment there were only a few patches of white blossoms, such as shepherd's purse and white deadnettle, which displayed any relief against the green. Generally the countryside was sinking into its drab almost colourless winter appearance.

High above them, the occasional kestrel flew in lazy circles, keen eyes watching for prey among the dying brownish bracken and evergreen gorse. A flash of red moved quickly as a fox went dashing for cover, more out of habit than fear of a kestrel, for its size made it quite safe. It was field mice, voles and hatchlings that the bird of prey was seeking.

As they rode along the track, it was the first time that Fidelma and Eadulf had been alone for some days. Eadulf had been watching his companion keenly.

'You are worried about the youth, Idwal, aren't you?' he said finally, breaking the silence.

She glanced at him and smiled briefly. 'You have a discerning eye.'

'You believe he is innocent?'

Fidelma pouted thoughtfully. 'I believe that there are many questions to be answered.'

'I think that you would have liked to take charge of Brother

67

Meurig's investigation,' Eadulf observed in gentle accusation.

'As the Blessed Ambrose said – *Quando hic sum, non ieuiuno Sabbato.*'

Eadulf frowned for a moment. 'You mean . . .'

'I mean, I follow the local law and custom. I do not have the right to dictate to a *barnwr* of this country. I have no wish to take over from Brother Meurig.'

Even as she spoke, Fidelma realised, with an inward sense of annoyance, that she was lying. She flushed and hoped that Eadulf did not notice.

'Well, Brother Meurig seems competent enough.'

'So long as Brother Meurig asks the right questions, there is an end to it. No one can dictate his interpretation of the answers. We, however, must concentrate on our commission. The sooner we resolve this matter, the sooner we can continue to Canterbury.'

They fell silent for a while.

The road from the township to the community of Llanpadern was an easy one, hardly more than three kilometres. They soon came within sight of the complex of buildings below the hill which Brother Meurig had identified as Carn Gelli. The buildings seemed isolated; even had Fidelma not been informed of the disappearance of the community, she would have felt that something was amiss simply by the atmosphere emanating from the buildings. That inexplicable aura of solitude seemed menacing. Fidelma was sensitive to atmosphere. Perhaps that very intuitiveness was the reason why she excelled in her profession. It gave her the ability to sense liars. She felt the twinge of guilt again. She had wanted to take charge of the investigation into Mair's death for her instinct made her feel that Idwal was speaking the truth.

They continued to ride along the path to the gates and Eadulf leant forward from his mount and pushed against them. They were not secured from the inside and swung open. The courtyard beyond was deserted. Eadulf halted his horse and the breath hissed between his teeth in a nervous whistle. His eye was immediately caught by the great stack of wood which was clearly laid for bonfire. Fidelma walked her horse to a tethering pole and dismounted, hitching the animal's reins to it.

Eadulf found that he could not suppress a shiver as he glanced around at the silent buildings. Fidelma noticed his movement but said nothing. Things unseen did not cause her apprehension. It was things manifest and physical that brought danger. She waited until Eadulf had dismounted before she walked slowly back to the gates and stood looking down. Eadulf joined her. She glanced up at him.

'There are too many tracks here, too much coming and going, and there has also been rain over the last few days which has obscured anything which might tell us about movements here.'

'You do not trust Brother Cyngar's word when he told you that he examined the area for traces which would indicate how the community departed?' Eadulf asked.

Fidelma was irritated by the question. 'I accept that he spoke his truth. It is always a good thing to check whether it coincides with your own. We won't find much in the way of tracks. See the road by which we came from Llanwnda? And that other one to the west? Mostly stone-strewn tracks. We shall not be able to pick up traces on those roads unless we have good luck.'

She swung the gates shut before turning back into the courtyard and examining the scene thoughtfully.

'If this place was subjected to a raid by Saxons,' Eadulf said, reading her thoughts, 'then they were very neat and tidy. Nothing destroyed, nothing burnt, no bodies . . .'

'Yet this boy Dewi said there were bodies left on the beach where the Saxon ship anchored,' she pointed out. 'Now, where shall we start? Somewhere in this deserted place must be a clue to what happened here.'

Eadulf did not appear convinced. 'What if that which happened here is inexplicable?' he muttered.

Fidelma actually laughed, low and musically. '*Omne ignotum pro magnifico est.*'

Eadulf recognised the line from *Agricola* by Tacitus. He had heard it used several times before when his mentors had mocked his Saxon superstitions. 'Everything unknown is thought magnificent.' It was often used to point out that the unknown was thought to be supernatural when, in reality, it could easily be interpreted once the facts were known. He felt hurt by her remark, for he felt it was aimed at his Saxon background, so he did not respond.

She was already striding towards a door. It led into the sleeping quarters of the community.

Like Brother Cyngar before them, they found the beds neat and tidy, nothing disturbed. The same was true of the chamber of the Father Superior.

It was when they entered the gloomy refectory that Eadulf

found the noxious odours in the deserted room almost overpowering. The food was still mouldering on the tables.

'Must we?' he muttered, raising a hand to cover his nose, as Fidelma moved resolutely into the hall.

Fidelma's glance was one of rebuke. 'If we are to uncover the mystery, then we must be prepared to examine everything in case we miss something which would give an indication of the cause.'

Reluctantly, Eadulf followed Fidelma as she walked slowly between tables on which lay the remains of the last meal that had been served to the brethren of the community of Llanpadern. There was evidence that scavengers had entered and made free with the food on the tables after it had been deserted. The mouldering bread and rotting cheese had clearly been attacked by the sharp teeth of rodents. Yet it was not this that Fidelma was concentrating on.

She was observing the knives and spoons, laid often carefully aside. A knife left halfway through cutting a loaf, still in the bread itself. A meat knife left lying on the floor. Fidelma halted suddenly, looking down. Nearby was a plate which had once contained a roast joint, judging from what little remained of it. The plate seemed to have been dragged out of place for it had pushed several other plates into an untidy heap. Fidelma's sharp eye caught sight of a knucklebone on the floor some way away. Her gaze then returned to the knife on the floor. Its slightly rusting blade was discoloured and she realised it was stained with dried blood.

Bending forward, she picked it up and examined it closely. Unless the meat had been exceptionally rare, the profusion of blood which had caused the staining must have come from some other source. But what?

'Eadulf, can you find a candle and light it?'

Although it was a bright morning outside, in here, in these buildings, all was shadowy gloom and it was difficult to see in any real detail.

Eadulf glanced round. Most of the candles had burnt away to streams of tallow. Brother Cyngar had told them that when he had entered the buildings, the candles, or most of them at least, had been alight. Eadulf spied one that had been toppled from its holder. A good few inches of unmelted tallow remained. Eadulf always carried a tinderbox with him: a small round metal box about three inches in diameter in which he carried charred linen cloth instead of wood chips, for he found it was a more combustible material, taking a spark better than dry wood.

From the box he took a piece of steel and held it in his left hand, the smooth edge above the charred material. Then he struck a sharp glancing blow downwards with the edge of the flintstone he held in his right hand. Tiny fragments flew off, glowing white hot, and fell onto the charred cloth which began to glow. He had a few dried bulrushes impregnated with brimstone and held one of these next to the glowing linen. It burst into flame almost immediately and he lit the candle. He closed the lid of the tinder-box to extinguish the flame in the cloth, reopened it to return the flint and steel, and then carried the candle over to Fidelma.

The operation had taken a little time, but Fidelma waited patiently. She had no other option, for every light in the buildings seemed to have been extinguished. In most houses a lamp or a fire was kept continually alight so that a flame could be passed on without the necessity for the long performance of igniting a fresh one.

By the light of the candle Fidelma examined the blade of the knife and then she bent to the floor, motioning Eadulf to hold the light as low as he could. She drew in her breath sharply.

'What is it?' demanded Eadulf.

'There seems to have been a great effusion of blood here. This was not caused by cutting meat at a meal. I believe someone was cut by a knife . . . this knife.' She gestured with the hand that held it.

A sudden sound in a dim recess of the refectory caused them to fall instantly quiet. It was like a low growling from the inner depths of the throat. Eadulf slowly turned his head into the darkness.

In a far corner of the room, the candlelight reflected against eyes that glowed like coals. He could barely make out the dark, round-shaped head. It was a silhouette only, the silhouette of a gargoyle.

The growl rose in volume.

Eadulf leant back unobtrusively against one of the tables, his free hand searching blindly for some weapon, for he knew he must not take his gaze from the menacing dark shape with its hell-like glowing eyes. It seemed to be crouching in the corner watching their every move. He could see by the movement of the dark shape that the creature, whatever it was, was gathering to spring. He felt, rather than saw, that Fidelma was trying to

71

hold herself perfectly still. His scrabbling fingers found a metal plate and he picked it up from the table, balancing it in his hand like a discus.

It was at that precise moment that the creature sprang forward, with a terrible scream, directly towards Fidelma's head.

'Down!' shouted Eadulf as he twisted round and let fly with the metal plate. It was almost a perfect discus cast. It impacted with the creature in mid-air. There was a terrible screeching cry, worse than its first scream, and it seemed to perform a twisting motion, changing its direction even in mid-spring.

In the grey light from the window, to which the creature now bounded, they had a momentary vision of a giant cat. It had black and yellowish-grey stripes in a brindle pattern, and was well over a metre in length. It leapt for the sill, paused, and then, with another snarling scream, the creature was through the window and away.

Eadulf set down his candle and turned to Fidelma. She was leaning back against the table, trembling slightly.

'What was that?' she demanded, trying to recover her poise.

'A wild cat.' Eadulf's voice was filled with relief. 'It's rare that they attack people. They usually live on rabbits, hares and small rodents. It must have thought that it was trapped.'

Fidelma shook her head in disbelief. 'But the size of it . . . I've known cats go wild, but . . .'

Eadulf smiled a little patronisingly, realising he possessed knowledge that Fidelma did not.

'That was not a domestic cat gone wild. These cats are another breed, larger and more dangerous if cornered. It is rare that they venture out of the forests. They hunt rather than scavenge. Do you not have them in the five kingdoms?'

She shook her head. 'Feral cats, yes, but not such beasts as that.'

'It probably came in here after rodents. There are plenty about,' Eadulf said, almost cheerful now.

Against threats of a tangible nature, Eadulf was fearless. Against anything that smacked of the supernatural, he was as apprehensive as a small child. Fidelma was smiling inwardly. It was almost the reverse with her. What was it that her mentor, the Brehon Morann, used to say? Nature is a strange architect.

'Let us hope that we do not encounter any more such creatures,' she observed, turning back to the task in hand. 'Bring the candle again, Eadulf.'

Once more she bent down to the dried bloodstains. 'I am sure that someone was stabbed with this knife and bled profusely here.'

She gestured to Eadulf to keep the candle low to the floor. Then she gave a little intake of breath, denoting satisfaction.

'A trail of blood spots. Let's see where this will lead us.'

They followed the occasional blood spot from the refectory. It was not easy, for the spots were few and far between, and in one place it took Fidelma some fifteen minutes of searching before she could find the next spot and thus pick up the elusive trail.

Eventually, they found themselves in the gloomy chapel.

'I think the trail takes us to that sarcophagus.' Fidelma paused at the door. The light was gloomy. The sarcophagus was a stone affair standing in the central aisle of the chapel before the high altar. It was an elegant structure made from a blue-grey coarse-grain rock. They could see as much from Eadulf's raised candle. It was constructed as a long, coffin-shaped affair and raised about a metre above the paved floor of the chapel, with tiny columns at its head and feet. On it was an inscription in Latin: *Hic Iacit Paternus.*

'The tomb of the Blessed Padern, founder of this community,' muttered Fidelma. 'There are certainly some blood spots here.' She pointed to the surface of the tomb.

Eadulf saw that it was true. Splashes of blood were visible on the stone slabs and against the side of the structure. He looked inquiringly at Fidelma.

'I suppose we must look inside?' He inflected the sentence to make it sound like a question.

Fidelma did not deign to answer. She was examining the lid of the sarcophagus. 'I think it was constructed to swing back,' she told him. 'Do you see where the stone is worn smooth?'

Eadulf nodded reluctantly. He set his candle aside and reached forward with both hands to test the strength of its resistance to his weight. To his astonishment, the lid of the sarcophagus moved easily. He glanced up in satisfaction.

Fidelma nodded quickly.

Eadulf pushed again and the stone swung effortlessly aside.

A smell of decay came immediately to his nostrils. He actually found it less unpleasant than the harsh odours of the decomposing food in the refectory.

Fidelma had moved to the side of the sarcophagus and was

peering into the tomb. Eadulf, more nervously, joined her in examining the contents.

Sprawled on the remains of a crumbling skeleton and decayed winding sheet lay a new corpse. A corpse that appeared to have been unceremoniously dumped inside, without ritual, without even the customary shroud. It was the body of a man who, by the state of decomposition, could only have been dead a day or two at the most. He lay on his back, and the dark stains across his chest showed how he had come by his death. He had been stabbed several times.

Eadulf was startled. 'This is no religious,' he observed, stating the obvious.

The body was that of a short muscular man with full beard, dark and swarthy and physically unlike any Briton that Fidelma had ever seen. His clothes consisted of a sleeveless leather jerkin, and leather patched pants which were rolled up to the knees. His legs and feet were bare. He wore bronze and copper bracelets on which were curious patterns and a neckpiece with a symbol like a lightning stroke. Around his waist was a belt from which hung an empty sword scabbard.

Eadulf let out an uncharacteristic whistle.

Fidelma regarded him with faint surprise. Not only was the whistle uncharacteristic but it was not often that Eadulf departed from deferential behaviour in a church.

'Does the body mean anything to you?' she asked quickly.

'Hwicce.'

Fidelma looked bewildered.

'The symbols on his bracelets indicate he is a warrior of the Hwicce,' explained Eadulf, pointing.

'That information leaves me none the wiser, Eadulf. Who-ekka?' Fidelma tried to pronounce the phonetics.

'The Hwicce comprise a sub-kingdom of Mercia which borders on the kingdoms of the Britons called Gwent and Dumnonia. The Hwicce are a mixture of Angles and Saxons, a fierce warrior people not yet converted to the true faith, and ruled by their own kings. I last heard that Eanfrith was their ruler. They supported the pagan king of Mercia, Penda, when he was alive. He had no time for Christian virtues.'

'So, the report received by Gwnda was correct,' Fidelma said thoughtfully. 'It does appear that there was a Saxon raid on this place and the community have been taken off as captives.'

Eadulf was leaning forward. He pointed to the man's necklet with its engraving of a lightning stroke.

'That is the symbol of Thunor, our pagan god of lightning.'

Fidelma looked down, her brows drawn together as she examined the lightning flash. Her mind was turning over the facts.

'Here is another mystery. The Saxon warrior is placed in the sarcophagus of the Blessed Padern. He has been stabbed to death. The evidence suggests that he was stabbed in the refectory with a knife being used to carve meat during the meal. If this was done in the course of a Saxon raid, why was he carried here and placed in this sarcophagus? Why didn't his comrades carry him away?'

Eadulf was frowning. 'It would be the normal thing to do,' he agreed. 'The Hwicce, especially, do not believe in letting their dead fall into the hands of their enemies if they can avoid it. He should have been removed and buried at sea. The Hwicce are still revered by the Saxon kingdoms.'

Fidelma examined him curiously. 'Why so?'

'They still follow the old ways. The dark paths of Frige and Tiw are beset with sacrifice and darkness.'

Fidelma was scornful. 'Nothing in that is worthy of reverence.'

'It might be because they are frontiersmen, still carving their kingdom out of the territory of the Britons who were most hostile to the advance of the Angles and Saxons. They have retained their belief in the original gods of the people. Their kings still claim that they are descended from Woden, the chief of the gods.' Eadulf hesitated.

'And?' Fidelma was not encouraging.

'In spite of the coming of the Faith, all our kings from the land of the West Saxons to Bernica still claim such a lineal descent from the god Woden.'

Fidelma pursed her lips cynically. 'At least my people do not have to claim they descend from gods and goddesses to seek leadership and obedience.'

Eadulf flushed slightly. While Fidelma was logically right, he still felt that criticism of his culture was implied. He decided to deflect the subject.

'Why would the Hwicce raid this godforsaken coast? We are nearly two hundred kilometres from their kingdom. Why would they raid here? Why leave the place so immaculate and why leave one of their number in a Christian tomb?'

'That is something which we must discover. Let us leave our

pagan friend in the sarcophagus for the time being. Our next step is to search for more evidence before we journey to – what was the name of the place where the young boy, Dewi, reported the Saxons had killed some of the brothers?'

'Llanferran.'

'That's right. Llanferran.'

Eadulf gave a deep sigh. 'None of this even begins to make sense to me. It is one unreasonable alternative facing another.'

'When you consider all the possibilities, it is the most reasonable explanation that provides an answer,' Fidelma assured him. 'Most things are illogical until you have the information which explains them. Come, let us see what else we can discover in this place.'

Fidelma helped Eadulf return the lid to its normal position. She was about to lead the way out of the chapel when something else caught her eye and she paused, staring intently at the altar.

'We almost missed that,' she said, nodding towards it.

Eadulf looked at the bare altar and frowned. 'Missed what?' he demanded.

Fidelma sighed impatiently. 'Come, you should know better. Look, observe.'

Eadulf turned back to the altar. 'There is nothing there,' he protested. 'What am I looking at?'

'Nothing,' said Fidelma. 'That is precisely the matter.'

Eadulf was about to question her further when the realisation finally came to him. 'There is no crucifix there. No altar candles; no icons.'

'Precisely. Just as we may expect after a raid, the valuables are gone.'

As they turned to leave, just behind the chapel door they discovered another curious object. It was the figure of a man made from twists of straw bound together with pieces of string.

Fidelma was examining it with a thoughtful expression when Eadulf interrupted.

'I can see no reason why the Hwicce would raid this place,' he commented. 'Surely the missing icons and treasures here would not constitute great wealth?'

'Your people keep slaves, don't you? Perhaps the incentive lay in the sale of the community.'

They found their way to the *dormitorium* and conducted a more thorough examination. It took them but a few moments, searching the sleeping quarters, to ascertain that nothing was missing from the personal belongings of the brothers. Toilet articles, a breviary and other small items remained at each separate bed.

In the chamber which was clearly that of the Father Superior, Fidelma's sharp eyes noticed that one small, iron-bound box lay discarded in an alcove. It was the sort of box that one might expect to find valuables in, but it was open and empty. Nor, as she pointed out, was there a crucifix in the room. The chamber of a Father Superior would usually contain a fairly valuable cross. That one had hung in the room until recently was evident by the dusty shadow marks outlining its position on the wall.

However, the Father Superior's personal belongings, toiletries and other items, and a collection of books in Greek, Latin and Hebrew, showing that Father Clidro had been something of a scholar, were all neatly stacked on a shelf. One even lay open on his desk with a metal page marker indicating the spot where he had left off reading.

'This is truly a strange affair,' observed Eadulf.

'That I'll grant you,' agreed Fidelma, but she could not help adding mischievously, 'but certainly not one that is sinister in the sense of any dark forces at work.'

'We have looked through all the buildings. Let us find our way to Llanferran. Our horses are restless.'

They could hear a protesting whinny from the animals they had left tethered outside.

'They remind me that we have not looked in the stables or animal pens,' replied Fidelma. 'We must be thorough.'

Eadulf screwed his face into a dismissive grimace. 'We know that there is nothing there. Brother Cyngar looked. He told us.'

'He also told us that he had looked round the community's buildings and found nothing. Yet we have found a great deal.'

Eadulf nodded glumly. She was right, of course.

They left the dormitorium and went outside. 'The gate seems to have blown open,' Eadulf remarked.

'Leave it,' Fidelma advised. 'It will not take us long to look at the animal enclosures.'

Brother Cyngar had been right. They were empty. All the livestock had gone. However, Fidelma insisted on looking carefully round, trying to spot the slightest thing that was out of the ordinary. From the enclosures they went to the large barn beyond, next to which stood a smith's forge. The brazier was filled with grey ash, and cold. It was some time since a fire had been kindled here. The barn doors were open. Fidelma halted

77

and looked inside. Cyngar had said he had gone to the barn and glanced inside but found it empty. Certainly, as they stood on the threshold they could see that there were no animals inside. There was nothing supernatural about their disappearance; the ground was stony and hard and the animals could easily have been driven off without trace.

'Brother Cyngar said that the community possessed two mules. Why are there half a dozen stalls?' asked Eadulf.

'Visitors, of course,' Fidelma responded. 'The community provided hospitality for travellers and pilgrims passing through here. It would be natural to provide shelter for their horses.'

She walked inside and carefully peered into each individual stall. When she reached the end of the line of stalls on the left, she turned round. Something caught her eye and she glanced up. Eadulf saw the expression on her face. He was still standing in the doorway and she was looking at something directly above his head inside the door.

'What is it?' he demanded, thinking that the wild cat had slunk back again.

Fidelma's features were grim. 'I think that we have found Father Clidro,' she said quietly.

Eadulf quickly walked a few paces inside the barn before he turned and looked up.

There was a pulley hanging from a rope attached to one of the main beams of the roof. Another rope stretched from a support beam to the pulley and was threaded through it. At the end of this hung the body of a man.

He wore the tonsure of St John and dark robes which marked him as not an ordinary religieux but a man of rank within the community. But they were ripped, torn and bloodied. The angle of the head showed that the rope had broken his neck. He was an elderly man. A frail man.

Eadulf exhaled sharply and genuflected.

'Release the rope,' Fidelma said quietly, pointing to it.

Eadulf went to where the rope was secured and loosened it, lowering the body gently to the straw-covered floor. It was clear that the man was not long dead, something which surprised Fidelma.

'I think you will find that the old man has been flogged before he was hanged,' muttered Eadulf. 'I saw the tears in the back of his robe as I lowered him.'

With Eadulf's help, Fidelma rolled the corpse over and

checked. 'A severe flogging,' she confirmed. 'What manner of man could do this to such an old one?'

'Do you really think that this is Father Clidro? But if so, he was not killed at the time the community was raided. Look at the way the blood is comparatively fresh! I would say that he was killed not more than a day ago.'

'There is no means of knowing for certain that he is Father Clidro but the odds are certainly in favour of it. He must have been of this community and he wears robes of rank . . .' Her voice trailed off.

Eadulf became aware that Fidelma's eyes had widened. She was staring over his shoulder.

He turned round swiftly.

There were three men in the doorway of the barn. The man in the centre stood with hands on hips. On either side, his dour-looking companions had bows in their hands. The bows were drawn, arrows ready, and aimed at Fidelma and himself.

Chapter Eight

Fidelma and Eadulf did not move from their positions. They froze as they saw the arrows pointing unwaveringly at them.

The man in the middle, standing with hands on hips, was smiling at them. He was a slim, youthful-looking man, quite handsome in a way. His hair was a tousled bushy crop of red-brown, his eyes blue and piercing. He was clad in the dress of a warrior, a close-fitting leather jerkin over a woollen shirt, and tight leather trousers and boots. A sword hung from his right side and a hunter's knife from his left.

Fidelma's eyes widened slightly as she beheld the gold torc which he wore round his neck. Years ago, in her own country, it had been the symbol of a hero, usually a princely warrior. The torc was a ring of fashioned gold, curved to fit closely round the neck. It was, she observed, highly decorative, ending in terminals which were the focus of elaborate engravings. Torcs were now old-fashioned in the five kingdoms and no one wore them any more except on some state occasions, and then only rarely. She knew from experience that the torc was common to many peoples in Britain and Gaul.

She also saw that he was wearing a more delicately wrought red gold chain which fell to his chest. It was of beautiful workmanship, exquisitely made and of some value. She wrinkled her nose in distaste. Wearing two such valuable and delicate objects detracted from the impact of each and created only an impression of ostentation and little taste.

'Well, well,' the young man finally intoned, regarding them with his smile still in place, 'what have we here?'

Fidelma slowly straightened up, keeping her hands slightly away from her body so that the bowmen could see that she posed no threat. Eadulf hesitated a moment and then followed her lead. The sounds of horses on the paved courtyard outside came to their ears. Clearly, the man and his two archer companions had an escort.

'I am Sister Fidelma and this is Brother Eadulf,' she began.

The young man's smile broadened. It was an expression that

81

caused Fidelma to feel uncomfortable. The smile was cold, merciless; the sort of expression with which a hunter might observe the helplessness of his prey.

'A Gwyddel and another Saxon, from your names?' He glanced at his companions. 'Well, lads, here are strange companions.' He turned back to them, still wearing his sinister smile. 'What are you doing here?'

'I am a *dálaigh*, what you call a *barnwr*—'

'I did not ask who you were,' interrupted the young man sharply. 'I asked what you were doing here?'

'I am answering you. My companion and I are acting under the commission of your king, Gwlyddien, to investigate the report of the disappearance of this community . . .'

To her surprise the young man burst out laughing. It was a laugh without mirth.

'Gwlyddien is no king of mine. Anyway, would a king of Dyfed employ a woman of your nation, not to mention a Saxon? Saxons are the enemies of our blood.'

One of the bowmen, the man who was covering Eadulf, raised his bow slightly as if in expectation of the order to shoot Eadulf.

'Look at the commission bearing the king's seal if you doubt my word,' Fidelma protested, gesturing to her *marsupium*. 'It will go ill with you if you murder a religieux and one employed by the king of Dyfed. Brother Eadulf has done you no harm!'

The man looked at her almost in pity. 'Ah, I forgot. The Gwyddel like to be friends with the Saxons, don't you? You are the ones who went to the Saxons to convert them to the Faith, to attempt to teach them to read and write and follow the ways of civilisation. We Britons knew them better. That was why we refused to try to convert them, even when the prelates of Rome came here demanding that we should do so. Have a care, Gwyddel; one day the Saxon will turn on you and do to you what they have done to the Britons who once dwelt all over this land.'

It was a speech which obviously stirred his companions who grunted in agreement, although their bows never wavered. It was the speech of an educated man who was used to command.

Fidelma did not flinch. 'I say again, what harm has this man done to you?'

'Have you not heard how the Saxons slaughtered a thousand

religious from Bangor to celebrate their victory over King Selyf of Powys?' demanded the young warrior.

'I have. That event happened nearly fifty years ago and none of us were born then. You certainly were not.'

'Do you think that because your missionaries have now brought Christianity to them, the Saxons have changed their character?'

'I cannot argue with prejudice, whoever you are. I say again that we are here on a commission from the king of Dyfed. We are in the territory of Dyfed, whether you acknowledge its king or not. Tell us who you are and why you dare ignore the law of this land.' Fidelma's voice was sharp and assertive.

The young man regarded her with surprise that this attractive young woman was not in awe of his threats and his obvious ability to carry them out.

'You seem very sure of yourself, Gwyddel,' he finally conceded. 'Have you no fear of death, then? Dyfed or not, it is I who am the law here.'

'I think not. You might have a transitory power by virtue of your friends with bows, but you are not the law. The law is a more sacred thing than the sword which you carry. As for fear, fear is not a passion that makes for virtue. It weakens the judgment, and I am a *dálaigh*.'

The man stood for a moment, his blue eyes staring into her fiery green ones. Then his smile returned and he chuckled appreciatively.

'You are right, Gwyddel. Fear betrays unworthy souls, so I am glad that you do not have any fear. I dislike killing those who are frightened to pass into the Otherworld with courage.'

He turned, raising a hand to his bowmen. Fidelma was determined not to allow her consternation to show, but she realised that the man did not speak simply for effect. He was ruthless.

'Would you kill religious?' she cried. 'If so, then I presume that you must be responsible for this outrage . . .' She gestured with her hand towards the body of the old religieux they had taken down from the beam.

At that moment another man entered the barn. He was clearly a member of the same band. It was hard to discern his age for he wore a war helmet of polished steel which enhanced his height but disguised his features. She had the impression of a handsome face and vivid blue eyes. He stood to one side watching Fidelma and Eadulf. His mouth was thin, and set in a grim expression.

The first man still stood with raised hand, and then one of the bowmen coughed nervously.

'Lord, what of Sulda? Some of these religious are often physicians.'

The first man hesitated.

'Kill them now and have done with it,' snapped the newcomer, vivid blue eyes regarding them coldly. 'Enough mistakes have been made these last few days.'

The first man glanced at him with an expression of open hostility. 'That was no fault of mine. I did not evolve so complicated a strategy. My man is right.' He turned to Fidelma and Eadulf. 'Are either of you trained in the art of healing?'

Fidelma hesitated, not sure whether Eadulf was able to follow the conversation clearly. 'Brother Eadulf studied at the medical school of Tuam Brecain,' she volunteered.

The man examined Eadulf with amusement. 'Then you have bought the Saxon a longer lease on life than he was about to enjoy. You will both come with us.'

'You still have not told us who you are,' Fidelma replied defiantly.

'My name will mean nothing to you.'

'Are you ashamed of it?'

For the first time a scowl crossed the young man's features. His companion with the polished war helmet moved unobtrusively forward and laid a hand on his arm. The movement was not lost on Fidelma. The warrior could be goaded and that knowledge might come in useful at some time. The young man made an effort to regain his composure and the cynical smile returned.

'My name is Clydog. I am often called Clydog Cacynen.'

'Clydog the Wasp?' Fidelma spoke as if placating a child. 'Tell me, Clydog, why is it that you wear that old symbol of a hero about your neck? Can it be that you have earned that distinction fighting against unarmed religious?'

The young man's hand automatically went up to touch his torc. Another flush of uncontrollable anger crossed his features.

'It was worn,' he replied slowly, 'at the defeat of King Selyf at Cair Legion. The Saxons will have good cause to remember that crime.'

The man in the war helmet cleared his throat warningly. 'We have bandied enough words. If you want these religious to look at Sualda, let us go now before another mistake is made. You two, walk in front of the bowmen. No tricks or they will shoot. I do not make vain threats.'

Eadulf felt able to intervene for the first time.

'Have a care, *Welisc*,' he said, using the Saxon word for a foreigner, which Saxons generally used as their name for the Britons. 'This is Fidelma of Cashel to whom you speak, sister of the king of Cashel.'

Fidelma turned to him with a frown of disapproval. 'Remember the adage, *Redime te captum quam queas minimo!*' she muttered.

The man with the war helmet glanced from Eadulf to Fidelma and burst out laughing. 'Well now! We find that the Saxon has a tongue, after all. Thank you for your information. A princess of the Gwyddel, eh? Well, lady, you need not remind your Saxon friend that one should strive to pay as little ransom as possible when one is taken prisoner. I doubt whether we shall trouble your esteemed brother with a ransom demand even though we now know your rank. He is too far away and such negotiations are troublesome.'

'So you are common outlaws?' Fidelma regarded her captors with defiance.

There was an angry flush on the cheek of the man who called himself Clydog. 'An outlaw? In Dyfed, I would not deny it. But not common; not I. I am—'

'Clydog!' The word came like a sharp explosion from the man with the war helmet. He turned abruptly to Fidelma and Eadulf. 'Enough chatter. Precede us!' He indicated towards the courtyard.

'Do you have a name also?' Fidelma was not to be intimidated. In fact, she was pleased that she was causing dissension among their captors.

The man with the war helmet regarded her for a moment. 'Among this band, you may call me Corryn,' he replied without humour.

'It is the first time I have heard of a wasp and a spider coexisting,' Fidelma said humorously, knowing that *corryn* was the word for spider.

'You might be surprised,' came the man's rejoinder. 'Now, shall we proceed?'

Outside, Fidelma was surprised to see half a dozen mounted men, all well armed and astride good horses. With them were two more men seated on a large farm cart which seemed to be filled but whose contents were covered with tarpaulin. She rebuked herself for not paying closer attention to the warning from their own horses, and the open gates.

'I see that you have come with your own mounts,' observed Clydog, examining their horses. 'Those beasts are richly accoutred thoroughbreds. You religious are well provided for.'

'They were provided for us by King Gwlyddien,' Eadulf pointed out defensively.

'Ah. Then the old man will not miss them. Still, as we have a distance to ride, you may still use them.'

'Where do we ride for?' demanded Eadulf. 'And why are you taking us as prisoners if you do not expect to ransom us?'

'Mount up!' snapped the man who called himself Corryn. 'Do not ask questions!'

Eadulf mounted. There was little point in doing anything else.

Clydog had turned to the two men on the cart. 'You know what to do? Rejoin us as soon as you have finished.'

He walked his horse to the head of the band as they closed in around Fidelma and Eadulf, and with a wave of his hand led them off at a brisk pace. They seemed to be heading directly towards the large mass of forest to the south. Fidelma was sure that at some point on their journey to Llanwnda Brother Meurig had referred to the name of this woodland. What had he called it? The forest of Ffynnon Druidion?

Of all the ill-luck. To fall in with a band of cut-throats. Brother Meurig had mentioned that there were robbers in the area but not such a large, well-armed band as this. Had she realised, then she would have demanded that Gwlyddien or even Gwnda provide them with an escort of warriors. In truth, she was now more concerned about Eadulf's safety than her own. Perhaps she should have listened more closely to Eadulf when he was talking about his feeling of discomfort at being a Saxon isolated in the lands of the Britons. It was not that she did not understand the depth of historical animosity between the two peoples but that she had thought good sense would prevail. She had forgotten that prejudice was often reason enough to inflict harm on someone.

She examined the figure of Corryn, riding beside Clydog at the head of the band of men. She had that curious feeling that his features were familiar. Had they met before? Or did he merely remind her of someone? If so, who?

He seemed intelligent and of good education. He spoke Latin;

certainly enough to pick up on her warning to Eadulf that he should be circumspect about revealing her identity because robbers would set a high price on a woman of rank whereas they might let a simple religieuse go without ransom.

Clydog, who seemed to be the leader of the band, also appeared to be well educated. There was the torc which he wore round his neck and the mysterious response he had made about it. Neither Clydog nor Corryn seemed to be typical of robbers and outlaws. But whatever the mystery was it was an infernal nuisance that their paths had crossed at this time. The first task was to escape. All told there were nine riders with them, including Clydog and Corryn. It would be hopeless to attempt to escape now because most of the outlaws carried bows of the type that were four feet in length and when strung would send an arrow over a great range. They would have to wait until they reached their destination and hope an opportunity would present itself there.

She glanced surreptitiously at Eadulf. She could see the grim lines of worry on her friend's face. She knew that Eadulf had only gone along with her decision to undertake this investigation to please her. He had been apprehensive; he had been apprehensive even before he accompanied her to the abbey of Dewi Sant to see Abbot Tryffin. Perhaps she should have respected his reservations, for Eadulf did not worry without reason. She would never forgive herself if her vanity, her arrogance, led to some harm's befalling him. They should have waited in Porth Clais and continued their journey to Canterbury without interruption. She set her jaw firmly. It was no use indulging in repentance now.

They reached the thick cover of the trees. Clydog obviously knew the tracks for he did not slow down but kept on at a rapid pace, while those following moved quickly into single file behind. Fidelma and Eadulf found that their companions were expert horsemen for they had negotiated their prisoners into a position in the middle of their column without slowing their pace. It was some time before the column of horses burst through a thick entanglement of evergreen undergrowth. Fidelma observed they had entered a clearing where a small stream bubbled into a large pool, not large enough to be called a lake. There was an old burial chamber at one end and some makeshift huts and tents nearby. A cooking pot hung over a central fire. A rail at the far end provided the only stable for the horses, being simply a spot at which the beasts were tethered.

There were half a dozen more men in the camp, who came forward, examining the prisoners with curiosity.

'Who are they, Clydog?' demanded one of them, a thickset fellow who appeared well used to the outdoor life.

'We picked them up at Llanpadern,' Clydog replied, slipping from his horse. 'This one's a healer.' He jerked his thumb at Eadulf.

'Do they know?' asked the fellow.

'Put a curb on your loose tongue!' snapped Corryn, joining him. 'That goes for all of you. No one speaks to the prisoners.'

The men regarded Fidelma and Eadulf with unconcealed curiosity.

'They are strangers, aren't they?' demanded a shrill-voiced youth, hardly old enough to shave.

'A Gwyddel and a Saxon,' replied Clydog.

There rose a curious murmur.

'Get down, Saxon,' ordered Corryn.

Eadulf dismounted. The outlaw grabbed him by the arm and propelled him towards a hut, thrusting him into its gloomy interior before he could exchange a further word with Fidelma. There was a man lying on the ground.

'If you are a healer, do something,' snapped Corryn, withdrawing and leaving him alone.

Eadulf looked down at the man, who appeared to be asleep, and then moved quickly back to the door of the hut.

Fidelma still sat on her horse surrounded by the dismounted men, but her reins were held tight so that she could not make any sudden moves.

'She asserts that the incompetent fool who claims to be king of Dyfed,' went on Clydog, 'gave them a commission to investigate the disappearance of Father Clidro's community.'

This raised a shout of laughter.

'Not even old Gwlyddien is senile enough to give a commission to a Saxon,' cried someone with a shrill voice.

'He gave the commission to me.' Fidelma's voice was soft and ice cold but demanded to be heard above the noise of their mirth. They fell silent and looked speculatively at her.

Clydog chuckled and moved forward. 'Allow me to present you, lady. This is Fidelma of Cashel, sister to the king of that place.'

'Where in hell is Cashel?' demanded one man.

'Ignorant fellow!' smiled Clydog. 'It is one of the biggest of the five kingdoms of the Éireann. Its territory could swallow this kingdom several times over and not notice it.'

Eadulf was astonished at the outlaw's knowledge.

'A rich place, eh?' demanded the shrill voice.

'Rich enough,' agreed Clydog.

'Why would old Gwlyddien ask her to investigate Llanpadern?' demanded another of the men.

'Ah, because she is a *dálaigh*, my friends.'

'What in the world is a *dawlee*?' demanded the man.

'A *dálaigh*, my ignorant friend, is the same as our *barnwr*; a judge, a person who investigates crimes and mysteries and pronounces on them.'

'Why send a Gwyddel? Aren't there *barnwr* enough in Dyfed?'

'Why, indeed? Perhaps there are none that he can trust,' grinned Clydog.

'Perhaps,' said Fidelma, her voice still cold, 'you might like to ask King Gwlyddien yourself? But perhaps you lack the courage to go to Menevia to do so?'

Clydog smiled up at her. His smile was an almost permanent expression and one that she realised she did not trust at all.

'Enough! Enough!' snapped Corryn, moving forward. 'Did I not say that no one should speak with these prisoners?'

Clydog stood his ground, looking in annoyance at his comrade. 'Would you deny my men a little fun?'

'Fun they may have after our purpose is achieved.'

'Yet it is an interesting point, Corryn. Why would the old fool give such a commission to this woman, even if she is a *dálaigh*? Why to a Gwyddel?'

His men murmured in support. Eadulf felt obliged to call out from the entrance of the hut, 'Sister Fidelma has a reputation in the art of solving mysteries.'

Clydog turned and grinned at him. 'Our Saxon friend is frugal of speech. As you can tell, lads, he is not an adept in our tongue, unlike the good sister here. However, when he speaks, he imparts no idle information.' He paused and turned back to Fidelma. 'Do you know the *Satyricon* of Petronius, lady?'

Fidelma was surprised by the question. 'I have read it,' she conceded.

Clydog bowed his head. 'He wrote, *Raram facit misturam cum sapientia forma*. This is a rare occasion.'

Fidelma flushed. The line that he had quoted meant that beauty and wisdom were rarely found together.

'You seem to have some degree of learning, Clydog. And a tongue that can drip honey. I give you a line from Plautus. *Ubi mel ibi apes* . . . honey attracts bees and you should remember that bees can sting.'

Clydog slapped his thigh and guffawed with laughter while his men looked on puzzled, not able to understand the nuances of the Latin that passed between their leader and Fidelma.

'It will be my pleasure to entertain you this evening, lady. I shall go personally in search of a deer to put on the spit.'

'How long do you mean to keep us prisoners?'

'For the time being, you are my guests.'

'You have no fear of what the king of Dyfed might do when he hears of this outrage?'

'*If* he hears of it, lady,' he replied with emphasis.

'Do you think that you can keep this act from his knowledge?'

Clydog was imperturbable. 'Assuredly.'

Fidelma felt angered by his nonchalance. She tried to stir him into some emotion. 'Even if Dyfed does not act, then my brother will—'

'Will do what, lady?' cut in Corryn. 'If you do not return to Cashel, he will mourn, that is all. Pilgrims vanish and are heard of no more. It is common. Saxons vanish all the time in the border areas between their kingdoms and the Cymry. Now, I think we have had enough banter.' He looked meaningfully at Clydog.

Clydog nodded. 'Have no expectation that you can talk yourself to freedom, or that some rescue party will appear to set you at liberty. You and the Saxon are guests of Clydog Cacynen and that is all you need to know.' He turned away, issuing orders.

Corryn swung back to Eadulf with an angry look. 'Did I not tell you to proceed with your healing art, Saxon?' he demanded, hand on his sword.

Eadulf turned back into the hut and bent down. The man who lay on the floor was clearly one of the outlaws, rough-looking and unkempt. He was not asleep, as Eadulf had thought at first, but semi-conscious. There was a flickering candle on a box to one side of the hut and Eadulf reached for it.

By laying his hand on the man's brow he realised he was in a fever. Holding the candle up, he drew back the blanket and immediate saw the cause of the man's illness. He was bleeding profusely from a cut on one side of the stomach. It was not a deep cut but it was jagged and infected.

Eadulf became aware that Corryn had entered the hut and stood staring down over his shoulder.

'Can you do anything?' the outlaw demanded.

'What manner of weapon made his wound?' Eadulf asked, as he examined it. 'How was it infected?'

'It was done with a meat knife. Hence the jagged tear.'

'Can any of your men be relied on to know hair moss when they see it?'

Corryn nodded. 'Of course. There is some growing by the stream.'

'I need some. I also need my saddle bag.' Eadulf always carried a small medical bag on his travels.

Corryn hesitated a moment and then turned out of the hut. Eadulf could hear him snapping an order to someone. The feverish man suddenly caught at his wrist. Eadulf found the eyes wide open, locked on him.

'I fixed him, didn't I?' The voice was intense.

Eadulf smiled reassuringly. 'You lie back. Just relax. You'll be all right.'

The man continued to clutch at his wrist. 'He took me unawares. Chased him into . . . into . . . took the meat knife. Got me. I . . . had to kill him . . . fixed him, didn't I?'

'Surely you did, my friend,' muttered Eadulf. The man suddenly fell back exhausted, as Corryn re-entered and put down the saddle bag.

'What's the man's name?' Eadulf asked.

'Sualda,' replied Corryn. 'Why?'

'Sometimes it reassures patients if their physicians know who they are,' Eadulf pointed out sarcastically. He took up his bag and began to busy himself, asking for hot water. The water and the hair moss arrived at the same time.

'What are you doing?' asked Corryn, after Eadulf had cleaned the wound.

'An infusion of valerian to decrease the fever and then, on the clean wound, a poultice from hair moss soaked in a distillation of red clover blossom, comfrey and burdock. Then there will be nothing left but prayer.'

Corryn went away, calling one of the outlaws to watch Eadulf. The man waited until Eadulf had finished his ministrations before escorting him roughly from the hut. His wrists were secured behind him and he was taken to a larger, darker hut, pushed inside and secured to the support post in one of the walls. As he left, the man suddenly punched Eadulf full in the mouth. Eadulf's head jerked back.

'That's for my brother, Saxon! He was killed by your people on a slave raid. Your death will be slow, I'll warrant you.'

The man went out, and Eadulf heard a movement on the opposite side of the hut. Fidelma's voice came out of the gloom.

'Are you hurt?' she asked anxiously.

'It could have been worse,' Eadulf replied stoically, licking his lips and tasting the salty blood. 'No broken teeth.'

'We've been in worse situations.' She attempted to sound reassuring as she tested her bonds. They had been expertly tied. She had resorted to speaking in their common language. 'What did they want with you?'

Eadulf told her briefly. 'I think we can be sure of one thing,' he said. 'Whatever fate he has in store for you, to him and his men I am a mere Saxon. As soon as it is known whether this man, Sualda, will live or die, I will become expendable.'

Fidelma gave a troubled sigh. 'Bear up, Eadulf. We have escaped from dangers before and will do so again.'

Eadulf had been struggling with his bonds, feeling them tight against his wrists and vainly searching for something which might assist in his loosening them. Fidelma listened to his ineffective efforts for some time before saying reprovingly: 'Eadulf, there is no use contesting with the inevitable until you have a choice.'

'What of the advice of your much quoted friend, Publilius Syrus?' demanded Eadulf in annoyance.

'Syrus?' Fidelma was confused.

'You are always quoting lines from Publilius Syrus. Don't you recall where he said that necessity can turn any weapon to advantage? Shouldn't we be searching for what weapons we can to aid us in our necessity?'

There was silence between them for a moment or two.

'It is no use arguing between ourselves, Eadulf,' Fidelma replied at last. 'Show me a weapon and I will turn it to advantage. As we have no weapon and no means of obtaining freedom at this moment, we can use the opportunity to reflect on our situation.'

Eadulf groaned inwardly. He could not argue with Fidelma's logic. 'There is little that actually makes sense,' he pointed out.

'I believe that Clydog and his men already knew that the

community had deserted those buildings. They might even have known that we were inside.'

'That's absolutely—'

'Ridiculous?' Fidelma broke in. 'Perhaps. But the only way they can have entered, without us knowing, is that they rode quietly up. They did not ring the bell. They came through the gates and across to the barn where they surprised us. I think they had been there before.'

'Well, for what purpose?'

'Solutions do not come as easily as questions arising from a contemplation of the facts, Eadulf. Was Clydog warned that we would be there? If so, by whom? How many people would know? And then, again, why would they want Clydog to come and take us away? To prevent us finding out the truth of what happened there? Was the old man the Father Superior, Father Clidro? How did he come to be hanged only a few hours before we found him?'

'You forget about the Hwicce in the sepulchre,' muttered Eadulf mournfully.

Fidelma smiled in the darkness. 'The Hwicce. No, I am not forgetting him. Indeed, if Clydog and his men had been at Llanpadern before, then his presence begins to make sense.'

Eadulf shifted his position so far as his bonds allowed. 'Well, for the love of Christ, do not mention the Hwicce in front of these fellows. They might think that I was connected with him. My span on earth is already more tenuous than I care to contemplate.'

Fidelma was still thoughtful. 'Perhaps Clydog already knows about the body in the chapel sepulchre.'

'Of course he does not.' Eadulf was emphatic.

'Why of course?'

'Because if he had known he would have made some remark about the fact. Once he knew that I was a Saxon, he would have made the obvious comment.'

She was quiet for a while and then she sighed deeply again.

Eadulf continued now and then to pull at his bonds without success. It irritated him to be so helpless. Having recently spent weeks in a grim cell in the abbey of Fearna awaiting death, he felt an uncontrollable rage, a frustration, at being a helpless prisoner again in so short a space of time.

From the silence across the hut, Eadulf surmised that Fidelma had retreated into meditation. It was the art of the *dercad* by which countless generations of Irish mystics had achieved the state of *sitcháin* or peace, calming extraneous thought and mental irritations. Eadulf wished he could accomplish this art. In the time that he had been with Fidelma, he had learnt that she was a regular practitioner of the ancient art in times of stress. But the Blessed Patrick himself had once expressly forbidden some of the meditative arts of self-enlightenment because they had been practised in pagan times. However, the churches of the five kingdoms tolerated the *dercad*, not forbidding it but not really approving of it. Fidelma had told him that it was a means of relaxing and calming the riot of thoughts within a troubled mind.

Time passed. Slowly the air grew chill and the shadows of early evening began to darken. They could see the glimmer of the fire outside and hear the noisy laughter of the men.

Fidelma stirred anxiously. 'One thing we can learn from that fire, Eadulf,' she observed quietly.

'Which is?' came Eadulf's response from the other side of the darkened hut.

'That Clydog and his men are not afraid that their fire will attract unwelcome attention. They must be pretty confident of the security of their position.'

She finished abruptly as a man's shadow appeared in the doorway of the hut. They could not see his features but it was the voice of Clydog which came out of the gloom.

'There, now, as I promised, the feast is ready and we are ready to welcome you, as our chief guest, to join us, my lady.'

Chapter Nine

Clydog came into the hut, bent down and untied Fidelma's bonds from the support post in the wall of the hut but did not loosen her hands. He drew her to her feet and gently pushed her before him towards the door. She stopped at the threshold when it appeared that he was ignoring Eadulf.

'What of my companion?' she demanded.

'The Saxon? He can remain where he is.'

'Doesn't he deserve food and drink?'

'I'll have something sent to him.' Clydog dismissed the subject of Eadulf. 'It was you to whom I extended the invitation to my feast. I would speak with you and not the Saxon.'

Fidelma found herself firmly propelled outside. A fire was glowing and above its fierce heat a deer carcass was being turned on a great spit. Two men were overseeing the roasting of the meat while others sat round drinking and engaging in boisterous talk.

Away from the fire, the evening air was chill and Fidelma was almost thankful for the warmth of the burning wood. Clydog led her to a log on the far side of the fire before an isolated tent made up of skins. It was one of a number which she had noticed were dotted about the clearing and presumably sheltered Clydog and his men at night.

'We offer but rough hospitality here, princess of Cashel,' Clydog said, pointing to the log and motioning her to sit. When she had done so, he reached to untie her wrists.

'There now. You can eat and drink in more relaxed form. But, lady, remember that my men are all about you and it would be futile to attempt to escape.'

'I would not leave my companion to the mercy of your company,' she said acidly.

Clydog grinned broadly and seated himself beside her. 'Very wise, too. We have no liking for Saxons, especially for Saxon religious.'

Corryn came forward. His thin features remained partially

hidden by his war helmet, which he had not removed. He handed her a beaker of a pungent-smelling mead. She noted that his hands were rather soft and well cared for, unlike the rough hands of a warrior or one used to manual work. Fidelma took the beaker but did not drink.

'This is not wise, Clydog,' Corryn muttered, turning to his comrade.

Clydog glanced up angrily. 'Each to his business, my friend.'

'Isn't our business the same?'

The outlaw leader laughed dryly. 'Not in this matter.'

Corryn stifled a sigh and turned back to the fire to rejoin the others. Clydog had noticed that Fidelma had not touched her drink.

'Do you not like our forest mead, lady?' he inquired, taking a swallow from the beaker he held in his own hand. 'It is warming on a night such as this.'

'You said that you would send food and drink to my companion.' Fidelma's quite tone was resolute. 'When he is able to eat and drink then so shall I.'

'The Saxon can wait,' Clydog replied nonchalantly. 'Our needs come first.'

'Not mine.' Fidelma rose so abruptly that Clydog was too surprise to stop her. 'I shall take this to him,' she announced, taking a pace forward before she was stopped. It was Corryn. He caught her arm in a grip that was like a powerful vice, in spite of his soft well kept hands. She gasped in surprise. Corryn's grin broadened.

'*Varium et mutabile semper femina*, eh, Clydog? You should watch out for this one. I told you that this was unwise.'

'Wait!' Clydog came to his feet. His face mirrored his annoyance. 'I will send food and drink to your Saxon friend if it means so much to you.'

Fidelma stood, unmoving, in Corryn's vice-like grip. There was nothing else she could do.

Clydog turned to Corryn with an angry gesture. 'Release her and see that food and drink are taken to the Saxon.'

The man did not immediately let go of her arm. 'What use is feeding a man who will die anyway?'

'Do it now!' snapped the outlaw leader, 'or we will have a falling out.'

Corryn suddenly pushed her away and she spun round to face him. She saw the blaze of anger and resentment in the man's vivid blue eyes. Then he controlled his features. He shrugged and turned to his companions at the fire, barking out orders. One of them reluctantly arose and cut off some portions of the roasting venison, and put them on a wooden platter. Then he took a beaker of mead and went to the hut.

Satisfied, Fidelma returned her gaze to Clydog, who had reseated himself but was watching Corryn with a strange expression on his pale face.

'So you mean to kill us?' Fidelma demanded quietly, standing before him.

'I am no friend to Saxons,' he replied shortly.

'Nor to anyone else, so it seems.' She glanced again to where Corryn was seated at the fire.

Clydog shook his head slowly. 'You are a determined lady, aren't you? Anyway, I am not responsible for the views of my men. It is I who give the orders here and so far I have not ordered anyone to be killed. So come and sit down again.'

Fidelma did not bother to respond.

'Sit down, Gwyddel!' The order was issued in a sharper tone. 'Be grateful that I saved you from Corryn. He would have killed you both at Llanpadern. I was only able to spare the Saxon's life because he was a healer.'

Fidelma sat down stiffly, her face expressionless. She was trying to work out Clydog's implication that he was somehow accountable to Corryn for his actions. Her captor chuckled in appreciation.

'I can see that you will be an excellent guest,' he mocked.

'What do you want of me, Clydog?' she demanded. 'Why do you wish to hold Brother Eadulf and myself as prisoners?'

'Should I want anything more than your company at this meal? Come, eat your fill and enjoy the conversation. You will find that I am an educated person who is sometimes starved for intellectual discourse.'

'You can surely speak to your companion there,' she sneered, nodding towards Corryn. 'One who can quote Virgil must be educated.'

Clydog frowned. Her comment seemed to worry him.

'Anyone can pick up Latin here and there,' he said, almost defensively. 'Now, relax and let us enjoy the meal.'

'I would rather be starving in the forest,' she replied spiritedly. 'At least the wild animals would be better company.'

'Can it be that you dislike me so much?' mused the young

man, still smiling. 'Dislike is but a dismal reflection of your own desire.'

Fidelma could not suppress the smile which shaped her lips. 'I do not know you well enough to hate you, Clydog,' she informed him with amusement. 'But I certainly dislike you and that does have something to do with desire.' His eyes widened but she went on: 'My desire is that you should be a thousand miles from this place.'

Clydog took a sharp knife from his belt, manipulating it ostentatiously before rising from his seat, moving to the spit and cutting slices of the roasting venison, which he placed on two wooden platters. He turned and handed one of them to her and then reseated himself.

'I am sure that someone with your intelligence, lady, has read Antisthenes,' he said, after a moment.

'You surprise me that common thieves such as yourselves have read the eminent philosophers. First we hear from Virgil and now of Antisthenes.'

Clydog did not respond to her jibe. 'If, lady, you claim you dislike me, then perhaps you should recall those words of Antisthenes. Pay attention to those you dislike, to your enemies, for they are the first to discover your faults and mistakes.'

Fidelma bowed her head slightly. 'Publilius Syrus is my favourite philosopher. Perhaps you have read him?'

'I have some knowledge of his moral maxims.'

'He said that there was no safety in gaining the favour of an enemy. You may call the enemy your friend only when he is dead.'

'Publilius Syrus,' sneered Clydog. 'Who was he but a slave from Antioch who was brought to Rome and managed to win his freedom by writing plays which pandered to the sensibilities of his masters?'

'Do you disapprove of his maxims, of his plays, that he was from Antioch, or because he was a Roman slave who won his freedom? Many of your ancestors followed that same path.'

'Not my ancestors!' Clydog snapped with an anger which surprised Fidelma.

'I mean those Britons and Gauls who were taken as slaves to Rome and won their freedom.'

'Let them speak for themselves. I will speak for myself.'

'You are obviously an intelligent man, Clydog. Who are you?' Fidelma suddenly asked. 'You are too intelligent to be a mere outlaw.'

The young man glanced at her. The shadows caused by the flickering fire disguised the expression on his face.

'I have told you who I am.'

'Clydog the Wasp, an outlaw,' Fidelma acknowledged. 'Yet what made you so? You were not born a thief.'

The young man laughed brusquely. 'I am what I am because I want more in life than it has been my fortune to have been given. But it is not to talk about me that I asked for your company at this feasting.'

There was the sound of raised raucous voices from the other side of the fire. Fidelma was amazed to see that Corryn had been persuaded to take up a stringed instrument which reminded her of a *ceis*, a small, square-shaped harp whose strings were set diagonally, much played in her own land. The voices died away as Corryn struck up a song. His voice was a tenor, melodious and sweet.

> 'Winter's day, thin are the stags,
> swift and sturdy is the black raven,
> the wind is as swift as a storm cloud,
> woe to him who trusts a stranger,
> woe to the weak, woe to the weak.'

Fidelma sniffed deprecatingly. 'Is that your philosophy, Clydog? Woe to the weak?'

'What better philosophy?' agreed the outlaw. 'It is the strong who shall inherit this earth.'

'Then you are not a Christian? Our Lord said that those who are blessed with a gentle spirit shall have the earth for their possession. You do not share that sentiment?'

'I am not a Christian. I do not share the teachings that deny men courage and strength. Your God is a god of slaves and encourages them to remain slaves. He encourages people to remain poor, to be hungry, to be without clothes. Your God is a god invented by the rich to enslave the poor. Away with such nonsense! Away with such teachings of slavery!'

Fidelma examined the young man with interest. His voice was edged with passion.

'Were you poor and enslaved, Clydog?'

99

He turned angrily on her. 'What do you—' He caught himself. 'I did not say . . .'

Fidelma smiled gently. 'I see there is an anger in your heart and you are prepared to forgive nothing. Luke wrote: "Where little has been forgiven, little love is shown."'

'Don't preach your faith to me, Gwyddel. We do not need it. Anyway, you should approve of sinners like me, being a Christian.'

Fidelma was puzzled and said so.

'Do not your teachings tell us that the greater the sinner, the better saint he makes? The more he has sinned, the more your Christ will forgive him?'

'Who taught you that?' demanded Fidelma.

'It is there in your Christian writings. Your Christ said, "I tell you, there will be greater joy in heaven over one sinner who repents than over ninety-nine righteous people who do not need to repent." It is there in your holy writings.'

'So you are adept at sinning? Is that your path to peace and contentment?' Fidelma sneered.

Clydog was not put out. 'You should not provoke me with your intellectual games, Gwyddel, although I am told that in your religious houses in Éireann your people practise such things.'

'Surely the honing of the mind is not confined to my land. I am told that the Cymry even play a game similar to our *fidchell*, the wooden wisdom, as a means of training a sharp mind.'

Clydog nodded absently. '*Gwyddbwyll*, we call it. Our great warrior, Arthur, was a master of the game.'

'Therefore, you should be as adept at intellectual sport as any Gwyddel,' Fidelma said waspishly.

Clydog reached for the jug of mead and made to fill her beaker again. Fidelma shook her head. He filled his own, staring speculatively at her.

'You are an attractive woman,' he finally said.

Fidelma shifted with an abrupt feeling of unease at the change in his tone.

'Why is such an attractive woman a member of the religious?'

'Attraction is relative. Is there a reason why one's physical appearance should preclude one from following a particular calling in life? One's outward appearance often disguises what is inside. You, for example, Clydog, ought to be a rough, ugly little man with warts and blackened, broken teeth.'

Clydog hesitated and then chuckled appreciatively. 'A good answer, Gwyddel. A good answer. Beauty often hides a black soul, eh? So what does your beauty hide, Fidelma of Cashel?'

The question was sharp, and confused Fidelma for the moment.

'I would debate that I am—' she began but he interrupted.

. 'I hear that there are some of your faith who claim that all religious should live lives of celibacy. You are not celibate, are you?'

The question caused Fidelma to flush.

'Your face seems to have betrayed you,' he went on, when she did not answer.

'It is none of your business,' she snapped. 'But it is not commanded by the Faith as well you know. Rome would prefer that abbots and bishops did not marry but there is no law which states that this should generally be so.'

She was becoming aware that this man's temper was like dry tinder. The smallest and most innocuous spark could set off the flame of his changeable personality. His temperament was unstable. The more she could moderate his swings of humour the more chance she stood of extricating Eadulf and herself from this captivity.

Clydog was grinning lewdly at her. 'Of course you have had lovers. The only chaste woman is one who has not been asked. Is the Saxon your lover, eh?'

Fidelma felt her face reddening again. Once again she paused, trying to find the right words.

'You are intelligent, Clydog. You appear cultured. You would know that there are some topics of conversation that it ill behoves civilised people to engage in. Let us turn to some other subject.'

Clydog laughed harshly. 'You mistake me, Gwyddel, if you think that I am civilised. You forget that I am only an outlaw. That you are my captive and that we are alone in this forest where you are subject to my power. Does that not excite your senses?'

'Excite?' Fidelma thrust out her bottom lip. 'That is a curious word. Certainly it makes me apprehensive, but not for myself . . . for you.'

For a moment Clydog seemed bewildered, unable to grasp the meaning of what she had said.

'Apprehensive for me?' His smile was forced. 'I have had women weep and cry for mercy but I have not come across one who is apprehensive for me.'

Fidelma tried to suppress a shiver as she began to recognise the warning signs. 'You have denied the law and you have denied the Faith. Should I, a religieuse, not be apprehensive for your fate in this world and the next?' she replied gravely.

'Your apprehension for me is gratifying. It means that there must be some feeling in you for me.'

'Indeed. It is the same feeling that I would have for a leper or a blind beggar who refuses charity,' she returned quickly.

Clydog suddenly exploded with an oath. He came to his feet, towering over her. 'Enough of this. Let us get down to the reality. There is my tent. Precede me. You know why you are here.'

Fidelma heard the breathless note of pent-up passion in his voice. She found herself unable to move as her mind raced, trying to find a way to escape.

'That is something you have so far avoided telling me,' she found herself parrying weakly. 'Tell me why I am here?'

Clydog was frustrated by her obstructive wordplay. He had never encountered a woman who had withstood him in this matter.

'Don't be obtuse, lady,' he snarled. 'You are too intelligent to pretend ignorance. Does the Saxon receive all your favours?'

Fidelma met his licentious eye. 'You are impertinent, Clydog. I will accept that you have had too much mead and lay the blame on that. Now . . .' She rose. 'I shall go back to the hut to join my companion.'

Clydog lurched forward, grabbing at her. 'No you don't, lady. You are coming to my tent to entertain me this night!'

One or two of his men at the fire had turned to watch and now called out a few ribald remarks, laughing in lascivious fashion.

'Having trouble taming her, Clydog? Take a stick to her!'

'His night tonight, mine tomorrow!' yelled out another.

Fidelma took a swift step backward to avoid Clydog's out-stretched hands.

'So you are merely an animal after all, Clydog?' she sneered. 'An animal without morals? You would force your sexuality on a religieuse? Then you are but the recrement of animal dung; no more, no less.'

Clydog stood breathing heavily now. 'You think to try to shame me with insults, Gwyddel? I am afraid you will not succeed. My blood is as good as yours. The difference is that I know what I am. I am inured from the frothings of prelates and their acolytes. There is no place you can escape to, so you may as well drop your cold pose. A woman as attractive as you cannot pretend to be indifferent to the attentions of a real man.'

Fidelma's mouth was tight and dry as she regarded him though narrow eyes. 'A real man? No, I might not be indifferent to a real man. But as you are not such a one, I merely pity you for a pathetic animal.'

Clydog's men were laughing. Some clapped their hands together, shouting encouragement to Clydog to teach the foreign woman a lesson. Fidelma could see that Clydog's expression had hardened. She had pricked his vanity.

He suddenly lunged forward again, swearing at her.

She half twisted so that his momentum caused him to stumble by her. He caught himself, whirled round to face her again. This time his eyes were evil in the firelight. He launched himself forward once more, hands outstretched to grab her.

Fidelma balanced herself and seemed to reach out her hands to meet him but then, hardly appearing to move at all, she pulled Clydog past her, over one hip, using his momentum to throw him stumbling to the ground.

She positioned herself in a defensive attitude. It appeared that Clydog had no knowledge of the old art of her country. When missionaries journeyed far and wide through many lands, taking the word of the Faith, they were vulnerable to attacks by thieves and bandits. It was believed wrong to carry arms to protect themselves, and so they developed a technique which was called 'battle through defence' – *troid-sciathaigid*. Fidelma had been taught this method of defending herself without the use of weapons from an early age.

Clydog rolled over and came to his feet again, shaking his head in bewilderment. His men's raucous laughter rang in his ears.

'Some warrior! He cannot even defeat an unarmed woman!' cried one of them.

'Do you want some help to tame her?' called another.

'Let me at her,' jeered a third, 'I won't need any help.'

Clydog was provoked beyond reason now. 'I'm going to teach you a lesson, Gwyddel,' he growled.

'You think that you are man enough to teach it?' sneered Fidelma. 'Your men believe that you are in need of being taught yourself.'

She was being deliberately provocative, for she knew that anger caused mistakes. With a cry of rage, Clydog ran at her again. She realised that surprise was no longer on her side and that, angry as he might be, he was now prepared to counter her movements. She could not repeat herself. As he ran, he lurched to the side as a feint. She was prepared for such a tactic and stepped quickly back, balancing on one leg and bringing her other foot sharply upwards as he lunged back to his previous position. There he was met with a sharp springing kick straight at his genitals.

Clydog screamed in anguish and fell back writhing on the ground.

Fidelma hoped to seize the advantage but Clydog's men were now standing in a menacing semicircle around her. There was no escape. Two of them had drawn their swords. Another ran forward to help Clydog, who was vomiting on the ground.

'He's in a bad way.' The man turned to his companions.

'Kill the bitch,' Corryn ordered unemotionally. 'And the Saxon. They should both have been killed at Llanpadern. Sualda will recover on his own.'

One of the men raised his sword.

Fidelma tried not to flinch.

'No!'

The cry came from Clydog. Even in the shadows of the flickering firelight, Fidelma could see his face, white and pain-racked. He had been helped to his feet and now staggered forward, leaning on one of his comrades' arm.

'No! No harm is to come to her yet. She might still have a use.' His mouth split in a mirthless grin. 'You will regret what you have done, Gwyddel,' he told her between clenched teeth.

'I only regret not having taught you a harsher lesson,' she responded acidly, hiding her relief that she had been reprieved from immediate death.

Corryn was frowning. 'Do you insist on continuing this charade?' he demanded.

Clydog ignored him. 'Take her back to the hut. Bind her.'

She flet rough hands grab her arms and twist them behind her back, the rope drawn so tightly round her wrists that she gasped with the pain. The unkind hands propelled her towards the hut. Then came Clydog's voice.

'Bring out the Saxon! We'll have some sport with him before we dispatch him to meet his true god, Woden.'

'You can't!' Fidelma screamed, twisting in her captors' grasp. 'Why punish Eadulf for what I have done? Can't you take defeat like a man?'

104

'Maybe you would like to watch?' sneered Clydog. 'Ah, but your presence may give the Saxon courage enough to face his death with stoicism. I have seen such things before. Saxons run to meet death with the name of their god on their lips, believing they will be accepted in their immortal Hall of Heroes. No, you may console yourself by listening to his pitiful cries for mercy. Bring him out now!'

They pushed her into the darkness of the hut. She was thrown to the ground, the breath driven from her body. Even so, she was in an agony of torment as she was bound in her former place against the wall of the hut.

'Hurry!' she heard Clydog yelling from outside. 'Don't take all night. Bring the Saxon to me. I am impatient for the fun to begin.'

'Eadulf!' Fidelma finally managed to gasp.

Then she heard an astonished cry from one of the robbers. She blinked and tried to focus as the man raised a torch high to illuminate the interior of the hut.

She looked across to where Eadulf had been bound. He was not there. His severed bonds lay discarded and, nearby, a wooden platter on which the slices of venison still lay uneaten. Her heart lurched with a quick beat of hope.

There came to her ears the whinny of a distant horse, and the receding sound of the animal crashing along the trail beyond the clearing.

Then there came a cacophony of several voices crying at once.

'One of the horses has broken loose!'

'The Saxon! He is escaping!'

She heard Clydog's almost hysterical cry: 'The Saxon? Is it true? Has he gone?'

The outlaw came pushing into the hut, saw the severed bonds, and glanced down at Fidelma. His teeth clenched.

'Have no fear, Gwyddel. We will find him. These woods are well known to us; we know them like the backs of our hands. When we bring him back you will both enjoy a pain so exquisite that you will be pleading for me to kill you in order to put an end to it. Death will come as a merciful release.'

'First you will have to catch Eadulf,' she spat back angrily. 'So far, Clydog, you have not been able to fulfil any of your boasts. I doubt whether you can you fulfil this one.'

She saw murder in his eyes there and then. As she braced

herself, Corryn suddenly appeared at his side and caught his arm.

'The Saxon is escaping!' he hissed. 'No time for this now. Your personal vengeance can wait.'

Clydog hesitated, eyes blazing. It seemed several moments before he had his temper under control. Then he turned out of the hut, shouting orders. Fidelma heard a movement in the clearing, the sounds of horses being mounted, and the snap of undergrowth as they departed. She was left alone in the darkness of the hut.

One part of her rejoiced that Eadulf had managed to escape and hoped that he would be able to avoid his pursuers. The other part of her mind sank into a troubled feeling of gloomy isolation as she realised that she was now alone and helpless at the hands of Clydog and his band of cut-throats. Clydog's temper would be uncontrollable when he returned. She lay listening to the sound of the receding horses, and wondered where Eadulf would make for. She presumed that he would try to head for Llanwnda and seek help from either Brother Meurig or Gwnda, the lord of Pen Caer. But, even if he succeeded, it would be some time before he could bring rescuers back to this place, even if he could find it again, and provided Clydog did not move camp in the meantime.

She tugged futilely at her bonds. They were firm enough. She wondered how much time she had before Clydog and his men returned.

She prayed that Eadulf would elude them.

Then, in the darkness, she heard a sound. Turning, she saw the shadow of a man entered the hut.

Chapter Ten

Fidelma tried to struggle up to defend herself as best she could.

'Quiet!' hissed a voice.

Fidelma gasped in disbelief. 'Eadulf!' she whispered, partly in relief and partly in consternation. 'What are you doing here? I thought you were long gone.'

Eadulf dropped to his knees beside her. She felt his hands working quickly at her bonds.

'My hope is Clydog and his carrion thought the same as you; that I had escaped on horseback,' came back his cheery voice.

'How did you manage to free yourself?'

'Simple. When the man brought me the venison, I asked him to loose one hand so that I could lift the food to my mouth. The idiot did so, thinking that he had restricted me enough, but I was soon able to pick at the knots and—'

'Clydog will kill us both if he captures us again,' she interrupted.

'I know. I heard what was happening. Are you harmed at all?' His voice was slightly embarrassed.

'I am not hurt. But Clydog is hurt in more than his pride,' she replied with grim satisfaction.

'I knew that you would be able to keep him entertained with your defensive techniques. I was going to wait inside the hut and then release you. But when I heard Clydog had decided to make me a martyr in the fullness of my youth, I decided not to encourage such an ambition. I slipped into the woods unobserved and watched them take you back to the hut. Then I let loose one of the horses and gave it a slap on the flanks to encourage it to gallop off down the trail.'

He gave a quick exhalation of breath and Fidelma felt the rope round her wrist suddenly slacken.

'I'm free!' she said quickly, rubbing her wrists to restore the circulation.

Eadulf helped her to stand up.

'What now?' she asked him, knowing that he would have already thought out some plan.

107

'I saw that they had left our two horses still tethered. I suggest we take them and ride in the opposite direction to the one which they have taken.'

They started out of the hut and then Fidelma suddenly pulled him back. He realised why almost immediately.

'Halt!' cried a voice. An outlaw who had been left on guard came racing towards the hut. They saw the flash of firelight on the naked blade of his sword. 'Stand still. You cannot escape.'

Eadulf acted swiftly. He reached down, picked up a handful of mud and threw it at the man. It was not thrown with any degree of force but simply to distracted the outlaw, who parried it with ease. At the same time, Eadulf dived towards a wood pile and seized the first log he could from the stack. He swung round, almost in the same rolling motion, and came into a defensive crouch as his assailant recovered, realising there was no danger from the makeshift missile. Not waiting for the outlaw to move, Eadulf was on him, brandishing the wood above his head. The men were too close for the sword to be used effectively, and a moment later Eadulf had sent the wood crashing against the side of the man's head.

'Come on!' he called to Fidelma, even before the outlaw had fallen to the ground. Fidelma was already untying the horses. With Eadulf leading, they set off in a brisk canter along the track which led in the opposite direction to the trail which Clydog and his men had taken.

It was fairly dark and the woods with their canopy of branches increased the darkness. A sudden wind was whipping at the treetops. Fidelma glanced up into the darkness.

'It will be raining before long, Eadulf,' she called. 'This wind is a harbinger of a storm, I'll warrant it.'

'Then it might help rather than hinder us,' replied Eadulf. 'At least it might hide any tracks.'

She could not be sure how far they had travelled, except that it was a fair distance, when a short time later the sky suddenly lit with a momentary flash of lightning, followed almost immediately by a harsh rumble of thunder which caused the horses to shy and whinny in protest. Rain, like cold, icy pinpricks, began to fall, quickly increasing in intensity.

'We are not going to get far at this rate,' Fidelma called. 'Any idea where we are?'

'I could not see the stars. There were too many storm clouds before this set in to be sure,' replied Eadulf, 'but I think we are heading west or south-west. The forest was due south from Llanpadern.'

His words were punctuated by another flash, and almost immediately the crash of thunder reverberated once again.

'We'll have to find some shelter out of this,' Eadulf said. 'This rain is too intense.'

'It might be providential as the rain will wash away our tracks,' replied Fidelma. 'We'd best dismount and lead the horses. The thunder and lightning are making them skittish.'

Eadulf reluctantly acknowledged that it was the best course. He knew Fidelma was an expert horsewoman, learning to ride almost before she could walk. He was more used to travelling on foot. They dismounted and began to lead the animals along the track, feeling it turning to a muddy slushy mess beneath their feet as the rain gushed down through the trees.

It was just after another bright flash that Eadulf halted and pointed along a small pathway leading off the main track which had been illuminated by the lightning.

'I thought I saw a rock face along there. I am sure there was an overhang. It might provide shelter. It would be better than nothing at all.' He had raised his voice to be heard above the sound of the torrential rain and the rolling storm.

Fidelma simply nodded.

'Wait here!' yelled Eadulf. 'I'll make sure that it is safe along there.'

He turned along the path, leading his horse. Soon he had disappeared in the darkness and sheeting rain. Fidelma stood impatiently, waiting by the head of her nervous mount, gently speaking to it and stroking its muzzle in an attempt to keep it calm.

Then Eadulf reappeared. 'It's all right,' he called. 'Come on. The overhang leads into a large cave where we can shelter with the horses. I've left mine there. It's big and dry.'

She followed, guiding her horse carefully along the muddy path through the whipping branches.

If anything, the rain was increasing in its intensity. The storm seemed to be circling round in the forest as if some angry storm god were trying to seek them out, sending his lightning forks sizzling down to the ground seconds before following them with a thunderous explosion. One must have struck nearby for they saw, on what must have been a hill, a fire break out among the trees only to be quenched moments later by the torrent of rain.

109

Fidelma found herself entertaining the irreverent thought that the Saxon thunder god Thunor had prepared this vengeance for them. It was not so long ago that her people measured storms as a manifestation of the power of the gods and goddesses. It occurred to her to wonder why Thunor sounded so similar to the Irish thunder god Torann and to his British counterpart Taranis, but then she dismissed the thought.

The overhang was quite large and Fidelma had no difficulty leading her horse under its shelter. As Eadulf had said, a dark, almost pitch black cavern yawned beyond. His horse was hobbled inside; he had taken the reins and tied the beast's forelegs to prevent it walking far, for there was nothing to tether it to. Fidelma smiled to herself, approving of his forethought. She'd make a horseman of him yet. She quickly followed his example.

The cave seemed large and dry but they were both saturated and cold.

'I don't suppose there is a chance of a fire?' she asked.

'I doubt whether I could find dry kindle or wood,' replied Eadulf, a shadowy figure against the mouth of the cave, lit only when the lightning flashed. 'Even then I am not sure whether it would be prudent. We have not come so very far from Clydog's camp. We don't want to attract any attention.'

'He and his men would surely give up the chase while this storm lasts,' she decided. 'Let's see what we can do.'

As soon as it was light enough and, they hoped, the storm had abated, they ought to try to increase the distance between themselves and Clydog and his cut-throats. In the meantime, there was the problem of being wet and cold to overcome. Eadulf was right: there was no dry fuel to be found, and so they resigned themselves to making the best of the situation.

Eadulf, more by touch than an ability to see anything in the darkness, had removed the horses' saddles. He found a smooth boulder to one side of the cave and Fidelma heard him arranging things.

'I've put down the saddle blankets here. They are pretty damp, but better than the cold rock. I suggest we try and get warm together and perhaps our garments will dry on us.'

Fidelma and Eadulf huddled together against the boulder. Their embrace was one of animal necessity, each needing the warmth of the other's body. Outside the cave, the storm was drifting away, but the dark rain clouds still rolled over the forest, sending cascades of water pouring across the landscape.

'It'll be clear by morning,' muttered Fidelma as she nestled into the crook of Eadulf's arm.

Eadulf was silent for a moment. 'If we head due west in the morning we ought to reach the coast. But perhaps we might find a southerly road before that.'

'Why southerly?' she asked, momentarily perplexed.

'So that we can find our way back to the abbey of Dewi Sant.' He felt Fidelma stiffen a little.

'We have not fulfilled our commission from Gwlyddien.'

'Surely we have? We know that Llanpadern was attacked by sea-raiders. We found the body of the Hwicce warrior. I think it is obvious what happened to the community and to the king's son.'

'I don't think it is obvious at all. I want to go to Llanferran to see Dewi, and hear more about the bodies he found.'

Eadulf's facial muscles tightened in dismay. 'How can we remain here with this madman Clydog in the vicinity?' he demanded. 'There is no way that we can move about seeking information, not with this band of maniacal killers on our heels.'

'I cannot retreat now, Eadulf,' she answered quietly. 'That would be to deny my oath as a *dálaigh*, not to mention my acceptance of Gwlyddien's commission.'

'But surely . . .' protested Eadulf helplessly. He realised that he would not win against the remorseless logic of her decision.

'You may return to the abbey if you wish,' Fidelma interrupted without rancour. 'You can await me there. But there is too much evil here to allow me to admit such a defeat without trying to resolve the questions that spring to mind.'

Eadulf was quiet for a moment. 'Do you plan also to go back to Llanpadern?'

'Not to Llanpadern. Clydog would doubtless think of following us there. For the time being we have learnt all we can from that sad, desolate place. As I have said, we must see what information we can pick up at Llanferran.'

'And after that, where then?'

'Back to Llanwnda. I must inform Brother Meurig and Gwnda of the presence of Clydog and his men. Doubtless Gwnda is equipped to protect his people against them and I will also seek that protection. Brother Meurig and Gwnda might know something about this Clydog and his outlaws.'

'What more do you want to know other than he is a thief, a rapist and a would-be murderer?'

'I want to know much more,' Fidelma assured him. 'Both Clydog and Corryn are educated. They have the bearing of men born to authority and used to rule. That intrigues me.'

'Yet what has that to do with Llanpadern? That is surely what we must concentrate on if you are determined that we must remain here to solve this mystery.' He felt Fidelma relax a little at his quiet acceptance of her decision.

'You'll stay with me, then?' she asked.

Eadulf sniffed uncomfortably. 'Did you have any doubt?'

He heard her sigh. 'Of course I didn't,' she confessed. 'Anyway, I am going to prove you wrong.'

He frowned in the darkness. 'Wrong? What do you mean?'

'You said that Clydog had nothing to do with the disappearance at Llanpadern. I think he knew more than he said, which, admittedly, was not much.'

'You forget that Saxon sea-raiders were seen. That some of the brethren's bodies were found, and the body of the Hwicce at Llanpadern. What more evidence do you want as to what happened there? What connection would a thief like Clydog have with Saxon raiders?'

'Remember that I said that he must have been there before, or been forewarned that we were there, hence the silent approach he made with his men?'

'There is another explanation for it.'

'Which is?' Fidelma was surprised that Eadulf had been giving the riddle some thought.

'He could have seen our approach to Llanpadern, watched our entry and then waited until we were inside before slinking up on us.'

'As I recall, we were inside for well over an hour before going to the barn. That is a long time for him to wait, if he had been watching before deciding to entrap us there.'

'You obviously have a theory,' Eadulf said in resignation.

To his surprise she gave a negative shake of her head. 'At this stage, I have only questions.'

'But what makes you think there is some connection? The fact that he surprised us in the barn is hardly reason to think he was connected with the Saxon raid.'

'You said that he did not know about the Saxon in the crypt.'

'Yes. Otherwise he would have made some remark when he knew I was a Saxon.'

'He did.'

Eadulf stared at her in the darkness, although he could see nothing but the deeper blackness of her head against his chest. 'Well, I did not hear it,' he said defensively.

'His first words when I told him who we were. Don't you remember?'

'He simply made some remark like "A Gwyddel and a Saxon."'

'He did not. What he said was "A Gwyddel and *another* Saxon." Who was the other Saxon if not—'

'The Hwicce?' supplied Eadulf quickly.

'Who-wicca.' Fidelma struggled again with the pronunciation. 'Why do you Saxons have such unpronounceable names?'

'Because,' Eadulf snapped testily, 'we are a different people. Every language is easy to pronounce to those who speak it. Every language is phonetic once you know the phonetics!'

'*Absit invidia*,' Fidelma murmured pacifyingly. 'There is no offence intended. I simply make a statement as it appears from my own viewpoint.'

'I'm sorry,' muttered Eadulf. 'A curse on languages, anyway. They are twisty things, words upon words, with sly meaning and never any precision.'

'On the contrary, Eadulf, the only thing that creates an enemy of language is insincerity. Language can only be our friend if it is in accordance with the truth of the speaker.'

Eadulf groaned softly. 'Is this the time and place for philosophy?'

'All times and all places are conducive. Language has betrayed Clydog's knowledge. Clydog knew the Hwicce was in the tomb. When he heard that you were a Saxon, unconsciously it slipped out – *another* Saxon.'

Eadulf was silent as he considered the matter. Then he said: 'So he must have known that the body was in the tomb?' Suddenly he gave an audible groan. 'What a fool I am. Sualda!'

'Exactly. I think that the Hwicce was cornered by Sualda in the refectory. He picked up that meat knife and stabbed Sualda, who in turn killed him.'

'But why hide the body in the sarcophagus?'

'That is a question that we cannot answer yet.'

Eadulf clicked his tongue in annoyance. 'I would place a wager that Clydog knows something about this mystery. If only I had tried to make sense of Sualda's ramblings.'

He heard Fidelma yawn sleepily, and glanced towards the cave mouth. It was still dark and raining outside.

'We'd better try to sleep a while,' he advised. 'At first light we must try to pick up the road to Llanferran and hope we don't encounter our friend Clydog again.'

There was no sound except the regular rise and fall of his companion's breathing. Fidelma was already asleep.

The noisy chorus of birds woke Eadulf. It was still dark but one could feel the onset of the dawn. He was surprised that he had even fallen asleep. It seemed only a few moments ago that he had been thinking that sleep would be impossible as he half lay, uncomfortable in his damp clothes, against the hard rock on the cave floor with Fidelma nestled in the crook of his left arm.

He tried not to make too sudden a movement but turned his head slightly and looked down at her still sleeping form. She seemed so vulnerable, so unlike the Fidelma he was used to seeing; the face so confident and, perhaps, a little arrogant.

He moved his gaze back to the cave mouth and saw the sky was not really dark but getting lighter all the time. The cacophony from the birds increased. It was time to be moving.

He stirred, moving his muscles gently. Fidelma moaned a little in protest. He reached over with his free arm and shook her gently on the shoulder.

'Time to be going,' he said quietly.

She moaned again and then blinked. In a moment she was sitting up staring about her. She shivered in the chill.

'Have we overslept?' she asked, rubbing her eyes.

'No,' Eadulf assured her. 'But it will be dawn in a moment or two.'

Fidelma looked at the cave entrance and saw the sky. 'We'd better make a start then,' she said, rising to her feet and stretching. She felt chilly and her damp clothes were uncomfortable. The horses were standing patiently, blowing and snorting in the cool air, their breath like little puffs of steam.

'At least it seems to have stopped raining,' Eadulf observed as he walked to the cave mouth and looked out. 'But it is still cold.'

114

The ground outside had been saturated by the rain and the sky was still filled with menacing heavy clouds. He muttered something in Saxon which sounded like a curse. Fidelma raised an eyebrow in disapproval. Eadulf shrugged and indicated the wet ground with a jerk of his head.

'It will make our tracks easy to follow, if Clydog is still out looking for us.'

Fidelma began to saddle her horse. 'He will be,' she assured him. 'With luck we can find some rocky trail or perhaps a stream to follow.'

'I'd give anything for a drink and something to eat,' Eadulf sighed, following her example and putting the saddle blanket on his mount.

Fidelma was abruptly reminded that they had not eaten since the previous morning. She wished she had eaten the plate of venison she had been offered on the previous night. Eadulf was in the same position, having forsaken his meal to effect his escape.

'Let's hope we can find somewhere to refresh ourselves on the journey. We need to find our way to Llanferran,' she said brightly. 'Don't forget our horses are just as miserable as we are. They haven't been rubbed down or watered and fed either.'

Eadulf led the way out of the cave and back along the small twisting mud path towards the main track from which they had departed on the previous evening. It was a chilly, grey-stone morning. Even the bird song seemed desultory now.

They mounted and began to proceed along the trail. Although they seemed to sit at ease on their horses a close observer would have noticed that their muscles were tensed and now and then they turned their heads as if in expectation of pursuit.

Fidelma wondered how long it had been before Clydog had overtaken the riderless horse and realised how he had been tricked. How long before he had returned to the camp and found that she was gone as well?

They came to a spongy turf clearing among holly and sessile oaks. On one side was a clump of wild pear, leaning together, with their narrow outlines and sparse branches. A few months earlier and they could have eased their hunger with its fruits.

Eadulf was sitting on his horse peering about him. He let out a low exclamation and turned his horse towards a group of trees. Among them he had noticed some tall specimens with deeply

115

furrowed bark. He dismounted and was soon cutting away with his knife.

'What is it?' Fidelma called.

'Hopefully, breakfast,' he replied. 'I noticed these elder trees and hoped we might be lucky.'

'Lucky?' She was perplexed. She came closer and peered down at what he was cutting away from the tree. 'Ugh!' she grunted in repulsion. 'It looks like a human ear.'

Eadulf grinned up at her. 'It's actually called Judas's Ear.'

Fidelma realised it was a fungus; liver-brown, with translucent flabby flesh.

'Is it edible?' she asked uncertainly.

'It is not a delicacy but I have known people who eat it both cooked and raw. It might take the edge off our hunger.'

'Or give us indigestion,' observed Fidelma, examining with distaste the piece he handed her. 'Why is it called Judas's Ear?'

'There is a tradition that Judas Iscariot, who betrayed the Christ for thirty pieces of silver, hanged himself on an elder tree. This fungus only grows on the elder.'

Fidelma nibbled experimentally. The taste was not too unpleasant, and she was hungry. A short time later, they found a small spring and slaked their thirst. Here they were also able to pause and let their horses drink and graze for a while on the wet grasses that surrounded the spring. Then they were on their way again, directed westward by the sun rising against their backs.

Soon the woods began to thin and they found themselves in a small twisting valley through which a small stream gushed, widening occasionally into moderately sized pools. At Fidelma's suggestion they walked their horses through the shallow waters, whose swirling eddies hid their passing.

After a while the wooded cover ended and low plains of marshy ground stretched before them. They were aware of the plaintive crying of gulls and the noticeable tang of salt in the air.

'The sea can't be far away,' Eadulf observed unnecessarily.

'So we have to turn north now,' Fidelma replied. 'I can see some buildings . . .'

'Maybe we can get a proper meal there.'

Fidelma smiled ruefully at her companion. 'I confess that if it were a choice between going hungry or having another meal of your Judas's Ear, I would prefer starvation.'

They rode to some rocky high ground that, to the west, swept down towards a deceptive cliff edge. Below was a broad bay

116

with a sandy beach, backed by shingle. Further up was a deep inlet through which a river came tumbling to the sea. They had to ride around this cleft, with cliffs on one side and marshy land on the other, to find a place to cross.

The buildings appeared to be a small hamlet with a hill rising behind it. Fidelma had noticed several ancient stones including a stone circle not far off. Smoke rose from the hamlet and they could see people moving about.

Eadulf sighed in relief. 'Civilisation and food.'

'Let's find out where we are first.'

As they came closer, Fidelma realised that the place was not even large enough to be called a hamlet. There was only a large smith's forge and outbuildings and what looked like the sort of hostel that was common in her own land, where people gathered to drink, eat or stay for the night.

An old man carrying a large stack of twigs on his back was approaching them from a path on the inland side of the track along which they were proceeding.

Eadulf decided to try out his improved knowledge of the language.

'*Shw mae! Pa un yw'r fford i . . .?*'

The old man stopped and stared at him. His eyes widened. '*Saeson?*'

'I am a Saxon,' admitted Eadulf.

To their surprise, the old man dropped his bundle of sticks and went scuttling away towards the buildings shouting at the top of his voice.

Fidelma looked grim. 'It seems that they do not like Saxons in this part of the world.'

Before Eadulf could protest, Fidelma was moving on resolutely in the wake of the old man, who had now halted, waving his arms and still shouting. A broad-shouldered man, who was clearly the smith, and a couple of other men had grabbed what appeared to be weapons and watched them with caution as they approached. There were no expressions of welcome on their faces.

'What do you want here?' called the broad-shouldered man as they drew within speaking range.

Fidelma halted, Eadulf by her side. '*Pax vobiscum*, my brothers. I am Sister Fidelma of Cashel.'

'A Gwyddel?' The smith frowned. 'The old man said that you were Saxons come to rob and kill us.'

Fidelma smiled reassuringly and slid from her horse, motioning

Eadulf to dismount also. 'My companion is a Saxon. Brother Eadulf. We have come neither to rob nor to kill. We are of the Faith.'

The tension of the group relaxed a little but the smith still stood regarding her mistrustfully.

'It is unusual to find a Saxon travelling in this country as a religious. Saxons are more likely to travel in raiding parties as we, on this coast, know to our cost. We have lost many loved ones in raids.'

'We mean no harm here. We are seeking a place called Llanferran.'

'And so?'

Fidelma was bewildered for a moment. 'We would also like refreshment and fodder for our horses for they are exhausted. Then if you would direct us to this place, Llanferran, we will be on our way.'

The smith stared at her for a second or two and then shrugged, putting down his weapon.

'You have found Llanferran. My name is Goff.'

Chapter Eleven

'Now, what is it you seek here apart from hospitality? It is not often that strangers come here merely to seek food and shelter, least of all Saxons.' Goff the smith looked suspiciously at Eadulf.

'We hold a commission from your king, Gwlyddien, to investigate the disappearance of the community of Llanpadern . . .'

The smith scowled suddenly. A young man who stood at his side, white-faced and anxious, let out a nervous gasp.

'We were told by Gwnda, lord of Pen Caer, that someone called Dewi had information on this matter.'

The smith reluctantly indicated the youth. 'This is my son, Dewi. I named him after the blessed founder of our church.'

Fidelma smiled at the apprehensive boy. 'Then we have much to discuss. However, can we beg some food and the warmth of your fire while we talk of this matter?'

The smith hesitated before making up his mind. 'If you are true religious then you are welcome at my hearth. We will go up to the house.'

He turned to one of his companions standing in the sullen, suspicious group about the old man they had first encountered, who was glaring at them with hatred.

'Take charge of the forge,' instructed Goff. He was about to turn away when Fidelma stayed him.

'Can the wants of our horses also be met? They need a good rub down, also water and feed.'

'See to it,' Goff ordered.

With murmured thanks, Fidelma and Eadulf followed Goff and Dewi across a yard and up a small rise to the large building which, as Fidelma had guessed, bore all the hallmarks of the hostels kept in her own land, where food, drink and a bed could be purchased.

A round-faced woman was standing before a cooking pot hanging over a roaring fire.

'Rhonwen!' called the smith. 'We have guests. Religious on their travels.'

119

The round-faced woman came forward, wiping her hands on an apron that hung around her ample girth.

'This is Rhonwen, my wife,' Goff said.

'Have you broken your fast this morning, Sister?' the pleasant-faced woman asked. 'Can I get you something to eat and drink?'

Soon fresh-baked bread and dishes of cold meats and cheeses were set before them. The smith and his son, Dewi, joined them in beakers of good mead.

Fidelma had reached into her *marsupium* and pushed the vellum bearing King Gwlyddien's seal in front of the smith. He glanced at it and handed it to his son with a shrug.

'Dewi has been taught to read,' he muttered apologetically.

'It is a commission from the king, father. The Gwyddel is a lawyer, like our *barnwr*.'

'Very well. What can we tell you about Llanpadern, Sister?' asked the smith. 'We know that it was raided.'

'So Dewi told Gwnda.' Eadulf entered the conversation for the first time. 'Tell us about this raid.'

The youth glanced at his father who nodded.

'We heard that there was a Saxon warship anchored off Penmorfa nearly a week ago,' Dewi began. 'Then seven religious were found near the cliffs there. They had all been killed. It was obvious who had caused their deaths.'

Fidelma looked at him inquisitively. 'Why obvious?' she demanded.

'One moment, Sister.' The smith rose and went to a cupboard at the back of the room. A moment later he had returned bearing a round warrior's shield, a broken sword and a knife. 'These were found with the bodies of the religious. Do you need me to identify their markings and their origin?'

Fidelma turned to Eadulf, who was looking at the markings with an uncomfortable expression. She knew what he would answer before she asked the question.

'They are Hwicce,' he confirmed.

'Can you be sure?' she pressed.

Eadulf nodded. 'Observe the double lightning stroke on the shield, the symbol of Thunor, god of lightning? If that is not enough, one can see the riveting and construction . . .'

'Indeed!' interrupted the smith, smiling maliciously. 'No Briton would do this work. This is a Saxon shield and weapons.'

120

'And you say that these were found by the bodies of the religious? Who discovered them?' The questions came sharply from Fidelma.

'Some travelling merchants brought us word. Dewi with two companions went down to Penmorfa to confirm their story.'

'Did you see any Saxons, Dewi?'

The youth shook his head. 'There were only the bodies of the slain religious.'

'Did you see any sign of the Saxon ship?' she asked.

His father, Goff, laughed sourly. 'Saxons raid swiftly. They come and then are gone. Once they have attacked, they do not wait for retribution.'

'Tell me more about the bodies you found, Dewi,' invited Fidelma.

'What more is there to say?' The youth frowned uncertainly.

'Did you recognise them as being religious from Llanpadern? How were they lying? How were they killed?' Fidelma shot the questions in rapid succession.

Dewi gave the questions some consideration before replying. 'I have frequently been at Llanpadern, so I was able to recognise two or three of the brothers.'

'Did you know Brother Rhun?'

'The son of the king? He served as the steward of the abbey at Llanpadern. He conducted the business of the abbey with traders and merchants. I met him often.'

'My son drives our cart, transporting the goods I make to those who cannot come to the forge to collect them,' explained his father.

'I remember a forge at the abbey,' Eadulf said reflectively. 'By the barn.'

'They had their own smith, but now and then he needed help or materials. Is that not so, father?'

Goff nodded slowly.

'From what you say, I presume that Brother Rhun was not one of those slain?' pressed Fidelma.

'I can name only two of the brothers who were. He was not one of them.'

'And you are sure they were all of the community?'

'Positive.'

'And there were seven bodies?'

'Seven,' the young man confirmed.

'And you were going to tell me how they were killed.'

'Sword strokes mainly.'

'In what manner?' pressed Fidelma.

'Mostly from behind, across the back of the neck.' The young man apparently understood what was wanted of him. 'One was stabbed from the front, through the heart, while another had an upward stroke to the stomach. They lay in a small group, as if they had been huddled together for the purpose.'

Fidelma's brows were drawn together. 'In a group, you say? Where were the shield and weapons found?'

'Just by them.'

'Just by them?' She turned and took the broken sword. Its blade had been snapped off. 'This was where, exactly, in relation to the bodies?'

'It lay at the feet of one religieux.'

'Did you wipe the blood off?' The weapon she held was clean and almost shining.

'It was like that when we found it,' Goff the smith put in.

'And where was the other part of the weapon? In one of the corpses?'

'No, the wounds were clean and—' Dewi stopped abruptly as he suddenly realised the significance of the question.

'And the knife and the shield? Were they just lying close by?'

The young man considered. 'The shield was on top of one of the bodies and the knife alongside another.'

'So what happened after this discovery?'

It was Goff who answered.

'Dewi came back to fetch some more of us down to Penmorfa. I retrieved the weapons and searched the bodies in case there was a means of identification. There was none. No jewellery or crucifixes – nothing. So we buried them by the cliffs where they had fallen.'

'Are you sure that they were killed at that spot?' asked Fidelma.

'Oh yes. There was a great deal of blood on the ground around the bodies.'

'And then?'

'When we had ensured that we were safe, I told my boy, Dewi, to ride to Llanwnda and tell Gwnda, the lord of Pen Caer, what we had found; the slaughter and the sighting of the Saxon warship along the coast. It does not need much imagination to work out what happened.'

122

'That Saxon raiders attacked the community at Llanpadern? Are you sure of that?' Fidelma asked. 'Are you sure that they carried off the community and, for some reason, slaughtered seven of them on the cliffs before they went back onto their warship?'

'Of course. This is what must have occurred.'

'Do you know that there is no sign of an attack at Llanpadern? No building is burnt or destroyed. Nor are there signs of any religious slaughtered there.'

Goff grimaced.

'That's easily answered, Sister. The Saxons came at night and surprised the brethren so that there was no opportunity to defend themselves. They were rounded up like lambs for the slaughter.'

'But—' began Eadulf. Fidelma silenced him with a sharp look.

'And has there been any further sign of this Saxon ship, either before or since?' she asked.

'We keep a special watch along the coast for such raids. There has been no further sign of it.'

Fidelma suppressed a sigh. 'You have been most helpful, Goff. You, also, Dewi.'

'Where do you go now?' asked Goff, offering them more mead.

'Back to Llanwnda. We will rejoin our companion from the abbey of Dewi Sant there.'

'I hear there is also trouble at Llanwnda.'

'That is so,' confirmed Eadulf, now tucking into some bread with relish. 'Our companion, Brother Meurig, is investigating—'

'Meurig the *barnwr*?' Rhonwen moved to the table, her round face suddenly serious. 'Is he investigating the death of poor Mair?'

'Did you know Mair?' Fidelma asked.

'Here, under the shelter of Pen Caer, Sister,' Goff nodded towards the distant peak, 'we are a close community. Besides, Iorwerth is a fellow smith and news travels quickly from forge to forge.'

'So you knew Iorwerth as well?'

'We were apprentices together at the same forge when we were young. For two years I slept cheek by jowl with him before our smith-master drove him out.'

Fidelma was immediately interested. 'Drove him out? Can you be more precise?'

Goff looked sombre at the memory and glanced towards the serious face of his wife.

'That I can, Sister. Our smith-master had a daughter. Some nights I would awaken to find that the bed of my fellow apprentice was empty. You understand?'

'I think I follow you,' agreed Fidelma.

The broad-shouldered man scowled in disapproval. 'With Iorwerth, it was more a question of lust than love. I don't think Iorwerth really cared for anyone. Maybe not even his daughter. I know his wife died some years ago and his mourning was brief.'

'Indeed it was.' Rhonwen sat down suddenly at the table. She looked at Goff and some hidden message passed between them.

'I don't think we need you any more, Dewi,' he said. 'Best get down to the forge and see all is well.'

Reluctantly, the youth rose and left them. After he had gone, Rhonwen leant forward.

'Iorwerth's wife was a friend of mine. Esyllt was a beautiful girl. How she was ever persuaded to marry Iorwerth, only God would know. It was not a marriage that I would have said was favoured in heaven. Her death was almost predictable.'

'What happened?' asked Fidelma.

'She simply took ill and died one day. You know how it is? Some ague. The fever carried her off, poor dear. One thing, she went to a better place than she had occupied with the living. Iorwerth is a petty and vengeful man. I often wondered why poor Esyllt stayed with him. I asked her once if she would like to come away and stay with us, when we knew Iorwerth was beating her. After all, Esyllt was my closest and dearest friend.'

'Tell me, Goff, where was this master-smith under whom you and Iorwerth were apprentices?'

'He was smith of Dinas. Gurgust of Dinas. Poor man.'

Fidelma raised an eyebrow. 'Poor man?'

'His daughter, you see.'

'Poor man from the point of view that his daughter was having an affair with Iorwerth?'

Goff shook his head. 'From what happened afterwards. It was a few weeks after Iorwerth was chased out of Dinas, after Gurgust had discovered that his daughter – Efa was her name – had succumbed to Iorwerth's attentions, if you understand me? Gurgust was in such a rage that he threw his daughter out of his house as well.'

124

'Did she go off with Iorwerth?'

'She did not. Iorwerth had vanished and the girl was on her own. It seems that poor Efa took up with an itinerant warrior and had a child by him. Then Efa died.'

'Did she die in childbirth?'

'She was found in nearby woods, strangled, when her child was a few months old.'

'Strangled?' Fidelma was not often overtly startled but she set down her mead carefully.

'It was very sad. Poor Gurgust gave up the forge after that. I did hear that he tried to find and claim custody of Efa's child.'

'Did he succeed?'

'Not that I know of. The warrior had already given up the child and vanished in a host that marched on Ceredigion. I left Dinas and moved to the smithy here in Llanferran. It was only some years later that I heard that Gurgust had been killed in one of the border raids. In spite of his actions, he loved his daughter, Efa, and when she was murdered . . .' He ended with a shrug.

'Did they ever find out who was responsible for Efa's death?' asked Fidelma when he paused.

Goff shook his head. 'There was speculation that the warrior who had befriended her was the murderer. But no one knew who he was nor was he ever caught. There was even some argument that it was none other than Iorwerth himself.'

'Was Iorwerth ever questioned about it?'

Goff was not surprised at her query. It had doubtless been asked many times over the years.

'Of course. But Iorwerth had left Dinas as soon as Gurgust had thrown him out. At least no one could find him. It was thought that he had been in one of the hosts which marched on Ceredigion. Then, some years later, it was found that he had set up his own smithy at Llanwnda. Then he married Esyllt, my wife's friend, and Mair was born. There was nothing to connect him with the death of Efa except rumour. Some felt that a wandering beggar had killed her, because the golden chain that she always wore – a chain of red gold which Gurgust had fashioned for her and which she had prized – was missing. It carried a strangely shaped gold pendant with jewels ending in the likeness of a hare. It was the symbol of Andrasta, the old pagan goddess of my people.'

'Andrasta?' queried Fidelma. 'I have not heard of this goddess.'

'They say the great queen, Boudicca, invoked her before she drove the Romans out of her kingdom,' explained Goff.

'And this gold chain and pendant was missing?'

'It was. The conclusion was that she had simply been robbed and killed.'

'Nevertheless, Iorwerth was suspected?'

'He is an evil man, Sister,' interrupted Rhonwen. 'I would not put anything past him.'

Fidelma sat awhile, frowning. 'Is Dinas far from here?'

'It is a long way around the coastline. But if you went to the coast a few kilometres north-west of Llanwnda, then took a boat across the great bay there, Dinas is the island on the far side of the bay: a distance of perhaps five kilometres. Often the island is the object of attacks from Ceredigion just along the coast. But Gurgust and his daughter Efa are long forgotten. This happened twenty or more years ago. There is nothing there now.'

'It seems a curious coincidence that both the daughter of Gurgust and the daughter of Iorwerth should meet their deaths in similar circumstances.' Fidelma was reflective.

'How can there be any connection?' demanded Goff.

'You said that Gurgust was killed in some border war?'

'I did.'

'Are you sure?'

'It is what I heard.' The smith's eyes suddenly lightened and he smiled. 'If Gurgust lived, and believed that Iorwerth had killed his daughter, then he would have sought revenge long ago. Gurgust is long dead.'

Rhonwen leant forward across the table and laid a hand on his arm. 'Even so, husband, the good sister must have a reason for asking the question. Are you saying that you believe Idwal to be innocent of young Mair's death? Does Brother Meurig also believe this?'

Goff interrupted before Fidelma could respond.

'You told us that you had come here to investigate the raid at Llanpadern. What is your interest in the death of Mair of Llanwnda?' he demanded suspiciously.

Fidelma reassured him. 'We journeyed to Llanwnda with Brother Meurig. He is there to investigate the killing. It is natural that our curiosity is piqued by the affair, and what help we can render to Brother Meurig we are willing to give.'

'So you do believe that Idwal is innocent,' Rhonwen said

shrewdly. 'No *barnwr* would waste their time on such questions unless they suspected that all was not as it seemed.'

'How well do you know Idwal?'

Rhonwen answered with a smile. 'As Goff said, we are a small community.'

'What do you make of him?'

'Make of him?' Rhonwen was puzzled.

'Do you think him capable of murder?'

'Who is and who is not capable of taking a life given the circumstances?' countered Goff. 'We are all capable of doing so, I should imagine.'

'I think Sister Fidelma means, what is your assessment of Idwal? Is he a likeable boy? Would he kill without justification?'

Goff rubbed his nose. 'He is a half-wit.'

Rhonwen made a tutting sound and shook her head. Fidelma turned to her.

'You disagree with that assessment?'

'He isn't a half-wit. He is merely slow. Almost childlike. He did not have a pleasant childhood after Iolo the shepherd died. Iolo fostered the boy as a baby. He was still a boy when Iolo's brother, Iestyn, drove him out. Since then Idwal has had to earn a living as an itinerant shepherd.'

'I'll not deny that the boy has a fairly gentle nature,' agreed Goff. 'There is no denying that. He would weep every time one of his lambs died. But who knows what provoked him? We all have the instinct to kill when presented with the right circumstances, and the boy was deep. He kept his thoughts to himself. Who knew what angers lay beneath his quiet exterior?'

'So you believe that he is guilty?' asked Eadulf.

'I believe what I am told by men whose opinions I respect.'

'And who is it that you respect who told you Idwal was guilty?' Fidelma asked sharply.

'Why, Iestyn of Llanwnda, of course.'

Fidelma saw Rhonwen screw her features into a brief expression of dislike.

'You do not think much of Iestyn, do you?'

Goff's wife made her views clear. 'When I think of him throwing that young boy out to fend for himself . . . and now he has the gall to level the finger of blame.'

Goff tried to defend his opinion. 'Iestyn has been a good friend to me. And perhaps he was right to throw the boy out years ago. Perhaps he saw what was coming.'

'I know this is a small community, but when did you speak with Iestyn on this matter?' Fidelma probed.

'A day or so ago. He came by with a cart that needed a repair.'

'I thought he was a friend of Iorwerth. Surely Iorwerth was closer at hand and would have been able to mend his cart?'

'What my husband means,' sniffed Rhonwen, 'is that Iestyn was delivering a cartload of hides to a trader near here when his cart broke. Easier to call here than drag it all the way back to Llanwnda.'

'I understand. So Iestyn was the one who told you what had happened and said that Idwal was guilty.'

'He was,' said Goff, rising abruptly. 'And now, pleasant though it is to gossip, I have my forge to get back to.'

Fidelma stood up and Eadulf followed reluctantly. She knew when she had been dismissed.

'We have a journey to complete. But let me ask one more question before we depart.'

Goff made a gesture which seemed to indicate the invitation to put the question.

'You say that this is a small community and everyone knows one another?'

Rhonwen was beginning to clear the remains of the meal from the table. She smiled. 'Are you seeking information about someone?'

'I am. What can you tell me about a man who calls himself Clydog Cacynen or another who goes by the name of Corryn?'

The jug which Rhonwen had been holding fell to the floor and shattered into a number of pieces, allowing the little remaining mead to splash over the wooden boards. Goff moved forward, frowning, as Rhonwen began to apologise nervously and start picking up the pieces.

'How did you come across the name of Clydog?' he demanded.

'We heard that there was a outlaw in this area and were warned to be careful of him,' she lied easily. 'I simply wanted to know who he was.'

'If you want to ask about him, ask Father Clidro. He once tried to negotiate a peace with him.'

'But Father Clidro—' began Eadulf.

'Father Clidro, as you will recall, is no longer at Llanpadern

128

nor is any of his community,' interrupted Fidelma quickly, with a warning glance at Eadulf.

'Then we can answer no more questions,' Goff said firmly. 'I would merely add my voice to those you have heard already and urge you to avoid meeting with Clydog. He is a scourge on our people. He has sharp ears and punishes swiftly. We will say no more. I give you God's speed on your journey.'

His expression was resolute. It was clear that his wife was upset at the mention of Clydog but also clear that Fidelma and Eadulf had outstayed their welcome at Llanferran.

Goff refused payment for the hospitality that he had provided, muttering the usual formula that prayers offered up by the religious on behalf of his wife and himself were worth more than gold or silver. Fidelma and Eadulf responded with the usual blessing. But there was an emptiness about the ritual; it was performed without feeling.

As soon as it was over, Fidelma and Eadulf retrieved their horses from Dewi at the forge and took the trail which the youth indicated as leading to Llanwnda.

'Curious,' observed Eadulf, after they had travelled without speaking for a while.

Fidelma, immersed in her own thoughts, glanced absently at him. 'What?'

'Remember Rhonwen's reaction when you asked about Clydog? The smith also seem scared to death of the man.'

'With cause, no doubt,' she agreed. 'Unfortunately, we can no longer ask Father Clidro about him. From the look on Rhonwen's face, I suspect that Clydog is not beyond rape as well as pillage.'

'Short of being able to ask Clydog, which I do not propose doing,' responded Eadulf in grim amusement, 'I think we will not be able to resolve that mystery. However, so far as the disappearance of the brethren of Llanpadern is concerned, I think we may now offer an explanation to Gwlyddien, as much as I am embarrassed by it.'

Fidelma answered with a short laugh. 'We may offer an explanation, but is it the right one? Come, let me hear your version.'

Eadulf look slightly pained at her sceptical response. 'My explanation is the same as I offered before.'

Fidelma was still smiling softly. 'And that is . . . ?'

'I do not make excuses for my people, but you know that

many Saxon ships raid the coast for plunder and slaves. A Hwicce ship landed here, raided the community at Llanpadern. In the raid, one of them was killed . . . the man we found in the tomb. The raiders then marched their captives back to their ship. Something happened when they reached the cliff overlooking the ship. Perhaps an attempt to escape. Seven were cut down. The evidence of Hwicce weapons and a shield show who did it.'

Fidelma glanced at Eadulf without approval. 'It is a good theory,' she admitted.

Eadulf frowned in annoyance. 'Theory? You do not accept it?'

She smiled softly. 'Not in the form in which you give it. You forget that Father Clidro was not killed at the time of this attack. His blood was freshly spilt when we found him.'

'I had forgotten.' Eadulf looked disappointed.

'I think you may well be right in certain matters. A Saxon ship . . . I would not know whether it was from this strange kingdom you mention – the Who-ekka?' She forced her tongue over the unfamiliar syllables. 'But if, as Goff said, a Saxon ship did anchor off shore here, then I suspect they did play a part in whatever happened at Llanpadern.'

'But the rest must follow,' protested Eadulf.

'The facts do not support what you have said. Forget that you are a Saxon.'

Momentarily Eadulf's features broke into a humorous grin. 'That is a difficult thing to do in this land where I am constantly reminded of it,' he observed wryly.

'In any raid by Saxons on a community – and we have had many such raids in Laigin and Muman so we know of them at first hand – what usually happens?'

Eadulf pursed his lips to give her question some thought.

'What happens is that Saxons burn and destroy, carrying off plunder,' went on Fidelma, without waiting for him to answer. 'They take young men and girls as slaves, and kill the rest. Where is the evidence that such a raid was carried out at Llanpadern?'

'Father Clidro was—'

'Father Clidro was flogged, taken to the barn and hanged. He was not struck down by sword or spear. But his body does not appear there until well after the Saxon ship has left. Where has he been during the last few days?'

Eadulf had considered the anomaly. Her reasoning had not

been entirely lost on him. He had been worrying about it but had no logical explanation.

'But what of the slaughter of the seven brothers on the foreshore? What of that?' he protested.

'That is a singular event, Eadulf. Consider it. Most of them were killed by a sword blow from behind. A blow to the neck. They were all killed in the same spot, which does not indicate that they were attempting to escape their captors, does it? And, having killed the seven, what warriors do you know who would cast down a shield, a knife and a broken sword by the bodies and leave them?'

Eadulf compressed his lips as he remembered the questions that Fidelma had asked about the broken sword. There had been no blood on it and the broken end was not in any of the bodies.

'Are you saying that this was deliberately done in order to make people think that Saxons were responsible?' he asked, bewildered. 'Are you saying that there is no Saxon connection?'

Fidelma shook her head immediately. 'The Saxon in the tomb and the Saxon ship anchored off the coast are somehow connected with this mystery. But I am not sure how.'

He regarded her in surprise. 'But if it was not a Saxon raid, what else would bring a Saxon ship here?'

'That is the mystery which must be solved. All I know is that the facts are complicated and inexplicable based on the knowledge we currently have.'

Eadulf remained silent for a moment. 'Then I doubt that we shall produce an answer.'

Fidelma turned a disapproving eye on him. '*Tempus omnia revelat,*' she said reprovingly.

'Time may well reveal all things but can we afford to wait?' he replied sharply.

'Wait we must,' she replied calmly. 'We must be patient.'

'Have you forgotten the threat from Clydog and his men?'

'I have not. As I have told you, I think he also provides a key which may unravel this mystery.'

The countryside in which they were riding fell away on their left to a coastline consisting of dramatic cliffs and deep rocky coves. Here and there they could see seal pups cavorting in the water, while mingling with the sea birds were a few buzzards emitting their mewing 'kiew' as they scanned the ground for small mammals. Buzzards preferred these open hillsides over which they were now travelling, for it was ideal territory for catching rabbits. The track was now leading by another hill, turning inland. They could see the deserted walls of an ancient hill fortress standing some two hundred metres from them. They followed the contours of the south side of the hill towards the east where Llanwnda lay across the main hill of Pen Caer. Eadulf knew that 'pen' meant a head while 'caer' was a fort.

'I'll be glad of a bath and fresh, dry clothes,' observed Eadulf cheerfully as he realised they could not be far away from Llanwnda.

Their clothes had dried on them before they reached Llanferran and left them with an uncomfortable sensation, the linen and wool rough and irritating to the skin. Eadulf, after such a long time in the five kingdoms of Éireann, had grown accustomed to Irish ways. There the people bathed every day, generally in the evening, while in the morning they only washed their face and hands. Eadulf had always considered this toilet rather excessive. In his own land, bathing was often confined to a swim in a nearby river and then only infrequently. But the Irish made a ritual of cleanliness, and used a cake of a fatty substance called *sléic* to create a lather which washed away the dirt.

Now Eadulf missed the heated bath water, the immersion in the tub called a *debach* in which were placed sweet-smelling herbs, the vigorous towelling with a linen cloth. He had to admit, after his initial caution, that the ritual made him feel refreshed and invigorated.

Fidelma shared his longing for a bath and clean clothes. The previous night's adventure, such as it was, had left her with a feeling of besmirchment that she felt it would take many baths to eradicate. But there was another anticipation with which Fidelma was returning to Llanwnda. She had not been able to rid herself of concern for young Idwal. Nor could she shake off the belief, albeit based on pure emotion rather than deduction, that the boy was innocent of the death of Mair. She was looking forward to hearing how Brother Meurig's inquiry had developed. Perhaps the information she had gathered about Mair's father, Iorwerth, might be useful.

The track was now leading them down into a thickly wooded valley beyond which the settlement of Llanwnda was situated. Fidelma realised that this was probably the very wood in which the girl had been strangled. She wished that she knew for certain. She would have liked to have examined the spot, even though she knew that no clues would remain there after so long an interval.

Fidelma, however, liked to see the places where victims met their deaths, insofar as she was able. It helped her envisage the scene more clearly in her own mind.

She mentioned this fact to Eadulf, and he looked glum.

'Isn't it best not to interfere in Brother Meurig's investigation?'

Fidelma was vexed by his attitude and showed it. 'Interference? Eadulf, you know that as a *dálaigh* I cannot stand aside and ignore crime.'

'But this is not your—'

'Not my country? You have not stood aside in our adventures before and claimed that you should not be involved in them because you were a Saxon! Crime is crime in any land. *Justitia omnibus* – justice for all.'

Eadulf blinked at the sharpness of her tone. 'I meant—' he began.

She made a cutting motion with her hand. 'I know what you meant.'

They lapsed into an uncomfortable silence.

Fidelma often regretted her outbursts of irritation. She knew that her quick temper and sharpness of tongue were faults. Then she remembered that her mentor, Brehon Morann, was fond of saying that the person without a fault is without life. Even so, perhaps she should try to curb her moods.

'I am sorry,' she suddenly said, surprising Eadulf. 'Since we came to this place, I have had a curious feeling that there is much evil here. A mystery which is like a complex of threads of which we have been given several. We follow the thread a distance and find another and another but none of them lead to any centre. I think it is important that the mysteries of the death of Mair and the disappearance of the community of Llanpadern are resolved.'

Eadulf did not respond for a moment.

Fidelma decided to continue. 'I know you want to proceed to Canterbury as soon as possible but I could not be at ease with myself if I did not pursue these matters to a conclusion.'

Eadulf was forced to respond with a resigned smile. 'I really expected no less. It is just that I am worried for your safety . . .' He hesitated and raised a shoulder, letting it fall eloquently. 'For *our* safety,' he corrected. 'I have felt danger before but never the hostility that I have encountered here. And the threat from such a person as Clydog is something that causes me concern. If you

133

or I should fall into his hands again . . .' He did not finish the sentence, but his meaning was clear enough.

'Then we must ensure that we do not fall into the hands of that outlaw,' Fidelma replied brightly, with more assurance than she felt.

They were entering a small clearing in the wood and saw that it was occupied by a woodsman's hut.

'Best check that we are on the right track to Llanwnda,' Eadulf advised.

They noticed that the door stood partially open and Fidelma drew rein and called a hello. There was no answer.

The small hut was a tiny affair and outside it was a pile of wood in the process of being cut, for a large-handled axe stood embedded in one of the logs, as if abandoned by the woodsman in the middle of his attempts to sever it.

It was Eadulf who noticed it and he turned to Fidelma and silently pointed to the axe.

Fresh blood was dripping from its blade onto the wood.

Perhaps the woodsman had cut himself while swinging his sharp-bladed axe at the log.

'Hello!' cried Fidelma again. 'Are you hurt? Can we help?'

There was no sound; no movement.

Eadulf swung down from his horse and moved to the door of the hut. For a moment he stood on the threshold staring in and then he let out an exclamation.

'The man is here and unconscious, so it seems,' he called to Fidelma, before moving into the dark interior. Fidelma was in the act of dismounting to join him when she heard his voice upraised in surprise.

'What is it?' she demanded, starting forward.

Eadulf had emerged and was leaning against the door jamb, his face pale. He stared at her for a moment as if unable to form words. 'He's in there . . .'

Fidelma frowned. 'The woodsman?' she demanded, surprised at his attitude. After all, Eadulf had studied to be an apothecary at Tuam Brecain. He was surely used to injury and violent death. 'Is it a bad wound? Come on, Eadulf, let us help the poor man. I've not known you to be so squeamish before.'

'It's too late,' Eadulf breathed.

Frustrated, Fidelma pushed him aside and entered the small hut. The light from the door spread over the figure on the floor. She bent towards the body which was stretched just inside.

Three facts came to her in quick succession.

Firstly, the man's neck was nearly severed. This had been no accident. Someone had taken the axe and swung its sharp blade with the intention of killing the man. Then, leaving him dead or dying on the floor, the assailant had returned the axe to the woodpile outside, embedding it in the log before departing.

Secondly, the man was not a woodsman. He was wearing the robes of a religieux.

Thirdly, she recognised the twisted, agonised features of the victim. It was Brother Meurig.

Chapter Twelve

They rode into Llanwnda in silence. Fidelma had spoken little on the journey from the woodsman's hut. As they crossed the bridge over the stream into the township, they heard the clang of metal on metal from the smith's forge, heard the rasp of the bellows and saw Iorwerth the smith at work, swinging his hammer with his muscular arm. He barely glanced in their direction as they rode by. In the square beyond the bridge, where two nights before they had watched the abortive attempt to hang Idwal, there now stood a tall stack of wood, piled high and obviously ready to be ignited into a gigantic bonfire. Children were playing here and there in groups, unconcerned, riotous, normal. There were a few groups of people in the single street. Some stood gossiping, a few cast glances filled with curiosity in their direction.

Eadulf looked at Fidelma. He could see that she was perturbed. Indeed, the murder of a religieux was a heinous crime. When he had tried to speculate on who might have done this terrible thing, she had simply replied with her customary advice: 'It is no use speculating without facts.' She had refused to engage further with him, although he felt that she must be examining possibilities in her own mind as they rode along. That irritated him.

Fidelma was not immune to Eadulf's frustration but she was in no mood to speculate aloud. She was too busy turning matters over in her head. She had spent some time carefully examining Brother Meurig's body. She had also inspected the hut, the axe and the surrounding area. She had found nothing at all which could be called a clue. What had Brother Meurig been doing in the woods? Had he been searching for the spot where Mair had been killed? If so, what had he stumbled on to cause him to be killed in such a vicious and maniacal fashion?

It was no use sharing these questions with Eadulf. He would know the questions well enough but it was answers that were needed and there were none – yet. Without further information, questions remained simply questions.

The tranquillity of Llanwnda was in sharp contrast to what they had seen in the woodsman's hut and their experience at

Llanpadern. No one seemed surprised to see them again. No one appeared to be interested in their arrival.

'We'll go directly to Gwnda,' Fidelma said to Eadulf as they walked their horses slowly down the street towards the hall of the lord of Pen Caer.

It was only when they had dismounted and were hitching their mounts to the posts in front of his hall that Gwnda himself appeared. He seemed ill at ease to see them.

'What news from Llanpadern? You are soon back from there,' he said in greeting. It was clear that there was no enthusiasm in his voice.

Fidelma examined his features closely. 'What do you know of Brother Meurig's whereabouts?' she asked.

Gwnda's mouth tightened a little at her response. 'I don't know where he is. He left here this morning.'

'Going where?'

Gwnda shook his head. 'He did not tell me.'

'When did he say that he would return?'

'He did not say.'

Fidelma tried to control her exasperation.

'Did he tell anyone where he was going?' Eadulf decided to enter the questioning.

'A secret man, is the *barnwr*.' Gwnda smiled without humour. Then he noticed the condition of their clothes and their tired and dishevelled appearance. 'You appear to have slept rough. Could you not find shelter at Llanpadern? There was a bad storm last night.'

'We had to shelter in a cave,' Eadulf explained shortly. 'Baths and the possibility of finding some fresh clothing would be a welcome thing.'

'You are my guests until you depart again for the abbey of Dewi Sant,' the chieftain acknowledged without enthusiasm.

'Then we . . .' began Eadulf, and then paused, suddenly catching sight of Fidelma's warning look. She was not sure what he was about to say but the look expressed her alarm in case he mentioned the finding of Meurig before she was ready. '. . . we accept,' he finished lamely.

They followed Gwnda into the hall and he clapped his hands for attention. The tall blonde woman entered and her eyes narrowed a little as she beheld them.

'Buddog, Sister Fidelma and Brother Eadulf are once more

our guests. See that baths are prepared and refreshment brought. Also see that their horses are cared for and fed.'

The woman inclined her head slightly. 'It shall be done.'

While Gwnda was issuing his instructions, Fidelma managed to whisper to Eadulf: 'Let me do the talking about Meurig.'

They were seated before the fire when Buddog brought in their drinks and announced that the bathing preparations were being made. When Gwnda had seated himself and taken his drink, Fidelma said quietly: 'Father Clidro is dead.'

The lord of Pen Caer stared at her for a moment. 'So it was a Saxon raid, after all? How many of the brethren have died?' There was a note of triumph in his voice.

'Some seven others, so far as we can deduce, and then there is Father Clidro. He was hanged in a barn at Llanpadern while the others were, as was reported to you, slain on the beach near Llanferran.'

Gwnda sighed deeply. 'Our coastline is vulnerable to Saxon raids.'

'Do you know of an outlaw called Clydog?'

Gwnda actually started so much that some of his drink spilled on his hand.

Fidelma smiled grimly. 'It is obvious that you do know of him,' she observed before the chieftain could compose himself.

'Most people around Pen Caer know that name and many are acquainted with him to their cost,' conceded the chieftain, recovering his poise.

'What do you know of him?'

Gwnda examined them both thoughtfully. 'Why bring Clydog into this?' he said slowly.

'I merely want you to share with me what you know of this Clydog the Wasp.'

Gwnda paused thoughtfully. 'Clydog Cacynen.' He almost sneered the name. 'Six months ago we had reports of wayfarers being robbed in the forests around Ffynnon Druidion. At first, none of them were killed, merely robbed and sent on their way. They spoke of an outlaw named Clydog, who seemed quite cultured and who robbed them with a laugh. He had a small band of warriors, presumably adventurers, thieves and murderers escaping justice. A dozen or so men who took to the forests with Clydog.'

Fidelma was a little impatient. She felt that he was not telling

139

her anything that she did not know. 'You said that none of his victims were killed at first. That implies that others were killed later.'

Gwnda nodded in confirmation. 'That is so, Sister. Several people have been killed as Clydog's raids have become more reckless. King Gwlyddien once sent a band of warriors to scour the woods to destroy Clydog, but without success. Clydog knows the forests of Ffynnon Druidion like the back of his hand.'

'Gwlyddien had to send warriors? You are lord of Pen Caer. Why couldn't you raise your own band of warriors to flush him out?'

Gwnda chuckled without humour. 'If I searched all Pen Caer I doubt whether I could find a dozen trained warriors. Most of the young menfolk are already serving with the Lord Rhodri to protect our borders with Ceredigion.'

'So, apart from this one attempt, nothing has been done about Clydog since?'

'So long as Clydog does not strike at any of the major settlements of Pen Caer and confines himself to the highways, he is no great threat to the peace of the area.'

'So your policy is to let Clydog alone and hope he lets you alone?' Fidelma was disapproving. 'What if he were responsible for Llanpadern?'

Gwnda started in astonishment. 'Are you saying that it was not a Saxon raid? Are you saying Clydog was responsible for killing Father Clidro and the others? That is nonsense. What purpose would it serve?'

'I am asking, what if he were responsible?' she pressed.

'Then I suppose that King Gwlyddien would have to raise men to go against him. Send warriors in such numbers that he would be flushed out. But it would take a fair number to comb the woods of Ffynnon Druidion, and the kingdom cannot spare many trained warriors. Not at this time.'

'Cannot?' Fidelma emphasised the word.

'Artglys, the king of Ceredigion, is pressing on our borders, searching for weaknesses in the hope of taking over this land. Our borders are long and our warriors stretched to maintain the peace along them.'

Fidelma sat for a moment considering the information. 'We know what Clydog is, but I would like to know who he is.'

Gwnda was puzzled. 'Who?'

'Surely this outlaw did not suddenly appear from nowhere?'

The lord of Pen Caer surprised them by nodding slowly. 'That is precisely what he did.'

'You mean that he is not a local man?'

'Not so far as we know.'

'If he is not from the area, how does he have such a good local knowledge that he can avoid the warriors of the king when they search for him?' Eadulf asked.

Gwnda sniffed deprecatingly. 'A good point, Brother Saxon. A good point. But no one who has seen Clydog has been able to identify him as being related to anyone in this area. Perhaps it is one of his men who has the local knowledge.'

Fidelma was disappointed. She had been sure that Clydog must have some local connection; a connection which she was hoping would link him to the mystery.

Buddog re-entered. 'The baths are ready for our guests, lord,' she announced. 'Alas, we have no robes suitable for religious. However, if the sister and the brother will consent to put on ordinary garments for a day, we will wash their own robes and return them.'

Fidelma slowly rose. 'That will be acceptable. Your hospitality is most welcome, Gwnda.'

As Buddog left the chieftain also rose, along with Eadulf. 'It is my earnest hope that the affairs that have brought you here are speedily resolved,' he said.

'It is our hope also, Gwnda,' Fidelma replied with the same solemnity. 'However, it may take some time. You see . . . Brother Meurig has been murdered.'

Eadulf had been waiting to see what dramatic moment Fidelma would choose to reveal the find in the forest.

The expression on Gwnda's face changed only slowly. Then he shook himself like a shaggy dog. 'Are you saying that Brother Meurig is dead?'

'His body lies in the forest,' confirmed Fidelma.

Gwnda let out a long, whistling sigh. 'Murdered, you say? Why did you not tell me immediately?'

'You said that you did not know where Brother Meurig had gone or when he would return. What could you have told me if you had known before?'

'Nothing, but . . .'

'But?'

'Only that his death hangs heavily on my conscience. Perhaps

I should have warned him more insistently before he left. I might have prevented this catastrophe.'

Fidelma exchanged a quick glance with Eadulf. 'Warned him? Prevented his murder? It sounds as though you knew far more than you have revealed to us about where Brother Meurig's investigation was leading?'

'It's not that.'

'Not that? You maintain that you did not know where he was going but that you could have warned him not to go and thus prevented his murder?' There was a cynical tone in Fidelma's voice.

Gwnda's expression was defensive. 'I might have prevented it,' he insisted. 'I'd better take some men to the woodsman's hut and retrieve Brother Meurig's body.'

'Before you go, I think that you should explain,' Fidelma said quietly.

'Explain? When Brother Meurig left here, I could have demanded that he go alone, that's all.'

'Go alone?' Fidelma frowned quickly. 'You mean he left here in the company of someone else?'

'Isn't that what I am telling you?'

Fidelma let out a sharp breath of exasperation. 'In the name of the Holy Saints, man, tell us in whose company Brother Meurig left and why you think that person was responsible for his death?'

'He left with Mair's killer, that's who.'

'Mair's killer?' echoed Eadulf.

'The young boy, Idwal. He left with Idwal.'

An hour later Fidelma and Eadulf had emerged from their baths both refreshed and wearing more comfortable clothing. Buddog informed them that Gwnda was waiting in the main hall and a meal had been prepared for them.

It was gloomy and dark now and Fidelma realised that it would soon be evening, for autumnal darkness descended early.

Gwnda was, indeed, waiting for them.

'I have sent two of my best huntsmen and trackers to see if they can pick up signs of Idwal,' he reported. 'But he will have most of this day's start on us and we will not be able to set out in pursuit before tomorrow's first light. In death, it seems, Brother Meurig has proved the guilt of the boy, at least.'

Fidelma admonished him with a look. 'That the boy left with

Brother Meurig is not certain proof of his guilt either in Mair's case or in the death of Meurig.'

Gwnda stared at her for a moment and then chuckled grimly. 'Surely, Sister, you can entertain no doubt about the boy's guilt now?'

'There are questions to be asked still. But you are right, Idwal must be found. I hope that the men you sent out are instructed not to harm him but to bring him back here if they find him?'

'They know that they are tracking a killer. They will act accordingly,' replied Gwnda.

'Brother Meurig was a *barnwr*. I am a *dálaigh* holding an equivalent legal rank,' announced Fidelma. 'Therefore I am going to take charge of this case.'

Gwnda was silent for a moment. The corners of his mouth turned down as he pressed his mouth tight shut for a moment. 'By the Holy Cross, you are not!' he finally responded with firmness.

Fidelma returned his look without flinching. 'Do you challenge my authority?' Her voice was soft. Eadulf knew that it was when she spoke softly that she was at her most dangerous.

'You have no authority here. Not in this matter, anyway.'

Fidelma stiffened. 'I have the authority of King Gwlyddien of Dyfed,' she retorted.

'No you do not.'

Fidelma's eyes widened in disbelief. 'Brother Meurig told you so when we arrived. You accepted it then.'

Gwnda shook his head. 'King Gwlyddien authorised you only to investigate the disappearance of the community of Llanpadern. He sent Brother Meurig here to judge the case against Idwal. You have no right to intervene in this matter. I am lord of Pen Caer and I shall be magistrate in this affair.'

Fidelma swallowed sharply. It was true. Gwnda was right under the absolute letter of the law. She had no jurisdiction here. She thought for a moment and then realised that she could do nothing but back away.

'Then I must plead with you, Gwnda. I believe that an injustice is happening. I should investigate this matter further if justice is to be served.'

'You have authority to investigate at Llanpadern. That is all.' Gwnda's expression was determined. 'You are welcome to the hospitality of my hall for this night. I presume that you will want to return to the abbey of Dewi Sant tomorrow. Until then I suggest that you do not wander far from the protection of my roof.'

Fidelma's eyes narrowed in annoyance. 'That sounds suspiciously like a threat, Gwnda?' Once more Eadulf heard dangerously quiet quality to her voice.

Gwnda's expression was impassive. 'There is no threat at all in what I say, Sister. I am but warning you for your own safety and the safety of your Saxon companion.'

'That certainly sounds like a threat to me,' observed Eadulf sourly.

'When the news of Brother Meurig's death has spread, there will be many who will be angered. The fact that Idwal was obviously responsible for Mair's death was acknowledged by most people in Llanwnda. Now it appears that Brother Meurig has been killed by him. The people will be reminded that you stopped them taking their revenge on Idwal. Had they done so, Meurig would be alive now.'

'It was not we who prevented the mob from murder,' corrected Eadulf. 'Brother Meurig was the one who stopped their foolhardiness.'

Gwnda smiled thinly. 'Brother Meurig has paid the price for his mistake. However, if you start wandering around Llanwnda, the people might recall that you were with him and bear collectively the responsibility for a further death here.'

'That is a totally illogical way of thinking,' snapped Fidelma.

'I speak not for myself, of course, but for the people,' Gwnda said evasively. 'They are notoriously illogical when it comes to curbing feelings of vengeance against any who have wronged them.' He turned to the door. 'If you need anything further just ring that hand bell. Buddog will come to attend to your wants.'

They heard his steps retreating outside and a short time latter a horse left the stable.

Eadulf was resigned. 'So that is that! We return to the abbey of Dewi Sant tomorrow. At least we can—'

He was brought up short by Fidelma's scornful expression. 'Do you think I would run away now?'

Eadulf gazed into her fiery green eyes and suppressed a sigh of resignation. 'I suppose not.'

'Precisely so.'

'Then what do you intend?'

'I have never retreated from a mystery that I was pledged to resolve. Nor will I now.'

144

'Then you will need to get the authority of King Gwlyddien to overrule the lord of Pen Caer.'

She glanced at him and smiled. As usual, Eadulf had that ability of getting right down to the practicality. Her smile broadened. Eadulf read what was in her mind and groaned inwardly.

'You want me to ride to the Ábbey of Dewi Sant and seek authority of King Gwlyddien?'

She nodded affirmatively and added: 'It is the only way.'

'Do I have time to eat first?' he asked petulantly.

'Naturally. And to sleep as well. The best way to do this is for both of us to pretend that we are leaving tomorrow at first light. Then I shall find somewhere to stay outside Llanwnda while you go on to the abbey. If you ride fast, and the abbot provides you with a fresh horse, you could be back within twenty-four hours.'

'What will you do for twenty-four hours?' demanded Eadulf. 'You will not be able to move around asking questions and there is the additional danger of our friend Clydog and his men to be avoided.'

Fidelma looked rueful. 'I will do what I can. But you are right, I will be very restricted until you return.'

'I think that it is better we rethink this plan,' Eadulf went on. 'There is no way you are going to be able to ask questions about Idwal. Besides, Gwnda is right, you know.'

She looked at him belligerently. 'Right? In what way?'

'This matter of Idwal is not really our affair. Our task was to—'

She held up her hand to stop him. 'Spare me what I have heard a thousand times,' she snapped waspishly. Then, almost at once, she smiled apologetically. 'Sorry, Eadulf, but you have pointed this out before – several times.'

He agreed gloomily. 'Facts are facts no matter how many times they are stated,' he added in self-justification.

'The fact is that I am coming to the belief that there is some common factor in all these events. I want to know what that connection is.

'This is not the first time you have implied there is a connection. How can you say so? I have seen no evidence of any connection.'

'I feel it.'

'It is not like you to rely only on intuition.'

'I do not rely on it, as well you know. But Brehon Morann

once said that often the heart and emotions will see before the head does.'

'And often the heart and emotions will be blind while logic shows the way,' grunted Eadulf.

'I thought we could work together,' Fidelma found herself protesting. 'Instead we seem to be arguing all the time. What has happened to us, Eadulf?'

Eadulf considered the matter.

He realised that it was true. Since they had come to this accursed country of Dyfed there had been a growing friction. It was not that argument was new to them. Indeed, they had often argued but each had retained their respect for the other; both had retained their sense of humour. Eadulf knew that Fidelma always teased him over their conflicting opinions on the Faith, over their differing philosophies. But the arguments were always good-natured and there was no enmity between them. Yet now, now . . . what was wrong? There seemed a growing bitterness behind their words.

He rubbed his chin thoughtfully.

'I think it is this atmosphere, Fidelma,' he answered weakly. 'I feel it is oppressive.'

'You have been gloomy ever since we came on this shore. Perhaps I should have taken notice of what you said. Maybe we should have waited in Porth Clais and found another boat.'

Eadulf knew that she did not believe what she was saying. She was in her element here, studying this mystery. To deny her that would be to totally misunderstand what made her function.

'The fault lies with me,' he said, after a moment or two. 'I am the one who is the cause of the problem.'

Fidelma looked quickly at him to check whether he was being sincere. Then she shook her head. 'I think the fault might lie with the decision I took at Loch Garman.' Her voice was without emotion.

Eadulf compressed his lips. He said nothing.

Fidelma waited a moment or two and when he made no other comment she added: 'The sages say *ne cede malis*, but that is precisely what we seem to be doing. We are yielding to misfortune. We have never done so before.'

'There is a curse on this land,' growled Eadulf angrily.

'A curse?' Fidelma actually smiled, a swift glimpse of her old urchin grin of mischief. 'I have never seen you retreating back into the superstition of your people, Eadulf.'

Eadulf's face reddened. He was well aware that most Christians from other lands did not regard the newly converted Angles and Saxons as truly Christian. He had not forgotten the body of the Hwicce in the tomb at Llanpadern and the talk of a Saxon raiding ship. He knew just how much the Britons of these kingdoms hated Saxons. He had always felt himself above the misdeeds of his people in their centuries-old struggle to drive the Britons ever westward and take over their lands. The Saxon wars were nothing to do with him. They were a matter to be condemned by the Church and he was no part of them. To have Fidelma associating him with . . .

He paused in his misery. Someone had entered the room and crossed to the table where they were sitting. It was Buddog.

'I have come to set the table,' she announced quietly, and suited the action to the word, beginning to place the plates from a wooden tray.

Fidelma regarded the dour, taciturn woman with a speculative eye. 'Have you heard the news?'

The blonde servant did not pause. 'Concerning Brother Meurig? I have.'

'Gwnda is claiming that he was killed by Idwal.'

'That is not my concern.'

'I thought you were anxious to point out to Brother Meurig, when we were last here, that Idwal was deserving of some sympathy.'

'I did not say that,' the woman said brusquely.

'Then what did you say?'

'I said that if Idwal killed Mair then she deserved it.'

'Ah yes,' conceded Fidelma. 'So you did. You felt that she was flirtatious and led men astray. Why was that, now? Remind me of your reason for saying so.'

'Because Mair was sly. Capricious. She twisted men around her little finger. She could make them do whatever she wanted.'

'Ah, so I remember. But what you are saying is that she was hardly the virgin depicted by her father Iorwerth.'

'What did Iorwerth know of what she was up to? A virgin, indeed,' sneered the woman. 'She used men's lust as a weapon against them.'

'You seem to have known her pretty well? More so than her father,' pointed out Eadulf.

'I knew her. She was around here enough times.'

'Ah, yes. She was Elen's friend, wasn't she? But as for using men's lust against them – who do you say were her victims? Are you speaking of Idwal?'

'And others.'

'What others?'

The door opened abruptly. They looked up and saw a dark, attractive young girl enter the room. It took Eadulf a few moments to remember that she was Elen, the daughter of Gwnda, lord of Pen Caer. She hesitated when she saw Buddog. But the blonde servant took the opportunity to leave, her eyes lowered.

'Is it true?' The girl's first words were a breathless gasp as she faced Fidelma. 'Is it true that Brother Meurig has been killed and that you are looking for Idwal to kill him in revenge?'

Fidelma motioned the girl to a chair by her. Automatically, Elen obeyed the unspoken order and sat down. When she had done so she repeated with emphasis: 'Is it true?'

'It is true that Brother Meurig was hacked to death in the woodsman's hut in the forest. However, it is not true that we are looking for Idwal to kill him. Indeed, your father made plain that we have no role in the matter. Nevertheless, we would like to find Idwal if only for his own safety.'

The girl remained silent for a moment. 'Brother Meurig told me that you were a famous lawyer from Cashel.'

'When did you speak with Brother Meurig?' asked Fidelma.

The girl pouted thoughtfully. 'He asked me some questions yesterday before I left.'

'Before you left?'

'I have just returned from Cilau and heard the news in the township.'

'Cilau?' Fidelma frowned. 'I seem to have heard the name before.'

'It is a small settlement not far from here. I have a cousin there,' explained the girl. 'I left there at midday to get here before dark.'

'Did you know that Brother Meurig was going into the forest?'

'I knew that he planned to go to the forest this morning to see where Mair was killed,' Elen agreed.

'Did you know that he was taking Idwal?

'Didn't he need Idwal to show him the spot where Mair was murdered?'

'As I recall, you did not believe Idwal killed your friend Mair?'

'Idwal would not harm anyone. You spoke with him so you must know that he is a simple youth. Simple but nice . . . and he is so gentle. Sometimes, when a sheep or lamb under his care falls from a rock and injures itself, he can hardly bring himself to kill it. Only the fact that life is a greater misery with the pain of its injury gives him the courage to do so.'

'You really like Idwal, then?' Fidelma remarked encouragingly.

'I know that he could not kill Mair.'

'Have you heard that your father is convinced he killed Brother Meurig?'

'My father never liked Idwal. I do not believe he could kill Brother Meurig any more than he could kill Mair.'

'You seem to be thinking with your heart rather than with your head,' Eadulf observed dryly. 'Emotion is no judge of the facts.'

Fidelma knew that there was an implied rebuke to her in his words and she looked at him quickly, but he did not catch her eye.

'There is another question I would like to ask you, Elen, before we proceed,' Fidelma said. 'The servant, Buddog. She disliked your friend Mair very much. Has she been in this household a long time?'

'Since before I was born,' asserted Elen. 'Poor Buddog.'

'Poor? Why so?'

'She is my father's mistress. But I think that my father has now grown tired of her.'

Fidelma relaxed a little. This explained much about Buddog's attitude.

'How well do you really know Idwal, Elen?' Eadulf asked, interrupting her thoughts.

The girl considered the question and then understood its deeper meaning. Her eyes widened. 'I am not . . .' She hesitated. 'There is nothing between us, nothing sexual that is. Nor will there ever be. He is just a simple, friendly boy for whom many feel sorrow. He is four years older than I am. He was abandoned in his youth and raised by a shepherd . . . Iestyn's brother, but I forget his name.'

'We have heard Idwal's story,' cut in Eadulf sharply. 'Your relationship is no more than that?'

The girl flushed in annoyance. 'I have said so.'

'It seems curious,' Fidelma said slowly, 'that you are so

149

adamant that Idwal could not have killed your friend Mair and that this opinion is based on no more than your feelings about the youth. I would imagine that we all have the propensity within us to kill if the circumstances were right. What I mean is that if we were outraged enough, or pushed into it by an overriding necessity which was more urgent than our moral code . . .'

'I cannot imagine any circumstances in which Idwal would be driven to such rage that he would do such a thing,' Elen replied firmly.

Fidelma regarded the girl thoughtfully. She appeared sincere enough. 'Tell me more about your friend Mair.'

Elen looked disconcerted for a moment. 'What would you want to know?

'How long had you known her?'

'We grew up together. Here in this small township everyone knew everyone else, especially children growing up. Mair and I were the only two girls of our age. We almost looked alike and a few times visitors thought we were sisters.'

'I believe that you know that Idwal is not guilty of the crime he is accused of for another reason . . . another than simply a vague emotion of your heart.'

Fidelma made her suggestion without preamble, surprising Eadulf.

Elen was quiet, and Fidelma decided to explain further.

'When Idwal was accused of raping Mair and taking her virginity, you knew that was not the case, didn't you?'

The girl shrugged. 'Mair was not a virgin,' she agreed. 'She told me so many months ago.'

'If Mair had a lover, the loss of her virginity is not a factor for compensation under the law, as her father is claiming.'

'How did you know about her lover?' Elen asked curiously.

'Because Idwal implied it without intending to do so.'

'Idwal is not artful enough to keep a secret for long,' she agreed. 'Did he tell you who it was?'

'He would not even have told us that Mair had a lover if I had not drawn it out of him by a ruse,' replied Fidelma. 'He refused to give a name. He said that he had sworn an oath to Mair not to tell who it was. She wanted a certain message delivered. Idwal refused to take it. That letter was to her lover.'

Elen lowered her head sadly. 'He is a very moral boy. That's a further reason why he could not have killed Mair.'

'Granted that, do you know who this lover was?'

'I do not. She was very secretive. She only told me of how it was, that first night. You know, the way girls talk about their relationships. The way it felt. Mair was very cynical. She was actually poking fun at this nameless lover. She told me that he was very clumsy and not at all expert in the techniques of love.'

'And was Mair such an expert at the techniques of love?' inquired Eadulf cynically.

Fidelma suddenly leant forward towards the girl, her eyes searching. 'Brother Eadulf does have a point. This conversation you say you had with Mair, was that truly the time when she lost her virginity or had she had experiences before?'

Elen considered the question carefully, realising the implication, and then she shook her head. 'At the time, she was boasting about losing her virginity. She was always a flirt. Always attracted to men – older men at that. As I recall, it was the first time that she had talked about sex, but I think she was implying that her lover was elderly and clumsy and that she felt superior to him.'

'Elderly?' Fidelma sat back thoughtfully. 'As Mair was very young, it might be someone who was merely older than she was.'

'Elen, you have absolutely no idea who this man was?' demanded Eadulf.

Elen shook her head firmly.

'Think carefully,' he pressed. 'This might be the very man who killed her if, as you claim, your friend Idwal did not.'

'I do not think Mair's lover killed her.'

Eadulf was sardonic. 'Another emotional deduction, I presume?'

'Not so,' replied the girl with some spirit. 'You see, I believe that I was supposed to be the victim that day.'

Chapter Thirteen

There was a moment of utter silence. Even as Fidelma was about to form the question that Elen's statement obviously demanded, there was a noise outside the room. Gwnda came through the door and paused. He looked anxious.

'They have—' he began, saw Elen and stopped abruptly. Then he said: 'Elen, please leave us.'

'But, father, what—' the girl began to protest.

Gwnda stamped his foot on the floor, a strangely petulant action which caused Fidelma some amused surprise. She had heard of people stamping their feet in annoyance but this was the first time she had actually observed such a demonstration of emotion.

'Go to your room, at once!'

Reluctantly, the girl rose, glanced at Fidelma with a look which seemed to indicate that she wanted to continue the conversation with her, and withdrew.

Gwnda waited until she had gone. 'I didn't want the girl to hear,' he explained brusquely.

'That much was obvious,' Fidelma assured him dryly. 'What is it that Elen should not hear?'

'The boy—'

'Do you mean Idwal?' Eadulf interrupted.

'Idwal. He has been found.'

Fidelma rose immediately. 'Then we need to ask him some questions immediately,' she said decisively.

Eadulf was also rising when Gwnda made a negative gesture.

'It is too late for questions. I said that the people would be angry when they heard of Brother Meurig's death. Iorwerth and Iestyn led the crowd. They . . . they have lynched the boy.'

'Is he dead?' asked Fidelma after a pause. She realised that the question was superfluous as soon as it came to her lips. Of course the boy was dead. Gwnda's face confirmed it.

'I have rebuked Iorwerth and Iestyn for what they have done,' said the lord of Pen Caer. 'I have accepted that it was not done

153

within the law. But I believe it was a just outcome and will explain as much to King Gwlyddien's chief *barnwr*. The boy is dead. That ends this sad affair.'

'Does it?' Fidelma's anger was clear in her voice. Eadulf shifted his weight uncomfortably.

'It is, indeed, a sad story,' Gwnda went on, oblivious of the glitter in her eyes. 'I am only sorry that the matter resulted in the death of such a learned *barnwr* as Brother Meurig.'

'That is certainly to be regretted.' Fidelma's voice was dangerously brittle.

Gwnda clapped his hands and Buddog entered a moment later. He demanded mead be brought.

'I have had the boy's body taken to Elisse the apothecary. He will see to it that the boy is buried properly. At least, here is an end to the matter,' he said, seating himself. 'My daughter knew Idwal,' he added, as if by way of explanation. 'I didn't want her to hear what happened just yet.'

'She will soon find out,' Eadulf pointed out.

'Indeed, but I will find a gentler way of telling her. I needed to tell you both immediately.'

'It is outrageous that people have taken the law into their own hands,' Fidelma said, her anger a little more under control now. Eadulf had thought she was going to explode in fury but she seemed to be fighting the emotion. 'Do you still intend to prohibit me from making inquiries about the death of Mair and Brother Meurig?'

Gwnda seemed astonished. 'Inquiries? But we have resolved this matter. Not in accordance with law, but it is resolved.'

'I have not resolved it.'

Gwnda frowned in irritation. 'I have already told you that you have no jurisdiction in this. The matter, so far as I am concerned, is now ended. I will send to the abbey of Dewi Sant to inform the court.'

Fidelma stood with head bowed in thought. 'Very well; yet you have no objection to my pursuing inquiries about Llanpadern.'

Gwnda was suspicious. 'You know I do not. You have the permission of the king.'

'Then I shall continue to pursue those inquiries.' She turned and motioned to Eadulf to accompany her, leaving Gwnda gazing in annoyed perplexity.

Outside Eadulf examined her with a baffled expression. 'What was that supposed to mean?' he asked.

Fidelma smiled wanly. 'I intend to question Iorwerth and Iestyn.'

'But Gwnda said—'

'Gwnda said that he had no objection to my pursuing inquiries concerning Llanpadern. You will recall that Idwal passed through Llanpadern on the morning Mair was murdered. What concerns Llanpadern might concern Idwal.'

She turned into the kitchen and sought Buddog. 'Where can I find the lady Elen?' she asked.

The blonde woman shook her head. 'She left the house when her father arrived. I do not know where she has gone.'

Fidelma compressed her lips in annoyance but thanked the woman.

'A pity,' she said to Eadulf after they had left the kitchen and stood outside in the yard. 'I want to hear what she meant by saying Mair was killed in mistake for her. Until we can find her, let us go down to Iorwerth's forge and have a word with this outraged smith.'

Eadulf moved reluctantly after her. 'I doubt if Gwnda is going to interpret matters in the same light.'

'Probably not,' agreed Fidelma briefly. 'That is why I still want you to ride to the abbey of Dewi Sant tomorrow and secure Gwlyddien's authority for me. Gwnda's prohibition must be cancelled. In the meantime, let us see what Iorwerth says about Idwal's death before you leave.'

Eadulf was glum. 'I do not like to leave you here on your own.'

'But the permission of Gwlyddien is now necessary and urgent.'

There were several people about in the township as they walked from Gwnda's hall down to the forge. It was late afternoon and there was a hint of dusk approaching. Many of the people they met now avoided eye contact and hung their heads, scuttling away into their houses.

'The madness of the lynch mob has been dispelled,' Eadulf commented cynically. 'Now they feel their individual guilt at taking a human life.'

'And that guilt will only last a day or two before they begin to find justification for their actions,' agreed Fidelma.

As they came upon Iorwerth's forge they saw a horse tethered outside. A figure that seemed familiar was dismounting and untying a heavy saddle bag. The young man turned at their

155

approach. Fidelma recognised the son of Goff the smith whom they had encountered earlier that morning.

'Dewi!'

The young man greeted them with a smile. 'I thought that I might see you here,' he said.

'But what are you doing at Iorwerth's forge?' asked Eadulf, his eye falling to the heavy saddle bags.

'My father promised Iorwerth some gold to work with in his forge. I have come to deliver it.'

'Do you have any objection to that, Gwyddel?' snapped a voice angrily.

Iorwerth, the thickset smith, was standing at the door of his cabin with his muscular arms flexing, a pair of tongs clenched almost menacingly in one hand.

Fidelma smiled softly. 'Why should I have any objection?'

Iorwerth looked disconcerted. 'What are you hanging about my forge for, anyway?' he demanded ungraciously.

'We have come to have a talk with you. But we have no objection to you concluding your business with Dewi first.'

Iorwerth looked doubtfully from Fidelma to Dewi and back again. 'How do you know this Gwyddel, Dewi?' he demanded gruffly.

'We met Dewi at his father's forge this morning,' Fidelma intervened innocently. 'Does that worry you? Or is there any other information you would like?'

Iorwerth glowered at her, not sure how he should answer.

'Can you read, Iorwerth?' was her next unexpected question.

Iorwerth's expression was not pretty. 'I have no call for reading,' he replied gruffly.

'A pity. Dyfed is known as a literate kingdom. However, perhaps Dewi here can read . . . ?'

The young man flushed a little in embarrassment. 'Father Clidro taught me,' he affirmed.

Solemnly Fidelma took out a piece of vellum from her *marsupium* and handed it to him. 'Perhaps you could tell Iorwerth what this says. I fear that if I tell him he will not trust me to tell the truth.'

Iorwerth's eyes narrowed in continued annoyance.

The young man took the vellum and read quickly through it. 'You showed this to my father. It is a commission from King Gwlyddien.'

'Saying what?' prompted Fidelma.

'Saying that you act on his authority and advising everyone to co-operate with you . . .'

Fidelma reached forward and took the vellum from Dewi's fingers. 'Do you understand that, Iorwerth?' she asked.

Eadulf found himself hiding a smile at her sleight of hand. He knew that she had not allowed the young man to read out that the co-operation related to the specific inquiry about Llanpadern.

The smith's jaw came up stubbornly.

Dewi was apologetic. 'It is what the words say, Iorwerth, and I have seen the king's seal often before at the abbey of Dewi Sant when I have delivered father's work there.'

The smith remained hesitant but then admitted defeat. 'If that is what the words say,' he conceded reluctantly, 'I will answer your questions.'

'When you have finished your business with Dewi,' Fidelma told him, 'we will go inside your cabin and talk.'

The young man unslung his saddle bag and handed it to Iorwerth. 'There is little business to conduct, Sister,' he announced. 'I merely came to deliver the pieces of gold that my father promised Iorwerth for his forge.'

Iorwerth took the bag and emptied out the pieces of metal, looking more like jagged rocks than precious gold.

'Excellent,' Iorwerth said as he examined them. 'It is as agreed. Give my salutations to your father, Dewi.'

The youth returned the courtesy and turned towards his horse while Iorwerth said to Fidelma: 'You may enter and tell me what you want of me.'

As Fidelma was about to follow him, Eadulf said: 'I will join you in a moment. I just want a word with Dewi.'

She raised an eyebrow to show her curiosity. Eadulf caught her gaze and half nodded towards a corner of Iorwerth's forge. She just had time to control her surprise. In a corner was a figure of a man made of twists of straw. It was not the same but it was similar to the straw man which they had found in the chapel of Llanpadern.

'Well, Sister?' Iorwerth was demanding as he stood at the door of his cabin. She recovered from her astonishment and joined him, and he led the way into his small living quarters. The space was claustrophobic and dark. She had to bend slightly, for she was tall and her head almost connected with the low beams. The heat of the fire was almost stifling. Fidelma did not wait for Iorwerth to ask her to be seated, for she knew that she would wait in vain.

'What do you want?' Iorwerth demanded gruffly.

'Let us talk about Idwal.'

Iorwerth blinked rapidly. 'But Gwnda said . . .'

Fidelma turned icy cold eyes on him.

'Yes?' she prompted. 'What did Gwnda say?'

Iorwerth gave a half-shrug. 'The matter of my daughter's murder is closed.'

'Not so. You heard that I have a commission from King Gwlyddien, didn't you? Things are closed when I say they are.'

'Idwal killed my daughter and he killed Brother Meurig . . .'

'And you killed him?' ended Fidelma.

At that moment Eadulf entered and took his position just behind her.

'I did not kill him,' Iorwerth was protesting. 'Not the way you imply it. The people killed him.'

'Ah,' smiled Fidelma. 'The people. Tell me how the people killed him.'

'When Gwnda told us that Brother Meurig had been killed, we all knew that it was Idwal. After all, Idwal had raped and killed my daughter. Had you and Brother Meurig not interfered, justice would have been done before now.'

Fidelma decided to let this pass. 'You still have not told me what happened.'

'I knew a likely spot where the boy might hide out, an old oak tree a little way on from the woodsman's hut.'

Fidelma was curious. 'How did you know this spot?'

'The boy was a creature of habit. I knew he used to play there a lot when he was younger. So did Mair and Elen and many of the young ones of the township.'

'Go on.'

'We went there, a dozen men of the township . . . Idwal was there. When he saw us he tried to escape. I am not sure who it was but the next thing was that he had been strung up on the oak.' The smith looked at her defiantly. '*Vox populi vox Dei.*'

'What was that you said, Iorwerth?' asked Eadulf in surprise.

'*Vox populi vox Dei,*' repeated the smith. It was clear from the way he pronounced the words that they were not familiar to him.

'That is an interesting expression. You know what it means?'

'It is our exoneration,' replied the smith.

'The voice of the people is the voice of God,' translated

Fidelma, musingly. 'The wishes of the people are irresistible, eh? That excuses you from killing Idwal, I suppose?'

Iorwerth was silent.

'Was Gwnda with you during this madness?' Fidelma continued.

'You should ask him.'

'I suppose that he fed you this little bit of Latin to use as some magic amulet for your defence?'

Iorwerth did not answer.

'Did you know that your daughter was not a virgin?' Fidelma asked the question without warning. 'You made a false claim to seek higher compensation, didn't you?'

Iorwerth's face went crimson with rage. He moved a few threatening paces forward but Eadulf placed himself quickly before Fidelma. The smith stood for a moment with large fists balled as if he were going to strike out.

'You dare slander my daughter's name?' he finally gasped.

'So, you claim that you did not know? Nor did you have any idea of who her elderly lover was?'

Iorwerth was staring at Fidelma in anger but able to control himself now. 'Were you told that by that simpleton? Did Idwal tell you these lies?' he snarled.

'Why are you so sure that they are lies?'

'Because Idwal would try to protect himself from his accusers. He fooled you, Gwyddel. He fooled you!'

'But if another witness made the claim and not Idwal? What then?'

Iorwerth's eyes were suddenly filled with suspicion. 'What witness? It is a lie. My daughter had no secrets from me.'

'Even in normal circumstances, a daughter will not often confess to her father when and how she lost her virginity.'

Fidelma examined him carefully now. The phrase *vultus est index animi* came to her mind. The expression on one's face is a sign of the soul. Iorwerth's soul was in anguish.

'Tell me about Mair,' Fidelma invited. 'What sort of daughter was she?'

The brawny smith suddenly sat down and buried his face in his hands. To their surprise a sob racked his big frame.

'She was not a good daughter. But she was all I had left of her mother. She was the image of her mother. Poor Esyllt. I did her grievous wrong. She died when Mair was young. I tried to make it up . . . to Mair.'

'I understand,' Fidelma's voice was more compassionate. 'You compensated for the loss of Esyllt by spoiling Mair. In what way was she not a good daughter?'

'She was strong-willed, like me in some ways. She did what she wanted. She was . . . an individual, strong-headed, like a horse that has not been broken. She would not obey me.'

'So you would definitely not be told if she had a lover.'

'She knew how important it was for . . . for both of us, to go through with the marriage that had been arranged with Madog, the goldsmith of Carn Slani.'

'This was an arranged marriage?'

'It was.'

'Did Mair consent?'

'She knew that we required the money that a union with Madog would bring.'

'But given free choice she might have wished for another match?'

'She was headstrong.'

'Gwnda, as I recall, once told us that she was a dutiful daughter.'

Iorwerth gestured disdainfully. 'Gwnda would not know more than what he was told.'

'So he did not know that Mair was headstrong?'

'Most people knew. Anyway, Gwnda's daughter Elen was close to Mair, closer than a sister. It would be hard to ignore the fact that Mair was her own person.'

'So when we are told that you forbade Mair and Idwal to meet one another, you might have been fairly certain that Mair would ignore your orders?'

Iorwerth sniffed irritably. 'She might. But Idwal certainly feared me. He was a fairly timid creature.'

'Indeed?' Fidelma was surprised. 'Timid, but you claim that he killed your daughter.'

'He was timid with men, and a coward is often shown to be the most cunning of killers.'

'Turn your mind back to the morning of the day that Mair was killed. I would like you to tell me something about it – say, from the time you rose in the morning.'

Iorwerth looked bewildered. 'I don't understand . . .'

'Indulge me,' Fidelma invited.

'Well, I was up at dawn and started my fire at the forge. Not long afterwards Mair came to say goodbye.'

160

'Goodbye?' Eadulf questioned.

'She was going to her cousin at Cilau.'

'Cilau? Doesn't Elen have a cousin there?'

Iorwerth inclined his head in agreement.

'I believe so. She left and I was busying myself when I saw Idwal entering the township. He was running. At the time I thought it was odd. To see him running, I mean.'

'You say he was entering the township?'

'He came over the bridge outside—'

'Just a moment. Which route did Mair take leaving the township?'

'Across the bridge.'

'So Idwal must have passed her?'

'The track, as you know, lies through the forest in which she was found. It leads to the west and also to the south.'

'But this was early in the morning and not long after you had seen her set off on the path to Cilau?'

Iorwerth nodded.

'And Idwal came running into the township?'

'I think that he went straight to Gwnda's hall.'

'Do you know what caused him to run to Gwnda?'

'Gwnda later said that it was Idwal who first reported that the community at Llanpadern had vanished.'

'What then?'

'About half an hour later, I saw Idwal returning across the bridge and vanishing into the forest. I simply carried on with my work.'

'It was, so far as you were aware, a morning in which nothing was out of the ordinary apart from Idwal's strange entrance into the township?'

'That is so. I had worked for an hour or perhaps a little more when my friend Iestyn came to the forge. He was very agitated. He told me that he had seen Mair and Idwal in the forest and they were having a fierce argument. He had hurried directly to inform me.'

Fidelma changed her position in the chair. 'Why didn't Iestyn intervene?'

Iorwerth was dismissive. 'Iestyn knew my daughter. If he had tried to intervene it would not be thanks that he would be getting from her.'

'So he came directly to you? And you were angry at this news?'

161

'Of course I was angry. I was furious that Idwal should disobey me. I meant to teach him a lesson. There were a few friends in the forge and they offered to come with me. I set off with Iestyn to the place where he had seen Idwal with my daughter.

'We hurried on until . . . until we found the body of my daughter. A short distance away was Gwnda who had captured Idwal. He would not let us harm the boy but sent for a *barnwr* to judge him. Everyone was angry and finally the people broke into Gwnda's barn and took the boy. Gwnda was told to remain in the house if he had no stomach for justice. We were about to hang the murderer when . . .'

'When we arrived with Brother Meurig and saved you from your folly,' finished Eadulf.

'Knowing you were going to kill Idwal, did Gwnda try to stop you?'

'Of course not . . .' Iorwerth hesitated. 'I mean, we were too many for him. Didn't you see that we had guards at his hall to watch over him?'

'There is one thing I am uncertain of,' Fidelma said reflectively, ignoring his question.

'Which is?' demanded Iorwerth.

'Where was Gwnda when you left the township to go in search of Idwal and Mair? He must have been in the forest already?'

The smith gave a shrug. 'It was good that he was there to capture Idwal.'

The door suddenly burst open unceremoniously. The lord of Pen Caer stood framed in the opening. Behind him stood two men with swords brandished in their hands. He scowled angrily at Fidelma.

'So I have been informed correctly. I was told that you were here at Iorwerth's forge.'

'As you see.' Fidelma smiled, with irony.

'Did I not say that you had no authority to ask questions, Gwyddel? I am lord of Pen Caer and I am the law here. Now you and your Saxon friend will pay the price for ignoring me.'

162

Chapter Fourteen

Fidelma rose slowly and faced Gwnda. She did not flinch from his angry, threatening stare.

'Ignoring you, lord of Pen Caer?' she asked with feigned innocence. 'But the last words you said to me were that you had no objection to my investigating the affair at Llanpadern. Did you not mean what you said?'

A puzzled frown creased Gwnda's forehead.

'I am sure that you would not go against the wishes of King Gwlyddien,' she added.

'What tricks are you trying to play with me, Gwyddel?' Gwnda demanded, but the certainty had left his voice.

'I am investigating the matter of Llanpadern,' she said. 'Idwal was at Llanpadern and he brought the first news of the disappearance of the community here. That is what I was investigating.'

Iorwerth tried to correct her. 'But you were talking about Idwal and my daughter.'

Gwnda turned triumphantly to Fidelma. 'I did not expect a religieuse to lie. Perhaps that is the fashion among the Gwyddel?'

'On the contrary, Gwnda,' replied Fidelma, an iciness making her eyes glisten. 'It is not my fault that the matter of Mair's death overlaps the return of Idwal from Llanpadern. Are you Solomon of the Hebrews that you propose to precisely sever along the border of the two parts?'

Gwnda's jaw clamped shut, a muscle twitched in his face. He realised the point that she was making. Finally, he said: 'You are very clever, *dálaigh* of Éireann.'

'*Utcumque placuerit deo*, lord of Pen Caer,' intoned Fidelma with bowed head. 'However it shall please God.'

Gwnda sniffed in annoyance. 'Do not place all your trust in God,' he replied sourly.

'Do you still continue to raise objections to my investigation?'

Gwnda abruptly turned to his companions and dismissed them in disgust. 'My objections continue as ever,' he said as the armed men left. 'You have no authority in the matter of the deaths of Mair and Meurig.'

'Nor of Idwal's murder, I presume?' she added, glancing at Iorwerth, who flushed angrily. 'But I am investigating what Idwal saw at Llanpadern and what he told people about it on the morning that he returned here.'

Gwnda compressed his lips for a moment as he realised the dilemma. 'If you keep to that subject, then I shall have no objections.'

'Then let me ask you some questions,' Fidelma went on. Her voice rose a little as Gwnda made to leave, compelling the lord of Pen Caer to pause and turn to face her.

'Idwal was seen running to your hall that morning by Iorwerth.' She indicated the bewildered smith, who had not really understood much of their exchange. 'What did Idwal tell you that morning?'

'Nothing. I was not there. He spoke to Buddog. You will have to see her.'

'When did Buddog inform you that Idwal had come to the hall?'

'When?' Gwnda seemed to have trouble with the question.

'I was wondering why you did not order a search party to go to Llanpadern.'

Gwnda blinked for a moment. 'We were busy with the affair of Mair's death,' he said defensively.

Grim amusement edged Fidelma's mouth. 'You will note that I did not bring up the matter of Mair's death?'

Gwnda's expression was sullen. 'It was not until much later in the afternoon that Buddog remembered to tell me about Idwal's visit.'

'So,' said Fidelma, 'Buddog did not tell you what Idwal had said until after the boy had been brought back to your hall. Having then heard the news, why did you not send a party down to Llanpadern?'

The lord of Pen Caer shrugged. 'By that time, I had sent a messenger to the abbey of Dewi Sant asking for a *barnwr* to come here, so I decided to wait and seek his advice on both matters. Then the morning of the day you arrived, Dewi, the son of Goff, came from Llanferran with news of a Saxon raiding ship and the bodies. It would have been dangerous to go to Llanpadern in case of an attack here on the township.'

'Can you remember what Buddog told you?'

'Why not ask her?'

'I shall, but I would like to know what you recall.'

164

'Idwal had arrived asking for me. Then he told Buddog that he had been passing Llanpadern. It was early that morning. He thought he saw one of the brethren leaving on the road south . . .'

'That must have been Brother Cyngar,' interrupted Eadulf and was silenced by a sharp look from Fidelma.

Gwnda continued: 'Idwal went to the community expecting to break his fast. There was no sign of anyone and so he came on to tell me.'

Eadulf was about to say something when he caught another warning glance from Fidelma.

'Which brings me to another question,' she continued. 'Just as a matter of clarification, you'll understand. How was it that you found Mair's body and Idwal?'

'I have told you that you have no authority to inquire into the subject of Mair's death,' he replied testily.

'I was talking about Idwal.'

'The same thing.'

'Not at all. Idwal called to see you about Llanpadern but you were not here. It is natural to ask, how did you meet up with Idwal?'

'I was out in the woods, that's all.'

'And you came across him purely by chance?'

'That is so. I think I have answered enough questions.'

From his curt tone, Fidelma realised that she would be able to extract no more information from him. She smiled with good grace. 'Thank you for your time, Gwnda. You have been most helpful,' she said. 'And, you, too, Iorwerth.' She motioned to Eadulf to follow her as she turned to leave.

'Remember, Gwyddel,' Gwnda snapped, 'your authority ends with the matter of Llanpadern.'

'I shall remember that, lord of Pen Caer,' she replied softly.

They walked back along the street towards Gwnda's hall. As soon as they were out of earshot, Eadulf spoke. His voice was almost bubbling with fury.

'The man is hiding something! Why didn't you let me press him?'

'Because it would have done little good except to alert him against us.'

Eadulf jaw slackened. 'You knew he was lying?'

'I know that he was not telling the whole truth. But it would be pointless to pursue him unless one had solid ground to stand on.

Eadulf considered the matter. 'I know that Gwnda was involved with the hanging of poor Idwal. He put Iorwerth up to reciting that Latin phrase as a defence.'

'I realised that Gwnda was not averse to the killing of Idwal even on the evening when we first arrived in this place,' Fidelma agreed. 'Iorwerth let the truth slip when he indicated that Gwnda made no effort to protect Idwal.'

Eadulf was startled. 'You suspected him that first evening?'

'Do you remember the story that was given to us? That Gwnda was a law-abiding ruler who had sent for the *barnwr*, and that it was Iorwerth and Iestyn who led the mob who dragged Idwal from his custody by force?'

'I remember. Gwnda was held prisoner in his own hall by the mob.'

Fidelma smiled dryly. 'Held prisoner? There were two young men at the door of his hall and both were unarmed. Yet when we arrived, Gwnda came bounding out with a sword in his hand. If Gwnda had been held prisoner, it was effected by two unarmed men against an armed one well versed in the use of weapons.'

Eadulf considered the event, reflecting on the details. 'He did seem over-anxious to forgive his people for their rebellion against him. By why the subterfuge? These pieces of fact do not seem to fit into a pattern.'

'I am not sure that we have even the framework, let alone sufficient pieces to make a pattern.'

They had reached Gwnda's hall, but before entering Fidelma laid a hand on Eadulf's arm.

'You must ride for the abbey of Dewi Sant immediately. I need that authority of Gwlyddien to set aside this blockage by Gwnda.'

Eadulf grinned smugly. 'There is no need for me to leave you alone here and unprotected.'

Fidelma stood uncertainly. 'Of course there is need.'

Eadulf shook his head firmly. 'While you went in to question Iorwerth, I had a word with young Dewi. He is a bright lad. I asked him if he would be willing to ride to the abbey of Dewi Sant and deliver our message to Abbot Tryffin.'

Fidelma received the news with a moment's silence. 'Do you trust him to do so? After all, until we know what is happening in this place, we should be wary of whom we trust.'

'You are a wise counsellor. But I trust the boy and I trust the silver piece which he will receive from me when he returns.'

'I see. And the message you sent?'

'That Brother Meurig was dead. That we were being prevented from investigating and that there was an armed band in the area from whom we had a narrow escape. That we needed the authority of Gwlyddien to negate Gwnda's objections to our presence.'

Fidelma gave her reluctant approval. 'You really feel that you can trust the boy?'

'I have backed my trust with our lives,' pointed out Eadulf. 'There is danger here and I think it wise not to leave you alone.'

Fidelma quickly reached forward and squeezed his arm. 'Faithful Eadulf,' she said in an unexpected moment of tenderness. Then she added: 'You *are* sure about the boy?'

Eadulf nodded. 'He also told me why his parents, Rhonwen and Goff, became scared when you mentioned the name of Clydog. Clydog had called at their forge and treated them both harshly, robbing them and promising to return and do something worse if they spoke about him.'

'That would explain the fear,' agreed Fidelma. She suddenly became silent and Eadulf followed her gaze.

Down the street came Iestyn, the dour-looking farmer, seated on a two-wheeled farm cart pulled by a sturdy little donkey. He glanced towards them, his features forming in an expression of dislike, then quickly returned his concentration to guiding the cart along the track.

'This is luck,' Fidelma said in a quick aside to Eadulf before stepping forward and raising a hand. 'Iestyn! Hold a moment. I need a word with you.'

In spite of himself, Iestyn felt compelled by her commanding tone. He pulled on the reins and sat glowering expectantly down as she approached the cart.

'What do you want of me, Sister?' he demanded gruffly.

Fidelma returned his sullen look with a faint smile. 'Answers,' she replied brightly. 'Answers to a few questions.'

'What questions?' came his suspicious response.

Eadulf had joined Fidelma. 'If you alight from your cart for a moment, we will tell you.'

'I am busy,' replied the farmer, but in spite of his unwillingness he twirled the reins around the brake which he had applied and climbed down to join them.

Fidelma, who was tall anyway, seemed to tower over him and he stared defiantly up at her.

'Well? What questions? I did not say I had the rest of the evening to waste time in.'

'Do not be concerned, Iestyn.' Fidelma ignored his pugnacious rudeness. 'We do not suspect you of anything. We merely need to clarify a few matters with you.'

Iestyn was perplexed by her reply. 'Suspect me? Of what? Anyway, you are no *branwr*, but a Gwyddel. You have no right to stop me.'

'We have every right,' Fidelma assured him, with such conviction that she surprised even Eadulf, who groaned inwardly. It only needed Gwnda to arrive again and denounce her authority to cause more trouble.

'What do you want?'

'Let us talk about the death of Mair.'

'What of her death? She was the daughter of my good friend, Iorwerth.'

'We have been talking with Iorwerth. He tells us that on the morning Mair was killed, it was you who came to his forge and told him that you had seen Mair and Idwal arguing with one another.'

Iestyn sniffed defensively. 'So?'

'Tell us about it.'

The farmer was suspicious. 'There's nothing to tell. I was coming through the woods . . .'

'What took you there in the first place?' asked Eadulf innocently.

'My farm is by the stream that runs through the woods. I was coming on foot to the township, having delivered some fruit to a neighbour of mine. In fact, I was coming to call on Iorwerth.'

'Go on,' Fidelma said when he paused.

'I heard voices raised. I recognised Mair's voice at once. Then I saw Idwal. They both seemed upset and Idwal was quite violent.'

'Violent? In what manner did that violence manifest itself?'

'His voice was raised. His expression and attitude seemed threatening.'

'What then?'

'I knew that Iorwerth had forbidden Mair to see Idwal and Idwal to see Mair. I hurried on to Iorwerth's forge to tell him.'

'Did you like Mair?' asked Eadulf, causing Fidelma to wonder what had prompted the question. 'I mean, did you find her attractive?'

168

Iestyn coloured. 'I am her father's friend and old enough to be her father myself,' he snapped.

'Just so,' agreed Eadulf cheerfully. 'But she was an attractive young girl. Didn't she have lovers, or men who would have liked to have been her lovers?'

'Her father had arranged a marriage for her to—'

'I know. But you must have found her attractive?'

Fidelma saw the anger gathering in Iestyn's eyes and, not wanting to lose him, decided to interrupt Eadulf's line of questioning.

'We were wondering why you left them in the middle of such a terrible quarrel, Iestyn. Why didn't you intercede in this argument?'

'I had no right to interfere. It did not occur to me that the boy was about to kill the girl, or I would have done so.'

'Ah, so you did not think the argument was that serious?' Eadulf observed quickly.

The farmer looked at him, a frown on his face as he tried to understand the implication of the remark.

'The argument was serious,' he said slowly. 'Otherwise Mair would still be alive.'

'It is easy to be knowledgeable in retrospect,' agreed Eadulf. 'But at the time you did not think that the argument was so serious that physical danger for the girl might result? Otherwise you would have stayed to help Mair, wouldn't you?'

'Of course I would!' snapped the farmer.

'Instead you hurried to Iorwerth's forge and told him that you had seen Mair and Idwal quarrelling in the woods?'

'I did.'

'Did you see anyone else as you came through the woods? Did you see Gwnda there, or pass anyone else?'

Iestyn shook his head. 'Not that I recall . . . oh, I saw Buddog on the path gathering mushrooms.'

'There is something which worries me,' Fidelma commented. 'You reported that Idwal was meeting Mair in spite of Iorwerth's instruction not to do so. You observed them quarrelling. Not seriously enough for you to intervene. Nor seriously enough for you to be concerned for the immediate safety of Mair. But this news is enough to set Iorwerth, yourself and several others racing into the woods to punish Idwal. Why was there this hatred of the boy?'

'The boy needed to be taught to obey, needed to be taught

respect. That's all,' replied Iestyn defiantly. 'We were all friends of Iorwerth and we thought that we should help him.'

'So what happened when you went into the wood?' Fidelma asked.

'I led them to the spot where I had seen Mair and Idwal. There was Mair, dead. Almost at the same moment we saw Gwnda, and Idwal stretched unconscious on the ground, a little further on. Iorwerth and the others . . .' He paused, and gave them a stubborn look. 'We were for hanging the boy there and then. Gwnda stopped us, insisting that the law must be upheld.'

'As a matter of interest, did Gwnda tell you what he was doing in the woods that morning?' asked Eadulf.

Iestyn shook his head. 'The path behind the woodsman's hut is frequently used by the villagers. It goes to Cilau.'

'I see. So you brought the boy back to the township? Knowing that a *barnwr* from the abbey would be arriving, why did you take it into your heads to imprison Gwnda, take Idwal from the stables, where he was being held, and attempt to hang him before we reached here?'

'There were many people involved. It was the will of the people. *Vox . . . vox . . .* the voice of the people is the voice of God!'

'*Vox populi vox Dei,*' supplied Fidelma in amusement. 'Yes, we've heard that justification before.'

Iestyn did not answer.

'I remember that you were brandishing a cudgel on the night we arrived. Was that to ensure the voice of the people was heard?'

'Had you not interfered then Brother Meurig would have still been alive.'

'Are you saying that you had no responsibility for Idwal's death?'

'The boy killed Mair. We have a way of dealing with killers in our township, Gwyddel.' For the first time Iestyn's bitterness broke through the barrier of restraint he had put up.

'It is a way that is denounced by your own law. Brother Meurig pointed that out to you in no uncertain terms.'

'The entire township was behind us.'

'Does that make it right? Morality is not often defined by the will of the majority.'

Iestyn scowled.

'I suppose,' Eadulf commented sarcastically, 'that it is the will of the majority which absolves you from responsibility for Idwal's death?'

The farmer was equally derisive. 'Are you saying that was wrong? Brother Meurig was a *barnwr* and a religieux. Are you saying that you do not want his killer punished? I thought you religious protected your own?'

'How did you know it was Idwal who killed Meurig?'

The farmer regarded him as if he were mad. 'What are you saying?'

'Simple enough. Who said that it was Idwal who killed Brother Meurig?'

'Why . . . everyone knew it.'

'Everyone stood as witnesses to Idwal's killing of Brother Meurig?' Fidelma was scornful.

'I did not mean that. If it was not Idwal who slew the *barnwr*, who did so?'

'A good question,' said Fidelma. 'One that should have been considered before Idwal was killed.'

'Who else was it but Idwal? He was taken to the wood in the custody of the *barnwr*. That was a stupid thing for Brother Meurig to do. He should have taken someone else to guard the boy. Idwal must have waited for the moment when he could kill the *barnwr* and escape.'

'He did not escape far, did he?' Fidelma put in quickly. 'In fact, he was waiting in a fairly obvious place only a short distance away.'

'The boy was simple-minded.'

'Simple-minded but an evil killer whom you had to hang immediately?'

'As I would do with a dog turned wild,' agreed Iestyn sourly.

'So you murdered the boy without giving him a chance?' Eadulf was moved to retort.

'Murdered?' The farmer was angry. 'Don't you dare to talk to me of murder, Saxon. Your people have enough murder on your hands. My grandfather was a wise and learned man who could read Latin. He studied at the school of Illtyd when Gildas the Wise was also a student there. He kept a copy of a book which Gildas wrote . . .'

'*De Excidio et Conquestu Britanniae*,' muttered Eadulf softly. 'I have read it.'

Iestyn was disconcerted for a moment. Then he said: 'I only know the name as it was translated to me. It was *Concerning the*

171

Ruin and Conquest of Britain. My grandfather used to read it to me and translate it. I learnt enough of Saxon perfidy from that work. Alas, that I have no Latin that I can read it now.'

'Had you been able to, then you might have recalled that Gildas kept his harshest criticism for the kings of the Britons whom he denounced for their iniquities,' replied Fidelma. 'His conclusion was that the conquest by the Saxons was a just punishment inflicted by God for the sins of your fathers.'

Iestyn clamped his jaw so tight that it seemed positively painful. Then, without a further word, he turned and swung back up onto his cart, unwound the reins and flicked the patient donkey into movement.

'What now?' Eadulf asked after a moment, as they watched the angry farmer moving away.

'Now,' Fidelma said decisively, 'we have upset enough people. Perhaps the stone we have cast into the pool will cause the ripples to come back to where we are standing. Why did you ask if Iestyn had seen anyone else on the path the morning he saw Mair and Idwal quarrelling?'

'Don't you remember that Buddog said she had seen him coming through the woods that morning?'

Fidelma's eyes widened in surprise and then she made a small hooting sound in her throat and her face dissolved into that mischievous grin which seemed so at odds with her calling.

'I'd forgotten, Eadulf. You are a treasure!'

Eadulf was bewildered and said so.

Fidelma tucked her arm under his and smiled confidently. 'I have a feeling those ripples may soon reach us,' she observed.

Chapter Fifteen

The evening meal was being served to Eadulf by a surly Buddog when Fidelma joined him. The blonde servant barely acknowledged her before leaving the room. Fidelma looked disappointed at finding Eadulf eating alone.

'What's the matter?' he asked, helping himself to a plate of stew.

'I was hoping that Elen would be here so that we could finish our fascinating conversation with her.'

Eadulf looked chagrined. He had almost forgotten the claim that Elen had made. They ate their meal in companionable silence. It was a young girl, nervous and gawky, who entered to clear away the remains.

'Everyone seems to be away this evening. Do you know where the lady Elen is?' Fidelma asked her.

'She's gone, Sister.' The girl glanced anxiously around, apparently to ensure they were alone.

'Gone?' Fidelma's voice was sharp.

'She left shortly after you came back.' Suddenly the girl cast a frightened glance towards the door and pulled out a small rolled parchment from beneath her blouse. 'She asked me to give you this when you were alone. There's writing on it, but I can't read and she would not tell me what it was about.'

Fidelma glanced at it. The goatskin square contained a note written in Latin. She turned to the girl and smiled encouragingly at her. 'You will forget all about this, won't you?'

'Of course, Sister. Elen is good to me. One day I hope . . .'

'Hope what?'

'I am a hostage, Sister. Two years ago I was taken in a raid on the kingdom of Gwent by lord Gwnda. I don't want to end up like Buddog. She has been a servant here for a lifetime. Elen promised me that one day I may be set free.'

'*Deo volente*,' Fidelma sighed solemnly, adding, as the girl did not understand Latin, 'God willing.'

The young servant bobbed a sketchy curtsy and hurried from the room.

Eadulf, who had been waiting impatiently for Fidelma to reveal the contents of the parchment, asked: 'What is it?'

'A message from Elen, in Latin.' Fidelma waved the parchment. 'It simply says, "Meet me at the woodsman's hut if you can after the evening meal. Tell no one."'

Eadulf pursed his lips sceptically. 'Rather dramatic,' he observed. 'Do we go?'

'Of course we do,' replied Fidelma.

It was very dark by the time they reached the clearing in the woods where earlier that day they had found the body of Brother Meurig. It was still only early evening but the sky was pitch; black rain clouds had swept in abruptly from the west and a fine drizzle had started to fall, so that the skies were starless and oppressive, without even the relief of moonlight. It was quite chilly.

'A curious place to request a meeting,' muttered Eadulf as they approached, walking their horses quietly. The hut was only half an hour's ride from the township. They had debated whether to leave their horses behind so as not to be noticed; it was easier to avoid unwelcome scrutiny on foot than on horseback. But they realised it would make their journey longer and more unpleasant. 'Clearly the young woman is not troubled by thoughts of spirits. After all, a religieux was murdered here barely twelve hours ago.'

'*Mortui non mordent*,' Fidelma reassured him as they negotiated the track.

'Dead men may not bite but . . .' Eadulf paused and shuddered. '*Absit omen!*'

A light moved at the entrance of the hut: a figure holding a lantern.

'Sister Fidelma? Is that you?'

It was Elen's anxious voice.

'It is I and Brother Eadulf,' Fidelma called as they moved forward into the light and dismounted. Eadulf took their horses to the side of the hut where Elen's own mount was tethered.

They followed the girl inside. The interior had been cleared apart from the dark telltale stain on the floor which marked where Brother Meurig had met his death. Elen placed the lantern on the table, and seated herself on a bench in one corner. Fidelma sat on a small wooden stool opposite Elen while Eadulf looked about and then positioned himself awkwardly on the end of the bench which the girl had occupied.

'A curious place to meet,' Eadulf reiterated. 'And cold,' he added with a shiver.

The girl agreed, but added: 'It is better to be uncomfortable but secure from prying eyes and ears than warm where we can be overheard.'

'Do you want to explain that remark now,' Fidelma asked, 'or shall we take up at the point where your father interrupted us?'

The girl was suddenly hesitant.

'Did you really mean it when you said that you thought Mair was killed in mistake for you?' pressed Fidelma.

Elen nodded unhappily.

'Who do you think would want to kill you and why?'

'There is an outlaw in these parts called—'

'Clydog?' interrupted Eadulf. 'Clydog Cacynen?'

'You know of him?' asked the girl in wonder.

Fidelma smiled grimly. 'We have had the pleasure of his company. Why would he kill you?'

'Last week I was riding in those woods to the south of here. My horse picked up a stone in his hoof and I dismounted to remove it. As I was bending down, I heard voices raised in anger not far away. I left my horse and moved closer. I . . .' She paused and then gestured slightly defensively. 'I am of a curious nature and wondered what the argument was about.'

There was a brief silence while she gathered her thoughts.

'There were three men in a small clearing away from the track which I was following. They were so busy with their argument that I was able to come up behind some bushes to observe them closely. One of them was a religieux, a broad-shouldered man. I felt that he was somehow familiar, but I could not recognise him.'

'Why did you think that he was familiar?' interrupted Eadulf with interest.

The girl pouted as she gave the question some consideration. 'I can't say. Perhaps I was mistaken. It was simply a feeling.'

'Continue,' invited Fidelma. 'Did you recognise the others?'

'I knew only one of them. That was Clydog Cacynen.'

'How did you know him?'

'Because once, some months ago, I was returning with a companion to Llanwnda and we had stopped for refreshment at the hostel of Goff the smith.'

'I know the place,' Fidelma said.

'While we were there, Clydog and his men rode in and

175

demanded that Goff shoe one of their horses. They were in too much of a hurry to notice two young girls. I saw Clydog then. That's how I recognised him in the forest.'

'What about the third man?' asked Eadulf.

Elen shook her head. 'I did not know him at all. He was a warrior.'

'One of Clydog's men?'

She gave a negative movement of her head. 'Perhaps.'

'Was he wearing a war helmet, blue-eyed?'

'He was not wearing a helmet. I think that he had sandy hair but as for the colour of his eyes . . . I am not sure.'

'And this argument, what was it about?'

'Little that made sense. The curious thing . . .' She hesitated. 'The curious thing was that the religieux seemed to be issuing orders to Clydog and to the other man.'

'Can you recall exactly what was said?'

'Not really. I remember Clydog was saying something about the plan being . . . what was the word? . . . convoluted, that's it. Convoluted and without guarantee of success.'

'What plan?' demanded Eadulf.

Elen shrugged. 'That I do not know. The religieux turned to Clydog and said something like he must obey his instructions or it would not go well with him. Something like that, anyway.'

Fidelma looked thoughtful. 'What did Clydog say to that?'

'He was defiant, but he seemed to show some deference to the religieux.'

'That does not sound like the Clydog we saw,' muttered Eadulf. 'He seemed to have no respect for members of the Faith.'

Elen smiled wanly at him. 'You are right, Saxon. Clydog is no respecter of the Faith. The stories about him are legion . . . he is said to be a very cruel and evil man. The king himself sent warriors to flush him out of the woods, but without success.'

'But he was deferential to this religieux?' mused Fidelma. 'Well, continue, Elen. What then?'

'The other man, the warrior, seemed to be siding with the religieux. He said something like "The king has worked out this plan himself" – I remember that. And that it would succeed if it were followed to the letter.'

Eadulf glanced at Fidelma. 'The king? Gwlyddien?'

Elen shrugged. 'He just said "the king". Gwlyddien is certainly king of Dyfed. Clydog was dismissive. He said something about seizing power at the point of a sword. The religieux said that it would put all the kingdoms against them unless it was seen to be a legal claim. It was then that my horse became fretful, snorted and stamped.

'Clydog and the warrior rose, startled. They looked directly towards me. I turned and ran. I heard them shouting and running after me. I leapt for my horse and galloped away down the track. They must have left their horses elsewhere for they did not pursue me.'

Fidelma sat back thoughtfully. 'So what brings you to the conclusion that you were the intended victim of the murder and not Mair?'

'Mair and I were of the same age, build and colouring. We were sometimes taken for sisters, looking much alike. It was only after I began to think about Mair's death, and knowing that poor Idwal was incapable of it, that I began to realise.'

'Realise what?' demanded Eadulf.

'That Clydog must have had a glimpse of me as I fled. He must have thought that I had overheard something that was important; something secret which they had been discussing. I think that Clydog came upon Mair in the woods and mistook her for me. I think Clydog killed her.'

Fidelma digested the claim in silence before asking her next question. 'Did you tell anyone about overhearing this conversation?'

Elen shook her head slowly.

'Surely, you told your father? As lord of Pen Caer he is the local authority. He should know of any conspiracy within his lands.'

The girl shook her head defensively. 'I thought it was best to keep this to myself. I was fearful of Clydog's vengeance and, as it later proved, with good reason.'

'But after Mair was killed,' Eadulf suggested, 'did you not think it wise to tell your father?'

'I did not. Perhaps I was being selfish, perhaps callous. I felt . . .' She suddenly gave a sob and her face creased in anguish. It took a few moments for her to regain control. 'I could only feel relief. When I realised that Mair might have been killed instead of me. I thought that there was an end to it. That Clydog would not come after me. That I was safe. That was all I thought. May God forgive me.'

Fidelma leant forward and patted the girl on the arm. 'It was a natural reaction, Elen. So you have kept your secret until now?'

Elen wiped her eyes and nodded.

'Why now?' demanded Eadulf. 'Why do you feel that you can tell us now?'

The girl looked disconcerted for a moment, and Fidelma smiled encouragingly at her.

'It is a good point,' she said. 'You could have continued to remain silent about this. You did not have to tell anyone.'

Elen was silent, lips compressed, head bowed.

'Come, there must be a reason?' Fidelma coaxed.

The flash of lightning created such a brilliant white glitter that they were blinded by its intensity for a moment; a fraction of a second. Then the crack of thunder almost deafened them. Nearby, a crash and a splutter of flame showed where a tall tree had been struck.

There came a chorus of frightened whinnies from the horses and a thud as one of the animals reared up and caught its front hooves against the side of the woodsman's hut.

The girl had sprung up in panic.

'Be calm. It is just the storm breaking,' Fidelma said. Unruffled, she went to the door of the hut. The rain was a torrent, pouring straight down, churning the ground around them into a river of mud. It cascaded on the roof of the hut like a shower of stones, cracking and hissing. As she looked up at the sky, another bright flash caused her to blink rapidly. This time there was a more discernible pause between the flash and the accompanying crack of thunder. 'I'd better attend to the horses.'

Eadulf moved forward. 'You can't go out there,' he protested. 'I'll do it.'

He was met by an amused look. 'Eadulf, you are the first to confess that you are not the best of horsemen. I know the beasts. I will go and calm them.'

As she turned back to the door, another flash came and Eadulf mentally counted the seconds between it and the crack of thunder.

'It is moving away,' he announced, more in hope than certainty.

Fidelma drew her heavy woollen cloak around her head and went out to where the horses were tethered. It was difficult to hear in the pounding rain but Elen thought she could make out her voice calming the beasts. It was some time before she returned, thoroughly drenched. Eadulf had examined the hut and found some bundles of dry wood. With the aid of the tinderbox he carried, he had started a fire. Fidelma shook off her cloak and stood before the leaping flames to dry her clothing. The thunder was distant now, the rain easing to a fine trickle. The storm had raced in from the sea to the west and was rapidly heading inland.

'Now,' Fidelma said, after a few moments, as the steam began to rise from her sodden clothing, 'perhaps we can get back to our discussion.'

'I was asking why Elen had decided to tell us at this point when she could have remained silent about the matter and no one the wiser,' Eadulf prompted.

'Ah yes,' Fidelma said, turning to the girl, who had now reseated herself on the bench. 'And why tell the story to us when you could have told it to your father?'

'I did tell my father.' Elen's voice was soft.

'Does he know that you are now telling us?'

She gave an affirmative gesture. 'I told him so.'

'So Gwnda knows that you are meeting us and telling us these facts?' Eadulf could not keep the incredulous note from his voice.

'I have said so.'

'You have not answered the question as to why you have now decided to tell your story when you might have remained silent,' Fidelma insisted.

Elen turned frightened eyes upon her. 'I have seen the warrior again, the one who was with Clydog. I think he recognised me.'

'When?' demanded Fidelma.

'This afternoon, when I returned from Cilau.'

'Where?'

'In Llanwnda. Don't you understand?' Her voice rose desperately. 'He was in Llanwnda. I am sure, sure that he recognised me. My life is in danger. He will tell Clydog and Clydog will realise that he killed the wrong person.' She ended with a gasping sob.

'Very well, Elen,' Fidelma said calmly. 'But where in Llanwnda did you see this warrior?'

'It was at Iorwerth's forge.'

Fidelma glanced quickly at Eadulf. 'Iorwerth's forge, you say?'

'I was passing by, returning from Cilau as I said. The warrior was there, seated near the forge drinking mead. Iorwerth was examining his horse. He saw me passing by and I am sure he recognised me. I hurried on by but glanced briefly back and I saw that he had risen from his seat and was speaking to Iorwerth. They were both gazing after me.'

'And all this you told your father?'

'He said that I should go away for a few days while he tried to sort things out.'

'Did he?' murmured Fidelma.

'I said that I ought to tell you.'

'And he did not protest?' demanded Eadulf in astonishment.

'He thought it the best course of action.'

'I see,' mused Fidelma.

'Do you?' Elen seemed agitated. Her voice suddenly had an hysterical note. 'Don't you realise that Iorwerth is somehow linked to this, to the very people that killed his own daughter? He even allowed himself to be used to cover up the fact by being part of the mob who killed poor Idwal.'

Chapter Sixteen

'You are only surmising that Iorwerth is involved,' Fidelma said, seeking to calm her.

Elen shook her head stubbornly.

'Be logical,' insisted Fidelma. 'This warrior could have been there merely having his horse shoed at Iorwerth's forge. Why do you believe that he and Iorwerth were connected?'

'Because they were laughing and drinking together when I passed by. What else could that mean other than that they were plotting together? I know he recognised me and asked Iorwerth who I was.' The girl seemed adamant.

'Do you know what your father has done about this matter? Is he challenging Iorwerth about it?'

'I do not know what his plan was. He told me to leave until it was sorted out.'

'He did not raise any objection at all when you insisted on telling us?' mused Fidelma. She turned to Eadulf. 'It is strange that he said nothing to us when we spoke at Iorwerth's forge.'

'Perhaps he did not want to alert Iorwerth about the matter,' Eadulf suggested.

'Perhaps,' Fidelma unwillingly agreed. 'Tell me, Elen, do you think that Iestyn is also involved in this matter?'

'He is Iorwerth's friend.'

'But what manner of man is he?'

The girl was impatient. 'He is a farmer today but he fought as a warrior in many campaigns. He is old now. Old and bitter because he says the young ones do not pay him enough respect.'

'Where exactly is his farm?' Fidelma asked with interest.

'You know the bridge over the stream into the township . . . where Iorwerth's forge is?'

'I do.'

'Before you cross that bridge, you turn right along the track. Follow it for a kilometre or so along the side of the stream. At the end of the track you will come to his farm.'

'Is he married?'

'He was.'

'Children?'

'All killed fighting for Gwlyddien in the wars to protect the boundaries of Dyfed. That also is a cause of his bitterness.' Elen paused and looked from one to another. 'Time is passing. Have you learnt enough from me?'

Fidelma told her that they had.

'What do you plan to do, then?' Eadulf asked as the girl stood up and wrapped her cloak around her shoulders.

'I mean to leave here. I have told my father's servants that I am going back to Cilau to stay with my cousin. But I shall not go there.'

'Where then?' asked Fidelma. 'Do not worry, you may trust us completely. But if I resolve this mystery, which I fully intend to do, then I shall need to know where you are in case you are needed as a witness.'

'You will not tell anyone?' the girl pleaded.

'I will not.'

Elen glanced at Eadulf, who nodded his agreement.

'To the south-west of here is a community called Llanrhian. I have a friend there. I shall be there.'

'Do you mean to ride there tonight? In this weather?'

'Better at night. I know the road well enough and no one will see my passing.'

There was a distant clap of thunder. The girl started nervously. Suddenly she plunged her hand into the folds of her skirt and came out with an object which she handed to Fidelma.

'I want you to keep this. Idwal gave it to me it for safe keeping. It was the only valuable thing that he possessed. He felt that it would be stolen by his gaolers.'

Fidelma took the object. It was a red gold chain from which dangled a bejewelled pendant on which was an image of a hare.

'When did Idwal give you this?' asked Fidelma, turning it over in her hands.

'On the day he was brought back to the hall as a prisoner.'

'On the day Mair was killed?'

'The same day. He had not been searched then and he felt that it would be stolen if discovered upon him. You see, he trusted me. He told me that it had belonged to his mother. Iolo, the shepherd who raised him, had given it to him.'

Elen turned to the door and looked out into the darkening night.

'I have told you what I know. I must be gone. Pray for me, for I realise what wrong I have done by keeping quiet for so long and by actually feeling relief at poor Mair's death.'

'We will pray that you come safely to your destination, Elen,' Fidelma agreed gravely. 'You alone must come to terms with your conscience about Mair. You may be right, but you may also be wrong. Whether you be right or wrong, there is no blame on you, believe me.'

The girl smiled quickly and left the hut. They heard her mount her horse and ride away.

Eadulf looked at Fidelma as she still stood before the fire drying herself.

'Well, it seems that the mysteries are being cleared up one by one. You were right about Idwal's innocence. It was obviously Clydog who killed Mair.'

Fidelma frowned and shook her head. She held up the chain with its glittering piece of jewellry.

'On the contrary, Eadulf. I think that the mystery is deepening and we can take nothing for granted. I would certainly not accept the idea that Clydog killed Mair in mistake for Elen without more evidence.'

'But you heard what the girl said? Surely it all fits?'

'What about the role of Gwnda? You suspected him. He was an accessary to the killing of Idwal. Why? To stop him from speaking? About what? If Gwnda really believed Idwal was guilty, why now agree to his daughter telling us her story? It is all very confusing. Or is it?'

'Would Gwnda be an accomplice in some plot in which the murder of his own daughter was envisaged? What was that plot? Why prevent her speaking about some chance meeting in a wood about a matter she clearly did not understand? Surely not? I don't know what path we can take from here.'

'One obvious place,' rejoined Fidelma, glancing out of the hut door and observing that the rain was easing still further.

Eadulf raised an eyebrow.

'We will have to have another word with Iestyn,' Fidelma said. 'After that, we'll go back to Iorwerth and see what he has to say about the strange warrior.'

Eadulf sighed deeply. 'I had wondered why you were so keen to learn more about Iestyn.'

Fidelma picked up her still sodden cloak and flung it around her shoulders before going out to the horses. Eadulf kicked out the remains of the fire and followed her outside. The drizzle had stopped, but it was still a cold, damp evening.

They rode back towards the bridge in silence, letting their horses walk casually with a loose rein. Just before the bridge, Fidelma turned along the path which Elen had indicated, following the track along the bank of the stream. The dark waters were running on the left side while the trees and undergrowth presented an almost impregnable wall to the right.

Eadulf leant forward in his saddle, straining his eyes to see ahead. It was really dark. The heavy rain clouds still hung low and oppressive, shutting out all light. There was no moon, no stars, to light the path. In such circumstances, Eadulf acknowledged Fidelma's better horsemanship by not attempting to guide his animal but allowing it its head, and freedom to choose its own safe path along the river behind Fidelma's mount.

It was a longer trek than Fidelma had estimated. Eventually she saw a light ahead and realised that the dark looming shapes were buildings: Iestyn's farm. She turned to Eadulf, just a dark shape in the blackness behind her.

'Let us not announce our arrival yet,' she called quietly.

She guided her horse round one of the farm buildings, which looked like a barn, and halted in its shade before dismounting. They found a bush on which to hitch their horses' reins and then moved towards the edge of the barn. A faint light was issuing through the windows of the farmhouse, sending a gloomy ray across the stable yard.

'What is it?' demanded Eadulf, struggling to peer forward into the semi-darkness.

'Quiet!' hissed Fidelma. 'There are a couple of horses in the yard before the house.'

'Why does that cause you alarm?' replied Eadulf, dropping his voice to match hers.

'They are not farm horses.'

'I don't understand,' he muttered, stepping in the cloying mud and groaning in irritation.

'Those are war horses, not farm horses. And what warriors would call at a farmhouse at night?'

'Clydog?' whispered Eadulf, suddenly anxious.

'They could be anyone. Friends. Even relatives. But it is best to be prepared.'

Eadulf screwed up his face in distaste in the darkness. He could feel the chill of the wet mud sticking to his sandals. He wanted to protest but then shrugged. He just uttered a prayer of thanks that the storm had passed and the rain had ceased.

Their horses were out of sight. Fidelma led the way cautiously forward round the farmyard, coming to the side of the farmhouse. She eased her way silently to a window and took a quick peek through, but could see nothing through the rough opaque glass. She glanced back to Eadulf and shook her head.

'I can't see anything,' she whispered, 'nor hear anything clearly. But I think Iestyn and his visitors are inside.'

'What now?' asked Eadulf ruefully. 'Do we wait out here in the damp or should we simply knock on the door?'

Fidelma pursed her lips in temper.

Directly in front of the house, on the opposite side of the farmyard, was the big barn behind which they had tethered their horses. Fidelma touched Eadulf's arm and pointed across to it. Keeping low she led the way back across the yard and had almost reached the black gaping door, with Eadulf close behind, when a shadow moved.

A menacing growl, ending in a string of high-pitched yelps, gave them a second's warning before a large, muscular dog leapt out from the barn at them. The great dog was a matter of a metre from Fidelma when its barking ceased in a yelp of pain and it seemed to Eadulf that the giant beast hung suspended for a moment in its mid-air leap. Then it fell to the ground, whining and yapping in pain and frustration.

In the gloom Eadulf realised that the dog had been tethered. Had they been nearer to the barn or had the lead been longer then the story would have ended otherwise.

The horses in front of the farmhouse started to whinny and grow restless. The dog continued to snarl and bark in frustration. Eadulf looked desperately around and then, grabbing Fidelma's arm, he took off towards a small building, surrounded by a low wall. He jumped the wall, helped Fidelma over it and dragged her down behind it. Shapes began moving around them. Eadulf realised by the stench that he had leapt into a pig pen. Pigs snuffled inquisitively at them before settling down with total indifference to their presence.

Cautiously, Fidelma and Eadulf raised their heads. Across the yard, the door of the farmhouse had swung open. A man stood holding a lantern high. The dog was still barking furiously.

'Shut up, Ci!' the man snapped. 'What the devil's the matter with you?'

They recognised Iestyn. He was joined by another man. Fidelma gave a sharp intake of breath, and moved her lips to Eadulf's ear to whisper, 'It's Corryn.'

The dog was whining petulantly now in the presence of its master.

'What set the dog off?' Corryn was demanding.

'There's nothing out here,' replied Iestyn. 'The horses are skittish. Maybe they spooked the dog.'

'Maybe,' agreed Corryn reluctantly, peering round into the blackness.

A third man had joined them. 'You are well away from the township,' he said. 'Surely no one would pass by here? It would be awkward if they did so at this time.'

Iestyn chuckled sourly.

'No one is likely to come by on a night like this. There is only the one track between here and the township. You know that. Anyway, why be worried now? I would have been more worried about riding into the township in broad daylight. You might have been recognised.'

The third man chuckled in reassurance. 'I don't think so. I recognised the girl but I am certain that she didn't recognise me. Anyway, I know who she is now. Gwnda's daughter.'

'Exactly,' intervened Corryn. 'What if she had raised some alarm? It was a dangerous thing to do. It could upset all our plans.'

'Only if she overheard anything. She probably did not hear anything at all about the plan. Anyway, it is progressing too slowly. Ceredigion is not prepared to wait for ever.'

'If Artglys wants Dyfed to be allied with him, then he must wait,' snapped Corryn. 'We have spent too much time bringing this plan towards fruition to abandon it now. And what is Artglys's alternative? He has none.'

The third man shrugged. 'The warriors of Ceredigion are trained and ready. We can move immediately.'

Corryn's tone held a bantering note. 'And do you think that Dyfed has bred weaklings? How many times has Ceredigion come in battle array into Dyfed? Since the time of Ceredig you have looked enviously upon this kingdom. Many times you have attempted to seize it but it has withstood you. It will not fall because Ceredigion comes in battle array: it will fall only by subterfuge. So let us hear no more about Artglys and his impatience. Let us stick to the plan which we have so carefully constructed.'

The third man's jaw rose angrily. 'The plan will be followed so long as my lord Artglys says it must be followed.'

'Then you had better consult your king as to whether he wants an alliance or not.' Corryn began to turn away.

'And you had best consult Clydog as to his intentions,' the warrior called.

Corryn spun round. 'Clydog's intentions are not my intentions!' he snapped. 'Go and tell Artglys's jackal, Morgan, that he best proceed with the next stage. We must ensure that Gwlyddien starts his action soon and he obviously needs more bodies to stir his rage. A few more religious slaughtered on the beach will help to increase his temper. Do you understand?'

The third man stood hesitantly. Then he seemed to shrug indifferently. 'Very well. Now I understand why they call you the spider, my friend. Waiting, plotting, watching, and then . . . Let us hope we do not get impatient. I shall tell Artglys what you require.'

Without further ado, he left his companions and went to his horse, mounted and vanished into the gloom without a backward glance.

Iestyn remained holding his lantern with Corryn by his side, as if watching the vanishing figure.

'The man is arrogant, my lord,' came the farmer's disapproving tone.

'Truly said,' agreed Corryn. 'And in the days ahead, it might be appropriate to take the measure of him. Remember that this is not a *foedus amorum* but a treaty of convenience which, when its aim is accomplished, can be severed.'

'Do you trust Clydog, lord?'

'Not at all.' Corryn laughed sharply. 'Nor, I doubt, does his father. That is why he has sent Clydog here to create trouble in Dyfed rather than allowing him to remain at home. Which reminds me, I must rejoin him. Is there any further word of that woman . . . the Gwyddel and her Saxon friend?'

'They have returned, and have even questioned me and Iorwerth. The stupid woman is more concerned about finding out who killed Mair than anything we may do.'

'Could Iorwerth have told them anything that can be traced to us? That Ceredigion idiot should not have taken his horse to Iorwerth's forge.'

Iestyn shook his head quickly. 'What can they learn? Information requires informants. Iorwerth knows nothing; there is no means by which they can discover our plan before it is too late.'

Corryn was silent for a moment. 'You may well be right, my friend. Yet the Sister is no fool. I have heard that these advocates of the courts of Éireann are clever and resourceful. She certainly is. So is the Saxon. I could not believe how simply they tricked Clydog and escaped from his camp. But seeing is believing.'

'When the time comes, you will be able to deal with them, lord,' Iestyn said. 'Anyway, they cannot know anything.'

'Nevertheless, Iestyn, I do not like the fact that they are here asking questions.'

Iestyn chuckled reassuringly. 'I am ready for them, lord. Have no fear. The plan is safe. It is Mair's death that seems to concern them.'

'I shall rely on you, Iestyn,' replied the other evenly, 'for you know what betrayal merits.'

There was a sudden silence between them. Then Corryn turned to his horse and mounted it.

'Keep me informed through the usual sources, Iestyn. If Morgan obeys his orders, then we should expect some action from Gwlyddien soon. Once he begins to move . . . the kingdom is ours!' He raised his hand in farewell, and set off into the night.

Iestyn stood watching him vanish in the darkness and then turned back to his dog. It had been lying down outside the barn, head between its paws, watching. It now uttered a faint whine.

'Get back, Ci, you stupid animal.'

The dog rose and barked.

Iestyn hesitated and glanced round. Fidelma and Eadulf sank lower behind the pig pen wall.

'Oh, I know,' came Iestyn's voice. 'I forgot to feed you. Don't worry. I have a bone for you.' He turned back into the house.

Fidelma grabbed Eadulf's arm and was up over the wall in a moment. The dog saw their movement and began to bark again. They heard Iestyn's irritable voice faintly.

'Shut up, stupid! I'll bring your bone in a moment!'

In the darkness, Fidelma led the way as hurriedly as she could to the horses. 'Come on, let's be away from here,' she whispered.

They turned their mounts away from the barn, and the moon suddenly emerged from between the cloud banks. It was pale and low down on the horizon and did not really illuminate the darkness.

'We can't go back on the track,' said Fidelma. 'If Iestyn unleashes the dog it will overtake us, and Corryn's already on that path. He might turn back.'

Eadulf examined the stream. 'We can cross here. It appears shallow enough. Lead on, Fidelma.'

Obediently, she entered the water and urged her horse across. The sound of her passage was muted by the fact that a little way upstream, the stream gushed and cascaded through a barrier of boulders and rocks, almost like a waterfall. Eadulf followed swiftly behind. He could still hear the dog's frenetic barking behind them.

The horses mounted the bank with ease and were soon immersed in the mass of dark trees growing along that side of the river. Finding a path was difficult but eventually they came across a very narrow track which allowed them to proceed in single file. It seemed to lead in the direction of the township.

It was when they had moved quite a distance along it that Eadulf, who had been suppressing a number of questions which had come to his mind, finally allowed them to bubble over. He broke the silence.

'Why didn't we remain and question Iestyn as we intended?'

They came to a clearing and Fidelma halted her horse to allow it to rest. 'It would not have been a good time,' she said.

'Corryn had gone,' pointed out Eadulf. 'Our appearance might have surprised Iestyn. Made him confess.'

She shook her head. 'On the contrary, I think that even Iestyn might have realised why his dog had been making such a fuss. As it is, we now have an opportunity to go back armed with knowledge which Iestyn does not realise we possess.'

'I must admit that I am totally confused,' confessed Eadulf. 'Every time I think matters make sense they get even more obscure.'

Fidelma patted the neck of her horse absently. 'I am beginning to see a faint light for the first time, Eadulf,' she said confidently.

'How so?'

'What we have stumbled on is a conspiracy to overthrow Gwlyddien and take over the kingdom of Dyfed. I think that what happened at Llanpadern is connected with the conspiracy.'

Eadulf thought for a moment. 'A conspiracy from this neighbouring kingdom of Ceredigion?'

'Ceredigion plays a central role.'

'Are you saying that the Hwicce are involved with Ceredigion in this affair? I cannot believe that. The Hwicce of all people would not interest themselves in the ambitions of a *Welisc* ruler.'

'Doesn't it depend on the incentives, Eadulf?'

'You might have a point if you spoke about any of the other Saxon kingdoms, but the Hwicce are a frontier people. They simply would not involve themselves in the affairs of the *Welisc.*'

'Are you so sure?'

'I would wager money on it. Having learnt of this conspiracy,' Eadulf went on, 'don't you feel that we have outstayed our welcome in these parts? Should we not get back to the abbey to tell Gwlyddien that his kingdom is under threat?'

'We will certainly warn him,' agreed Fidelma, 'but this is not the time to desert our investigation. There are too many unanswered questions here to simply leave and then let Gwlyddien attempt to sort out who is behind this conspiracy against him.'

Eadulf groaned inwardly. Deep down he had known this would be Fidelma's reaction. For the first time, however, he was driven primarily by apprehension; a desire to leave this place of his blood enemies and return to the land of his fellow countrymen: to get back to Canterbury. He had had enough of the dangers of being among the *Welisc.*

'What else is there to know?' he demanded. 'We know that Clydog and Corryn are involved and this man Iestyn is in their secret. We know that an Hwicce ship is sailing round the coast and you claim that it is somehow involved in a conspiracy.'

'Knowing these things hardly helps,' pointed out Fidelma patiently. 'Knowing exactly how they interrelate would be more useful. Perhaps knowing the answers to the myriad questions that arise . . . that would be useful as well. Did Clydog murder Mair? If so, who killed Brother Meurig and why? Why was Idwal so conveniently killed? What is Gwnda's involvement in this? Why is Iestyn so respectful to Corryn? You heard the manner in which he addressed him. You see the many questions that pile up one after another?'

Eadulf held up a hand as if to still the stream of her remorseless queries. 'I concede that there is much that we do not know. Why doesn't Gwlyddien send some of his own *barnwrs* here to find out? Why us?'

'Because you may remember that we accepted his commission.'

'I remember,' said Eadulf in resignation.

'It is not in my nature to leave a task half finished,' added Fidelma. '*Finis coronat opus!*'

'In other circumstances I would agree,' muttered Eadulf. 'But I cannot help a feeling of fear while in this kingdom.'

'You do not have to tell me that, Eadulf.' Fidelma's voice was grim. 'I have never seen you so nervous of your surroundings before. Not in Rome, nor in my own land nor, indeed, when you faced death in Fearna. What is it about this land, this people, that makes you so apprehensive?'

Eadulf's lips were a tight thin line as he contemplated the matter. 'I have told you before that there is enmity between my people and the Britons. The *Welisc* are enemies of my blood.'

'Come, Eadulf. You are a Christian. You are an enemy to no one.'

'Not so. An enemy can be perceived as well as real. Just the very name Saxon is enough for some people to want to encompass my early death.'

'I feel that is more in your perception than in others'. Perhaps if you did not fear these people, they might not hate you in return?'

Eadulf was intelligent enough to realise that she was talking logic, but centuries of attitude were hard to cast aside.

'There are other things to consider apart from my fears and hates,' he said sulkily. 'What are your plans now?'

He did not see the look of sad sympathy with which Fidelma regarded him in the darkness. 'You are right. We are wasting time. I think we should return to Gwnda's hall. It is no use going to see Iorwerth now. I want, however, to question him about what we have learnt from Elen this evening. I also want to see what we can draw out of Iestyn.'

'What about warning Gwlyddien of this plot?'

'If young Dewi is to be trusted, he or someone from the abbey of Dewi Sant will be back here by tomorrow afternoon. We can send a message back by them.'

They had reached the township and were riding by the great unlit bonfire. On top of it, they noticed, the straw man from Iorwerth's forge had been placed. Fidelma halted her horse, staring at it, and then, to Eadulf's surprise, she broke into a low chuckle.

191

'What is it?' demanded Eadulf.

'What a fool I am. I could have answered one of our questions some time ago.'

Eadulf waited impatiently. 'I've just realised what tomorrow is . . . the bonfires and straw man.'

'What?' demanded Eadulf.

'It is the Samhain festival.'

Eadulf frowned, recognising the name of the native Irish festival: 'You mean the eve of All Hallows Day?'

'The one night of the year when the Otherworld becomes visible to this one and when the souls of those we have harmed in this life can come back and exact retribution from us,' confirmed Fidelma.

Chapter Seventeen

Fidelma was already awake and dressed when Eadulf arose the next morning. She was seated eating a meal of fresh-baked bread and honey washed down by sweet mead. She looked up as he entered and smiled a brief greeting.

'Is there is any sign of Gwnda yet?' he asked as he sat down and reached for the bread.

When they had returned on the previous evening, the lord of Pen Caer was not in his hall and Buddog told them that she did not expect him to return. He was visiting some friends. So they had eaten a frugal supper and gone directly to bed.

As if on cue, the door opened and Gwnda entered. To their surprise he greeted them with a smile and a civil tone.

'Elen has spoken to us,' were Fidelma's first words.

Gwnda joined them at the table. 'Did she tell you that it was I who suggested that she do so?' he asked.

'She told us that you offered no objection to her telling us the story,' replied Fidelma. 'Frankly, I am puzzled. When we last saw you, you were totally opposed to our involvement in this matter.'

The black-bearded lord shifted uncomfortably in his seat.

'I might have been wrong in my opinion about Idwal,' he confessed, yet without any indication of remorse. 'I felt it best that you hear her story.'

'You might have been wrong?' There was a bite to Fidelma's voice. 'The boy has been killed.'

'When my daughter told me her story, I began to see that there could be another explanation for Mair's death.'

'Which would mean that Idwal was innocent,' pointed out Eadulf.

'It would mean that a great wrong was done to the boy,' Gwnda admitted, although his tone was hardly that of a penitent. He seemed almost cheerful.

'A wrong in which you have played both an active and a passive part,' Eadulf sternly reminded him.

'If any wrong has been done then I am willing to take my

share of the blame in the matter,' said Gwnda. 'But the fault first of all lay with the outrage of the mob.'

'Let us examine your share of the blame,' Fidelma said. 'You were the first person on the scene when Mair was murdered and you caught Idwal. What did you say brought you to the woods at that hour?'

Gwnda considered the question. 'I can't remember. I was just out riding.'

'It seems that several people were in those particular woods that morning. Mair and Idwal. Iestyn . . . even Buddog.'

Gwnda's facial muscles suddenly tightened. His mood seemed to change and for the first time he appeared anxious. 'The woods span the main track to the south. It is not surprising people were about.'

'Until your daughter spoke to you, you had no doubts about Idwal's guilt. But now you have?'

Gwnda shifted his weight again as he considered his words. 'My daughter has the doubts. I am not convinced that she is right.'

'Did you come upon Mair and Idwal by accident that morning?' Fidelma asked.

'I did. I found Idwal actually bending over her body. That I have said before. I went through the details with Brother Meurig.'

'Brother Meurig is dead, so tell us what happened that morning again.'

Gwnda shrugged indifferently. 'I came across Idwal bending over Mair. She was dead. Within moments, I heard the sound of voices raised. Idwal stood up and started to run and so I caught him. Moments later Iorwerth arrived with men from the township. You surely know the rest?'

'All along, you have maintained that Idwal was guilty. You have even defended his lynching. You refused to let us make inquiries about it. But now . . . now you appear to suddenly change your mind. I cannot help but wonder why?'

'I am lord of Pen Caer. I am not answerable to you,' Gwnda responded. 'Anyway,' his voice softened, 'if my daughter's life is in danger then I am willing to admit a mistake. Didn't I send for the *barnwr* to try Idwal in legal fashion?'

'It did not prevent him from having no trial at all,' Eadulf observed dryly.

'Whether he killed Mair or not, I still believe that he killed

Brother Meurig in his attempt to escape. Therefore his death was not without justification.'

'Were you there when he was hanged?' Eadulf suddenly asked.

Gwnda shook his head vehemently. 'I did not arrive until afterwards. Someone told me that some of my people had caught the boy and by the time I reached the spot he was dead.'

'As lord of Pen Caer it is your task to see that justice is done. Yet you seem to have exonerated those who killed him.'

'I understood their anger against the boy.'

'But now you say that he might not have been guilty of Mair's killing?' pointed out Fidelma.

Gwnda was silent.

'You were vehemently opposed to our making inquiries into this matter yesterday afternoon, yet a short time later you approved of Elen speaking to us.'

'There is nothing strange in that. I have not changed my attitude. I still maintain that you have no right to interfere in this matter. You are here only to deal with the mystery of Llanpadern. Nothing has changed. But Elen wished to tell you about Clydog as you seem to have the ear of King Gwlyddien. I do not object to that. As I hope I have made clear, I am willing to listen to Elen's doubts but my opinion is that Idwal killed Brother Meurig. There is an end to the matter. It is now up to King Gwlyddien to clear the forests of Clydog and his men and resolve this matter of conspiracy which Elen overheard.'

There was a pause before Fidelma sighed as if in realisation that he would tell her no more. 'We appreciate your help in this, Gwnda. One thing more. What do you make of the meeting to which Elen says she was a witness?'

Gwnda rubbed the bridge of his nose thoughtfully. 'Clydog is a well-known thief in these parts. He and his outlaw band have held sway in the forests of Ffynnon Druidion for several months now. I cannot conceive of any involvement he might have with a religieux. I have no means of knowing what plan they were talking about.'

'You have told me that nothing is known about Clydog's background,' asked Fidelma. 'If we knew something of that, we might be able to understand something of this matter. What about his compatriot, Corryn? He seems to share the leadership of these outlaws?'

'I have never heard any stories of him. Only of Clydog.'

Gwnda rose abruptly, signalling an end to the conversation. He glanced through the window and smiled. 'A clear sky today. There has been no more rain since last night. You will have a good ride back to the abbey of Dewi Sant.'

Fidelma exchanged a look with Eadulf. 'What gave you the impression that we were returning to the abbey today?' she inquired.

Gwnda's eyes narrowed dangerously as he swung round on her. 'I told you that you would not be welcome here after last night. There is nothing to keep you here.'

'On the contrary,' Fidelma said, also rising to her feet. 'There is much to keep us here.'

She could see Gwnda attempting to control his temper. Just as he was about to articulate his anger there came a shouting outside the door and a moment later it burst open. A youth with wide frightened eyes came into the room with a rush, saw them and skidded to a hold, gasping for breath.

'A raid!' he managed to get out after a moment. 'A raid! Saxon warships.'

'What do you say?' gasped Gwnda, staring at the young man. 'Saxons raiding? Where?'

Eadulf groaned inwardly as he rose to his feet.

'Can you be more specific?' Fidelma demanded sharply of the youth. 'Where are these Saxon warships?'

The young man was agitated and did not reply until Gwnda took him by the arm.

'Speak, lad!' he thundered. 'Where are the Saxons landing?'

'My father is the cowherd Taloc, my lord. His cattle graze on the pastures at Carregwasted, a few kilometres to the north. You must know it – the old point, overlooking the bay.'

'Yes, yes. I know it. How many Saxon ships?' demanded Gwnda impatiently.

'We were tending the herd beyond when my young sister came running to tell us that a strange ship had entered the bay—'

'Are you saying there is only one Saxon warship?' intervened Fidelma.

'One's enough,' cut in Gwnda quickly. 'Go on, lad. How many warriors? Where are they now?'

The youth looked from one to another in bewilderment, and decided to continue. 'We went to look at it. My father said it was a Saxon ship, because of the markings on it. He said there was something strange about it.'

196

'Something strange about the markings? What?' interrupted Eadulf.

'Forget the markings. What happened then?' urged Gwnda.

'Some small boats put out from the Saxon ship and came to the rocky beach below. About a score of Saxon warriors with battleaxes and round shields came ashore at the point . . .'

Gwnda groaned loudly. 'I know the place. There is an easy path up from there. They mean to raid us, and I can only raise half a dozen able-bodied men. We will have to abandon the township; take shelter in the woods.'

Fidelma leant forward towards the youth. 'Did you see them preparing to come up from the beach?'

The young man shook his head. 'My father shouted to my sister and mother to take what valuables they could carry and hurry towards the forest shelter where they might hide. He went back to the herd to try to get them to safety while he ordered me to come and warn the township.'

Gwnda stood helplessly. 'We do not have enough warriors to defend the township,' he groaned. 'We must evacuate immediately!'

'Better that we first attempt to discover their intentions before you send your people into a panicked flight,' suggested Fidelma.

'Intentions?' Gwnda laughed sourly. 'They are Saxons. What other intentions have they but to rape, pillage and burn. They are barbarians!'

Eadulf flushed. 'Not all my people are barbarians.' His voice was tight with anger.

'I suppose you mean to tell me that your countrymen are here to trade peacefully with us?' Gwnda sneered.

Eadulf took a threatening step forward. Then he halted, controlling the impulse. 'We do not know why they are here. Nor will we find out if you run away or attack them.'

'Have we not learnt from the raid at Llanpadern? Or do you reject the evidence? I suppose you think I should go to the point and politely ask them what they want?'

'It might be an easier option than what you are suggesting,' Eadulf replied without thinking.

'But not a prudent one,' Fidelma said, rising and laying a hand on his harm, for she saw that Eadulf's temper was getting the better of him. She knew that his pent-up anger was caused by the guilt he had been made to feel about his Saxon heritage.

197

'If there is no man among the people of Llanwnda to go and meet with these Saxons, then I shall go myself. I shall find out what they want,' he said.

Gwnda stared at him in surprise for a moment and then he chuckled softly. 'Of course, you are one of them. You will go to them to save your own neck.'

Fidelma let out an angry hiss and stepped in front of Eadulf, more to protect Gwnda from her companion's physical rage than to protect Eadulf.

'That is unworthy of you, Gwnda. Brother Eadulf is a man whom I trust with my life and the lives of everyone in this place.' She hesitated and turned to Eadulf. 'It is a good idea that we try to parley with them, whoever they are, or at least get close enough to see what their intentions are.'

Eadulf was still simmering at the insult. 'I did not make the offer to go from self-interest,' he growled. 'But I shall go.'

'*We* shall go,' corrected Fidelma with a smile.

Eadulf shook his head firmly. 'I go alone. Gwnda is partially right. They are less likely to harm a fellow Saxon if their intention is warlike.'

'Perhaps,' Fidelma admitted reluctantly. She could understand his argument. 'But I will come as far as I can and—'

'Time is pressing,' interrupted Gwnda. 'I shall give the order for the township to be evacuated into the forests. I cannot wait for you to see what these barbarians are about.'

'You must do as you think fit, Gwnda.' Fidelma turned to the youth. 'Boy, point us in the direction of this landing place.'

The youth pointed northwards. 'Keep going along the northern track until you come to the sea. It is only a kilometre or two, directly to the north. You cannot miss the bay.'

Fidelma and Eadulf went to the stables and saddled their horses. As they left the township, Gwnda had already begun to sound an alarm bell. The place had become a scene of frenetic activity as people ran here and there collecting their children and belongings. Fidelma called to Eadulf: 'As soon as we come within sight of them, I'll hang back and you go on. But, for the sake of all you hold dear, Eadulf, please be careful.'

Eadulf gave a quick smile. 'I do not mean to throw my life away to make a point to that cretin Gwnda.'

'If you can make contact with these Saxons, try to find out if they were the same ship that was sighted where the brethren from Llanpadern were found and what they know of that raid.'

198

After that, they followed the path northwards in silence. Beyond an isolated copse, they came within sight of the sea. But it was not the view which halted them. It was a curious rhythmic sound; a musical chant, but not exactly so. There was something almost menacing about it. Eadulf signalled to Fidelma to draw rein and pointed to the shelter of the trees.

'They are coming,' he announced quietly. 'That's a Saxon war chant. Stay hidden. If anything happens . . . well, ride as if the furies of hell were on your heels.'

Fidelma raised her hand in acknowledgment, turned her horse and walked it in among the cover of the trees.

Eadulf waited until she was well hidden and then began to walk his horse towards the curious percussion-like noise. As he came round the corner of a rise he saw below him what to an untrained eye would look like a strange serpent moving slowly along the path, the sun reflecting off odd scales running along the sides of the monster. To an eye which had beheld the sight before it was a double column of men, large round shields giving protection on both sides so that little could be seen of the warriors who held them. He could make out their horned metal helmets and the double-bladed battleaxes held ready.

The column marched in unison, leather boots stamping the ground. And, with a regular monotony, the arms holding the axes would be raised heavenward before striking the weapons down on the metal shield rims so that the noise was a fierce drum beat, hypnotic, unrelenting. In the pause before the next beat came the cry 'úp the eorl! úp Eanfrith!' and then the remorseless bang of axe on shield again. It was unnerving and it was designed to be so. Eadulf was no stranger to the sight of Saxon warriors marching in a battle phalanx and issuing the war-cry calculated to terrify their enemies.

Abruptly the column halted and was silent.

Someone must have seen Eadulf on his horse and given the order. He hoped that no one in the column of warriors was armed with a bow and would decide to use it before he came within shouting range. He guided his horse slowly down towards the waiting column.

'Welcome, brothers!' he called, halting about five yards away from the head of it. 'What do you seek in this land?'

The column stood in silence and then a Saxon voice answered him.

'Who are you who speaks our tongue?'

'I am Eadulf of Seaxmund's Ham in the land of the South Folk.'

'A Christian?' The voice was still suspicious.

'I am.'

'We are Hwicce!' came the cold response.

Eadulf felt a coldness go through him. Here were the very people he had told Fidelma about. Saxons whose fighting prowess was legendary and who still clung to the old faith, worshipping Woden the Allfather, chief of the raven clan.

'I have heard of the Hwicce.' Eadulf managed a smile. 'The Hwicce are renowned among all the kingdoms of the Saxons, Angles and Jutes. But the Hwicce I have heard of are brave and generous warriors who are courteous to strangers – even to Christian brothers in strange lands.'

There was a moment's silence and someone muttered something and then there was a shout of laughter. Eadulf tried not to show his unease.

'You have a way with words, Eadulf the Christian,' came the voice. 'Tell us what you are doing here.'

Eadulf decided to be sparing with the truth. 'I am travelling with a companion to the kingdom of Kent, to Canterbury. A storm drove my ship ashore here a few days ago.'

'And you, a Saxon, have encountered no animosity from these *Welisc*?' demanded the voice in surprise.

'I have encountered many expressions of dislike but I have survived. But they are Christian in this land and do not kill without good reason.'

'Being Saxon is often considered reason enough. Doubtless, your Christian ways make these dogs spare you, Eadulf,' the voice replied. 'Tell me, do you know where the *Welisc* warriors are? Are we likely to be attacked?'

Eadulf thought quickly. Which would be more effective? The truth or some lie claiming that warriors were nearby? He felt it better to be truthful.

'There are no warriors nearby, Hwicce. This is a land of peaceful shepherds and herders of cattle.'

'Will you take an oath on that? Swear by the sword of Woden?'

Eadulf shook his head. 'An oath on the sword of Woden would be meaningless to me. I will swear on the cross of my Christ, though.'

'Good enough. Do you so swear?'

'I do. There are no large bands of *Welisc* warriors within a morning's ride of us. I swear this by the Holy Cross!'

The column of warriors broke up at a word of command. The shields came down and the phalanx dissolved and Eadulf came face to face with the person whom he had been addressing. The man set down his war shield and took off his helmet. To Eadulf's surprise, the speaker was a blond-haired youth, certainly not far advanced into his twenties. He had a handsome face, highlighted by deepset eyes so grey as to be almost violet in colour. He was tall, muscular and looked like a man to whom the profession of warrior came naturally. Eadulf took an instant liking to his open, youthful features.

'Well met in this land of the *Welisc*, Eadulf the Christian,' the young man grinned. 'I am the Eorl Osric, thane to Eanfrith, king of the Hwicce.'

Eadulf dismounted from his horse and took a few steps towards the eorl. 'Then well met, Osric of the Hwicce. *Pax tecum!*'

Osric grinned again. 'I have no Latin, Eadulf. Speak in good Saxon. I am not Christian. The gods of my forefathers are good enough for me.'

'I was going to ask you for a *quid pro quo*, but as you speak no Latin, I shall translate. Something for something. I have told you there are no *Welisc* warriors here. Now you tell me something.'

Osric chuckled. 'Were you a merchant before you joined this curious brotherhood of Christ, my friend?'

'I was hereditary *gerefa* of my people,' Eadulf assured him.

'A lawgiver. I might have known,' replied the young thane with a wry grimace. 'Then we shall cease to bargain. What is it that you wish to know?'

'What are you doing on this shore? Do you mean to harm the people living here?'

Osric pointed to the woods beyond. 'We are here to cut down the tallest tree we can find.'

It was a totally unexpected reply and Eadulf's face showed it.

Osric was still chuckling. 'My *gerefa* friend,' he said, 'it is quite true. Our ship has been demasted and we managed to make it into a bay beyond that point.' He waved a hand over his shoulder. 'We need to get a new mast. But as this is the land of *Welisc* we came prepared to fight for it.'

'And that was why you were shouting your war-cry?'

'We thought that it might frighten people off long enough for our purpose.'

He turned and snapped an order which sent his men racing towards the nearby wood searching for a tall tree.

One of the men, obviously the chief carpenter, pointed to a tall, fairly thin oak. Two axemen came forward and set to work with a will, the smack of their metal blades into wood echoing across the landscape. They did not waste time. The work was done quickly and efficiently.

'Was it your ship that was anchored down the coast some days ago?' asked Eadulf.

Osric turned to him with an amused grin. 'Another question? I thought your Latin merchant's term was question for question?'

'If you want to ask me questions, I'll be happy to answer them,' Eadulf offered, feeling suddenly comfortable with the young man. Hwicce or no, pagan or no, these were his own people and he felt at ease with them.

'Well, you are right. We have been up and down this coast during this last week or so. We have been chasing a *Welisc* ship.'

'Did you by any chance raid the *Welisc* religious community near here . . . to the south?'

Osric shook his head firmly. 'We had better things to do.'

Eadulf was surprised by the answer. 'You did not?' he pressed.

'Why do you ask? Do the *Welisc* claim that they were raided by us?'

'Some do. A Saxon ship was observed moored in a cove in that direction some days ago.' He indicated the position with his hand.

'That was my ship, the *Wave-Breaker*,' agreed Osric.

'Not far from where you anchored, Osric, there was a religious community called Llanpadern. The Father Superior was hanged and the community were taken. Several of the brethren were found slain on the foreshore and some Hwicce weapons were found nearby.'

'I was not responsible,' insisted Osric.

Eadulf decided to be bolder. 'There was also a body of a stranger found at the religious place.'

Osric's eyes narrowed. 'I have a feeling, my *gerefa* friend, that you are going to tell me that this body is significant.'

202

'It was the body of an Hwicce.'

Osric regarded him with a serious expression. 'Describe the body to me.'

Eadulf did so, and the young thane let out a long, low sigh. 'It was the body of Thaec.'

'Who is Thaec?'

'One of my crew. The night that we anchored in the bay you have described, he went ashore with another man. They both spoke the language of these *Welisc* and offered to attempt to pick up some intelligence. Only one man, Saexbald, came back.' Osric suddenly glanced around at his warriors. 'Saexbald! Come here!'

A tall warrior detached himself from the group and came running forward.

'Saexbald, tell the *gerefa* here what happened on the night you went ashore with Thaec.'

The warrior turned to Eadulf. 'We had scouted along the shore when, without warning, a group of *Welisc* horsemen came on us. We fought but Thaec was swiftly overpowered, even though he did his best to get himself killed rather than be taken as captive. I was separated from him in the fight and forced to abandon him. I only just managed to get back to the safety of the ship.'

'Thaec is dead,' Osric told the man.

'May he have met his death with sword in hand and the name of Woden on his lips,' the warrior intoned.

'Did you know who these *Welisc* were?' asked Eadulf.

'Warriors, no doubt. They fought well.'

'Did you hear any names shouted by them during the encounter?'

'Names? No. The only shouting I heard was . . . actually it was strange, come to think of it. One of the *Welisc* warriors seems to have been stung.'

'Stung?' queried Eadulf.

'There was some shouting about a wasp.'

A slow smile of satisfaction spread over Eadulf's face.

There was a resounding crash as the tree was felled. Almost immediately, the warriors started to strip the branches and the bark, using their powerful axes. Osric signalled the tall warrior, Saexbald, to return to his comrades.

'Did they torture poor Thaec before he died?' he asked.

'He was not tortured. It seems that he was stabbed in the chest with a sword.'

Osric rubbed his chin thoughtfully. 'Do you think he died fighting?'

'I am sure of it. I also know that he sorely wounded his assailant.'

'It would be good to tell his parents that their son died with sword in hand and the name of Woden on his lips, so that he could be gathered up into the Hall of Heroes where the immortals live.'

Eadulf looked disapproving. 'I cannot subscribe to pagan beliefs.'

'A man of principle, *gerefa*? Yes, I suppose you are. But did you see or hear anything which would contradict the story?'

'Nothing. But why would he have been taken to the community and killed?'

'Are you trying to tell me that the *Welisc* religious would not have killed him?'

'They would not have harmed him unless in self-defence. It was the *Welisc* warriors who captured him who killed him.'

'I know nothing of this religious community. We anchored in the bay because it was nightfall and we did not know these waters.'

'Did you not make a search for your missing crewman at first light?'

'We do not abandon our own unless we are forced to. You know that, *gerefa*. Of course a search was made at first light. From the shoreline we saw that a *Welisc* peasant had spotted us and, finding nothing, we reluctantly abandoned the search. It was madness to continue after we had been spotted, for we did not know how many enemy warriors were in the vicinity.'

'Just a minute,' Eadulf said. 'You knew that there were some. What of the band of warriors who took your man Thaec? Why did they not attack you at dawn?'

Osric made a gesture with his hand as if dismissing them. 'They had disappeared. Taken Thaec and vanished.'

'So what did you do then?'

'We put to sea again.'

'That brings me to another question. What are you doing so far from your own country?'

There was a pause and the young thane examined Eadulf's expression for a moment as if searching for something there.

'I answer because I think I can trust you, *gerefa*. I believe that you are a man of principle. We are chasing a *Welisc* ship.

Have you heard of a prince called Morgan ap Arthyrs? He is the king of Gwent, a territory which borders our kingdom.'

'I know little of affairs in this part of the world,' confessed Eadulf.

'Well, this Morgan is an enemy worthy of our steel. He is cunning and ruthless. He has ruled Gwent for many years.'

'Morgan?' Eadulf tried to remember where he had heard the name recently.

'We are chasing one of his ships. He raided on our side of the River Saeferne which marks our common border. We gave chase and a long chase it has been. But the ship has eluded us. Now we must return to our own land to prevent our families mourning the loss of more than Thaec and Wigar. Wigar was lost overboard in a storm: the same storm which snapped our mast.'

He indicated where his men had finished stripping and trimming the tall oak tree.

'It's not the best of times to cut a tree,' he observed, glancing to the sky, 'but we cannot choose our seasons. So long as it gets us home we shall be happy.'

Eadulf nodded absently. 'I still do not entirely understand. Ships often raid and chases occur. That I comprehend. But you have chased this one many a mile. Why are you so dogged in the pursuit of the *Welisc*, Thane Osric?'

Osric frowned momentarily. 'You ask a lot of questions, Eadulf the Christian.'

'It is because I hate mysteries,' Eadulf replied spiritedly.

'I will answer you, then. During the raid the *Welisc* took several hostages. Among them was Aelfwynn, the ten-year-old daughter of King Eanfrith. That is why I have pursued this ship of Morgan's so closely.'

One of Osric's men came forwarded and saluted him. 'We are ready, lord.'

'That is good. Let us prepare.'

The man turned and barked an order. The trunk of the tree had been rolled onto the long axe handles of the warriors and now they bent and picked up their burden as easily as if it had been a light branch. At another sharp command, the warriors began to move as one, returning on the path in the direction they had come from.

'You are welcome to continue your journey with us as far as the land of the Hwicce,' Osric offered, then added, glancing slyly at him, 'although I think you have other plans.'

205

'That I have,' agreed Eadulf. 'I will ensure that Thaec has a Christian burial.'

Osric shook his head as he shouldered his shield and took up his war axe again. 'That would dishonour him. No, let him lie where he is. Do not bother to find out how he died. His family will rest content that he now plays dice with the Immortals in the Hall of Heroes. Old men will sing of his courage around the fires in the evening. His memory will become immortal too. That will be more than poor Eanfrith will boast of lost little Aelfwynn. Alas, I can pursue the *Welisc* ship of Morgan no longer.'

He raised his axe above his head in salute. 'Farewell, Eadulf the Christian, sometime *gerefa*.'

Eadulf felt a sudden panic. He was sure that Fidelma would have asked more questions, discovered more facts, but his mind was blank. All he could say was: 'God send you a good wind home, Osric of the Hwicce.' He stood watching as the warriors, bearing their load and followed by Osric, went trotting down the hill.

Behind Eadulf, Fidelma emerged from the woods on foot, leading her horse. He turned to meet her. There was relief on her face.

'It seems that the Saxons were friendly after all,' she observed.

'Their ship was demasted and they were looking for a new mast to replace it,' he explained.

'That much I could see.' She smiled. 'Did you learn anything else? You spoke a long while with the young man who led them.'

'Osric was his name; thane to Eanfrith, king of the Hwicce.'

Her eyes widened slightly. 'So these were the Hwicce?' She stumbled again over the pronunciation. 'Then it was . . .'

'It was their ship that Goff the smith told us of. And the dead Hwicce at Llanpadern was one of their crew, a man called Thaec.'

Fidelma said quietly: 'Then you'd better tell me exactly what passed between you and Osric.'

Eadulf did so, keeping as close to the actual words as he could remember. Fidelma nodded from time to time, asking a question merely to have a point explained. When he had finished she was looking troubled.

'This information merely adds to our mystery,' she finally said, unable to keep the frustration from her voice.

There was a mournful smile on Eadulf's face. 'The Fidelma I once knew would have said, *Vincit qui patitur.*'

There was an angry flash in Fidelma's green-grey eyes, gone in a moment. 'Indeed, he prevails who is patient, Eadulf,' she replied tightly. 'I did not know that you judged yourself a paragon of patience?'

Eadulf flushed at the waspishness of her reply. 'I meant—' he began, but she interrupted.

'You have added another small piece of the picture but we do not know where it fits, that is if we are to believe your Saxon friend. We have an Hwicce warship chasing a ship of Gwent. It anchors in a cove at night. A crewman goes ashore to reconnoitre and is captured. The ship continues on its way, abandoning him. He then is found in a sarcophagus at Llanpadern having been stabbed to death. Does knowing this bring us any nearer an explanation?'

Eadulf had never heard Fidelma's voice filled with such frustration before. He tried to think of something to say that would be helpful, but could not and so retreated into silence. He was troubled on another level. Ever since they had arrived in this land of Dyfed they had been arguing with one another and he could not understand why. What had gone wrong with their relationship since they had left the shores of Laigin? Or had there been something wrong before?

He had persuaded Fidelma to join him on his return to Canterbury. Had he been blind? Had it been against her will? After all, she had left him at Cashel to proceed to the Tomb of St James while he had set out to Canterbury by himself. It was only in order to save him from the unjust accusation of murder that she had returned to defend him. Now he was confused. Anger grew out of his confusion. He realised that she was speaking again.

'Let's return to Llanwnda and stop the panic that must have set in among Gwnda's people.'

He suppressed a sigh as she mounted her horse, expecting him to follow. 'No,' he said abruptly. She stared down at him in astonishment.

'No,' he repeated, as he mounted his own horse. 'I shall ride to the point first and check whether they erected their new mast and told me the truth about their intention to sail south.'

She stared at him for a moment or two and then, without

207

speaking, jerked the reins of her horse, turning it to ride off to Llanwnda.

Eadulf sat astride his mount for a few moments, watching until she had disappeared among the trees. Then he turned his horse and headed after the Saxon warriors. When he reached the point overlooking the small bay, the Saxon ship was immediately discernible below. The main mast was indeed missing, and warrior-seamen were hard at work clearing the tangled ropes and rigging, preparing for the new mast to be set in place.

Osric and his men were already rowing their small boats towards the vessel, bearing their newly cut mast with them. Eadulf admired the ease, born of a lifetime at sea, with which they propelled their craft towards the long, low warship. He could admire their skill, for he considered himself something of an expert on seamanship. Not that he had ever been a seaman, but he had made many voyages now. Four times he had crossed the great sea between Britain and the land of Éireann; four times had he crossed the seas on his pilgrimages to Rome. And he had sailed along the turbulent eastern shores of Britain to attend the great Council of Whitby.

Eadulf liked the sea and yet, at the same time, he feared it. Was fear the right word? No; he did not take the sea for granted. He respected it. The sea was cruel and had no charity. Yet without the sea man would be insignificant, for the sea was like a great road between peoples and without contact with one another men would be isolated and there would be no progress between them. But the sea was patient, watching and waiting and ready, like a murderer on a dark night, hiding in an unilluminated lane with a knife to strike at the unexpected moment.

Eadulf broke off his thoughts with an impatient sigh. He dismounted and tethered his horse, seating himself on a boulder from which he could observe the warriors repairing their ship. The late autumnal sun was lukewarm in the cloudless sky. For the first time in days Eadulf felt that he could relax and give his thoughts to the matter which was worrying him.

Fidelma.

Where lay the fault for the deterioration of their relationship? What was it that he had once been taught by a sage of the South Folk? No one can understand anyone else unless, while being true to his own nature, he respects the free will of the other. Well, he once thought, perhaps arrogantly, that he understood Fidelma. Yet he had to admit that seven languages were more easily mastered than the understanding of the woman.

He heard a distant shouting and looked up from his revelry, glancing down to the bay. Something moved in the corner of his eye. He looked towards the northern headland and saw a second ship under full sail sweeping round into the bay. It was a sleek-looking fighting ship, and across its taut sails was the image of a large red dragon.

Chapter Eighteen

Eadulf leapt to his feet.

The shouting had come from the Saxons who had spied the oncoming vessel. There was no mistaking the intention of the other ship, nor that it was manned by *Welisc*. The dragon battle flag seemed common to most of the Britons. It had been the symbol of the great Macsen Wledig, whom the Romans had called Magnus Maximus when he was declared emperor of the western empire by the legions stationed in Britain. It was curious what thoughts came in moments of adversity. Macsen was betrayed and put to death. His wife, Elen, returned to Britain to become the most influential figure in the Christian movement, her sons and daughters founding many kingdoms of the Britons.

Eadulf watched the oncoming *Welisc* vessel with consternation. It was clear that the Saxon ship would have no chance to escape or manoeuvre. The new mast had only just been lifted on board and it would take a while to put it in place, let alone hoist the rigging and sails. Osric's ship was lying helpless.

Eadulf found himself squeezing his hands into fists in his frustration, so tightly that the nails dug into the flesh of his palms. Osric's men had grabbed their shields and weapons and rushed to the side of their vessel in a desperate attempt to repel borders. And then a curious thing happened.

When there was still several metres between the high prow of the *Welisc* ship and the side of the Saxon vessel, the red dragon ship turned aside and almost slewed round, still moving rapidly, so that it passed swiftly away from the Saxons. Eadulf heard shouting and saw several burning brand torches being thrown across by the Britons, landing on the Saxon deck and starting several small fires which were quickly extinguished by Osric's men.

Eadulf was baffled. He had been expecting a barrage of arrows from the bows which the Britons often used, or a boarding party with sword and shield. Yet the *Welisc* ship passed swiftly on, the sailing master obviously knowing the currents of this bay. Even as the vessel swung away, Eadulf saw several dark objects fall from its stern. Even from this distance he could recognise the shapes as human beings, and from the way they fell and floated in the water he realised that they were dead.

Bewildered, he watched the *Welisc* ship race out of the bay back the way it had come, round the headland. He waited for quite a long time, fully expecting to see the vessel reappear. When it did not, he decided to make his way down to the shore.

The Saxons were back at work on their ship, hoisting the newly cut mast into position. Others were clearly on watch, for he heard a shout and saw someone gesturing at him as he walked down the shingle. A couple of bodies lay in the surf, face down, moving gently to and fro as the waves washed ashore.

He had been recognised, for he saw Osric and a couple of his men climbing down into a boat and pulling away from the ship towards the shore.

Eadulf walked over to the nearest body.

It was that of a young man, clad in the brown woollen robe of a religieux. The young man's hair was cut in the tonsure of St John, the style worn by the religious of the Britons as well as the five kingdoms of Éireann. He was but recently dead, perhaps killed at the moment he had been thrown overboard. The wound – his neck had been cut – was still bleeding.

Eadulf bent down, grabbed the young man's shoulders, and heaved him out of the surf further onto the shingled beach. In doing so, he saw something which had been looped round the man's left wrist and arm. To a quick examination, it might appear that he had grabbed something from his assailant. It was a piece of cloth on which was embroidered one of the symbols which pagan Saxons still affected. Eadulf recognised it immediately as an Hwicce emblem, and exhaled sharply.

The crunch of shingle trodden underfoot made him look up. Osric came hurrying across to him while his two men stood guarding their small boat, ready to push off back to their ship if danger threatened. The eorl appeared angry.

'Did you have anything to do with that?' he demanded immediately, gesturing towards the headland round which the *Welisc* ship had disappeared. Eadulf realised that Osric was holding his sword menacingly in his pointing hand. 'You said that there were no *Welisc* warriors in the vicinity.'

'I did,' Eadulf said, raising himself up. 'The appearance of that ship was as much a surprise to me as to you.' He pointed down to the corpse. 'Did *you* have anything to do with this?'

Osric, disconcerted, glanced down. 'You saw the *Welisc* throw those bodies overboard from their ship, didn't you? Why would we have anything to do with this?'

'Look at the object looped round the arm of this man.'

Osric bent down. 'By the blood of Woden!' he swore. He looked back to Eadulf with a frown. 'What does this mean?'

'It means,' Eadulf said quietly, 'that anyone who examines these bodies will presume that they were killed by Hwicce.'

Osric was silent. Eadulf turned and went to the other body that had been washed ashore, drawing it also out of the reach of the waves. It, too, was a religieux, not as young as the first one. In his back, quite deeply embedded, was an Hwicce dagger. As Eadulf was laying the body down on the shingle, a groan came from its lips.

'*Deus misereatur!*' cried Eadulf, bending closer. 'This one is still alive.'

Osric came over and bent down by his side. 'Not for long, my friend,' he muttered. 'I have seen wounds like this and no man recovers. Stop!' Eadulf had been about to remove the Hwicce dagger from the man's back. 'If you remove the dagger he will die immediately. Turn him slightly so that he may speak before he dies.'

Eadulf turned the body on its side. 'Can you hear me, Brother?' he asked, in the language of the Cymry. He had been speaking to Osric in Saxon.

The man's eyelids fluttered and he gave a sound like a barely audible moan.

'Can you speak?' urged Eadulf. 'Who did this thing to you?'

The man's mouth moved slightly. Eadulf bent his ear to the lips.

'Break . . . break up the bronze . . . bronze serpent that Moses made,' came the painful whisper.

Eadulf did not understand. 'Who did this to you?' he whispered again, more urgently.

'Evil in our midst . . . the creature of the damned, the evil spider . . . casting his net . . . ensnared us all . . . He was one . . . of us!' The man abruplty coughed blood and was still.

Osric stated the obvious: 'He's dead, my friend. Did you learn anything?'

Eadulf shook his head. 'I think he was rambling. In a fever, perhaps.' He rose and glanced at Osric. 'I don't suppose that you recognised the ship which attacked you?'

213

The young Saxon thane nodded. 'That was the ship of Morgan, the one we had chased from the mouth of the River Sauferne out along the coast of these kingdoms.'

'They could have destroyed your ship.'

Osric did not demur. 'They could have done so. They might still, if they have courage to come back to match our mettle.'

Eadulf was rubbing his chin thoughtfully. 'I do not think they lack courage. Yet it is hard to understand why they did not finish off the job. Why simply dump these poor bodies overboard?'

'Who are they?'

'Religious. I have a suspicion that they might be part of the missing community of Llanpadern. Though why that should be I do not know.'

'I don't understand.'

'No more do I. I also suspect that whoever sails that red dragon ship . . . Morgan, did you say? . . . is trying to put the blame for these deaths onto you. Bodies of the religious found where you had anchored offshore also had Hwicce weapons near them. Why would they take pains to do this?'

Osric smiled grimly. 'It is not the first time the Hwicce have been attacked by the *Welisc* and not the first time we have killed *Welisc* Christians. So we do not care about bearing the blame for these deaths.'

Eadulf was thoughtful. 'Why is there a need to lay the blame on the Saxons in order to stir up enmity? The very name of Saxon is enough to rouse these folk to hatred, Christian or pagan. Is there some deeper meaning to this?'

'It is not for me to ponder on any deeper meaning, Eadulf the Christian. My only regret is that my ship was not ready otherwise I would have destroyed that ship of Gwent. Now it has probably found some hiding place further up the coast.'

Eadulf looked towards the Saxon ship. 'How long will it take to repair your mast?'

'We'll have done within the hour. As soon as the mast is raised I mean to out the oars and row further down the coast just in case the *Welisc* returns to the attack again. We'll repair the rigging while we are under way.' He hesitated. 'What about you? Surely you are not safe in this kingdom now?'

Eadulf was inclined to agree with him, but he accepted that Fate led him on another path. 'I must return to Llanwnda. There are things to resolve before I can see my homeland again.' While he had been speaking, his eyes had been examining the beach and the cliffs behind it. He had spotted several dark openings. 'Those caves there will be useful,' he said suddenly.

'Useful for what?'

'The bodies of the religious with their carefully planted items of Hwicce origin were tossed overboard for a purpose. That purpose seems obvious: those that discover them are to infer that the men on your ship did the killing. It could be that the *Welisc* have gone to raise the alarm somewhere along the coast and then will come back and destroy you.'

'But they don't need such a justification to do that,' pointed out Osric.

Eadulf was momentarily dejected. 'That I also know. But the fact is they did it as justification. At whom that justification is aimed is the mystery; not the justification itself.'

'Then what are you saying, *gerefa*?'

'Until I can discover that fact, I would rather put some grit in their newly churned butter.'

'How would you do that?'

'May I borrow a couple of your men to bring those bodies still floating in the sea to shore, and then use them to help me hide the dead in one of those caves? The fact that they will not be found immediately might destroy whatever plan the *Welisc* have devised.'

Osric grinned and slapped his thigh. 'Spoken like a man of action and a true *gerefa*, Eadulf the Christian. I thought that all you of the new faith spoke of peace and love and honesty. Why, you are a man worthy of service in the company of Tiw, mighty god of war and strategy.'

Eadulf allowed the compliment to pass. After all, it had not been so long ago that he had been content to worship Woden, Tiw, Thunor, Frig and the pantheon of Saxon gods.

Osric began to issue the necessary orders. His two companions launched their boat and rowed towards the bobbing bodies making their slow progress towards the shore line.

Osric turned back to Eadulf. 'I'll help you with this one.'

Together they lifted the body and clambered up the shingled beach. At the fast of the cliffs they laid it down while Eadulf went to examine the few cave entrances. He chose one which was deep enough for a cursory examination not to reveal the bodies, and he and Osric carried the first body inside. By the time they returned for the second body Osric's companions had brought up the third. They returned for the fourth while Eadulf

215

ensured there were no telltale signs that would lead anyone to the cave.

'What now, Eadulf the Christian?'

'Now I shall return to Llanwnda to try to sort out this mystery.'

Osric smiled and shook his head. 'You are a brave man to remain among these barbarians.'

'Have you ever reflected, Osric,' Eadulf replied with a grimace, 'that it is a strange world when two peoples each believe it is the other who are barbarians?'

'One day I will find time to learn something about your Christian faith, Eadulf. Who knows, perhaps it has something to teach us?'

'Perhaps it does,' Eadulf agreed solemnly.

Osric raised a hand in farewell and, with an order to his men, set off down the beach to his boat. Eadulf turned and made his way quickly up the path to the top of the cliff, to the point where he had left his horse tethered. When he looked back, he could see that the new tall mast was already in position. It would not be long before Osric's ship was moving out of the bay.

He mounted his horse and set off at a quick trot in the direction of Llanwnda.

'You have been a long time! I have been waiting for you.'

Eadulf was approaching the small bridge across the stream that marked the boundary of Llanwnda. Fidelma was seated on a fallen log, her horse tethered a short distance away.

He halted and dismounted. 'Something unusual happened which delayed me,' he replied.

She examined his features and read the grim lines of his face. 'Do you wish to tell me about it?' she inquired.

He glanced towards the apparently deserted buildings of the township. 'Where is everyone?'

'Still hiding, I presume. They do not trust the Saxons. I did inform one of Gwnda's men that they had nothing to fear, I don't think he believed me.'

The two of them walked their horses side by side across the bridge into the township. Sparing no significant detail, Eadulf quickly told her what had happened and what he had done.

She remained deep in thought for some time after he had finished. 'That is intriguing,' she said at last.

216

Eadulf raised an eyebrow. 'Intriguing is not the word I would use.'

'Yet there is no other way to describe this event. Tell me – and do not stand on any false idea of kinship – did you trust this man Osric in all he said?'

Eadulf scowled momentarily. 'What do you mean by trust?'

'Did you believe his story? Believe it when he said he was chasing a ship of this Morgan of Gwent and that it was the same ship that sailed into the bay?'

'I think, insofar as my ability to discern those who are frugal with the truth goes, I would say that he was telling the complete truth. Nor could he understand why the red dragon ship did not destroy him and his men while it had the chance.'

Fidelma nodded swiftly. 'That is the most remarkable thing. Surely, whoever commanded that ship would know that Osric would not wait around to be attacked further? Why such a futile action? It was obvious, as you concluded, that this Morgan merely meant to dump those bodies in the bay. That the Saxons were intended to be blamed for the slaughter is also obvious. But why?'

'I have asked myself that question several times on my way here. There is no simple answer.'

'If these were bodies of the religious of Llanpadern, and if Osric's men did not raid the community, why would this Morgan do so and why is he trying to place the blame on the Saxons?'

'I am sure that we have heard the name Morgan recently and I am trying to remember where.'

'You are right, Eadulf. It was Corryn who mentioned the name last night. But was it the same Morgan?'

'Good questions, as you have often said. Now we must find good answers.'

'Exactly so,' agreed Fidelma cheerfully.

They had halted just beyond Iorwerth's deserted forge. The pause in their conversation now brought a sound to their ears: the unmistakable noise of galloping horses. Three or four of them, at least. Some instinct made Fidelma motion to Eadulf to follow her and run quickly with her horse round the corner of the building next to the forge.

'What is it?' demanded Eadulf.

She shook her head and placed a finger to her lips.

The thunder of the approaching horses had diminished. The gallop slowed to a trot and then came the sound of their riders

217

pulling up. Fidelma moved to the edge of the building and peered round. Eadulf was surprised when she swiftly pulled back.

'It's Clydog!' she hissed.

Eadulf glanced round, seeking a hiding place or a means of escape.

'Wait!' whispered Fidelma, leaning forward to peer round again. 'He's not dismounting. He has two men with him.'

To their surprise they heard the door of Iorwerth's cabin open and heard a well-known voice greeted Clydog. It was Iestyn.

'You are a fool to tell me to meet you here!' snarled the farmer.

Clydog uttered his typical sardonic laugh. 'Is this the way a host should greet a traveller, friend Iestyn?'

'Any moment Gwnda and the others might return. So might that meddlesome Gwyddel and her crony, the Saxon.'

Fortunately, it seemed Iestyn was standing at the entrance to the forge and Clydog and his men were making no effort to dismount.

'Ah, I would like to meet with them again. They owe me the pleasure of vengeance,' came Clydog's voice.

'They escaped from you once,' sneered Iestyn. 'They'll probably do so again. Our mutual friend, Corryn, told me all about it. In the meantime, your bungling has nearly ruined everything. They are asking too many questions, getting too near the truth of this matter.'

'Why should you worry? Artglys of Ceredigion will guarantee you protection.'

'Every moment the Gwyddel and the Saxon stay in Llanwnda is dangerous for our cause. That was why you were supposed to take care of them.'

'So I shall. But there are more important matters to see to first. There is plenty of time.'

'When will we get the word?'

'As soon as we hear that Gwlyddien is marching east.'

'I cannot stay longer. You were a fool to come to this place. Why did you summon me here?'

'To tell you that Morgan carried out his part. Now you must do yours.'

'Don't worry. I'll make sure that word gets to Gwlyddien about the latest Saxon outrage. Did everything else go to plan?'

'So far.'

'I still say that the Gwyddel woman and her friend could destroy everything.'

'Have no fear, Iestyn. The word will soon come. The people of Dyfed will believe anything about the Saxons. I have sent one of my men to the abbey of Dewi Sant with news of the Saxon raids. If this does not stir that old fool Gwlyddien to march then his people will start taking matters into their own hands. Whatever way, we will be victorious. Make sure that some of your people bear witness to the bodies and see the Saxon ship.'

'What if this does not work?'

'It will work. As soon as Gwlyddien is forced to march against the Saxons, Artglys of Ceredigion will march south into the kingdom and within a day or two you will be looking at the new king.'

'There is an old saying, Clydog, "The end of the day is a good profit,",' Iestyn replied pessimistically.

'Just make sure that you get witnesses to see the Saxon ship and the bodies,' snapped Clydog, kicking his horse and leading his men back across the bridge into the forest.

Fidelma and Eadulf waited until they heard Iestyn leave the forge and disappear into the woods in the direction of his farmstead. Eadulf gave a long whistling sigh.

'I think I am more confused than ever,' he confessed, standing back from the door.

Fidelma shook her head. 'On the contrary, things have been made abundantly clear.'

'Clear?'

'It is now clear that Prince Cathen's suspicions about Dyfed's neighbour, King Artglys of Ceredigion, have a firm foundation. Ceredigion is trying to create a situation where Gwlyddien and his army are persuaded to attack the Hwicce. While they are away, Artglys will march into Dyfed to set up a puppet ruler answerable to him.'

'Do you mean Clydog?'

'It is possible.'

'So what you are saying is that the affair of Llanpadern was staged to force Gwlyddien's hand? That this Morgan marched on Llanpadern because Gwlyddien's son Rhun was a religieux in that community?'

'Precisely so.'

'I still do not understand the details . . . why take all the members of the community prisoner and then wait a day or

219

two before killing some of them and staging that first elaborate charade of an Hwicce attack?'

Fidelma was nodding thoughtfully.

'I think that might be explained. Brother Cyngar and the boy Idwal were not expected to arrive at Llanpadern that morning. Whoever did the deed did not even know that they had visited Llanpadern and found the community missing. Why the wait before starting to kill their prisoners? Because whoever took the community had to wait until the Saxon ship was sighted before staging the first "attack". Cyngar and Idwal upset the plan from the first by arriving on the scene too early.'

'But what of the death of the girl Mair?'

'We still have to work that into the scheme of things.' She stood up. 'There are a couple of people we need to question before we can clarify matters there. Come.'

She led the way into the township. A few people were beginning to drift back to their houses, having been assured that the Saxon ship had sailed.

'Should we try to stop Iestyn taking some townsfolk to see the Hwicce leaving?' asked Eadulf.

'Are you sure that the bodies of the religieux are well hidden?' Eadulf asserted they were, and Fidelma went on: 'Then we will leave that matter for a while and finish our other business.'

They had halted before a small building by which stood a stone statuette of a woman on horseback with a basket of fruit. Fidelma knew it was the old pagan horse goddess Epona, whom the ancients regarded as the symbol of fertility and health. The building was clearly the township's apothecary shop. There was light and movement behind the thick, opaque glass windows.

Fidelma went inside. Eadulf followed, mystified. An elderly man was sitting at a bench pounding some herbs in a mortar with a wooden pestle. He looked up as they entered.

'Ah, you are the *dálaigh* from Cashel, eh? Exciting times, eh? But not the first time we have had to abandon our township and take to the forests. The Ceredigion have sailed into the bay more than once in my lifetime, not to mention the Saxons.' The old man was clearly of a loquacious temperament.

'I presume that you are Elisse the apothecary?' Fidelma asked.

'I am. How can I be of service?'

'Did Brother Meurig seek you out before he was killed?'

'Ah, that was a sad death. Sadder that the people lost their senses and killed that young boy. Justice should not be an act of mere vengeance.'

'Did Brother Meurig ask your opinion on the death of Mair?'

The apothecary shook his head. 'He did not, although I was told that he wanted to speak with me. However . . . his time was short.'

'Then will you answer a couple of questions for me? I know what he wanted to ask you.'

The apothecary regarded her expectantly. 'I am at your service, Sister. Ask away,' he invited with gravity.

'You were called to examine the body of the girl Mair, weren't you?'

Elisse nodded in affirmation. 'Sad when one so young departs this life. Sad indeed.'

'What was the cause of death?'

'I would say that she was strangled first. Bruising and abrasions around her neck showed that.'

'Strangled *first*?' Fidelma picked up on the word.

'The other wounds were made after death, as if in some frenzy.'

Fidelma was leaning forward eagerly. 'Other wounds? What other wounds?'

Elisse regarded her in surprise for a moment. 'You were surely told about the knife wounds?'

Fidelma glanced at Eadulf. 'We have heard no mention of knife wounds. I heard that there was blood on her lower clothing. But we were told that this indicated that she had been raped and that she was a virgin.'

'No, that was the conclusion that Gwnda leapt to when he pointed the blood out to me. He and Iorwerth claimed that the girl must have been raped before death. Iorwerth believed his daughter to be a virgin.'

'What are you saying exactly? That she was not?'

'I am afraid not. I paid particular attention to the matter for when my wife was cleaning her body for burial she was troubled by wounds made on the upper inner thigh. I realised that two wounds had been made by a broad-bladed knife. This was the source of the heavy bleeding.'

Fidelma was silent as she contemplated what she had been told.

'I explained that there' – the apothecary gave an embarrassed

221

PETER TREMAYNE

shrug – 'there was no sign of sexual molestation. And I would
guarantee that she was no *virgo intacta*.'

'Could you tell by examination?'

'My wife did that. She also told me that she was not surprised,
for a year ago the girl had approached her and asked about ways
to prevent pregnancy. I speak boldly, Sister, but you must know
how women hand down such lore.'

'Mair asked your wife this question?'

'You may ask her yourself.' The apothecary turned as if to
call her but Fidelma restrained him with a shake of her head.

'There is no need. Your word as an apothecary is good enough.
That is all I want to know. It makes things very clear.'

They left the apothecary shop and Eadulf noticed that Fidelma
was walking with a light step and smiling to herself. There were
many more people in the street now. It seemed that everyone
had returned and there was no longer any fear of a Saxon attack.
To Eadulf's surprise, Fidelma turned back in the direction of
Iorwerth's forge.

'Where now?' he asked.

She indicated the forge at the end of the street. 'A final link
to be put in place,' she said mysteriously.

They could hear Iorwerth at work before they reached the
forge. He was rekindling his fire and they could hear the rasping
of his bellows as he tried to get the wood to catch. He looked up
with a scowl as they hitched their horses to the fence and entered
the forge.

'What now?' he demanded ungraciously. 'Are your Saxon
friends going to attack us?'

'There are just a few points that we need clarification on.'
Fidelma responded to his brusque manner with a pleasant smile.

Iorwerth set down the bellows and folded his arms, glaring
defiantly from one to the other. 'Gwnda claims that you have
no right to ask questions about the death of my daughter. I shall
not answer those questions.'

'That is fair enough,' agreed Fidelma easily.

Iorwerth started in surprise at her ready agreement. 'If not my
daughter's death, then what do you want to speak to me about?'

'Yesterday you had a visitor to your forge.'

Iorwerth's jaw clenched. 'I have many come to the forge. It
is my business.'

'This man was a warrior and, I am told, a stranger to this
district.'

222

The smith was frowning. 'I do not usually have warriors . . .'
He paused, and his expression told them that he had recalled the
man. 'Why do you inquire after that man?'

'What do you know about him?'

'As you say, he was a stranger, a warrior. His horse had loosed
a shoe. I fixed it.'

'You had never seen him before?'

'Never. He spent a short time here. He asked for mead to drink,
for which he paid, and spent a pleasant time exchanging some
gossip while I fixed his horse's shoe. That was all.'

'Tell me,' Fidelma pressed, 'did Elen, Gwnda's daughter, pass
by at that time?'

'How did you know that?' demanded Iorwerth, slightly surprised at the recollection. 'She did. I remember that because the
warrior asked me who she was.'

'You told him, of course?'

'I said that she was the daughter of Gwnda, lord of Pen
Caer.'

'Did he tell you why he wanted to know?'

'I think he said something like, "There's a fine-looking girl,
who is she?"'

'Nothing else passed between you?'

Iorwerth shook his head. 'Nothing, as I recall. He passed the
time of day while I fixed his horse's shoe. We exchanged a few
jokes and gossiped. That is all.'

'Did he mention his name by any chance?'

Again, Iorwerth made a negative gesture.

'Nor where he came from?'

'No, although I could guess.'

'Really? And what was your guess?'

'He was either from Ceredigion or somewhere along its
borders.'

'Why do you say that?'

'Smiths are a close-knit community. It is easy to recognise
types of work. From what I saw of his horse and his weapons,
I could swear that the work was done in Ceredigion.'

'Very well.'

'Why do you ask about this man?'

'A matter of curiosity,' smiled Fidelma. 'Let me ask you
something else. Were you ever a warrior?'

Iorwerth looked startled. 'Never. I have always been a smith.'

'I understand that you learnt your craft in Dinas?'

223

The bolt went home. Iorwerth blinked rapidly. He did not reply for a moment or two. Then he said, slowly: 'It is many years since I was last in Dinas.'

'Twenty years ago?'

'That is about right. How did you know this?'

Fidelma had taken something from her *marsupium*. She suddenly held it before his eyes. It was the red gold chain with the bejewelled image of the hare hanging from it.

'Have you ever seen that before?' she demanded.

A paleness crept over Iorwerth's features as he stared at the pendant.

'Where did you get that?' he asked slowly.

'Do you recognise it?' she insisted.

'I last saw that twenty years ago. Where did you get it?'

'Iolo the shepherd, before he died, gave it to Idwal. Iolo told the boy that it belonged to his mother.'

Iorwerth stepped back as if he had received a body blow. His eyes widened and his mouth had opened slightly. He was looking at them but not seeing them. Then his features seemed to dissolve.

'Oh, my God!' he cried.

Then, before either of them could react, he had turned, grabbed the mane of an unsaddled horse, swung himself up and gone racing away over the bridge and into the woods.

Chapter Nineteen

Eadulf turned with grim humour. 'Well, he certainly recognised the necklet. But what does that tell us? Indeed, what can we deduce from anything?'

Fidelma was smiling with a dreamy satisfied air. 'The deduction is simple, Eadulf. I believe that we have now all the pieces to set up the picture of what has happened in this place.'

Eadulf's surprise was only slightly less than that displayed by Iorwerth. 'Surely you cannot mean that?'

'Surely I can,' replied Fidelma with dry mischief. 'Let us hope our young friend Dewi returns from the abbey of Dewi Sant soon.'

'What then?'

'Then we can explain this puzzle, apportion the blame, and return to Porth Clais in search of a ship. I am sure that you urgently want to continue the journey to Canterbury?'

Eadulf did not reply.

'Good,' went on Fidelma as if he had spoken. 'Tonight is a chance to enjoy ourselves. The eve of All Hallows Day. The ancient pagan festival of the dead. We can join in the feasting and bonfires.'

'Are you sure that you have a solution to this riddle?' Eadulf seemed unconvinced.

'I would not have said so otherwise,' replied Fidelma quietly.

The evening meal, served by the taciturn Buddog, was eaten in a gloomy atmosphere. Gwnda sat moodily at the head of the table, drumming his fingers occasionally on the table top. He seemed preoccupied with his thoughts. The main savoury dishes had been cleared away when Buddog brought in a plate of small cakes speckled with currants from the gooseberry bushes.

'These are good,' Eadulf said desperately, trying to ease the brooding ambience.

'Have you not seen them before?' asked Fidelma, feeling sorry for him. 'We call them speckled bread at home and also serve them at this time of year—'

Eadulf had bitten deeply and a spasm of agony distorted his face. He put his hand to his mouth and drew out a small metal finger ring which he held up, staring at it in surprise.

'What in the name . . . ?'

Fidelma was chuckling. 'Don't worry, you are not being poisoned. It is merely a tradition.'

Eadulf turned the ring over curiously. 'What does it mean?' he demanded.

He did not notice Fidelma colour a little.

'I'll explain later,' she said. 'It is a tradition of the feast at this time of year.'

From outside came the sound of music and voices, especially children's, raised in singing. Eadulf's expression clearly asked a question.

'It is for the eve of All Hallows,' Gwnda replied morosely.

'Oh, the new celebration.' Eadulf remembered that Fidelma had explained the bonfire to him.

'New?' said Fidelma sharply. 'Come, Eadulf, surely you know of the antiquity of the feast? You have been in the five kingdoms long enough, even if you did not realise that the Britons also celebrated it.'

'I know that it was Boniface, the fourth of his name to be Bishop of Rome, who introduced the celebration of All Saints' Day fifty years ago,' Eadulf replied stubbornly.

'Because he could not stop the Gauls, Britons and Irish from celebrating the ancient festival of the New Year, the feast of Samhain. So he merely gave it a Christian guise. Isn't that so, Gwnda?'

The lord of Pen Caer was still moody. 'What's that? Oh, yes. Our people have celebrated the Calan Gaeaf since the days beyond time.'

'We still call it Samhain,' Fidelma said. 'Many still believe it is the true start of the new year, for the old ones believed that darkness must come before rebirth and so we enter the period of darkness in these winter months before the rebirth of life. In fact,' she smiled briefly, 'the old ones used to say that this was the best time for women to conceive so that the baby could be born within the period of light.'

'I thought it was a ceremony of the dead,' Eadulf pointed out.

'In a way,' agreed Fidelma. 'Because the feast marks an end and a beginning. It is thought by the ancient wise men that this

226

was a night suspended in time when the borders of natural and supernatural become blurred. It is the period when the Otherworld becomes visible to this world . . . a time when those departed souls to whom you had done wrong in this life might return to wreak vengeance on you . . . to even the balance of good and evil . . .'

With a crash, Gwnda pushed back his chair, and strode from the room.

Eadulf smiled uneasily. 'He seems to have a problem with that,' he observed wryly.

'I think that many people have a problem with it, if they truly believe it. It was the old way of trying to ensure that everyone behaved in a moral fashion towards their friends and neighbours in this life.' She paused and held her head to one side, listening to the sounds of music and shouting from outside. 'Let's go and look at these celebrations. The bonfire will probably be lit by now.'

It was a black night. The moon was still hanging low on the horizon whenever it could poke out between the clouds, but across the hills they could see a several bonfires here and there, bright specks in the distance. Already the township bonfire was alight and the shouts and cries of the children could be heard over the wild notes of the pipes, the beating of goatskin drums and the blare of horns. Some of the older people were dancing in a circle before the bonfire. Fidelma and Eadulf walked down to join the crowd watching the ascending flames.

The straw figure they had seen in Iorwerth's forge had been burnt away to almost nothing. A few remains could still be discerned on top of the fire.

'Human sacrifice?' Eadulf grinned cynically.

Fidelma took the question seriously. 'In olden times, it was the custom to offer a god called Taranis, the god of thunder, offerings in a wooden vessel, some say in the figure of a man made of wood. The figure symbolised the messenger to the gods.'

Eadulf's attention had been distracted and he seemed to be searching the crowd by the bonfire.

'What is it?' asked Fidelma.

'I was trying to see if I could spot Iorwerth or our friend Iestyn,' he replied. 'I would have expected their attendance at such a celebration.'

Fidelma agreed. She turned, and abruptly found herself facing the grinning figure of Iestyn standing behind her.

'Not gone yet, Gwyddel?' he sneered.

'As you can see,' she replied evenly. 'However, it is to be hoped that tomorrow may be a good day for our departure.'

'Tomorrow? Are you leaving tomorrow?' His tone rose to a sharp interrogative.

Fidelma merely moved away, drawing Eadulf with her and leaving the farmer staring suspiciously after them.

Out of earshot, Eadulf turned to her with a worried frown. 'Why did you say that to him? You know he will tell his friend Clydog. They'll be waiting for us on the road.'

'I just wanted to add some fuel to the simmering pot, Eadulf,' she replied calmly. 'Tomorrow we will have reached a resolution to this matter. I am just hoping that your trust in young Dewi is not misplaced. He should have returned here by today or tomorrow at the latest.'

'I can't see what Dewi's arrival will do to help us now. I don't think the authority of Gwlyddien will count for much here. Clydog has many fighting men at his disposal.'

'That is true,' agreed Fidelma. 'I am gambling on the fact that Clydog will not attempt—'

They suddenly became aware of a rise in the level of the noise of the voices. The music of the instruments grew hesitant and then awkwardly trailed off. Even the shouts and screams of the children began to trail away. They heard cries of men, harsh and commanding. Figures moved in the darkness. Figures on horseback, bearing aloft brand torches and naked swords.

Fidelma turned in their direction. By the bonfire, seated on horseback, she could see a familiar figure. 'Clydog!' she hissed.

Then, grabbing Eadulf by the sleeve, she plunged away into the darkness between the nearest stone cabins. They paused in the shadows for a moment to regain their breath.

'This is something I did not expect,' she muttered. 'I did not think Clydog would show his hand until Gwlyddien had been persuaded to march against the Hwicce.'

'Perhaps Gwlyddien has already has been persuaded?' Eadulf offered. 'Anyway, what can we do now? Iestyn will tell him that we are in the township. There is no way we can reach our horses in Gwnda's stables from here without being seen.'

Fidelma motioned in the gloom to the darkness of the woods behind the township buildings. 'That is the only avenue of eluding Clydog and his robbers. Come on.'

She led the way quickly and silently from the buildings and into the woods. It was difficult to find a pass through the undergrowth but Fidelma seemed to stumble on a deer path along which their movement became easier.

'Let's hope that there is no truth in the old superstition,' muttered Eadulf, floundering behind her in the darkness.

'What do you mean?'

'We've been involved in bringing to justice many who have now joined the souls in your Otherworld. Let us hope that those vengeful souls do not have the ability to come back this night and visit vengeance on us!'

Fidelma did not bother to respond. She was still annoyed with herself for not having foreseen the possibility of this event. It had not occurred to her that Clydog would feel secure enough to ride into the township and take over.

'How long will it be before they realise that we must have taken to the woods?' grunted Eadulf. 'I doubt if we will get a long start on them.'

Fidelma halted so suddenly that Eadulf almost cannoned into her.

'What . . . ?' he began.

'Water, up ahead,' she replied. 'It must be the stream that borders the township. We'll have to find a place to cross.'

A moment later they came on the dark rushing waters of the stream. Here and there in the darkness were little patches of white water as the swiftly flowing current rushed and gurgled over the stones and rocks in the river bed.

'The deer track leads straight down to it,' she pointed out. 'The stream is no more than two or three metres wide here, and I think I can just see a path on the other side. That means that the deer use this as a crossing, and if a deer can cross here so can we. Are you ready?'

'Let me go first, just in case,' insisted Eadulf, moving forward.

Fidelma allowed him to go on. Sometimes she was so absorbed that she forgot that Eadulf's masculine pride could be wounded when she did not allow him to take the lead in those areas where he felt he should.

She waited while he stepped into the bed of the stream and heard him gasp as the coldness struck him. Then he began to pick his way across, swaying now and then as the deceptive force of the current pushed against him. The waters, however, did not rise above his knees and soon he was scrambling up the far bank. She did not wait for him to call to her but began to cross immediately. As she reached the bank he leaned forward and helped her out.

The clouds were bunching up now and obscuring what little light there had been from the low-lying moon, causing the woods to be almost in total darkness. There was, however, a faint gloom which allowed them to follow the deer trail with a fairly fast pace.

'We must be a fair distance from Llanwnda now,' muttered Eadulf breathlessly after they had been travelling for some time.

'I think we have only been moving in a semi-circle,' Fidelma replied cautiously.

A moment or so later, they came to a darkened building. Eadulf shivered as he recognised its outlines. 'It's the woodsman's hut. We have not gone far at all.' He sounded disappointed.

'But at least we have come upon the main track through the wood. If we follow this road we will come to the forge of Goff . . .'

Eadulf grunted in dismay. 'But that is about seven or eight kilometres from here, and without horses . . . why . . . !'

Fidelma suspected that if she could see his features in the darkness they would be extremely woebegone. But it was too dark and she had only his voice to go by.

'A good pace, Eadulf, and we should be there by daylight. We might be able to get horses from Goff and ride on to the abbey of Dewi Sant to prevent this conspiracy from bearing fruit.'

She halted abruptly. 'I thought I saw a movement ahead,' she whispered.

Eadulf strained forward, peering along the track. The trees seemed to converge on them in a dark twist of gnarled branches. He shivered slightly.

'Isn't one of these trees the one on which they strung up Idwal?' he muttered nervously.

Fidelma nodded before realising that he could not see her gesture in the darkness.

'I think so,' she agreed.

The clouds seemed to part abruptly and the moon emerged once again to cast a gloomy light over the woods. This time they both saw it.

A body was swinging from one of the lower branches of a

squat oak just ahead of them. It hung low to the ground so that the toes of the feet, fully extended, almost brushed the earth. The head was at a curiously disjointed angle to the body.

Fidelma moved forward, Eadulf nervously at her side. He wished that Fidelma had not told him the folklore of this night, the eve of All Hallows.

They halted before the body. Once again the moon had disappeared behind the clouds. It was impossible to see who it was, although Eadulf felt that there was something very familiar about it. They both came to the realisation at the same moment. It was Iorwerth.

'*Dabit deus his quoque finem,*' Fidelma sighed sadly.

'You don't sound surprised?' muttered Eadulf, recognising the line of Virgil which indicated that God granted an end to all trouble.

'I am not,' she replied. 'Though I thought he was made of sterner stuff. Otherwise I would not have shown him that piece of jewellery. Let's cut him down.'

Eadulf took out his knife and began to saw at the rope. 'I don't follow what you mean. Who killed him?'

'He did it himself.'

The rope split and Eadulf lowered the body to the ground. 'Why should he . . . ?'

Sounds broke the stillness of the night. Lights moved in the darkness; burning brand torches. Their provenance was obvious. Fidelma grabbed Eadulf's hand.

'Run! That's Clydog or his men looking for us.'

Together they sprinted away into the woods. A cry behind them told them that they had been spotted. A moment before Eadulf had been cursing the clouds obscuring the moon. Now he cursed the fact that the night was not dark enough to hide them.

Within moments they realised their flight was almost hopeless. Their pursuers were on horseback. They searched desperately for some narrow path which would lead them more deeply into the woods away from the main track; some way by which they might elude the pursuing horses. There was none. The undergrowth was thick and dark and shut them out.

A moment later, one of their pursuers had overtaken them and turned his horse to block their path. His swinging sword blade menaced them.

'Hold or be struck down!' he snarled. They halted reluctantly.

The mocking tones of Clydog came from behind them. 'Did

231

I not tell you that we would soon meet again? We have some unfinished business, you and I, Sister Fidelma of Cashel.'

They turned and stared at him in the moonlight. Fidelma did not reply.

'We have wasted enough time this night,' Clydog suddenly said in businesslike fashion. 'Bind their hands behind them and bring them along. We will return to Llanwnda.'

One of his men jumped down from his horse and roughly drew Fidelma's hands behind her and secured them with a rope. She gasped in pain. Eadulf, clenching his hands, took a step towards her but was halted by the pinprick of cold steel at his neck. The sword was expertly held in the hands of the warrior on horseback who had blocked their path.

The other man, having finished with Fidelma, turned on him with an evil expression and swiftly searched him, removing his knife. Then Eadulf found his hands being dragged behind him. He tried to resist but the warrior spun him round and slapped him viciously across the side of the head, sending him toppling. His hands were bound before he had recovered. In less than a minute, they were both hoisted onto horses behind two warriors.

Clydog gave the command to ride on. To Fidelma's surprise, it seemed that neither Clydog nor his companions had noticed the body of Iorwerth, for they passed by the tree without a glance. She realised that when Eadulf had cut the body down it lay in the high grass, and in the gloom had not been seen.

'What do you intend now, Clydog?' Fidelma called.

The outlaw chief glanced back at her. 'Still asking questions, Gwyddel?' he jeered.

'I am afraid it is part of my nature,' Fidelma responded cheerfully. 'You have grown very bold since last we met.'

'What is your clever tongue about now?' Clydog demanded suspiciously.

'Nothing clever. Last time we met you were hiding in the woods, like the scavenger you are, preying on wayfarers to rob and kill. Now you have decided to attack an entire township. That means that you have become bolder. I merely wonder why?'

'I believe that you are clever, woman,' grunted Clydog angrily. 'I have a feeling that you know more than you say. We shall find out exactly what you know when we return to Llanwnda.'

Fidelma realised there was little to be gained by trying to continue the conversation. She looked over to where Eadulf was struggling to keep his balance behind the warrior on whose horse he sat. Poor Eadulf. He was not a good horseman. It was difficult enough for her, with her hands bound behind her back, to keep her balance. It must be extremely unpleasant for Eadulf.

At least the group of horsemen made no detours. Clydog led them down the track straight towards the township and within moments they were crossing the wooden bridge over the stream, passing the darkened silent forge of Iorwerth.

In the shadows, she saw one or two armed men standing in the darkness. Clydog ignored them, for they were obviously under his ordrs. He led the way up the street, beyond the still glowing bonfire, to Gwnda's hall, where the robbers dismounted and Fidelma and Eadulf were roughly pulled from their mounts. One man took the horses on to the stables.

Clydog moved up the steps to the door of the hall and pushed it open. He turned on the threshold and called for his men to bring the prisoners forward. Then he led the way inside, his men pushing Fidelma and Eadulf roughly behind him. So intent were they on keeping their balance, difficult with their hands tied behind them and his thugs pushing them this way and that, that Fidelma and Eadulf had not realised that Clydog had halted abruptly. They stumbled into him and nearly lost their balance. In the time it took them to regain their equilibrium and look up they realised that Clydog and his companions seemed to have become like frozen statues.

There were half a dozen men in the hall with bows strung and arrows pointing at Clydog's men.

Chapter Twenty

It was Gwnda's voice which greeted them with a gruff humour.
'You are welcome to my hall, Clydog the Wasp.'

Fidelma moved sideways a little so that she could see who
was standing in front of Clydog.

Gwnda was there, of course, seated in a wooden chair, but in
his usual chair of office stretched a young-looking warrior with
a circlet of silver round his fair hair. He was quite handsome,
with almost violet-coloured eyes that seemed to have no pupils.
A boyish grin moulded his features. He was richly dressed but
one could easily discern that the sword which hung at his side
was no mere decorative piece. He looked familiar but it was only
after a moment or two that Fidelma recognised him as the man
they had met briefly at the abbey of Dewi Sant. It was Prince
Cathen, son of Gwlyddien.

'Lay down your weapons,' snapped Gwnda to the outlaws.

Reluctantly, Clydog and his men unbuckled their sword
belts and one of Cathen's warriors laid aside his bow to come forward
and gather them up. Another man, at a wave of the hand
from Cathen, moved forward to sever the bonds of Fidelma
and Eadulf.

They both stood for a moment, rubbing their wrists to restore
the circulation, a little bewildered and amazed at this turn of
fortune.

'Take these dogs and put them with the others,' Gwnda was
ordering, indicating Clydog and his men.

'Wait!' snapped Clydog. 'You cannot do this to me. It will
go ill . . .'

But the warriors were hustling him away, leaving Fidelma and
Eadulf facing Prince Cathen and Gwnda, the lord of Pen Caer.

Cathen had risen, and now came forward with hands out-
stretched to her. 'You had us worried for a while, Fidelma of
Cashel. Your royal brother, Colgú of Cashel, would never have
forgiven us if anything had happened to you while you were a
guest in our kingdom of Dyfed.'

'I am very glad to see you, Prince Cathen,' Fidelma said

with enthusiasm. 'Seeing you has put the final piece in our puzzle.'

Cathen looked perplexed, but when she did not explain further he turned to Eadulf. 'It is also good to see you again, Brother Saxon.'

Gwnda had risen, a little half-heartedly, in deference to the actions of his prince.

'Come,' Cathen invited them, 'be seated before the fire and let refreshment be brought.' This latter was said to the stony-faced Buddog, who left the hall to do his bidding.

'What has happened?' Eadulf was asking. 'How did you get here?'

'Your young messenger, Dewi, arrived at the abbey and told Abbot Tryffin what you had told him to say. My father and I questioned him about the situation here at Pen Caer. I saw beyond the mere message. It seemed that you might stand in need of a small band of warriors to enforce your argument. So I offered to lead them and we rode here as quickly as we could. We left young Dewi at his father's forge on our way here.'

'It seems that fortune has favoured your bold move,' Fidelma observed gravely. 'Luckily for us.'

Buddog re-entered, her nervousness at the presence of the young prince showing. Mulled wine and oat cakes were served.

'*Fortis fortuna adiuvat*, eh?' Cathen was smiling at Fidelma.

'Even as Terence says in *Phormio*,' agreed Fidelma. 'But the township was in the hands of Clydog's robbers. How did you . . . ?'

'How did we change that state of affairs? Easily enough. Clydog had no idea that any adversary was in the vicinity. He had left with four of his men to chase you. That left fifteen or so to guard the villagers. You tell them how it was done, Gwnda.'

The lord of Pen Caer still seemed ill at ease. He stared at the ground for a moment. 'We had been taken to the big hay barn behind here, the entire township . . .'

'Everyone was imprisoned?' demanded Fidelma sharply.

Gwnda blinked.

'Was Iestyn imprisoned with you?' pressed Eadulf, realising what Fidelma was getting at.

Gwnda shook his head. 'I have not seen Iestyn all evening. Nor Iorwerth, come to that.'

Fidelma turned quickly to Cathen. 'Can you spare half a dozen

236

warriors? Men in whose cunning you have faith, as well as their sword hands?'

'I can. Why?'

'Get one of the townsfolk to guide your men to Iestyn's farmhouse. They are to take Iestyn captive and anyone else who is there. Tell them to be prepared for violence, for there might be some more of Clydog's men present who are not prepared to lay down their weapons without a fight.'

Cathen called one of his men in and issued orders. Fidelma looked satisfied.

'Now we can continue. We would not want our net to allow some of the culprits to escape.'

Cathen was clearly puzzled. 'Are you saying that these men Iorwerth and Iestyn are in league with this outlaw Clydog?'

'There is more in this matter than mere robbery, Prince Cathen,' she assured him. 'But Gwnda was explaining how you came to turn this affair to your favour . . . ?'

She turned, giving Eadulf a warning glance. He finally realised that there was some reason why she wanted to keep secret the finding of Iorwerth's body. He did not know what it was, but he decided to go along with whatever scheme she had in mind.

Gwnda took up his interrupted tale. 'As I say, we were imprisoned in the barn. Clydog had set ten of his men to guard us. There were a few others outside.'

'Thus it was when we came to the township,' intervened Cathen.

'How many are there of you?' asked Eadulf.

'Fifty warriors of my father's bodyguard. Good men all.'

'It's a wonder Clydog's men were not alarmed by the arrival of such a large body,' Fidelma observed.

'I sent two men ahead to scout. They came across a man positioned at the bridge by the entrance to the township. He made the mistake of thinking my men were his companions returning and greeted them with words which immediately made them suspicious. So they disarmed him and brought him back to our main body and me. He was persuaded to talk a little . . .' Cathen broke off with a dry chuckle. 'Perhaps we should skip over that. Anyway, he was persuaded to tell us that Clydog's men had imprisoned Gwnda and his villagers in the barn, and even told us the disposition of his men. It was a simple task to disarm them and release the villagers. Learning that Clydog and some of his men had gone off chasing you and Eadulf, we decided to tell

237

everyone to go to their homes and remain there quietly without lights until Gwnda told them otherwise. We positioned ourselves and waited for Clydog to return, as we knew he must. The rest you know.'

Fidelma nodded approvingly as she followed his narrative. 'You seem to be a sound strategist, Cathen.'

'Even a good strategist needs luck, Sister.'

Fidelma gave him an appreciative look. Cathen was certainly no vain leader.

Gwnda cleared his throat. 'So now, Prince Cathen,' he said, 'thanks to you peace returns to Pen Caer. You have rounded up and captured our local band of robbers. And Sister Fidelma will tell you that our other mysteries are resolved. *Si finis bonus est, totum bonum erit.*'

Fidelma shook her head quickly. 'If this is an end to the mystery, it is not good nor is everything good that comes from it.'

Prince Cathen looked uncertain. 'I would agree that there are several questions to be answered before we can resolve all these matters. Do you have the answers to those questions, Sister?'

'First tell me, Cathen, when Dewi came to your father Gwlyddien, did he make a specific request on my behalf?'

Cathen nodded. 'That you be given the authority of *barnwr* to investigate all those matters you felt important.'

'Do I receive that authority?'

'My father was most willing to give you that authority. As I said before, we merely thought you might need a little physical backing.'

Gwnda was looking on in disapproval.

At that moment, a tap came at the door and one of Cathen's warriors entered. 'It was easily done, Prince Cathen. We have the man called Iestyn. He was at his farm with a couple of outlaws. We surprised them before they could even draw their swords, so no one has been hurt.'

Cathen grinned at Fidelma. 'Excellent. So do we have all the rats in our trap now, lady?'

Fidelma did not reply for a moment but turned to the young warrior. 'Was one of the outlaws a man with a metal skull cap? A war helmet? A man of some arrogance?'

'That must be the one who answers to the name of Corryn. He was arrogant,' agreed the warrior.

'Corryn was the man I wanted.' Fidelma sighed in satisfaction.

'There was another outlaw, apart from the man Iestyn. His name was Sualda.'

'Sualda?' Eadulf's eyebrows rose a fraction. 'So he survived?'

'Luck is definitely on our side,' Fidelma told him.

Cathen glanced questioningly at her. 'Are these men special?' he asked. 'I thought that Clydog was their leader?'

'Very special,' she confirmed. 'Keep them all separate but closely confined. They are all important in this game of intrigue.'

Cathen gestured for his warrior to obey Fidelma and turned back to her. 'I am not sure I understand any of this,' he began.

'I shall explain tomorrow. In the morning, with Gwnda's consent of course, let us gather in this hall. I will then endeavour to bring all the ends of these matters together.'

Gwnda was frowning in annoyance. 'I thought the matter was concluded? We have rounded up all the outlaws. What else is there?'

Fidelma gave him a sympathetic smile. 'There are many deaths to be accounted for, Gwnda, and also an explanation of the conspiracy against King Gwlyddien.' She turned to Cathen. 'Do I have the right and your approval to present the explanations?'

'Of course,' the prince replied.

'Then I shall need one of your men to act as steward for the court that I propose should sit in Gwnda's hall at noon.'

'Cadell is my trusted lieutenant, Sister.'

'Very well. Let me speak with Cadell and issue him with instructions on what should be done tomorrow, for I need this business conducted in a precise and special way.'

Cathen and Gwnda were clearly at a loss to understand what was in her mind. However, Cathen turned to the door and called for one of his men, asking that Cadell be found and sent to him. A moment or so later a young warrior entered. Cathen spoke quietly to him and the man crossed the hall to Fidelma, raising his hand in salute.

'I am at your service, Sister,' he said. He seemed brisk and efficient.

'Remain while Brother Eadulf and I give you instructions.' She turned to the others. 'The night is almost gone and it has been a long and tiring one. I suggest that you all retire. Brother Eadulf and I will not be long in following your example.'

They hesitated and then, seeing the glint in her eye, began to disperse.

The morning was intensely bright. There were no clouds in the sky and the sun shone with that late autumnal brightness which causes people to narrow their eyes in order to focus through its glare. In spite of the sun's rays, the air was chill and there was a hint that a frost had come and gone in the predawn hours. Droplets of water glimmered and sparkled on bushes and trees and even the grasses.

Fidelma had slept late. In fact, it was approaching the noon day. Even so, she was stirring long before Eadulf and went down to the kitchen to find Buddog washing dishes there. The woman greeted her dourly.

'There is much movement in the township this morning, Sister. Many are crowding into Gwnda's hall to hear what you have to tell them.'

Fidelma seated herself at a table and began to pick at a bowl of apples.

'Let us hope they will not be disappointed,' she said tightly. Buddog frowned and left her alone.

A moment later Eadulf entered. Fidelma noticed that he still looked exhausted. She probably looked haggard herself, for they had not gone to bed until dawn. They had spent some time questioning Sualda, who had recovered from his infectious wound thanks to Eadulf's treatment, and Fidelma's speculation had been confirmed.

'I see people are gathering in the main hall,' Eadulf said in greeting, helping himself to an apple. He had barely bitten into when Prince Cathen entered with Cadell at his side.

'It is a fine day,' he announced. 'The sun is near its zenith. Cadell has been scrupulous in obeying your instructions. Those whom you asked him to request to attend are already in their places. Clydog and his band of outlaws are still imprisoned, with the exception of Iestyn who has been brought to the hall under guard.'

'Have the smith Goff and his wife Rhonwen arrived?' asked Fidelma.

'They have come with their son, Dewi,' agreed Cadell.

'And the girl Elen?'

'She was most reluctant to return. It was lucky that she had broken her journey at Goff's forge and we did not have to send all the way down to Llanrhian to fetch her. I do not think she is happy to be back.'

'Everything stands in readiness, Sister,' Cathen summed up. 'Just as you ordered it should be.'

'And is Gwnda in attendance?'

'He is, and very unhappy about it,' replied Cathen. 'As lord of Pen Caer he would normally seat himself as judge, but I will take precedence in this court in accordance with your request.'

'It will be up to you, Prince Cathen, to ensure that this hearing is properly conducted. I have no judicial authority and it will be your decision what legal path must be taken after I have presented the facts.'

'It will be as you say.'

'Then go before us and we will follow in a moment.'

He and Cadell left and went into the hall. Fidelma could hear the hum of voices grow silent with expectancy.

Buddog was still busying herself in the kitchen.

'Buddog? Are you not joining us?'

The tall, blonde servant shook her head. 'I am only a servant, lady. I am not allowed to enter Gwnda's hall during official business other than to attend to the wants of the guests.'

'But you have the right to attend and listen to what has taken place. Eadulf will take you in and secure you a seat.'

Eadulf rose and motioned for Buddog to go with him. She did so, but only with reluctance and some protest. For a few moments Fidelma sat at the table drumming her fingers on its wooden top and frowning into space. Then she gave a deep sigh, stood up and entered Gwnda's Hall.

The hall was crowded. Prince Cathen had taken the chair of office with Gwnda, as lord of Pen Caer, seated to one side. Gwnda was clearly annoyed at being removed from the place that he had expected to fill and watched her coming with intense dislike. One of the men whom Cathen had brought with him was apparently a scribe, for he now sat to one side ready to record the proceedings. Cathen's men were posted strategically around the hall and Cadell stood ready to perform the task of marshal of the court.

Fidelma paused at the door. A silence descended over the people as they turned to looked at her. Fidelma saw a scowling Elen seated near her father. There was Goff the smith, his plump wife, Rhonwen, and their son Dewi, on whom she bestowed a smile. Without the boy's journey to the abbey of Dewi Sant,

241

this could have been a more fatal affair. Buddog was sitting awkwardly where Eadulf had found a place for her. Not far from her, but with a warrior on either side, sat Iestyn the farmer.

Cadell had carried out his instructions to the letter. Clydog and Corryn and their followers were not in the hall, but were being kept in Gwnda's barn as prisoners until she called for them.

Cathen glanced towards his scribe and the man knocked on the table with the pommel of his dagger. It was a superfluous action for already the hall was quiet.

'We are ready to hear you, Sister,' Cathen called.

Fidelma strode forward to the centre of the room, where Eadulf was already standing before Cathen. 'Prince Cathen, let this court acknowledge that I and Brother Eadulf come here to speak with the approval and authority of Gwlyddien, your father, king of Dyfed.'

'This is fully and readily acknowledged. Sister Fidelma of Cashel and Brother Eadulf of Seaxmund's Ham, being lawyers of their own peoples, came to Pen Caer under commission of my father, the king. To facilitate matters he has approved of their being designated honorary *barnwr*s of this kingdom. We sit in anticipation of hearing the results of their investigations.'

Fidelma solemnly looked around, as if gathering her thoughts, and then turned back to address herself to Cathen. 'We came to this place in the company of Brother Meurig. There were two matters calling for investigation. One was that for which King Gwlyddien had originally commissioned our help – the mystery of the disappearance of the brethren of Llanpadern. The second was that which Brother Meurig, as a learned judge, had specifically been sent to investigate – the murder of Mair, daughter of the smith Iorwerth of this township.'

There was a silence as she paused.

'Initially, it was thought that these two events were two separate, unrelated issues, isolated from one another. Then I wondered if there might be some connection, for both incidents shared some common protagonists.'

There was still no sound as she paused again.

'Prince Cathen, with your permission, I shall approach the explanation of these events by dealing first with the murder of Mair and its outcome—'

'I object!' Gwnda was leaning forward in his seat. 'This matter is not in the competence of this foreigner, no matter what reputation she has in her own land.'

242

Cathen silenced him with a gesture. 'I have already ruled on her competence,' he said sharply. 'My father has confirmed her qualification to investigate and bring evidence forward in the death of Brother Meurig, and as the *barnwr* was investigating Mair's death it seems to me that it is within her competence to put forward her arguments in this matter.'

'Brother Meurig was killed by Idwal. Idwal had killed Mair. The matter should be closed,' protested Gwnda.

'Do you deny that you had second thoughts about Idwal's guilt?' Fidelma asked. 'Your daughter, Elen, thought that Mair had been killed in mistake for her because she had overheard a conversation in the woods which endangered her life. Is that not so? You even agreed that Elen should tell me so.'

Gwnda scowled. 'I did not share her belief.'

Cathen leaned forward and searched out the frightened features of Elen. 'Is this true, Elen? Did you make this claim and did your father agree that you were to tell Sister Fidelma and Brother Eadulf?'

'It is true,' Elen agreed unhappily.

Cathen turned back to Fidelma. 'Then Gwnda's objection is overruled. Continue.'

Fidelma paused a moment as if putting her thoughts in order before continuing.

'The seeds of this tragedy – and here I speak of the death of Mair – go back many years. It is best if I tell the story as best I can and, should I place a wrong interpretation on events, then the witnesses gathered here can challenge and correct what I have to say. You will discover that the hand that struck down young Mair was not the same hand that struck down Brother Meurig.'

This caused a stir in the hall, quickly dispelled by a rapping on the table by the scribe.

'As I say, the seeds of this tragedy were sown many yeas ago, in a place not so far from here called Dinas,' began Fidelma. Goff stirred uncomfortably. 'Two young apprentice smiths were working at the forge of Gurgust there. One of those smiths was Goff and the other was Iorwerth, Mair's father. Gurgust, their smith-master, had a daughter named Efa.'

Elen had bent forward in her seat, a curious expression on her face.

'Iorwerth made Efa pregnant. In a fury, Gurgust drove his apprentice Iorwerth out. His fury did not abate and he also cast his own daughter from his home. Desperate for security, Efa took up with a wandering warrior, who was thought by most to be the father of her child. I can only speculate on what happened, although I hope the person concerned will have the courage to confirm what I may say in speculation. This warrior took up with Efa but, shortly after the birth of the child, he quarrelled with her. Perhaps he simply did not want to become father to another man's child.

'The warrior disappeared and Efa was found strangled. More-over, her baby had also disappeared. Now Gurgust, in happier days, had made a red gold necklet, with a bejewelled pendant bearing the image of a hare, for his daughter. There was no sign of it and it was thought that whoever killed Efa had stolen it.

'Some time afterwards a shepherd named Iolo started herding sheep at Garn Fechan. He was raising a boy named Idwal, who was not his son. Here in Llanwnda, Iorwerth the smith married a local girl called Esyllt and had a daughter whom they named Mair. Iorwerth did not treat his wife, Esyllt, well. She subsequently died. In his guilt he became devoted to his daughter. Idwal, foster son of Iolo, was a simple, kindly youth, and he and Mair appeared strangely drawn to one another.'

'Where is Iorwerth?' interrupted Gwnda, in a hectoring tone. 'He should be here to refute this outlandish tale.'

Fidelma turned towards Goff. 'In the absence of Iorwerth, can you and your wife, Rhonwen, tell this court whether the tale I have told is outlandish so far?'

Goff stared at the ground before him. It was his wife who answered.

'You account is correct. You have imagined nothing so far. My husband was the second apprentice at Dinas and, as all should know, Iorwerth's wife, Esyllt, was my close friend.'

'What was not known,' went on Fidelma, 'was that the attraction between Idwal and Mair was not a sexual one but something which went even deeper. Idwal and Mair were born of the same father but did not know it.'

'Prove it!' snapped Gwnda above the hubbub caused by her statement.

'Just before the old shepherd Iolo died, he gave Idwal some-thing which had been the property of his mother. It was a necklet of red gold with a figure of a hare on it.'

'Idwal is dead,' cried Gwnda. 'You cannot prove any part of this story.'

Fidelma smiled. She turned to Elen.

244

'It is true,' the girl whispered.

'Speak up, child,' Cathen said. 'If you have something to say, let the court hear.'

Elen raised her head. Tears were glistening in her eyes. 'It is true,' she said more determinedly. 'Iolo told Idwal where the necklet had come from. When Idwal was accused of murder, he realised that his precious possession might be taken from him. He wanted to keep it safe and so he gave it to me.'

'Then where is it?' demanded Cathen.

Fidelma moved forward, holding it up. 'Elen passed it to me when she told me how it came into her possession. It is so distinctive that I am sure Goff will recognise it as the one made by his smith-master Gurgust. It was the one worn by Efa all those years ago. Goff and Rhonwen had already described it when they had thought it lost.'

Goff had risen, staring at the necklet. 'It is the same one,' he acknowledged in a quiet voice. 'I would recognise it anywhere.'

There was a yell and a scuffle. Eyes turned to where Iestyn had been sitting. He had been silent all through the hearing, his face immobile. Now he had tried to struggle to his feet, his eyes wide, his face a mask of hate.

'Are you claiming that Iorwerth was Idwal's father?' he shouted. His guard pushed him back into his seat.

'Iorwerth should be here,' muttered Gwnda. 'He should hear this accusation. If what you say is true, he would also recognise this necklet.'

'He did,' affirmed Fidelma, without responding to Iestyn. 'In Brother Eadulf's company, I showed the necklet to him.'

'Then where is he?' demanded Gwnda.

'Recognising it, realising that Idwal was actually his son by Efa, he became demented. You see, he had actually helped hang his own son for what he thought was the rape and murder of his daughter.'

'Then where is he now, Sister?' demanded Cathen. 'He should have been present in this court.'

Cadell, responding to Fidelma's gesture, cleared his throat and took a step forward. 'My prince, his body is now at his forge. On Sister Fidelma's instructions, I went to a place described by her at first light and found his body beneath a tree where he had hanged himself. His body had been found by Sister Fidelma and Brother Eadulf last night and cut down moments before Clydog captured them.'

There was a gasp of horror from the crowd.

'Iorwerth could not live with the fact that he had killed his own son,' went on Fidelma. 'Nor that his son, so he thought, had lusted after and killed his own sister.'

'This shepherd, Iolo, the man who raised Idwal, was he the warrior of whom you spoke?' queried Cathen. 'Was Iolo the man with whom this unfortunate Efa took up after she had become pregnant with Iorwerth's child?'

To everyone's surprise, Fidelma shook her head. Instead, she turned to Iestyn. 'Iolo was never a warrior, was he, Iestyn?'

The farmer glowered silently back at her.

'There is surely no need to deny anything now, is there? There are people here who know that you were a warrior in your youth and that you were Iolo's brother. I presume that Iolo took pity on the baby, thinking that it was your own child by Efa? He took Idwal to foster, and you gave him Efa's chain. Was that how it happened?'

Iestyn said nothing.

'You became too old to follow the profession of a warrior and came to farm at Pen Caer. Idwal was nothing to you except that he was a constant reminder of your past misdeeds. Every time you saw him you were reminded of Efa. I think that you killed Efa?'

The farmer raised hate-filled eyes.

'You will never prove it, Gwyddel,' he said between clenched teeth.

'I don't think I need to. Your current involvement with the plot at Llanpadern, to which I will come later, is crime enough for punishment. However, it would be good to clarify these matters. Your lack of denial is sufficient. When Iolo died, you found yourself inheriting his property and the first thing you did was throw Idwal out to fend for himself. The lad had to survive as an itinerant shepherd, remaining in the district as an unwitting thorn in your flesh.

'When Idwal was charged with Mair's murder, you saw your chance of getting rid of the boy's accusing presence for good. You took a leading role in demanding vengeance, in stirring people up to such a pitch of hatred that they took the law into their own hands. Your own guilt was also your motivation for your part in his slaughter.'

'I was not alone in that!' cried Iestyn.

'Indeed you were not. The guilt lies with everyone who had a hand in the crime of Idwal's death. But the most tragic hand in

246

this was that of Iorwerth, Idwal's own blood father, and for that crime he has inflicted his own punishment on himself.'

'Just a moment, Sister Fidelma,' interrupted Cathen thoughtfully. 'You have told us a tragic story, and it seems enough people here can verify its details. It is a dreadful and sorrowful tale about Idwal's life and death. But you refer to his death as a crime. True enough. But what of the crimes of Mair's death and Brother Meurig's slaughter? Whatever Iestyn's past misdeeds were, you do not appear to be accusing him of involvement in these deaths, nor have you exonerated Idwal.'

Fidelma bowed her head and smiled softly. 'You are a sound judge, Prince Cathen. We have so far only set the scene and attempted to clear up a mist that has obscured the central action of this tragedy.'

She paused again.

'Iorwerth wanted to believe the best of his daughter, Mair. He argued that she was still a virgin and accused Idwal of rape. Mair had already come to sexual maturity. She was known by her friends to be promiscuous and preferred the company of mature men. She had a lover.'

'This is dangerous surmise. You cannot make such claims without evidence . . .' cautioned Cathen.

'Oh, if need be I can call individual witnesses to back up my claims. Even Elen, daughter of Gwnda. Do you think it necessary at this stage?'

'Very well. It is not necessary at this moment but be prepared to do so if you are challenged.'

'I shall stand ready. Mair boasted to Elen, her close friend, that she had started an affair with a man who was older than her. On the morning that she was killed, she met Idwal in the forest. Idwal knew about her promiscuity. Idwal was a very moral young man and when Mair asked him to take a message to her elderly lover he refused. That was the cause of the argument which was witnessed by Iestyn as he passed them in the woods.

'Iestyn witnessed the row and went rushing off to Iorwerth to stir things up, claiming that the disagreement was something more than it was. I will believe that Iestyn did not, perhaps, foresee that the event would result in Mair's death, but when he found it did, it suited his plan well. He probably only wanted Idwal to be driven from the territory. With a murder charge, he saw a chance to remove him permanently.'

'I am confused,' interposed Cathen. 'Are you saying that Idwal did or did not kill Mair?'

'He did not kill her. Iestyn, hurrying to alert Iorwerth, passed someone else in the woods. He barely noticed that person, so intent was he on his errand of hate. Meanwhile, Idwal had refused to take the message to her lover. He had gone off in anger and left Mair alone. The killer then came upon Mair and Mair, in naivete, asked this person to take the message.'

'Why naively?' demanded Cathen.

'Because the person she asked had been the mistress of Mair's elderly lover for many years. She was now feeling cast aside while her lover found solace with this young girl. She already suspected Mair and hated her. To be asked to take a message to her lover from his new mistress was too much. In passion, she throttled Mair, throttled Mair with her powerful hands and killed her. Isn't that how it happened, Buddog?'

Chapter Twenty-one

A din had arisen in the hall at Fidelma's accusation. The noise rose while Prince Cathen and Cadell shouted for order and calm.

Buddog sat without expression. By not even a blink of the eyes did she register her feelings. There was no hysteria, no denial. Just a blankness on her face. It was as if she were no longer in her body.

Elen was sitting in her seat staring at Buddog with horror on her pale face. 'But if . . . if Buddog killed Mair, then . . .' she swung back to her father, sitting tense and pale and tight-lipped. 'You and Mair were lovers!' She screamed at him in disgust. 'You and Mair—'

It took some moments before a semblance of order was brought to the hall again.

'As the woman, Buddog, does not deny or confirm the charge, you may continue your arguments,' Cathen instructed Fidelma.

'Buddog had been brought to Gwnda's house as a hostage as a young girl. Over the years Gwnda and Buddog had become lovers. Buddog developed a blinding love for him. I don't know how his relationship started with Mair. Maybe it was because of Mair's promiscuity. Maybe he was flattered at her attention.'

She paused when she realised that Gwnda was trying to speak.

'Buddog was dear to me; I would have done anything to protect her. But Mair . . . Mair was young and vital. She gave me strength. She reinvigorated me!'

Fidelma expressed satisfaction at his confession. 'I began to suspect Buddog's involvement in this affair on the first night I arrived here,' she went on calmly. 'The trouble was that it was not the mystery I had come to investigate so I left it to Brother Meurig, not realising the danger he would face if he began to unravel the threads which I had already seen.'

She paused for a moment before continuing.

'Gwnda was in the forest that morning. It may have been entirely chance that he came across Buddog just after she had

strangled Mair. Remember, Gwnda still cared for Buddog. He
has just told you so himself. In those few moments he decided
to attempt to cover up her guilt. He told Buddog to take the letter
and return to Llanwnda and he would deal with things. After
she had gone, Fate intervened. Idwal returned to find Mair and
apologise to her. Gwnda hid himself . . .'

Gwnda was groaning and nodding now. 'I did not plan anything
at first,' he said. All his strength and authority seemed to have
evaporated. He was an old man, hunched and frail. 'I hid hoping
not to be seen. Idwal came to the body and bent down. He could
not believe she was dead. He tried to revive her. Then I heard
the cries of the people coming. It was then that I knew what I
should do.'

'You caught Idwal and pretended to Iorwerth and Iestyn
that you had caught him in the act. You pretended to be
the conscientious and honourable lord and told your people to
imprison Idwal, sending to the abbey of Dewi Sant for a *barnwr*.
You had to be seen to be above reproach in this matter.'

There was a silence and then Elen said: 'There is one thing
wrong, Sister. There were signs that Mair had been raped. We
heard the story of blood showing . . .'

Fidelma held up a hand. 'It occurred to Gwnda that many
thought Mair was a virgin. This was the most distasteful part
of Gwnda's cover-up. He took his knife and stabbed the upper
inside thigh a couple of times to draw blood and went to pains
to point it out to Elisse the apothecary, claiming the girl was a
virgin and must have been raped before she was killed. What he
did not realise, in his haste to lay a false trail, was that Elisse's
wife, preparing the corpse for burial, would see the wounds.'

Elisse took up in his place and identified himself. 'I confirm
that the blood was made by such wounds, Prince Cathen. When
Gwnda tried to tell me it was hymenal blood, I had to inform
him that it was not so. Further, as my wife here will observe,
Mair was no virgin and sought my wife's advice as to methods
of avoiding pregnancy.'

'It must have seemed Fate to Gwnda when Idwal came back to
make amends to Mair and found her body,' sighed Fidelma. 'But
Gwnda was too clever by half. When he heard that the apothecary
would not support him about the rape, and he realised that the
barnwr for whom he had sent might ask too many questions, he
decided on the next best course of action. If Idwal was already
dead, what need was there of a trial?'

Gwnda straightened up, realising that he should attempt some defence. 'I was imprisoned in my hall when the mob seized the boy. You know that. I had no part in that.'

'I know that you, fully armed, were being held by two unarmed young men, whom I see in this hall today.'

Two men stirred uneasily at the back of the hall.

'Do they deny the charade? I believe that even if you did not persuade Iorwerth to fan the flames of the mob's emotions to lynch Idwal, you certainly took advantage of the situation and made no attempt to stop them. But you wanted the *barnwr* to believe that you were not part of that attempted lynching. You wanted to safeguard your reputation and deflect any suspicion from yourself. You allowed Idwal to be taken and thought he would be hanged. Once dead, that would be an end of the matter and no accusation could be levelled at Buddog, or at you for covering up her crime.'

Buddog had remained sitting like a stone statue. Fidelma was regarding Gwnda without pity. 'As you have told us, Gwnda, in spite of your affair with Mair, you still have feelings for Buddog. That's the curious part. Your compulsion to protect was such that when poor Brother Meurig came close to the truth, you followed him and Idwal to the woodsman's hut and killed him.'

Gwnda began to protest his innocence. Fidelma cut him short. 'When we told you that Brother Meurig had been killed, you feigned surprise. Then, without our telling you where he had been killed, you left us saying that you would take men to the woodsman's hut to retrieve his body. Isn't it curious that you knew where the body was when you did not even know that he was dead?'

Gwnda groaned despairingly as he realised his error. He held his head in his hands and rocked back and forth in his seat. It was a few moments before he started to make some articulate sound.

'He would not listen to reason,' he muttered. 'I tried to convince him that the boy was guilty. He argued. We struggled. He cried to the boy to run off, to find you, to tell you what was happening. I broke free . . . I swear I did not intend it . . . I was only defending myself. The axe . . . I just swung it . . .'

Fidelma gazed at him dispassionately. 'When you had killed Brother Meurig you came back to the township. Why didn't you chase after Idwal?'

Gwnda continued rocking back and forth, moaning softly; a

strange, almost frightening behaviour in a man of his years and position.

'I didn't know what to do. You and Brother Eadulf had returned and I had to wait to see whether Idwal had spoken to you. Only after I heard that you had no suspicion did I call on Iorwerth. He and some others started to hunt for the boy. He was found and . . . you know the rest. You were right that I persuaded them that they would not be punished.' Gwnda raised an arm and let it fall in a gesture of defeat.

'Were you there? Did you watch an innocent boy hang when you could have saved him?' demanded Cathen with loathing.

Gwnda seemed to have retreated in on himself. He made no reply.

Fidelma addressed herself to Cathen. 'My suspicions about Gwnda were confirmed when I saw that he realised I would not be shaken from my belief that Idwal was innocent. This was the point where coincidence played its hand. Coincidence plays a much stronger part in the progress of our lives than we ever give it credit for. Elen had, by chance, overheard a meeting between the outlaw Clydog and some others. She hid but was discovered and fled. Although she had escaped, she was in fear that she had been seen. Then Mair was killed. Because Mair and Elen superficially looked alike, Elen came to the mistaken belief that Mair had been killed in mistake for her by one of Clydog's men. Then, by chance, one of the men at the meeting in the forest passed through the township. Elen thought she had been recognised and it would be realised that Mair had been killed by mistake. She told her father and he saw a another chance to throw us off the scent. He agreed that she come to me with the story.

'Since he had been adamant about Idwal's guilt and even refused me permission to investigate further, this sudden change of heart made me very suspicious. Gwnda's weakness was this necessity to carry things to excess, to overdo his false trails – the blood on Mair's body, and then to swing from extreme non-cooperation to an apparent attempt to be helpful.'

She paused and looked slowly round the quiet hall.

'There, Prince Cathen, is the truth about the deaths of Mair and Brother Meurig to which you must add, as a crime, the death of young Idwal. The self-inflicted death of Iorwerth was but a sad consequence of this tragedy.'

Cathen sat back nodding reflectively. 'Cadell, place the lord of Pen Caer and the woman Buddog under guard. They will be returning with us to the court of Gwlyddien.' Then the young prince drew his brows together. 'But what of the mystery of Llanpadern? You are forgetting that, Sister.'

Fidelma shook her head with a grim smile. 'That is one thing that I am not forgetting,' she replied softly.

The court had taken a short recess while Buddog and Gwnda were removed and placed under guard. When the scribe called for order, it was Eadulf who now took the floor in front of Cathen. Fidelma stood ready to support him. They had agreed between them the course of the presentation.

'Prince Cathen, my knowledge of the speech of the Cymry is not so fluent as that possessed by Sister Fidelma. I trust you will bear with me if I stumble in my search for the right words and phrases.'

Cathen smiled indulgently. 'I have knowledge of Latin and of the language of Éireann should you wish to explain yourselves in either of those tongues. Have no fear, I am sure that there will be no misunderstanding.'

'Thank you. Sister Fidelma has explained one of the two mysteries with which we have been involved in at Pen Caer. But the greater mystery was the one which brought us here in the first place. The mystery of the disappearance of the brethren of Llanpadern in whose community your own brother, Rhun, lived and worked. I will now explain how that poor community was taken prisoner, and why most of them are now dead or taken into slavery.' Eadulf turned to Cadell. 'Bring forth the prisoner Clydog.'

There was a stir as two guards escorted in the handsome outlaw chief. He wore his usual twisted smile. He glanced about him defiantly as if indifferent to the proceedings. Then he saw Eadulf standing before the court as his prosecutor and sneered openly.

'Well, well,' he murmured, 'it seems the court of Dyfed has placed a Saxon in charge. Is there no talent among the men of Dyfed that you have to appoint your blood enemies to govern your courts?'

'I am presiding at this court, Clydog,' snapped Prince Cathen sourly. 'Whatever happens here, you will answer to me or to my father Gwlyddien. Continue with your presentation, Brother Eadulf.'

Eadulf examined the arrogant features of the outlaw for several moments. Then he asked sharply: 'Prisoner, do you wish to appear before this court of Dyfed as Clydog Cacynen – Clydog the Wasp, a common outlaw and thief? Or is it as Clydog, son of King Artglys of Ceredigion, that you would prefer to be heard?'

The silence in the hall was absolute.

Finally Clydog gave a low musical chuckle. 'Well, Saxon, it seems that you and your Gwyddel friend have sharp eyes. I will agree to answer as Prince Clydog of Ceredigion.'

Eadulf turned back to Cathen, who was regarding Clydog in astonishment. 'You were right, my lord, when you first suggested, at our meeting at the abbey of Dewi Sant, that Ceredigion was behind this intrigue. With your permission, I will adopt the same method of presentation as Sister Fidelma in attempting to explain what befell at Llanpadern and what it means. I will tell the story and should we need witnesses or explanations then they will be provided.'

Cathen gave an indication with his hand that Eadulf should proceed. He seemed too surprised to speak.

'Ceredigion has long cast envious eyes over Dyfed. You told us that. In their plotting, Clydog came here to this heartland of Dyfed to attempt to sow alarm and dissension. It was easy to hide with his men in the forest in the guise of outlaws.

'What was the plan? A very simple one. If Dyfed could be made to believe that some outrage had been committed against them by the Saxons, an outrage which would cause Gwlyddien and yourself to raise an army and march on the Saxon kingdoms, it would leave Dyfed totally undefended. Once its fighting men had left, the Ceredigion could march in and take over the kingdom. A simple enough strategy.'

Cathen shook his head. 'Simple but unworkable. The people of Dyfed would rise up and fight the Ceredigion. They would not accept the rule of a Ceredigion prince. Our warriors would march back and fight.'

'I will come to that problem, for it is one which had been catered for,' replied Eadulf. 'However, like all simple plans, it was open to mistakes. It started with two coordinated actions. One of Artglys's allies, Morgan of Gwent, was to raid the Saxon kingdom of the Hwicce. The plan here was to entice an Hwicce warship to chase Morgan along this coast. The Saxon ship had to be seen and rumours of a Saxon raid spread. That part of the plan succeeded but not in the time it was meant to.'

'What do you mean?' demanded Cathen.

'The second part of the plan, which Clydog was to fulfil, was where things went badly wrong.'

Clydog, still standing between his guards, interrupted with a sneer. 'Nothing went wrong except your interference, Saxon!'

Eadulf ignored him. 'Clydog was to raid one of Dyfed's religious centres and the news of this and the slaughter of its brothers by Saxon raiders would cause the people of Dyfed to demand swift retribution. Gwlyddien would be forced to march on the Saxons.'

'But what mistake was made?' pressed Cathen.

'As we now know, the community of Llanpadern was chosen for the raid. But Clydog raided the monastic settlement too early. Why? Only Clydog and his men know the answer. Perhaps it was the impatience of his character. Perhaps it was because he had received wrong information and thought the Saxon ship had already arrived. But the Hwicce ship had not yet been sighted off the nearby coast, and it was essential that local people see the ship at the same time that the community was attacked. That was the plan. The raid on Llanpadern worked well. Seeing themselves at the mercy of armed men, the brethren offered no resistance and were not immediately harmed. Clydog looted the valuables in the chapel and also took the livestock, presumably to sell. But the main thing was that Clydog now had prisoners and, according to the plan, had to wait for the Saxon ship to arrive.'

'I do not see the logic of this,' intervened Cathen. 'Why not slaughter the brethren at once? It was a risk to keep prisoners.'

'A greater risk to slaughter them before it could be shown to the local people that Saxon raiders were present. The entire plan rested on this, as I have said. When no word of the Hwicce ship was brought to Clydog, the prisoners had to be removed from Llanpadern. To keep them there would have been equally foolish. The prisoners were split into two groups, half, with Father Clidro, were taken to Clydog's forest lair, the other half to Morgan's ship which lay hidden in a secret cove.'

Cathen was beginning to look angry now. 'By the Living God! My brother was a member of that community. I did not see eye to eye with him but he was my brother. There'll be vengeance against Ceredigion for this sacrilege.'

'Let us wait for talks of vengeance until we have seen what happened,' Eadulf advised. 'Morgan's ship, as I say, had arrived and took half of the brethren on board. All twenty-seven members of the community were alive at this point.'

'Is my brother still alive?' demanded Cathen.

'Let me tell this story as best I can,' insisted Eadulf. 'Clydog's major mistake was raiding too early.'

Prince Cathen was shaking his head. 'In what way was a mistake made? I am not sure I follow this well.'

'No sooner had Clydog removed the brethren from Llanpadern than first Brother Cyngar and then Idwal arrived and found Llanpadern deserted. There was no sign of an attack on the community. They went off to relay the news of this mystery disappearance. Clydog did not realise this.

'It was not until the next night that the Hwicce ship, pursuing Morgan, sought shelter in a nearby bay. Nearby, Clydog's men were watching for its arrival. They had taken seven of their prisoners down to the shore.'

'Are you going to be able to prove any of this, Saxon?' interrupted Clydog.

'Oh, yes.' Eadulf turned to him with a quick smile. 'As the Saxon ship anchored, two men came ashore from her. You and your men attacked them and succeeded in taking one of them prisoner. This was an unexpected bonus. You had a real Saxon warrior in your hands.

'You and your men waited until dawn, hiding nearby. As you hoped or planned, some local people came along and spotted the Saxon ship which then set sail. It was then, Clydog, that you ordered seven of your prisoners to be slaughtered and left on the foreshore. Proof that they had been killed by Saxons was placed by their bodies. Are we correct so far, Clydog?'

The Ceredigion prince was disdainful. 'You do not need my approbation, Saxon, for your fanciful tale. Where is your proof?'

'Prince Cathen,' Fidelma interrupted, speaking to the prince of Dyfed. 'I wish to make an unusual request. I would like Clydog taken to the back of the court and gagged so that he cannot interfere until I am ready.'

'That is not legal . . .' protested Cathen.

'But necessary, I assure you,' insisted Fidelma, glancing meaningfully to Eadulf who nodded briefly.

Cathen sighed and gestured to Cadell to cut off the voluble protest that had arisen from Clydog.

'What now?' Cathen demanded when Fidelma's request had been fulfilled. She turned to Eadulf and gestured for him to continue.

'Bring forth Sualda,' he called.

A moment later, the thin, pale-faced man whom Eadulf had treated when he had been near death at Clydog's camp came cautiously into the hall.

'Give Prince Cathen your name,' invited Eadulf.

The man was hesitant. 'I am Sualda, in the service of lord Clydog of Ceredigion.'

'Do you recognise me?' asked Eadulf.

'We spoke last night.'

'But before that?'

'I do not recall, except that last night you said you were the man who treated my wound when I was near death in the forest camp.'

'How did you get that wound?'

'A Saxon gave it me.'

'This Saxon was a sailor whom Clydog's men had captured one night when he came ashore from a Saxon boat near Llanferran?'

The man hesitated and then nodded.

'We have heard,' Eadulf said, 'how Clydog had taken some of the religious from Llanpadern to that spot and had them killed.' He prayed that Cathen would say nothing to disabuse Sualda of the false impression that the matter had been established.

'I was not one of those who killed the religious,' muttered the man quickly. 'I was guarding the Saxon prisoner when that happened.'

Eadulf exchanged a triumphant glance with Fidelma. The ruse had worked. A confession had been made.

'So tell us what happened. After the religious were killed, what then?'

'We were ordered to march back to Llanpadern. Clydog told us that we had to make it look as though the Saxons had attacked the community there.'

'But you did not. Why?'

'Lord Corryn was waiting for us and he was angry when he saw us. He said that the bodies of some religious had to be left at Llanpadern. He had the old priest, Father Clidro, with him. We . . . that is . . . well, he hanged the old man in the barn while Clydog and his men went off to fetch the rest of the prisoners we had left under guard in the forest.'

'And the Saxon sailor?'

'He had been brought with us to Llanpadern.'

'How did he die?'

'It was while the lords Clydog and Corryn were arguing about the bodies of the religious that the Saxon escaped. I was told to go after him. That was when I was wounded. I chased him into the room where the religious ate. He seized a meat knife and cut me and I killed him with my sword. As I was being carried back to camp with lord Corryn's warriors, I heard that our men had killed the rest of the prisoners and were taking them by cart back to Llanpadern. By then, I was beyond caring. I had gone into a fever.'

Eadulf was smiling. 'Clydog did not appear to be aware of the fact that time was important. By the time he returned to Llanpadern to fake the scene of the attack, he found another problem. Sister Fidelma and myself.'

Prince Cathen called for the release of Clydog, and Sualda was removed to one side.

'Well, do you wish to deny anything, Clydog of Ceredigion? What I have heard is a twisted plan arising from a twisted mind,' Cathen observed. 'It was diabolical.'

Clydog stood in defiant humour. 'My first instinct was to kill the Saxon and the Gwyddel. I should have obeyed my instinct.'

'Your plan did not work,' Cathen replied coldly. 'There was confusion and, above all, King Gwlyddien has not raised a host to march on the Saxons. Brother Eadulf seems to be telling us that it was your mistakes that caused this.'

'You are right,' agreed Eadulf. 'However, King Artglys of Ceredigion was increasingly frustrated that no movement was happening, no calls for vengeance against the Saxons. He had already sent one of his men to meet with his son Clydog. That was the meeting observed by Elen in the forest. It had been agreed then to leave some of the brethren with Morgan of Gwent in case just such a contingency should arise, and now Artglys decided to prompt matters by sending the same messenger to order Morgan to put some more slaughtered brethren of Llanpadern in a conspicuous place. It was sheer coincidence that Elen saw him again as he was passing through Llanwnda on his way to Morgan's ship.

'Morgan had enticed the Hwicce vessel into pursuit, but the Saxon ship had lost its mast in a storm during the chase. It put in here to cut a new mast, and by another coincidence I was able to witness Morgan's ship put into the bay and toss the dead bodies of the brethren overboard, with items which would lay blame on the Hwicce.'

Clydog started to laugh harshly. 'This Saxon is tying to absolve his fellow Saxons from blame. Don't listen. The Saxons killed these religious.'

Prince Cathen smiled coldly at him. 'You already stand convicted out of your own mouth and that of your man Sualda. But tell me, Brother Eadulf, why did the Ceredigion not slaughter all the religious prisoners at once? Why divide them into groups?'

Fidelma moved forward again.

'To use to mislead people. Some were left dead on the shore; some would have been left at Llanpadern itself had Eadulf and myself not been present to frustrate the plan; and others were kept in reserve to fabricate just such a drama as they presented to stir the people to hatred against an imagined enemy. Brother Eadulf and I have estimated that Morgan may still hold captive half a dozen of the brethren of Llanpadern.'

'Indeed,' added Eadulf, 'it was lucky for us that Morgan neglected to ensure that all the religious were dead when he tossed them overboard. One of them was still alive.'

Eadulf did not lie. He merely did not explain that the poor religious had died before he could identify those responsible for the deed.

Clydog blinked rapidly as he absorbed this news, and Prince Cathen leaned forward in his chair.

'Do you still deny this, Clydog?'

The Ceredigion prince raised his chin disdainfully. 'It is war, that's all,' he suddenly said, as if dismissing any wrongdoing.

Cathen's face was working with anger. 'War? The brothers of the community of Llanpadern have been murdered! My own brother Rhun, old Father Clidro, whom I knew well, and others sacrificed by those involved in this devilish plot! Blood must answer for blood! Did you and your father Artglys really think that this twisted plan would work? Even had Ceredigion marched into Dyfed, do you think that no one in the kingdom would have fought back against them once Artglys declared himself ruler of Dyfed?'

'It was even more subtle than that,' Sister Fidelma said in a quiet voice.

'More subtle?' queried Cathen. 'How so?'

'The plot needed someone inside Dyfed to rally the people in

259

support. There are several minor traitors ready to sell themselves to Ceredigion. Iestyn, for example.'

'I was no traitor!' cried Iestyn from the seat where one of Cathen's men still had him confided. 'Gwlyddien was weak. It was time we had a new ruler.'

Fidelma ignored him but signalled Cadell.

A moment later, Cadell ushered in the tall figure of Corryn, still wearing his war helmet.

'Remove your helmet,' she ordered.

When Corryn hesitated, Cadell reached forward and did so for him.

Cathen started up from his chair, a hand to his breast, staring at Corryn. The outlaw, now displaying a tonsure, his bright violet eyes defiant, smiled cynically back.

Fidelma glanced at Eadulf in satisfaction before returning her gaze to Corryn.

'And how would you like to be known in this court?' she asked. 'As Corryn the Spider, as Brother Rhun of Llanpadern or as the Prince Rhun of Dyfed?'

Corryn shrugged indifferently. 'It makes no matter. It would seem that we have reached a checkmate . . . for the time being.'

Fidelma turned to Prince Cathen. 'The final mystery is solved,' she announced. 'Why was there no confusion amongst the brethren when Clydog arrived? Why no sign of attack? Because Brother Rhun was able to exert his authority over his fellow monks to persuade them to submit passively to Clydog and his men. Their blood is on his hands.'

Cathen sat back heavily in his chair, regarding his brother with a shocked and anguished expression. 'Is this true, Rhun? Have you plotted with Ceredigion, the enemies of this kingdom, to overthrow our father and seize power? Even now I cannot believe it. Did you really support this terrible plot?'

Corryn smiled crookedly. 'You were always gullible, little brother. He that does not bear adversity for a while does not deserve prosperity. I was able to bear my adversity in the attempt to gain the prize that I desired. I spent many months in the preparation of this plan. That was why I left court and pretended to become a religious. God, how bored I was with the passing months in that close confinement of Llanpadern. The moment when I was at last summoned to meet Clydog and his father's messenger in the woods of Ffynnon Druidion was one of the happiest of my life.'

Cathen shook his head in disbelief. Then his face hardened. 'They say that there is no action more malicious than treachery, Rhun. You have set yourself up as a fox in lamb's clothing. I must bring you before our father so that he may see your spite and deceit. Only that will keep you alive for a little while longer. If it were left to myself, you would be thrown over the nearest cliff.'

Corryn seemed unperturbed. 'It might be better for you if you do so. This feeble kingdom cannot last indefinitely against the ambition of Ceredigion. *Non semper erit aestas!*'

Brother glowered at brother for a moment and then Cathen motioned to his men, pointing at Corryn.

'Take . . . *that* from my sight.'

As they propelled the erstwhile religious to the door, Cathen suddenly called: 'Perhaps it is you, Rhun, who should consider well that line of Seneca which you throw about so freely. Truly, it will not always be summer. The day of reckoning will come shortly for you. Let your friends, the Ceredigion, attempt to invade now . . . we will be ready for them. They will be driven away, as we have driven them away in the past; driven away like smoke in the wind.'

Epilogue

'I think that you made a splendid presentation, Eadulf,' Fidelma said approvingly.

The coast of Dyfed was disappearing in the distance as they stood resting against the taffrail of the Frankish trading ship beating its way southwards across St Bride's Bay. It was a satisfying feeling to sense the bounce of the hull against the waves; see the rise and dip of the vanishing coastline; hear the crack of the thin leather sails, as they filled with the changeable winds which were now set fair for their passage. The captain had promised them that their next landfall would be at Tanatos, the island off the coast of the kingdom of Kent. They now had a few days to do nothing but enjoy the voyage. They felt relaxed and happy.

'I was guided by you,' admitted Eadulf. 'You were the one who spotted the similarity of facial features between Corryn and Cathen. What made you suspect Corryn of being Brother Rhun? Just the resemblance?'

'Not only that. I was sure that I had seen Corryn's features before. Those blue eyes of his should have made me realise sooner. But why did he always wear that war helmet? Obviously to hide his tonsure.

'And there was his attitude. You remember that he was supposed to be Clydog's lieutenant and yet many times he seemed to be in charge? He was certainly Clydog's equal. However, what clinched my suspicions was when you reported the words of the dying religious on the beach.'

Eadulf shook his head, trying to recall. 'I thought that the man was raving, poor fellow.'

'He was telling you something in among his dying thoughts. He said that evil had been in their midst. The evil spider. Brother Rhun was the evil in their midst. He had taken the nickname Corryn, and what does that mean?'

Eadulf groaned inwardly. 'Spider.'

'Just so,' smiled Fidelma. 'Anyway, you were the one who healed Sualda. Sualda proved to be the weak link, for without him we might never have known what happened to the Hwicce warrior.'

'Ah, Thaec. At least he did meet his end with a blade in his hand, believing he was being dispatched to the Hall of Heroes. I suppose you are right. Without Sualda, Clydog could have kept his mouth shut or denied everything. How did you guess that Clydog was the son of Artglys?'

'He was not an ordinary outlaw, that was for sure. Like Corryn, he was well read, educated. Then I remembered that Cathen had mentioned that Artglys had a son. It was guesswork, but guesses are often a short cut to the truth.'

'What will happen to Clydog? He was an evil man.'

'He is also a prince of Ceredigion. I suppose he will be held as a hostage against King Artglys's future good behaviour. Perhaps Artglys might offer the remaining missing brethren of Llanpadern in exchange for the return of his son; perhaps even the missing valuables from the chapel.'

'And what of the fate of Rhun, the renegade?'

'I have no doubt what Cathen would like to do with his ambitious sibling. But the decision will be Gwlyddien's. Although while Rhun remains alive, he will be a constant threat to his father and brother.'

Eadulf pursed his lips. 'It was amazing that he had no compunction about slaughtering his own religious companions at Llanpadern.'

'He was more evil in many ways than Clydog,' Fidelma mused.

'And more short-sighted,' added Eadulf. He met her amused glance with a shrug. 'Aesop said that one should never attempt to soar aloft on the wings of an enemy. That's what he tried to do. A slave has one master but the ambitious man will have as many as are needed to help him reach his objective.'

'Which philosophy means?' prompted Fidelma humorously.

'That even if he had become king of Dyfed through the help of Ceredigion, the price would have been too high. Ceredigion would have demanded remuneration which Rhun might have been unable to pay.'

There was a silence between them for a moment.

'I suppose,' Eadulf said, after a while, 'that the greater tragedy, in this story, befell Idwal and Mair.'

'A sad drama that was almost obscured by an unrelated conspiracy,' agreed Fidelma. 'Brother Meurig's death, Iorwerth's suicide and the deaths that went before – Idwal's mother Efa, for example. Where did that cycle start?'

'Who knows? We are into the game of "what if". What if Gurgust had not thrown his apprentice Iorwerth out? Or if he had not banished his daughter Efa from her home?'

'What if the person who came along at that time had not been Iestyn?' rejoined Fidelma.

'Iestyn!' Eadulf sighed. 'I'd almost forgotten him. What will happen to him?'

'I suspect that it has already happened,' Fidelma said grimly. 'He might have found forgiveness for the part he played in feeding Iorwerth's fears and hatred, and causing the death of Idwal, but he was in league with Rhun. I heard that he had served as a warrior with Rhun and his allegiance was personal. But, when it comes down to fact, he was a spy for Ceredigion. I think his fate was written in Cathen's eyes when they took him from Gwnda's hall.'

'And what of Gwnda and Buddog?'

'The Britons spent many centuries as a province of the old Roman Empire,' Fidelma reflected. 'They have adopted ways of punishment that we have not pursued in the five kingdoms. There is more of vengeance and retribution in their law. They punish more harshly.'

Eadulf shivered slightly. 'Well, I am glad that we are now on our way to Canterbury. I cannot say that I enjoyed my time in the kingdom of the Britons.'

'That was evident,' agreed Fidelma seriously. 'I have never known you to be so apprehensive and irritable.'

'I am sorry that I allowed my fears to show.' Eadulf paused and glanced quickly at her. 'There were times when I felt they were justified.'

Fidelma's features were suddenly pensive. 'I have behaved very badly towards you, Eadulf. I should have treated you differently. I confess that I was trying to distance myself from you.'

Eadulf, to her surprise, nodded slowly. 'I knew well what you were doing.'

Fidelma stared at him, slightly bewildered at his calm assertion of knowledge. 'But you seemed to take every insult that I threw at you.'

'As fearful and apprehensive as I was in the land of the *Welisc*, I knew that you were more uneasy and afraid. And you were not afraid of the *Welisc*.'

'I think that you should explain that,' she said, her voice slightly breathless with tension.

'It's an easy explanation. At Loch Garman, before we left the kingdom of Laigin, you finally admitted to your feelings for me and you made a decision to accompany me to Canterbury instead of returning to your brother's kingdom. Do you think that I was unaware of how difficult that decision was? That I did not know how frightened you were of having made it? You have been racked with apprehension these last days. But it is in your character not to display your fear. You simply disguised it under a cloak of disdain and even derision towards me.' Eadulf shrugged, his expression still serious. 'I knew what was in your mind, Fidelma. You were testing me. You wanted to see if I might break and thus confirm that you had made the wrong decision. I was not going to make it so easy for you. If you want to change your mind then it must be by your own determination and not by mine. My mind in this matter is steadfast.'

Fidelma regarded him quietly for a moment or two before, impulsively, reaching out and placing her hand firmly in his.

'I don't think that I was doing it deliberately, Eadulf. Perhaps some unconscious impulse? But you are wise. I think my apprehension is cured. Will you forgive me for it?'

'Fear comes from uncertainty. You have to be certain. Seneca wrote that where fear is, happiness has deserted that place.'

Fidelma looked solemn. 'I agree. Fear is not a virtue. I am glad you tolerated my fear, Eadulf. I believe I am certain now. But if I grow uncertain, I vow to be honest and not let fear dictate. I have learnt by this experience.'

'Speaking of learning,' Eadulf smiled, shifting the conversation to a lighter note, 'do you remember that you promised to tell me the meaning of that cheap metal finger ring hidden in that speckled cake that I ate the other night? I nearly cracked my teeth upon it.'

Fidelma coloured slightly. 'Oh, it is only an old superstition,' she said in an attempt to dismiss the subject.

'What sort of superstition?' he pressed firmly.

Fidelma saw no easy way out of it. 'At home, on the feast of Samhain, which Rome now calls the eve of All Hallows Day, it is our custom to serve the speckled bread – *bairin breac*, we call it. The Britons have the same custom and call the bread *bara brith*.'

'But what does the ring in the bread symbolise?' Eadulf demanded.

'Well, when the speckled bread is being made, a ring and a hazel nut in its shell are mixed in with the dough. Whoever gets the portion of the speckled bread with the nut in it will remain unwed for the rest of their life.'

'But I had the ring,' he pointed out. 'What happens to whoever gets the ring?'

'It means that they will soon be married.'

Eadulf grinned in happy satisfaction. 'That is a superstition I can live with. In fact, I think it is an excellent superstition.'

Fidelma inclined her head in thought for a moment, leaning against the rail of the ship. Then she reached into her *marsupium*.

'I also had something in my piece of cake,' she said quietly.

Her features were formed in a smile and so Eadulf did not observe the serious look in her eyes.

She held out the object in her hand and gradually opened her fist, palm upwards. A hazelnut lay on her palm.

Come explore the world of Sister Fidelma.

The International Sister Fidelma Society is an organization devoted to the readers of Peter Tremayne's Sister Fidelma Mysteries. Members receive three copies per year of its official publication, *The Brehon*. The magazine is primarily a forum for the fans of the series, containing articles, competitions, readers' letters, and photographs—including special contents such as the first-ever publication of a Fidelma short story, "The Blemish," (September 2002), among others.

Come visit the Society's Web site at www.sisterfidelma.com for further details, news, merchandise, and updates.

Annual subscription for members is $29.95
(U.S. funds drawn on a U.S. bank).
Checks to be made out to:

David Robert Wooten, director & editor
The International Sister Fidelma Society
PO Box 1899
Little Rock, Arkansas 72203-1899
U.S.A.
david@sisterfidelma.com